also by
Laura Thalassa

THE BARGAINER SERIES
Rhapsodic
A Strange Hymn
The Emperor of Evening Stars
Dark Harmony

PESTILENCE

LAURA THALASSA

Bloom *books*

Published by Bloom Books, an imprint of Sourcebooks
P.O. Box 4410, Naperville, Illinois 60567-4410
(630) 961-3900
sourcebooks.com

Originally self-published in 2018 by Laura Thalassa.

Cataloging-in-Publication data is on file with the Library of Congress.

Printed and bound in the United States of America.
WOZ 10 9 8 7 6 5 4 3 2 1

For Teresa, who cares fiercely, gives endlessly, and loves absolutely. The world needs more people like you.

Then I saw when the Lamb broke one of the seven seals, and I heard one of the four living creatures saying as with a voice of thunder, "Come." I looked, and behold, a white horse, and he who sat on it had a bow; and a crown was given to him, and he went out conquering and to conquer.

—Revelation 6:1–2 New American Standard Bible (NASB)

PROLOGUE

They came with the storm.

The sky surged, great plumes of clouds tumbling and roiling together. The desert air thickened, feeling damp and smelling unusually ripe.

Lightning flashed.

BOOM!

The world lit up like it was on fire, and there they were—four great beasts of men astride their terrible steeds. The monstrous mounts reared back, pawing the air as their masters stared out at the world with fearsome foreign eyes.

Pestilence, his crown perched upon his brow.

War, with his steel blade held high.

Famine, a scythe and scales in hand.

And Death, blighted Death, his dark wings folded at his back, a torch of bilious smoke tight in his grip.

The Four Horsemen of the Apocalypse, come to claim the earth and lay waste to the mortals who dwelled upon it.

The sky darkened and the steeds charged, their hooves kicking up dust as they galloped.

North. East. South. West. The horsemen rode to the four corners of the world, and in their wake, machines broke, fuses blew. The internet crashed and computers died. Engines failed, and planes fell from the sky.

Bit by bit, all the world's great innovations ceased to be, and the globe slid into darkness.

And so it was, and so it shall be, for the Age of Man is over, and the Age of the Horsemen has begun.

They came to earth, and they came to end us all.

CHAPTER 1

Year Five of the Horsemen

"We draw matches."

I level my hazel eyes on the tiny wooden sticks in Luke's fist. He strikes one against our rough-hewn table, and the flame flares bright for a second before he blows it out.

Around us, the fire station's overhead lights hum in that distressing way most electronics do nowadays, like at any moment they might sputter out.

Luke holds up the matchstick with the blackened tip. "Loser stays behind to see our plan through."

This was the painstaking decision we made. One person doomed to die, three more to live.

All so we could kill that ungodly son of a bitch.

Luke folds the tip of the burnt match into his palm with the three unburned ones, then dips his hands beneath the table to mix them up.

Outside, beyond our decommissioned fire trucks, all our necessary belongings are packed, ready for a quick escape.

If, of course, we're one of the fortunate three.

Luke finally lifts his hand, the matchstick stems jutting from his closed fist.

Felix and Briggs, the other two firefighters, go first.

Felix draws a matchstick…

Red-tipped.

He lets out a breath. I can tell he wants to fall back in his seat; his relief is obvious. But he's both too macho and too aware of everyone else to do so.

Briggs reaches for his…

Red-tipped.

Luke and I share a look.

One of us is going to die.

I can see Luke preparing himself to stay behind. I've only ever seen that expression on his face once before, when we were putting out a wildfire that had all but encircled us. The fire moved like the devil drove it, and Luke wore the expression of a walking dead man.

Both of us survived that experience. Perhaps we'd survive this devil too.

He holds his fist up to me. Two wooden sticks jut out. Fifty-fifty odds.

I don't overthink it. I grab one of the matchsticks.

It takes a second for the color to register.

Black.

Black means…black means death.

Air escapes my lungs.

I glance up at my teammates, who are all wearing various looks of pity and horror.

"We all have to die sometime, right?" I say.

"Sara…" This comes from Briggs, who I'm halfway positive likes me more than a colleague and friend ought to. "I'll go instead," he says. Like his bravery counts for anything. You can't date a girl if you're dead.

I close my fist around the match in my hand. "No," I say, resolve settling in my bones. "We decided this already."

Staying behind. I'm staying behind.

Deep breath.

"When all this is over," I say, "someone please tell my parents what happened."

I try not to think about my family, who evacuated with the rest of the town earlier this week. My mom, who used to cut the crusts off my sandwiches when I was little, and my father, who was so upset when I told him I volunteered to stay behind for the last shift. He looked at me then like I was a dead woman.

I was supposed to meet them at my grandfather's hunting lodge.

That's no longer going to happen.

Felix nods. "I got you, Burns."

I stand. No one else is moving.

"Go," I finally order. "He's going to be here in days." If not hours.

They must see I'm not dicking around because they don't bother arguing or lingering for long. One by one they give me tight hugs, pulling me in close.

"Should've been different," Briggs whispers in my ear, the last to let me go.

Should've, could've, would've. There's no use dwelling on this now. The whole world ought to be different. But it isn't, and that's what matters.

I watch through one of the large windows as the men

leave: Luke unhitches his horse from the garage, and Briggs and Felix grab their bikes, their things strapped to the back.

I wait until they're long gone before I gather my things. My eyes move over my pack, stuffed with all manner of survival gear—and a book of Edgar Allan Poe's best works—before landing on my grandfather's shotgun, the oiled metal looking particularly lethal.

No time for fear, not until the deed is done.

I may be doomed to die, but I'm taking that infernal fucker down with me.

CHAPTER 2

No one knows where the Four Horsemen came from, only that one day they appeared on their steeds, riding through cities and wildlands alike. And as they passed through town after town, human technology broke like waves upon the rocks.

No one knew what it meant. Especially when, all at once, the Four Horsemen disappeared just as suddenly as they had appeared.

Our electronics never recovered, but we began to rationalize the inexplicable events away: It was a solar flare. Terrorists. Synchronized EMP pulses. Forget that none of these explanations made any sense—they were more reasonable than some Biblical apocalypse, so we cringed and swallowed those half-baked theories.

And then Pestilence reappeared.

———

I sit at our table for a long time after my teammates—*former* teammates—have left, running my fingers over the polished wood of my grandfather's shotgun, getting used to it in my hands.

Other than reacquainting myself with the weapon over the past two weeks when I shot the crap out of some tin cans, it's been years since I handled a gun.

I've killed a total of one creature using this weapon—a pheasant whose death haunted my twelve-year-old dreams.

Going to have to use it again.

I get up, sparing another glance out the window. My bike and the trailer I jury-rigged to the back of it sit across the way, my food, first aid kit, and other supplies strapped to the back. Beyond my bike, the Canadian wilderness perches on the hills bordering our city of Whistler. Who would've thought a horseman would come to this lonely corner of the world?

On a whim, I head over to the fridge and grab a beer—the world may be ending but fuck it if there's no beer.

Popping the cap off, I cross over to the living room and click on the T.V.—one of a precious few in our town that survived the horsemen's arrival.

Nothing.

"Oh, for fuck's sake." I'm going to die a horrible, shit-sucking death, and the TV decides today is the day it stops working.

I slam a palm on top of it.

Still nothing.

Muttering oaths my grandfather would be proud of, I kick the good-for-nothing TV, more out of spite than anything else.

The screen sputters to life, and a grainy image of a newscaster appears, her face warped by the bands of color and contortions on the TV.

"...appears to be moving through British Columbia... heading toward the Pacific Ocean..." It's hard to make out the reporter's words under the staticky white noise. "Reports of the messianic fever follow in his wake..." Pestilence has only to ride through a city for it to be infected.

Researchers—those who remain dedicated to their work even after most technology has been wiped out—still don't know much about this plague, only that it's shockingly contagious and the primary vector of transmission is the horseman. But a name has been given to it all the same—the messianic fever, or simply the fever. The name was cooked up by spooks, but that's what the world has come to—spooks and saints and sinners.

After turning off the TV, I grab my bag and gun and head out, whistling the *Indiana Jones* theme song. Perhaps if I pretend this is an adventure and I'm the hero, it'll make me think less about what I'm going to do to save my town and the rest of the world.

I spend most of the day and a good part of the evening setting up camp off the Sea to Sky Highway, the route he's likeliest to take. Dear God do I hope the horseman will pass through while it's light out. I have shit aim in broad daylight; at night I'm likelier to shoot myself than I am him.

Seeing how my luck's going today, there's a chance, a good chance, I'll fuck this up. Maybe Pestilence makes a detour or decides to be clever and approach from another direction. Maybe he'll pass by without me ever noticing.

Maybe, maybe, maybe.

Maybe even wild, frightening things have a pinch of logic to them.

I grab my gun and extra ammunition, creep close to the highway, and settle in for the wait.

He comes with the first snow of the season.

The entire world is quiet the next morning as the powdery white flakes blanket the landscape and turn the road pearlescent. More snow flutters down, and it all looks so ridiculously beautiful.

Out of nowhere, the birds take flight from the trees. I startle as I see them all high above me, their bodies dark against the overcast sky.

Then, from a dozen different locations, wolves howl, the sound sending a primordial shiver down my spine. It's like a warning call, and in its wake, the rest of the forest comes alive. Predators and prey alike flee past me. Raccoons, squirrels, hares, coyotes—they all rush by. I even see a mountain lion loping among them.

And then they're gone.

I exhale a shaky breath.

He's coming.

I crouch in the dim forest, shotgun clutched in my hands. Then I check the gun's chamber. Remove and reload the cartridges just to make sure they're properly in place. Adjust and readjust my grip.

It's as I'm double-checking the ammunition in my pocket that the hair on the back of my neck rises. Ever so slowly, I lift my head, fixing my gaze on the abandoned highway.

I hear him before I see him. The muffled clomp of his steed's hooves echoes in the chill morning, at first so quiet that I almost think I imagined it. But then it gets louder and louder, until he comes into view.

I waste precious seconds gaping at this...*thing*.

He's sheathed in golden armor and mounted on a white steed. At his back is a bow and quiver. His blond hair is pressed down by a crown of gold, and his face—his face is angelic, proud.

He's almost too much to look at. Too breathtaking, too noble, too ominous. I hadn't expected that. I hadn't expected to forget myself or my deadly task. I hadn't expected to feel...moved by him. Not with all this fear and hate churning in my stomach.

But I am utterly overwhelmed by him, the First Horseman of the Apocalypse.

Pestilence the Conqueror.

CHAPTER 3

No one knows why the horsemen arrived five years ago, or why they disappeared so soon afterward, or why now Pestilence and only Pestilence has returned to wreak havoc on the living.

Of course, everyone and their aunt Mary has their own answers to these questions, most that are about as plausible as the tooth fairy, but no one has ever actually had a chance to corner one of these horsemen and pump them for answers.

So we can only guess.

What we do know is that one morning seven months ago, the news bleated to life.

A horseman, spotted near the Everglades. It took the better part of a week for the rest of the report to drift in. About how a strange sickness was taking the people of Miami by storm.

Then the first death was announced. They did a big spread on the woman for the few hours she held the sole title of tragically deceased. But quickly the death count doubled, then doubled again. It grew exponentially, first wiping out Miami, then Fort Lauderdale, then Boca Raton. It moved up the East Coast of the United States, right along with the movements of this shadowy rider.

This time when the horseman passed through a city, it wasn't technology he destroyed but *bodies*. That's when the world knew Pestilence had returned.

I stare at Pestilence. This is no human any more than his mount is a horse.

The last footage I saw of him, he was storming through New York City, nocking arrows into his bow and firing into the stampede of screaming people bent on fleeing from him.

I had to watch the newsreel five times before I believed it. And then I could watch no more.

Now here he is. Pestilence, in the flesh.

Clop—clop—clop. The rider and his horse move slowly. Snow gathers on his shoulders and in his hair. And somehow even the white flakes add to his strange alien beauty.

I hold still, afraid the mist from my breath will tip the horseman off. But he seems utterly unconcerned about his surroundings. He wouldn't need to be; no one except me would willingly get this close to the literal embodiment of plague.

Never taking my eyes off Pestilence, I raise my shotgun. It takes only a few seconds to line up the sights. I fix my aim at his chest, which is really the only thing I can hope to hit. My stomach churns as I watch the horseman.

I've seen men die. I've seen fire blister bodies beyond the point of recognition, and I've smelled the sickening scent of cooking flesh.

And yet.

And yet my finger hesitates on the trigger.

I've never *killed* (pheasant aside). Forget that this creature isn't human, that he's been carving a path of carnage through North America—he *looks* alive, sentient, *human*. That's reason enough for me to fight with myself.

I adjust my grip on the gun and close my eyes. If I do this, Mom will live, Dad will live, Briggs and Felix and Luke will live. My friends and teammates and their families will live. The entire world Pestilence has set his sights on will live.

All I have to do is move my finger an inch.

I've never thought myself a coward, but for a single second, I nearly fold.

Fuck your morals, Burns—don't make your death all for nothing.

I suck a breath in, exhale, then pull the trigger.

BOOM!

The explosive sound is almost more shocking than the shotgun's kickback, the blast echoing throughout the silent forest.

Ahead of me, the horseman grunts as the spray of pellets hit him in the chest, the force of it knocking him off his steed. His horse rears up, pawing the air and letting out a frightened shriek, then takes off.

My gut roils.

Going to sick myself.

The horse is still racing away.

Perhaps it's the horse that's spreading the plague and not the man. Or perhaps both are.

Can't risk it.

"I'm sorry," I whisper as I line up my sights once more.

It's easier to pull the trigger this time. Maybe it's because I did it once before, maybe it's that I'm ready to feel the jerk of the shotgun or hear the blast of fire and gunpowder, or maybe it's that killing a beast is easier than killing a man—no matter that neither is what they appear to be.

The steed's front legs kick up, its body briefly contorting as it lets out an agonized bray. It collapses onto its side a hundred feet from its master, and then it doesn't move.

I spend several seconds catching my breath.

It's done.

God save me, I actually did it.

After setting my weapon aside, I head for the road, my eyes glued to the horseman. His armor is a mess. I can't tell if the pellets bit through his breastplate or if they simply twisted the metal, but several of them tore through that pretty face of his.

Hot bile burns the back of my throat. Already a corona of blood blooms around his head, and even though his face is a mass of wounds, I hear him groan.

"Oh God," I whisper. This thing is still *alive*.

I barely have time to turn to the side before I retch.

His breath comes in wet pants. He reaches for me, his fingers brushing my boot.

I jump back, letting out a cry and nearly falling on my ass.

I didn't even realize how close I'd crept to him.

Need to end this.

I race back to my gun on unsteady feet.

Why did I leave it behind?

Through my haze of panic, I can't remember which tree I left it at, and *the horseman is still alive.*

I give up my search for the weapon and head back to the

little camp I set up for myself. Among my things are matches and lighter fluid.

My hands shake as I grab them. Mechanically, I head back.

Are you really going to do this? I stare down at the items in my hands. *He's still alive, and you're going to burn him while he breathes. You, a firefighter.*

Fire is no clean death. In fact, it's got to be one of the worst ways to go. I don't hate Pestilence nearly enough because I can barely stand the thought of what I'm about to do.

I step back up to the horseman and flip open the lid of the lighter fluid. I bite my lip until it bleeds as I overturn the bottle, the liquid glugging out of it. I douse him, head to foot. I pause to vomit again.

Then the bottle is empty.

I can't keep hold of the matches I pull out. My hands are shaking so badly, I keep dropping them. Finally, my hand steadies enough for me to grip one, but then the issue is striking the matchbox.

Again the horseman gropes for my ankle.

"...*leeeeeseee*..." he groans from the ruin of his mouth.

A cry escapes me. I think that was a plea.

Don't look at him.

It takes five tries, but finally, I light one goddamned match. I don't mean to drop it—if I had it my way, I probably would've stared at the flame until it burned down to my fingers—but alas, my hand shook and the match fell.

Pestilence's clothes light on fire immediately, and I hear him give an agonized shout.

The smell of burning flesh wafts up from him as the fire builds on itself.

I realize belatedly that his armor is blocking the bulk

of the fire, making an already slow death that much slower. He's burning too hot and too thoroughly to touch, or else I might've removed his armor or stamped out the flames.

I dry heave. I'm not sure I could've given this creature a dirtier death.

He screams until he can't.

No one deserves to go like this. Not even a harbinger of the apocalypse.

I back away, and then my legs give out.

This doesn't feel like some noble deed. I don't feel like the hero saving the world.

I feel like a murderer.

Should've packed myself a beer—or five. This is not something to watch sober.

But I do. I watch his skin bubble and blacken and burn off. I watch him die slowly, each second obviously agonizing. I stay rooted there for hours, sitting along this abandoned road that no one travels anymore. That entire time, my only witnesses are the trees that stand like sentinels around us.

Snow gathers along his body, melting against his smoldering remains.

At some point, I look up from him, only to notice his horse is gone, a trail of blood and trampled snow leading off into the woods. Rationally, I know I should retrieve my shotgun and follow the horse's trail until I find the beast, and then I should kill it.

Rationally, I know it—but that doesn't mean I do any such thing.

Enough death for one day. Tomorrow I will finish the job.

The sky darkens. And still I sit until the cold has seeped its way into my bones.

Eventually, the elements force me to my tent. I unfold my stiff limbs, my entire body sore and sick. I don't know if the creature's plague has taken hold of me yet or if this is simply what it feels like to neglect eating and drinking and finding shelter and warmth all day. Either way, I feel terribly sick. Terminally sick.

I collapse onto my sleeping bag, not bothering to pull it around me.

For better or worse, I did it.

Pestilence is dead.

CHAPTER 4

I wake to a hand at my throat.

"Of all the vile humans who've crossed my path, you just may be the worst."

My eyes snap open.

A monster looms over me, his face pockmarked with bloody holes, his skin charred and twisted and missing in places.

I wouldn't recognize him except for the eyes.

Angelic blue eyes. The shit they're always painting on the ceilings of churches.

This is my horseman.

Risen from the grave.

"*Impossible*," I say, my voice hushed.

He smells like ash and burnt flesh.

How could he have survived that?

He squeezes my neck tighter. "You foolish human. In all the time I've existed, had you really thought another hadn't already attempted what you failed at?

"They tried to shoot me in Toronto, gut me in Winnipeg,

bleed me out in Buffalo, and strangle me in Montreal. They tried to do all that and more in so many other towns with names I doubt you'd recognize because you fickle humans never bother to look beyond yourselves."

Someone else already...tried?

Tried and failed.

It's like taking a glass of ice water to the face. Of course someone else tried to end him. I should've known better. But I hadn't seen footage of it, hadn't heard any reports of the attempts. Whoever had tried to take him out hadn't managed to alert the public that *he can't be killed*.

"Everywhere I go," he continues, "there's someone like you. Someone who thinks they can kill me to save their malignant world."

It's hard to stare at his face, grotesque as it is. And yet it looks so much better than it did when I left him, back when he was nothing but ash.

Pestilence pulls me in close. "And now you will pay for daring to do so."

He yanks me up by the throat.

Whatever vestiges of sleep clung to me, they're now gone. I reach for his hand, yelping when I touch bone and sinew.

How can he possibly use a hand when all that's left of it is bone and tendon? His grip is like iron, unyielding.

Pestilence drags me out of the tent before throwing me to the ground. My palms and knees sink into the shallow snow.

A moment later, a knee digs into my back. He runs his hands over my torso, likely feeling me for extra weapons. I shudder at the sensation. He's touching me with raw *bone*. He reaches for my pockets, then empties them of my Swiss Army knife and my matchbook.

In the deep blue predawn glow, the forest has an almost

sinister feel to it. It's silent as the grave, its former inhabitants long gone.

Pestilence pauses after his inspection. "Where is your fight?" he asks derisively when I continue to just lie there. "You were fast to act before. Where is that damnable human fire now?"

I'm still trying to wrap my mind around the fact the lump of smoldering flesh I walked away from last night has somehow regenerated. And it *talks*.

"You have nothing to say to that? Hm." A moment later, he grabs my wrists before binding them together over my head with a rough twine rope I'm pretty sure he nabbed from my things. "Well, it's probably for the best. Mortal conversation always does leave something to be desired."

The pressure against my back abates.

"Up," he commands.

It takes me a second too long to process the order, so he uses the rope to drag me to my feet. Once again I get a good look at him.

He's even more monstrous than I first thought. His hair is gone, his nose is gone, his ears are gone, his skin is still blackened. Hardly a man at all and certainly nothing that should be alive.

His golden armor remains in place, looking unblemished even though it should be charred and bullet riddled. I can't see much of his arms under the armor, but they must be in bad shape judging by the way the metal rattles loosely around. And his hands...his hands are nothing more than white bone and bits of flesh, as are his feet and ankles.

At his waist, he wears one of my blankets, which he must've snatched while I was sleeping. I cringe at the thought.

Pestilence leads me back to the road by my bound wrists.

19

I blanch when I see his white horse waiting patiently for its master, its flank coated with scarlet blood. It paws the snow-covered asphalt, huffing. When it sees me, it anxiously whinnies, sidestepping away.

Heedless of his horse's mood, Pestilence secures the other end of the rope to the back of his steed's saddle.

I glance between my tied wrists and his mount. "What are you doing?"

He ignores me, hoisting himself onto his horse.

"You're not going to kill me?" I finally ask.

He turns around, that mess of a face looking embittered. "Oh no, I'm not letting you die. Too quick. Suffering is made for the living. And, oh, how I will make you suffer."

CHAPTER 5

All day, Pestilence drives his horse down the highway at a brisk pace, forcing me to run behind him or else be dragged by my wrists. It's a small favor that I'm a firefighter and not an office worker; I'm used to hours upon hours of laborious exercise. Still, while I may be able to keep up with rider and horse, it's fucking uncomfortable, and soon my warm clothes are dripping with sweat.

We pass through Whistler, and my eyes move from one familiar landmark to the next. This is my hometown, where I was born, where I spent winters snowboarding and summers splashing around Cheakamus Lake, where I learned to drive my family's car, and where I had my first crush and my first kiss and every other milestone that means something to me. I have to blow a kiss goodbye to it all as we leave the town behind.

Hours I run, until my wrists are rubbed bloody and weariness closes in on me.

Can't keep this up forever.

It doesn't help that the horseman gives no indication

when—or if—he'll stop. Each kilometer feels like an eternity. When he eventually turns off the highway, I want to cry with joy. I don't give two steaming shits about what horrors he may have in store for me next. So long as it means this run from hell is over, I'll take them.

We follow a snow-covered road until it leads us to a house. And then—praise the good Lord—we come to a stop in front of the house.

Pestilence hasn't bothered to glance back at me since this morning, and even now, when he hops off his steed and ties the reins against a nearby lamppost, I could be invisible for all the attention he gives me. But as soon as he comes back around his mount, it's clear he hasn't forgotten about me.

I suck in a breath at the sight of him. The angelic horseman I first laid eyes on is back, the torn-up flesh of his face now mostly healed. There are still some red patches and shiny skin where bullet and burn wounds are healing, but he's got a nose and lips and ears, so all the important bits are back. Even his hair has returned, though the golden waves of it are only just long enough to thread your fingers through.

Now that he's all put back together, I can't stop staring at him. I wish I could say it is just horrified wonderment that pulls my gaze to him, but then I'd be lying.

He's painfully beautiful, with his mournful blue eyes, his proud high cheekbones, and the deadly set of his jaw. One of my hands twitches as I self-consciously try to tuck a lock of my sweaty brown hair behind my ear.

What is *wrong* with me?

"Did you enjoy your run?" he asks.

"Fuck you." I don't have the energy to put much venom into the oath.

He curls his upper lip anyway as he unties my rope from the saddle.

Like his face, his hands are mostly healed. I see no bone, no cartilage, no veins and arteries, nor any other manner of *innards* that several hours ago were *outtards*. But they do look a little red and scabby.

He turns from me, and I get a good look at the golden bow and quiver at his back.

He's killed humans with those weapons, and he'll kill more with them in the future, and the world is fucked to hell because he can't die, and short of death, he won't stop the killing.

So much for ending him.

The blanket is still tied around Pestilence's waist, and that plus his bare feet and legs (also mostly healed) should look comical, but the horseman is formidable.

I stare for longer than necessary, and God forgive me, I can't help but notice his form is every bit as pleasing as his face. He's got massive shoulders and narrow hips, and I want to stab my eyes out now. There's got to be some rule against ogling the guy you tried to murder.

Ahead of me, he jerks on the rope. I curse as I trip over myself trying to keep up while he makes his way up to the house.

I take in the two-story home. It's pretty but fairly unexceptional: stained wood siding, forest-green front door, a snow-covered planter box under one of the windows.

Why in the world did the horseman come to this place?

Pestilence strides right up to the front door and, after lifting a foot, kicks it inward. That's one way to open a door. The other way is trying the fucking knob like a normal person.

He drags me inside by the rope, as though I'm a naughty dog he must keep leashed.

From the silence of the house, it's obvious the owners aren't around, and they probably haven't been since the evacuation warnings went out—thank God. Anywhere is better than here at the moment.

Pestilence crosses the living room, pulling me along by this damnable rope. Now that I'm not running for my life, all my other aches and pains are waking up. My wrists are throbbing, and the sweat that coats me is rapidly cooling against my body. I'm not even going to think about how sore my legs will be in the morning.

The horseman ties the rope to the stairway railing one, two, three times over.

"You do know the moment I'm out of your sight, I'm going to try to escape," I say.

"Do I look worried, human?" he asks, giving the knot a final yank.

"I can't tell—too many bits are missing."

Not true, but he probably hasn't seen his reflection yet, so he wouldn't know.

Pestilence stares at me for a long second, his dislike for me nearly palpable, then heads upstairs, his footsteps echoing throughout the house.

I wasn't kidding about the escape thing. The moment he's gone, I attack the maze of knots like my life depends on it, which it does.

I'm desperately picking at the ties that bind me to the railing—when the *fuck* did this horseman learn to tie a proper knot?—when he comes back down carrying a fresh set of clothes. Clothes and duct tape.

All we need are some assless chaps and a paddle to round

this party out. But I doubt Pestilence has *that* sort of suffering in mind. Probably for the best. I don't think it's appropriate to hate-bang the guy you tried to kill. At least not on the first night.

Pestilence tosses the clothes onto the couch, keeping an eye on me as he does so. He removes his armor piece by piece. Beneath it, the remnants of the shirt he once wore now disintegrate, revealing his naked torso.

Even injured, he's the pinnacle of masculinity. He has muscles for days, his arms both thick and cut, his pecs nicely rounded out, and his abs ridiculously defined.

His chest still looks raw and red in places. It must have been terribly painful riding through the freezing day in nothing but a blanket while his armor scraped against his burned flesh.

It takes a second for my eyes to register that wounds aren't the only things marring Pestilence's skin. Ringing his chest are a series of strange letters that *glow*. A second set of them start at his hip bones, curving beneath the edge of the blanket; they glitter like amber in the dim light.

I stare, transfixed. I've seen tattoos before but none that *glow*. If his undying nature weren't proof enough of his otherworldly origins, this would be.

His biceps bulge as he reaches for the edge of his toga-loincloth blanket, and I look away before I can see anything else.

A minute later, Pestilence returns to my side, duct tape in hand. The outfit he wears now—jeans and a flannel—is a far cry from the outfit he wore when I first saw him, but it does fit him surprisingly well, considering most men aren't nearly as tall or as broad-shouldered as the horseman.

He levels those piercing blue eyes on me as he unrolls the

tape. "Because you were so kind as to lay out your intentions—" He wraps the duct tape around the rope he's tied to the railing, then around my wrist bindings, sabotaging any hope of me escaping. "I think this should keep you immobile for now."

Pestilence rips the last of the tape off, then tosses the roll aside.

I glare at him, but the look is wasted. He's no longer even paying attention to me.

The horseman heads to the wood-burning stove and begins to build a fire.

"So what now?" I ask. "You're just going to keep me captive until I die of plague?"

Plague I most definitely haven't been feeling—or maybe I have. It's hard to say when you feel like three-day-old roadkill anyway.

Pestilence turns his head just slightly in my direction, then continues to tend to his fire. It takes mere minutes to get the flames roaring and another few minutes to really feel the heat.

He sits in front of the fire, his back to me, and he rubs a hand over his face.

"I begged," he finally says. "Broken and bleeding, I beseeched you for mercy, and you gave me none."

My gut twists. "You can't make me feel sorry," I lie, because he can. He already has. I was sorry before I even pulled the trigger and sorry again when I dropped the match. It doesn't change anything, but still—I was sorry. I *am* sorry. And it leaves a bitter, brackish taste in my mouth.

"I dare not hope for so much from the likes of your kind," he says, still not bothering to turn around.

"It was *you* who came to destroy *us*," I remind him.

Like I even need to defend myself. I don't know why I'm bothering.

"Humans have done a perfectly fine job of destroying themselves without my help. I am just here to finish the job."

"And you wonder why I showed you no mercy."

"*Mercy*." He spits the word out like an oath. "If you only knew the irony of your predicament, human…"

He returns his attention to the fire and rests his chin on his fist, so I guess the conversation's over. He stares and stares into those flames, and at some point, I think he forgets I exist altogether.

My mind drifts to my family. More than anything, I hope they're far enough away from the horseman to avoid his plague.

Unlike normal viruses, messianic fever doesn't follow the laws of science. You can be kilometers away from Pestilence, quarantined in your own home, and somehow still catch it. It's not clear how far away one needs to be to avoid the plague altogether, only that if you linger in a city Pestilence passes through, you'll die. It's as simple as that.

You haven't died yet, my mind whispers.

It's been over a day since I first came face-to-face with the horseman. *Surely* I should be feeling something by now.

Speaking of feeling something…

I shift my weight. It's not just my wrists and legs that hurt. My stomach has been growling for who knows how long, and my bladder is about ready to explode.

I clear my throat. "I need to go to the bathroom."

"Then go where you stand." Pestilence continues to stare into those flames like he can read the future in them.

He's making it easier and easier for me not to feel guilty about shooting and burning him.

27

"If you're hoping to keep me alive," I say, "I'll need to eat and drink and sleep and shit and piss."

Any regrets yet, buddy?

He sighs, then gets up. Pestilence strides over to me, his stature commanding; he's hardly the monster who woke me this morning, and that bothers me like no other thing.

Wearing the flannel shirt, jeans, and boots, he looks painfully human. Even his eyes, which seemed so alien when I first caught sight of him, now look full of life. Life and agony.

He hooks his fingers under the duct tape binding my wrists, and with a swift jerk, he rips it in two.

Note to self: this fucker is strong.

He tears the rest of the tape away and unties the rope from the railing. Once he has it in hand, he leads me down the hallway, only stopping once we get to the bathroom.

Problem number one occurs as soon as he closes the door behind us.

I glance at the massive chest that blocks the exit.

"It's called *privacy*," I say.

"I'm aware of the term, conniving human," he says, crossing his arms. "Why you think you deserve it is a question for a higher power."

I huff and turn from him.

Problem number two occurs after I try to undo my pants. I barely have feeling in my hands, let alone the dexterity needed for the task.

Damn it. "I need help."

Pestilence leans against the door. "I'm disinclined to give you any."

"Oh, for the love of—"

"God?" he finishes for me, raising his eyebrows. "Do you really think *He* is going to help you?"

The scholar in me is instantly piqued by his words, but now is not exactly the time to learn all the mysteries of the universe.

I blow out a breath. "Look, if you're regretting keeping me alive, then kill me, but if you're married to this idea of yours, I'd really appreciate it if you'd pull my goddamned pants down."

"Would it make you suffer to mess yourself?" he asks.

I hesitate. He has to know this is a loaded question.

Which answer is likelier *not* to screw me over?

"Yeah," I finally say, settling on the truth, "it would."

He leans against the door. "As I said, I'm disinclined to help."

He doesn't move to leave, however, and now I'm simply grateful I have a toilet to pee in.

I grit my teeth as I try again to unzip my pants. The rope digs into my chafed wrists, and they scream in protest. It takes an agonizing amount of time, but I finally manage to unbutton my jeans, then drag them, the long johns beneath them, and my underwear all down.

Pestilence's impersonal gaze is on me, looking at my lady goods, which are on full display.

Kill me now.

He curls his lip.

"I'm sorry," I say, "but if this fucking bothers you, then you can step outside." *And let me pee, then escape, in peace.*

"Empty yourself, human. I'm tired of standing here."

Muttering several curses beneath my breath, I do just that.

A horseman of the apocalypse is watching me pee.

Of all the sentences in the English language I could've come up with, *that* is not one I ever imagined thinking. I bite back a hysterical laugh. I'm going to die, but not before my dignity is murdered first.

29

Wiping myself, flushing, then pulling my pants back up takes even longer—as does washing my hands.

At least there still *is* water to wash my hands with. Unlike household electricity, running water was hit far less severely. The why beats the hell out of me, though I'm not going to complain. It's helped put out many a fire since the world ended.

Once I'm finished, the horseman leads me back down the hall, giving my restraints a jerk that nearly throws me off my feet. And then I'm tied to that damn railing once more, and he's back to the fire.

"So is this what you do?" I ask. "Go from town to town and invade people's homes?"

"No," he says over his shoulder.

"Then why did we stop here?" I ask.

He exhales, like I'm impossibly tedious—which I am, but honestly, homeboy has a long learning curve ahead of him because he ain't seen *nothing* yet—and ignores me.

That's his main move, I'm coming to find.

I turn my attention from his back to my injured wrists.

"What happened to the others?" I ask, more subdued.

"What others?" he responds gruffly.

I'm honestly shocked he's still engaging with me.

"The others who tried to kill you."

The horseman turns from the fire, his icy eyes catching the light from the flames. "I ended them."

I don't see any remorse on his face for those deaths either.

"So I'm your first kidnap victim?" I probe.

He huffs. "Hardly a victim," he says. "But I will keep you and make an example of you. Perhaps then your dim-witted kind will think twice about plots to destroy me."

Now and only now is my predicament really hitting me.

I'm not letting you die. Too quick, he said. *Suffering is made for the living. And, oh, how I will make you suffer.*

An unbidden shiver runs down my spine. Bloody wrists and aching legs may be the least of my concerns.

The worst, I'm sure, is yet to come.

CHAPTER 6

I'm still not sick.

And I'm still alive—albeit not exactly enthusiastic about it.

Everything hurts so much worse the next day. My wrists are one sharp, burning throb, my shoulders are stiff and sore from all the hours they've been stuck in this bound position, my stomach is actively trying to eat itself, and my legs are useless with pain.

Oh, and I'm still tied to this shithole railing.

The only silver linings have been the few glasses of water Pestilence brought to me (one of which I accidently poured all over myself rather than in my mouth because my hands are still bound and God legit hates me) and the fact the horseman has been kind enough to take me to the bathroom again so he doesn't have to smell my "vile stink."

I hate the pretty bastard.

"This above all: to thine own self be true," I mutter under my breath. The line from *Hamlet* comes to me from memory. The meaning of it has been worn down like river rocks from time and overuse, but the words still affect me all the same. "And it must follow, as the night the day—" My voice cuts off when I see Pestilence.

Last night he wore jeans and a flannel shirt, but this morning he's clad in a black ensemble that fits him like a glove. Both the fabric and cut of his clothes manage to look simultaneously archaic and futuristic, though I can't say precisely why. Maybe it's not even the clothes—maybe it's his crown or the bow and quiver slung haphazardly over his shoulder. Whatever it is, he's looking distinctly otherworldly.

"I am going to untie you from the railing, human," he says by way of greeting, "but mark me: If you try to flee, I will shoot you, then drag you back here."

I stare at the deep V of his dark shirt, catching just a glimpse of one of those glowing tattoos.

"Did you hear me?" he asks.

I blink, and my gaze moves to his face.

The last of the horseman's wounds have healed—even his hair has fully regrown. Only took a day for him to completely regenerate. How disheartening.

"If I bolt, I'm dead meat. Got it."

He furrows his brow, and he studies me for a second longer before grunting. With that, he pulls me along to the kitchen.

Using one of his booted feet, he kicks out a chair. "Sit."

I grimace at him but do as he commands.

Pestilence strides away from me, opening cupboard doors seemingly at random before closing them and moving on. Eventually, he opens the home's icebox and pulls out a loaf of bread—who refrigerates their bread?—and a bottle of Worcestershire sauce from it.

"Here is your sustenance," he says, tossing them to me. By

some miracle I manage to catch the bottle of Worcestershire sauce in my bound hands. The bread beans me on the head.

"You'll have to eat while you run," he continues. "I'll not be wasting time for human breaks today."

I'm still stuck on the bottle of Worcestershire sauce. Does the horseman actually think I can drink this?

He yanks on my bindings, making for the door, and I scramble to grab the fallen bread loaf from the floor. While Pestilence ties me to the back of his saddle, I manage to stuff two thick slices of bread into my mouth and shove another few into my pockets. And then we're off, and I'm forced to drop the rest of the bread so I can focus on keeping up.

Immediately, I'm aware today will not be like yesterday. My legs are too sore, and my energy is too depleted. Each step is agonizing, and no amount of fear can force me to run as fast or as long as I need to.

I make it twenty, maybe twenty-five, kilometers before I fall, hitting my back hard on the road.

The horse jerks against my weight, and I let out a scream as my arms are violently yanked nearly out of their sockets. The rope digs into my wrists, and I shriek again at the searing pain.

It doesn't end. The pressure in my shoulders and wrists is nearly unendurable. I gasp out a breath, ready to scream some more, but it's all so violent that it takes my breath away.

Pestilence must know I've fallen, he must feel the resistance, and I know he heard my screams, but he doesn't so much as glance back at me.

I hated him before now, but there's something about this cruelty that cuts more sharply than a knife.

He's here to kill humankind. What else did you expect?

I have to lift my head as my body drags along behind the

horse to prevent it from getting injured. Yesterday's snow has mostly melted away, and the bare asphalt now acts like sandpaper against my back. I can almost feel the layers of my thick coat disintegrating under the force of it. Once it goes…I don't know how long a human can last like this.

I never get the chance to find out.

Before I feel the bite of the road against my bare skin, Pestilence stops the horse in front of another house.

I lean my head against my arm, utterly exhausted by the pain. Dimly, I'm aware of the horseman untying my restraints from his mount.

His footfalls come to my side, then ominously stop.

"Up."

I moan in response. Everything hurts so damn *much*.

A second later, he bends down and scoops me up.

I let out a whimper. Even his touch hurts. I close my eyes and lay a weary cheek against the golden armor of his chest as he carries me to the house's stoop.

I don't see Pestilence batter down the door; I simply hear it. Shouts ring out from inside the house.

"Oh my God," a woman says. "Oh my God—oh my *God*."

I force my eyes open. There's a middle-aged lady staring at us with a look of abject horror.

Why hasn't she evacuated? What was she thinking?

"We're staying here," the horseman says as he brushes past her.

Her head jerks back in surprise as she watches him invade her home. "Not in *my* house!" she says shrilly.

"My prisoner will need to eat, sleep, and use your amenities," he continues, as though she hadn't spoken.

Behind us, I hear her choke on several words before she says, "You need to *leave*. Now."

Her words fall on deaf ears. Pestilence heads up her staircase. Once he gets to the second floor, he kicks more doors open, and there's not a damn thing she can do about it. He muscles us into a sparsely furnished bedroom before kicking the door shut behind him.

He lays me on the bed, then backs away, folding his arms over his chest. "You're slowing me down, human."

I glare at him from where I lie. "Then let me go." *Or kill me.* Honestly, death may be the kinder option at this point.

"Have you forgotten my words so quickly? I don't intend to let you go. I intend to make you suffer."

"You're doing a good job of it," I say quietly.

His disapproving look only deepens at my words. Strange, you'd think he'd be pleased by that.

He gestures to the bed where I lie. "Sleep," he commands.

Oh, like it's that simple.

Even feeling like I've been shit-kicked to near death, I can't just up and fall asleep, especially not when the sun lances through the window and I can hear the homeowner protesting on the other side of the door.

"I need you to untie my hands first," I say, raising my bound arms to him.

His gaze narrows all distrustful-like, but he comes over to me and undoes the rope.

He leans in close. "No tricks, human."

Because I'm so sneaky at the moment.

Once my wrists are free, blood flows through my hands, the sensation agonizing. A low groan escapes my throat.

"If you want my pity, expect to be disappointed," Pestilence says, backing up to the door.

This guy is insufferable—even if he is annoyingly handsome. Actually, that may be making it worse. He's like the most aggressive form of my already most hated male combo: the hot asshole.

My eyes move over Pestilence as he folds his arms, content to just watch me, a look of mild repulsion on his face.

Feeling's mutual.

"I'm not going to fall asleep with you just staring at me," I say.

"Too bad."

So that's how it's going to be.

I sit up and stiffly peel off my outer clothes, which are mostly rags at this point anyway. Tossing them aside, I slide under the sheets and try not to shudder at the fact I'm lying in the guest bedroom of a woman Pestilence's plague will soon kill.

This is all so epically twisted.

Beneath the covers, I rub my wrists, and I bite down on my lower lip when I realize it's too excruciating to touch. Even the soft flannel sheets are agony against the raw skin.

Pestilence sits on the floor, leaning his back against the door, and his unspoken message is clear: *I'm not going anywhere.*

I flip over so I can, for five seconds, pretend he doesn't exist and today doesn't exist and none of this exists.

I lie there for some time. Long enough to wonder if any of my teammates survived the fever. Long enough to once again fret about my parents. I force myself to imagine them holed up in my grandfather's rickety hunting lodge, playing poker by the fire like we used to when I was young.

They think I'm dead.

I remember my dad's tears earlier this week. How shocking they were. He'd been so proud when I joined the fire department. He never wanted me to go to university; it didn't matter that I'd been obsessed with English literature since I was little, that I went so far as dressing as Edgar Allan Poe for Halloween one year in college (yeah, I was what wet dreams were made of), or that I spent long weekends writing poems. Once the horsemen arrived, university was a beautiful reverie and nothing more.

Too impractical, my dad had told me. *What are you going to use a degree for, anyway?*

I wonder what he'd say to that now...

"Horseman," I call out.

Silence.

"I know you can hear me."

He doesn't respond.

I sigh. "Really? You're just going to ignore me?"

He heaves out a breath. *Yes.*

I pick at a loose thread of my borrowed bedspread. "We drew lots," I begin. "To decide who'd kill you."

Pestilence is still quiet, but now I swear I can feel his eyes on my back.

"There were four of us left," I continue. "Me, Luke, Briggs, and Felix. We worked together at the fire station, and for the last several days before you came, we helped the Mounties warn residents that they needed to evacuate. We weren't positive, of course, that you'd ride through our city. Whistler isn't all that big, but it lies right on the Sea to Sky Highway, the same highway the news had previously spotted you on.

"By the time we drew lots, all the other firefighters had already left with their families. Those of us without families of our own, we stayed behind." My father's face floats through my mind.

You have a family, just like Felix and Briggs and Luke do. You just don't have a spouse and kids. And in the end, that's why you all took the final shift.

38

Fewer people to miss us.

"There were four of us left," I continue, "and we thought maybe—"

"Why are you telling me this?" Pestilence interrupts.

I pause. "Don't you want to know why I shot you?" I ask.

"I already know why you shot me, human." The horseman's voice is sharp. "You wanted to stop me from spreading plague. All these justifications you're spewing aren't for my benefit—they're for yours."

That shuts me up.

I was trying to save the world. I'm not evil like you think I am, I want to say. But somehow his words burn those explanations away like acid.

The room is quiet for a long moment.

"You're right," I finally say, flipping over to face him. "They are."

My reasons make no difference to him; they don't change the fact that I shot and burned him. That I didn't listen when he begged me to stop.

The horseman has his forearms resting on his bent knees, his penetrating gaze on me. "What do you hope to gain by agreeing with me?" he asks.

"You're the one everyone calls *Pestilence the Conqueror*," I say. "Can't you even tell when you've won an argument?"

Pestilence frowns.

I pull at that loose string on the bedspread again. "For what it's worth, I'm sorry."

"About what?"

"Killing you—or attempting to, anyway." Twice, technically, since Pestilence probably only lived through the gunshot wound because he was undying.

He lets out a hollow laugh. "Lies. You're only telling me this now because you're my prisoner and you fear what I mean to do with you."

It's true that I'm afraid of whatever terrifying punishments Pestilence wants to exact on me, but—

"No," I say. "I don't *regret* trying to kill you. I absolutely hated what I did to you, and I'll never be the same because of it, but I don't regret my choices. Still, I am sorry."

The horseman is silent for a long time as he scrutinizes me.

"Go to sleep," he eventually says.

And I do.

CHAPTER 7

I wake in the middle of the night, ripped from sleep by the sound of crying.

I blink, looking around.

Thought the neighbors had all evacuated...

I grope for my bedside oil lamp before I realize there *is* no bedside oil lamp.

Not my room. Not my apartment.

Then the past few days wash over me like a cold shower.

Drawing matches, shooting Pestilence, the brutal runs I was forced to endure until I could no longer. As the memories flood in, so do all my lingering pains.

You made this shit sandwich, Burns, now you got to eat it.

The sound of crying cuts through my thoughts, and I remember the homeowner. How many hours has it been since we showed up on her doorstep?

Twelve? More? Less?

I grope around again for an oil lamp; now that power is spotty, people keep lamps and lanterns around. My fingers slide over a bedside table, but what they bump into isn't a lamp. I feel around the glass of water and the pitcher next to it.

Did Pestilence leave this here?

I balk at the thought. That would be far too kind for the likes of him.

After pulling off my blankets, I get out of bed and slip down the hall, ready to head toward the crying, which seems to be coming from a room at the back of the house. But then I hesitate.

What are you going to do, Sara? Comfort her? You're a stranger playing Goldilocks in her house. You think she wants anything to do with you?

I stand there, second-guessing myself, while my eyes pass over the dark hallway once, twice, looking for Pestilence. I prowl back to my room and peek inside. The darkness obscures a lot, but it can't hide a horseman, and there isn't one in my room.

He's *gone*.

I don't give myself time to wonder where Pestilence slunk off to. I've got who knows how much time until he returns.

Not going to waste it.

I force myself to ignore the woman's cries. Can't help her now. She'll die like the rest of them—like I *should* be dying—and there's nothing I can do about it.

I tried, I want to tell her, *I tried, but the horseman can't be killed, and I'm so sorry, but I don't think any of us are getting out of this alive.*

Except that I am. Tonight. Right now.

I grab the pile of clothes I shed earlier from where they lie next to the bed. As silently as I dare, I slip them on, my hands fumbling with the buttons as I shake.

Hurry, hurry. Before he comes back.

After grabbing my boots, I slip them on and pad softly to the window. I wiggle the pane open, wincing against the blast of frigid air that blows in, stinging my lungs and rustling my hair.

Damn it. *Really* don't want to go out there on a night like this.

I hesitate. I could stay with Pestilence; he's not trying to kill me after all.

He wants to make you suffer.

There will be more running, more bleeding wrists, and more days like today when I can't keep up. And that's assuming Pestilence doesn't decide I need to suffer more than I already am. I'd rather not stick around to see what creative punishments he comes up with.

Mind made up, I punch out the window screen. A moment later, I hear it thud softly as it hits the ground below.

Deep breath for courage.

I swing first one leg, then the other, out over the window ledge. Outside, it's snowing again, a thin layer of it carpeting the ground. It's that ground that has me nervous. Sitting two stories up as I am, the drop could break my legs. It would have to be a bad landing, but it could. Painstakingly, I lower myself until I'm dangling out the window by my hands and thanking the fates that firefighting has given me good upper-body strength.

And then I let go.

For one long moment, I'm weightless. Then the moment ends, and my feet slam against the ground. Slowly, I straighten. No rolled ankles, no broken bones—for once, luck's with me.

I give the house a final passing glance, and then I bolt.

I sprint for the road, even though my body is in no condition to run.

I'm free. Holy freaking shitballs, I'm *free*!

Behind me I hear a faint, slick hiss, a sound I mistake for the wind until what feels like a knife slams into my back, just below my right shoulder blade.

I choke against the pain, my feet stumbling as warmth spreads out from the wound.

Blood, my mind puts together. *You're bleeding because there's an* arrowhead *embedded in your back.*

I should've known better, but when I saw that empty bedroom, I couldn't *not* act.

Hope is a damnable thing.

And now—Jesus, Joseph, and Mary, the burn of the wound seizes up my windpipe.

I don't bother to glance behind me as I force my feet to continue moving. I know what I'll see. Proud Pestilence, bow in hand, sighting me like a hunter.

If I stop now, he's got me.

I fucking *sprint*, snow crunching under my boots as I make for the tree line ahead of me. If I make it to the forest, I may still be able to escape him.

With every pump of my arms and sway of my torso, the arrowhead cuts deeper into muscle.

You've endured worse, Burns. You've walked through fire, felt the flames sear your skin and cook your body. You will live through this.

I will live through it…so long as this arrowhead wasn't tipped with poison…or plague. I try not to think about that latter one. I try not to imagine what will happen if I get away. How I may escape him only to die of the fever.

I'm almost to the woods when the next arrow hits me, the tip of it driving into my lower back.

Again I stumble, nearly going to my knees. This one—this one feels like it hit more than just muscle. There's a sick tugging sensation that feels wrong every time I move.

Behind me I hear the pounding of hoofbeats.

Move! I scream at myself as snow flurries swirl around me.

I stagger to my feet, forcing myself to keep going. My energy is quickly flagging, and I feel more blood soaking into my ripped clothes, the fabric quickly turning icy.

It takes the horseman less than a minute to reach me, his mount's breath steaming in the night air.

I feel Pestilence's burning gaze on me, even though I don't dare look at him. Escape is now futile, but I still won't force myself to stop.

I hear the heavy clanking of his armor as he dismounts, his boots crunching into the snow and dead underbrush.

In two long strides, he's upon me. His hand wraps around an arrow shaft.

"*No*—"

Mercilessly, he yanks it out. I scream as the blade of it cuts into more muscle and sinew as it's removed.

He tosses it aside, never saying a word. I feel another sickening pull as he grabs the other arrow lodged into my back.

Please. It's on the tip of my tongue to beg him, but I have a feeling that is exactly what he wants—for me to plead for my life the way he did his. I grind my teeth. Damn him, I won't give him what he wants.

When he yanks the second arrowhead out, the pain has my legs folding out from under me. Rivulets of my blood drip down my back, the sickening sensation setting my teeth on edge.

"Because you've proven yourself to be every bit as conniving as the rest of your brethren," he says, his tone just as cutting as his weapons, "you will no longer sleep. It's a luxury you can no longer afford."

Roughly, he grabs my hands, pulling a rope loose from where it's been secured at his hip.

I tug against his hands. "What are you doing?" I ask, panicking in earnest.

Not the rope. Not again.

Oh God.

It's hitting me that I tried to escape and I failed and now everything is going to be so much *worse*.

Kneeling in the snow, he begins to bind my wrists, his expression grim and angry.

If I don't get away now, I am going to die.

I kick out at him, my boot landing heavily against his thigh. He doesn't so much as sway.

He tightens the knots on my wrists, and I cry out at the stabbing pain. His lips thin as he loops the other end through his saddle.

"No." *Please.* "No, no, no." I'm muttering almost senselessly, a couple of tears squeezing out of my eyes.

I have two open wounds at my back, and the night air is so cold it rips through my clothing and burns my skin.

"*Why* are you doing this?" The question is almost a sob.

Pestilence glares at me. "Have you forgotten what *you* so recently did to *me*?" He gives a yank on the rope. "Up."

I don't get up. I don't have it in me *to* get up.

The horseman doesn't stick around to see whether I follow his orders. He mounts his horse and makes another clicking noise.

The steed trots away, and I only have one swift second to get my feet properly under me before I'm forced to move.

And then we're off again.

CHAPTER 8

I don't know how long we travel in the dark, cold night, only that it feels endless. My hands are numb, my legs are stiff with chill, and my back throbs in strange painful ways that make me think my injuries are more than just flesh wounds.

Still, Pestilence drives us onward.

At first his horse moves slowly, though I don't think it's to show me any mercy. Rather, I assume it's to draw out my agony for as long as possible. The steed picks up speed until his trot becomes a canter, and then his canter eventually becomes a gallop.

I keep up for a while. That much I can say. Despite everything, I somehow do keep up.

But no one except this dastardly immortal creature can go on forever. The lack of sleep, the thin meals, the cold, my wounds, and my exhaustion—it's all worn me down.

I trip, falling backward onto the snow-covered road, and I don't get up. My wrists jerk over my head, the force of it yanking at least one arm out of its socket.

Now I scream. Now I lose it.

My body is on fire—a person could go mad from this sort of pain.

I didn't even know I could hurt this much, and *oh God, oh God, oh God, make it stop, please make it stop, I'm sorry I shot your beloved horseman, just make it stop.*

But it doesn't stop. If God has any mercy, it's not spared on me.

I'm dragged through the snow, and the cold hurts so bad it burns. Whatever protection my clothes afford me, it doesn't last long. I feel the icy road against my back, and I don't know where my agony ends and I begin. All I know is that I haven't endured worse than this.

I scream until my throat is ragged from use. My arms are going to be ripped from my body. There's no other way this ends. And I'm in so much pain that I *hope* they'll cleave away from me so I can bleed out and die quicker than this.

It doesn't happen.

There's pain and pain and pain, so much goddamned pain. I'm burning up with it even though there's no fire, I'm burning up, and *make it stop, please make it stop, please, please, please—*

CHAPTER 9

I wake briefly to an intense flare of pain in one of my shoulders. I cry out as hands release me and some of the agony abates.

The world around me is out of focus, just swathes of colors, and my body throbs in the most horrible way. *Why* does everything hurt?

Around me, the colors sharpen enough for me to make out a face. An angel looms over me, his face still somewhat blurry.

Am I in heaven?

Should I feel pain if I'm in heaven?

I reach out and cup the angel's face with a shaky hand, my wrists bloody and my fingers purple. He flinches, moving out of my reach.

"Am I dead?" I think I ask, but the angel doesn't respond. "Stay with me," I murmur. I grope for a hand. When I find what I'm looking for, I lace my fingers through it. "Please."

Not supposed to say that word.

Why am I not supposed to say that word?

Something about begging, but now I can't quite remember...

Everything is drifting farther and farther from me.

I squeeze the hand I hold tightly. "Stay with me," I say again.

But the angel and the rest of the world melt away.

———————

I blink my eyes open, staring at the popcorn ceiling above me. For a moment, my life is normal, my mind wiped free of memory.

Someone squeezes my hand, and I turn my head, bewildered. And then I see him.

I scream.

There's nothing—*nothing*—more monstrous than that beguiling face Pestilence wears, his golden crown resting proudly on his head.

It's only once he drops my hand like it burned that I realize the fucker was *holding my hand*. It takes another second for me to process why exactly that fills me with blinding fury.

Fleeing the horseman. Arrows to the back. Tied to his steed and forced to run. Falling. Dragging. Pain. Dying.

I gasp at the memory, and now the full force of my agony surfaces.

"I'm...alive."

It seems impossible in light of everything I went through. It felt as though I were being torn apart.

"Suffering is for the living," Pestilence replies from where he sits. I glance around at the room we're in. It's another guest room, in another house Pestilence decided to invade.

50

My hands delve into the worn sheets beneath me. He brought me to this room and laid me on the bed, and presumably, I've been here ever since.

I can't tell whether this scenario utterly terrifies me or whether it takes the edge off my fear.

He didn't let me die. He intends to let me heal—

Only so I can suffer more.

I push myself up in bed, biting back a yelp at the intense pain that flares across my back.

"Why am I here?" I ask.

"I won't let you die."

Again I don't know whether him saving me is a kindness or a curse.

It's obviously a curse, you bimbo. He ain't saving you to romance your ass.

"You shot me, then tied me up and dragged me through the snow." Just saying those words forces a shiver through me.

His blue eyes are steady on me. "I did."

I roll a shoulder, the joint achingly sore.

"My arm was pulled out of its socket," I say, remembering the excruciating sensation.

He gazes at me for a long moment, looking every inch the damnable angel, then nods.

I glance down at myself. My shirt is gone, replaced by some stranger's—likely a large woman with an outdated wardrobe, judging by the garish floral print of it.

Someone saw me topless. My eyes slide to Pestilence, who's staring at me passively.

It was probably him, which means he's now seen both my vagina and my boobs.

Ugh. Why me?

I move my hand, the action feeling constrained. Pushing

back a sleeve, I notice my wrists are bound in soft white linen. I thumb one of the bandages.

Did Pestilence tend to me?

I remember the vicious way he yanked the arrowheads out of my back.

There's no way...

I'm distracted by the horrible throb of my back. I sit forward to take some of the pressure off, and cloth digs into the skin of my stomach.

Lifting the edge of the shirt, I stare at my torso, which, like my wrists, is wrapped in layer upon layer of bandages.

I run my thumb over the linen. "Who did this?"

Pestilence levels an unreadable look at me.

"*You?*" I finally ask.

My blood burns beneath my skin with horror and embarrassment and...something else at the thought of him ripping away my clothes and mending me. I try to imagine him cleaning and dressing my wounds, and I find I can't. I don't want to.

His lips thin. "Remember my kindness."

"Your *kindness*?" I say in disbelief. "You were the one who *inflicted* these wounds."

And you'll do it again and again and again until it breaks me.

Gah, he was right when he promised me suffering.

His upper lip ticks, like he's fighting a grimace.

Pestilence stands, his large frame looming over me. "Don't try to escape again, mortal," he warns, and then he leaves the room.

"Pestilence!" I shout for the five billionth time.

I pause, listening.

Still nothing.

Of course, he can catch me fleeing in two point five seconds flat, but when I actually need him, he's nowhere to be found.

"Pestilence!"

In the distance, I think I hear a moan, which sobers me up real fast.

Is someone else living here?

Heavy footsteps interrupt that thought. The door opens, and there Pestilence is, looking like a prince from a fairy tale.

His eyes first go to the bed, where I should be, before dropping to the floor, where I am.

"What are you doing out of bed, human?" he asks, looking at me all suspicious-like.

Because I'm so ready to attempt escape again.

"I need help." It hurts a good deal of my pride to say this.

His brow furrows and he steps farther inside the room before closing the door behind him.

"You do understand I am reluctant to offer you any such thing, given our history."

Our history. He somehow makes it sound like there's this whole saga between us.

"I know," I say.

He waits for me to continue. But now that he's here, looking like some airbrushed male model, I'm losing a little of my nerve.

"Um," I say, fidgeting on the floor, my back screaming in pain, "I have to go to the bathroom." This is technically no different than the other time I asked him to help me to the bathroom, and yet it is because now I'm injured rather than bound, and my frailty makes me feel vulnerable.

That's why I'm sitting here on the floor. I tried to get out of bed and mosey over to the bathroom on my own. I just hadn't factored in how weak I'd be or how sharply my wounds would ache.

I made it halfway to the door before I gave up.

And now here we are.

For a long moment, Pestilence doesn't react. Then, silently, he comes over to me. I tense a little as he kneels at my side. I know I asked for assistance, but I can't help remembering all the agony he's inflicted on me.

It's a horrible twist of fate that I depend on the very person who put me in this position.

Pestilence's arms slide under my body, and he lifts me. I yelp at the sharp stab of pain that lances through me at the movement. To my eternal humiliation, I wrap my arms around the horseman's neck to ease some of the pressure on my back.

The position puts me uncomfortably close to the horseman's mouth, and I have the misfortune of noticing how his upper lip is fuller than his bottom one.

He carries me to the bathroom wordlessly before depositing me on the toilet, even though my pants are still on. I finger the denim covering my lower half. I'm wearing *mom jeans*, a.k.a. the minivans of the pants world. I most definitely didn't dress myself in these.

Which means…

Ugh.

Horseman saw my lady goods again.

Said horseman looms over me. "Try to escape again—"

"Yeah, yeah," I say. "I'm not going anywhere."

Pestilence scowls, then steps outside the bathroom, closing the door behind him. He must know I'm in no state to go anywhere, or else I doubt he'd leave me alone in here.

That, or he knows he can just shoot you down again if you try to hobble away.

I go to the bathroom, then flush the toilet behind me.

"Pestilence!" I call out when I'm done, leaning heavily against the counter where I managed to rinse my hands.

When he comes in, I all but collapse in his arms.

This time, when I wrap my arms around his neck, I feel too pitiful to even be humiliated.

He nudges open the door to my room and puts me back in the bed.

"I thought you forbid me to sleep," I say as he slides his hands out from beneath me.

This close to him, I can see the crystalline blue of his eyes. They're the color of the sky on a clear day. Above them, his crown sits, the sight of it a grim reminder of who he is.

Those eyes of his narrow, and his already pouty mouth turns down. "Don't make me regret my kindnesses."

I really think he needs to reevaluate what that word means.

Before I have a chance to respond, he slips out of the room, and I'm alone once more.

It's another two days before I'm strong enough to leave the bed on my own.

Until then, Pestilence took to feeding me (and judging by his food choices, he has no idea what people actually eat) and taking me to and from the bathroom.

In other words, it's been a spanking-good time.

Not.

When the horseman wasn't tending to me, I spent my

time sleeping. Sleeping and dreaming strange dreams where my parents hovered nearby, just out of reach, and they murmured to me, and sometimes they shouted, and in the end they just coughed weakly before fading from sight.

Now I step into the hallway on shaky legs, thrilling at the feel of finally being mobile. Not that I'm back to normal or anything. Everything still hurts, even my lungs, and I shouldn't be out of bed, but I need to pee, and I'm tired of having to flag down Pestilence.

It's only after I've used the toilet and dipped my head to the bathroom's sink to drink my weight in water that I decide to explore the home I've been crashing in.

When I leave the bathroom, I take a moment to listen. If the horseman is nearby, he doesn't make his presence known. But I seriously doubt he is. Now that the two of us have established some sort of routine, one where I shout and shout his name and he only sometimes comes, I'm beginning to think the only time he's actually loitering about in this house is when he brings me food and water or helps me to the bathroom.

Not going to think about the fact he's been tending to me. I'm going to remember that he shot me in the back—twice—then dragged me through the snow until the pain was so great I passed out from it. I'm going to remember that he's still moving from town to town, bringing plague with him and towing me along for the ride.

We're enemies, plain and simple. He hasn't forgotten that since I shot him. I should make sure I don't forget that either, no matter how helpful he's been since.

A buzzing noise draws my attention to the ceiling. Overhead, a light glows softly. That's the first time I notice that this house has electricity, a luxury for a home these days.

Lucky ducks. The apartment I lived in never did. It was oil lamps and lanterns all the way for me.

I walk down the hallway, moving toward what looks to be the living room and the kitchen beyond. Now that my most urgent needs are taken care of, I feel the twisting throb of my empty stomach beneath the sharper pains.

Anything at this point will be better than the strange food combos Pestilence thinks to bring me, like mustard and uncooked pasta. I'm just spitballing here, but if I had to guess, I'd say the horseman ain't too familiar with human cuisine.

The air in this place has a stale taste to it, like it's been shuttered for too long in the heat, leaving perishable goods to spoil.

The images hanging along the walls on either side of me catch my attention. Family photos. My gut clenches. It's easy to get swept away by the most obvious horrors of the apocalypse and forget that the people who've been affected have families just like I do.

My eyes move from photo to photo, the images arranged in sequential order. First it's embarrassing baby pictures—the kind where your parents pose you naked and think you're absolutely adorable until you're older and they're just the shit your friends make fun of when they stumble upon them.

These pictures are followed by sweet toddler photos, then toothless grins of elementary school kids. Inevitably, these morph into family photos that somehow look outdated, between the large lacy collar the wife wears, the giant bifocals that make her husband's eyes all the beadier, and the mullet-like haircuts of their two boys.

I touch the frame, smiling a little at the sight. How old are these two boys now? In their thirties? Forties? Do they have families of their own?

The photos come to an abrupt halt with the end of the hallway, and I step into the living room.

I swallow a yelp.

There's a man lying on a navy sectional, clad in only a pair of boxers, and something's very wrong with him. Everywhere that his clothes don't cover, hundreds of small lumps press up from beneath the skin. To my horror some of those lumps have split open, revealing blood and pus and other slick things that have me tasting bile at the back of my throat.

I've seen a lot of disturbing things during my few years as a firefighter, but nothing like this.

There's a cloying smell in the air, one I hadn't noticed earlier. It's the scent of infection—rot.

He's caught the fever.

A shameful part of me wants to get as far away from this man as I can. He's undoubtedly contagious.

You're a first responder, Burns. This is what it means in the end. Sacrifice and, if need be, death.

My eyes move back to the man's face. His hair is a dull brown that's losing its battle to gray, and his face has that worn, stretched appearance that skin starts to get in a person's forties. And his bloodshot eyes, they stare at me listlessly as his chest rises and falls just the barest amount.

Dear God, he's still alive.

CHAPTER 10

Pestilence wanted me to see this. I know it as surely as I know my own name. Physically hurting me was only part of my punishment for trying to end him. This is the other part—to watch death at its most abhorrent.

No, not just to watch it. And not just to be powerless to stop it but to accompany Pestilence like a coconspirator, to play some role in spreading the disease.

I stare at the man, rooted to the spot, trying to remember all the stories I heard about this plague.

The news mentioned the lumps. How they could swell and cover every inch of the body. And how, toward the final stages of the disease, they'd burst open like overripe fruit as the person's body decayed from the inside out.

Necrosis, they call it—the body rotting while the organism still lives.

The hairs on my arms rise. I should be suffering from this. No—I should be dead from it. Instead I'm alive and healthy enough to watch this man succumb to it.

I take him in again, open sores and all. This sort of death has no business in the modern world. It's the kind of thing that belongs in old horror movies and tales from medieval Europe. Not here, where in recent memory cars ran and planes flew, phones made calls and the internet existed.

But the modern world is gone. Killed in the months that followed the horsemen's arrival. And now everyone's scrambling to get on with life in an age when we have lost almost everything.

Even though I want to run, I take a tentative step forward. I'm a firefighter, damn it. I'm used to seeing scary shit every day. Seeing it and *fixing* it.

I stride forward, noticing how the man's listless eyes try to track me.

Alive and aware.

I crouch in front of him, smelling ammonia and human excrement. Pestilence might've been helping me to the bathroom, but he hadn't been so benevolent with our host— or whoever this man is.

Again I hesitate. A part of me worries that by trying to help, I'll only hurt the man more. Not to mention there's a good chance I'll catch the disease in the process, and this is not a good way to go. But then, I've been alongside Pestilence for longer than this man has. I've been restrained and shot and dragged through the snow, and I'm still alive— alive and untouched by the fever.

Somehow, it's skipped over me.

But even if it hasn't, even if I've simply managed to avoid it up until now, what's the worst that'll happen? I'll be in pain? I dare the fates to give me worse than what I've already endured. And if I die? Well, then at least I won't have to stomach more of the horseman's presence.

I'm all for silver linings.

I crouch in front of the man, taking his hand. It's hot to the touch.

He works his dry throat and makes a weak attempt at shaking his head.

"Shoun't...toush...me... Siccc," he whispers.

I squeeze his hand. "It's all right," I say gently. "I'm here to help you."

He closes his eyes. "Allll...dea..." He moans this, his face grimacing. "I...lassst."

My stomach plummets. That smell of rot may not just be coming from him. It may be coming from other people... people who are now just *bodies*.

And in all the time I'd been recuperating, I hadn't noticed there were other people in the house.

You were asleep for most of it, I remind myself.

Yet maybe I *had* noticed. Maybe all my fever dreams weren't fever dreams at all but the noises filtering into my room while I slept, noises my mind put faces to.

My attention returns to the man in front of me. He had to watch whoever else lives here fall ill and then die. And somewhere at the back of his mind, he might've been aware that he was going to die last, without someone to care for him.

I place the back of my hand against his forehead, then his neck. He's burning up. And now that I look beyond the lumps and open sores that transform his body into a grotesquerie, I can see his lips are split and scabbed.

I stand suddenly and stride into the kitchen. When I find a hand towel, I run it under the kitchen faucet. Then, after flipping through the cupboards, I pull out an empty glass and a bottle of Red Label that I come across.

Once I fill the cup with water, I take the goods back to the living room, trying and failing not to think about the fact that I got a bed in this house but this man didn't. Was that Pestilence's doing? Was that this man's?

After setting my items down on a coffee table near the couch, I grab the wet towel and gently run it over the man's face and neck. Meticulously, I move down his body, trying to avoid what I can of the lumps and sores, which look painful to the touch.

I grab the glass of water and the bottle of Red Label from the coffee table. Holding the two up, I ask, "Which do you prefer?"

There's not even a second's deliberation. The man's eyes go to the whiskey.

"Good choice."

I dump out the glass of water right onto the carpet—because no one's going to give a shit about a puddle in a house full of plague—and fill it halfway up with the liquor.

Sliding a hand under the man's back, I lift his body just enough for him to swallow, ignoring my own aches and pains that awaken with the exertion. Using my other hand, I hold the glass of whiskey to his lips.

He downs the liquid in five solid swallows.

"More," he croaks, and his voice sounds stronger.

Again I fill the cup halfway up, and again he downs it. And then once more.

It's enough alcohol to send me to the hospital, but I guess that's the point. There's no beating this plague. The kill rate of this thing is 100 percent. At this point all either of us can do is manage this man's pain.

Once he empties the third cup, I reach for the bottle again, but he lifts his hand, just slightly. *No more.*

"Thank you," he wheezes.

I nod, swallowing the thickness in my throat. I take his burning hand, and I hold it between my own. "Would you like me to stay?" I ask. I don't bother adding *For your last few hours.* Even staring death down, I can't seem to acknowledge it by name.

The man closes his eyes, his body already relaxing from the whiskey, and he squeezes my hand once, which I take for a yes.

My thumb strokes circles into his skin, and softly I recite Poe. "Lo! Death hath reared himself a throne / In a strange city, lying alone…"

The words to "The City in the Sea" rush out of me, words I read and memorized long ago. Once I finish reciting the poem, I move on, quoting Lord Byron's "And Thou art Dead, as Young and Fair" and then a few passages from *Macbeth*, pieces of poetry and prose I picked up here and there. The world might've stopped caring about these poets long ago, but their immortalized words are appropriate now more than ever.

Next to me, the man doesn't open his eyes again, but every so often he tilts his head just a little in my direction, letting me know he's listening.

At some point, he stops turning to me. His wheezy breaths slow as he nods off. I sit on my heels, holding his hand, and watch until the rise and fall of his chest fades to nothing. Even then I hold his hand, not releasing it until his skin begins to cool.

I never got his name. I held his hand and eased his suffering, and the sight of his plague-riddled body will haunt me for the rest of my days, but I never got his name.

That's going to bother me.

On a whim, I grab the bottle of Red Label and take several swallows of it. I tuck the bottle under my arm. I already know I'm going to need it again, and soon. There will undoubtedly be more torments ahead.

After all, my suffering is just beginning.

CHAPTER 11

We leave not an hour after the nameless man expires.
Pestilence leads me out with a hand on my shoulder, his
golden bow and arrows never far from my sight.

Just a reminder of what he can do to me.

His steed waits for us, its reins not tied to anything, just
standing there like the creature has nothing better to do than
wait on its master.

Pestilence grabs the rope that's been shoved into one of
the saddlebags. After unwinding it, he wraps one end around
my wrists, which are still covered in bandages.

All my aches and pains come roaring back at the sight of
my bound hands.

Running again. I should've known.

But instead of tying the other end to the back of his
saddle, he threads it through one of his belt loops.

I raise my eyebrows. That's unexpected.

Pestilence makes careful work of avoiding my eyes as he
turns to me and grabs either side of my torso. Even though
he's carted me to and from the bathroom over the past two

days, I still jolt at the press of his palms beneath my armpits. Before I can do more, he hoists me onto his horse. A second later he swings himself on behind me.

The leather creaks as Pestilence settles himself in the saddle. I hiss out a breath at the pain that flares up as I'm pressed against his armor. His left arm loops around me, hand splayed across my lower stomach. His other hand takes the reins.

He leans in close. "You jump," he warns, his breath hot against my ear, "I'll make you run behind me again."

I don't doubt him, but right now all I can think about is how repulsive and intimate it is having him this close.

Pestilence clucks his tongue, and his horse is off.

I'm riding with one of the horsemen of the apocalypse.

Holy shit.

I've now got a front-row seat to the end of the world.

Even with all the aches and pains that pull at me, riding is a far better means of travel than running, wrists bound, behind a horse.

"I was really close to death, wasn't I?" I ask, referring to when Pestilence dragged my injured body down the highway.

"Must you talk?"

So pleasant, this one.

"Must you spread plague?"

He doesn't respond, though I can feel him brooding at my back.

"Why did you save me?" I prod.

"I didn't *save* you, human. I kept you alive. There's a difference. And I kept you alive to make you suffer. I thought I had made myself clear about this."

I touch my chest. Beneath my layers of borrowed clothes are the bandages that bind my wounds.

"You went to an awful lot of trouble to keep me alive."

"True," he says, after a moment's pause. "But then punishing you over and over brings me great joy." His words are bitter, and yet—

I don't believe them. God, how I *want* to because, oh, how I despise him, but I don't believe him. Not wholly. And I don't know why.

We ride in silence for a few more minutes, our bodies swaying with the rhythm of the horse's gait, before I start in again.

"Where did you learn to clean and dress wounds?" I ask.

"What does it matter?" he says.

I glance back at him, meeting his icy-blue stare as the wind blows a few strands of hair across his face.

What a waste of beauty.

Pestilence's jaw locks when I catch his eye, and he tears his gaze back to the road.

"It doesn't, I guess. I'm just grateful." I really am. I find I'm not ready to die, even though it may be the easier option at this point.

"I don't care," he says stonily.

Caught him in a good mood, I did. Not.

"So…" I practically feel his temper blackening, but I continue. "I haven't gotten sick."

"Astute observation, mortal."

"Is that just luck, or do you control who gets the plague?" I ask.

"Were you born with all your organs intact?" he responds.

I can't see his face, so I have no way of knowing where he's going with this question. "Yes…" I say cautiously.

"Good," he responds, "then I expect you to use the one beneath your skull."

67

Damn. That insult burned a little.

"So you *do* control the disease."

He says nothing to that.

"And you spared me from it," I add.

"Again you insist my motives are altruistic. Do not for a moment assume I value your life. You are only alive to sate my vengeance."

Yeah, whatever.

I stare down at the horseman's tan hand, which is still splayed over my abdomen. "Where are we going?"

Pestilence's exhalation manages to convey his world-weariness.

"I mean," I continue undaunted, "where's your ultimate destination?"

That question haunts people the world over. Where Pestilence is riding to.

"I don't have one, human," he says. "I ride simply until my task is complete."

Until we're all dead. That's what he means. He's going to ride his horse across the world until he's infected us all.

The truth sits like rocks at the pit of my stomach.

Pestilence's arm tightens around my waist. "Enough idle chatter. Your questions tire me."

I don't have it in me to give him lip over that. After that last response, I really don't want to talk to him either.

And so the two of us ride on in awful, unsettling silence, and all the while the horseman spreads his plague.

Day is giving way to night by the time Pestilence stops us at a house. I eye the single-story home with wariness as the horseman hops off his steed.

Really, really hope whoever lives here evacuated.

Pestilence reaches for me. After sitting in front of him for an entire day, I manage to not flinch at his touch.

I stare at him as he helps me off his horse. It's a strange feeling, being vulnerable around someone who's both hurt you and tended to you. Bound as my hands are, I have to rely on this devilish man for even something as easy as dismounting a horse, and I'm looking for his kindness, his compassion, in every small detail. It's completely ludicrous of me to do so, considering he's the very evil that landed me in this situation, but it doesn't stop me from searching for those things.

Briefly, Pestilence's eyes meet mine, and for once they're free of the ire and bitterness usually in them. Of course, the moment I think that, they become guarded once more.

My legs nearly fold when he sets me down.

"Jesus, Joseph, and *Mary*," I swear under my breath. My inner thighs feel rubbed raw, and my thigh muscles *ache*.

I glance to the heavens. *I get it, Big Guy, I'm not your favorite person right now.*

The horseman doesn't spare me another glance as he begins walking. A couple of seconds later, I feel a tug on my wrists as the rope binding me pulls taut.

"Keep up, human," he calls over his shoulder.

How very much I despise this man.

I hobble after him, watching with disapproval as he kicks in the front door. He hauls me inside.

It takes several seconds for my eyes to adjust to our dark surroundings. The room smells musty, like it's been sitting in its own juices for a while. Between that and the way my breath mists in front of me, it's obvious that whoever normally lives here is currently gone.

Pestilence steps up to me and takes my hands gruffly.

"You know the rules," he says as he undoes the knots. "You run, and my kindness ends."

I flick my eyes to Pestilence's quiver, where the feathered ends of a dozen golden arrows peek out from over his shoulder. I can still feel the points of those arrows in my flesh. My back throbs in response.

"You've really latched on to that word." *Kindness.*

Kindness is chopping firewood for an elderly couple who has neither the money nor the means to acquire it. Kindness is a warm hug or a soft smile.

Kindness is not this fuckery right here.

The rope falls away, and I eye Pestilence while I rub at the gauze bandages.

Giving the horseman a last sullen look, I head over to the fireplace. The owners have logs, matches, and scraps of old paper laid out. I stack the wood and place the kindling in a few choice locations. All the while I studiously ignore the horseman whose gaze I feel on my back.

"Are you done?" I call out.

There's a pause. "With what, human?"

"Staring at my backside—have you looked your fill?" I ask, my voice dripping with disdain.

"Am I supposed to be insulted by that?" He sounds genuinely baffled.

If he's going to make me spell it out, then... "Yes."

He grunts. "I'll try to remember that the next time you cut me down with your *scathing* words."

I can just about feel his pleasure at his little comeback.

Good one, horseman. You really got me by the tits this time...

I look over my shoulder at him. His armor and his crown gleam in the darkness. "You are *such* a creeper," I note.

His brow pinches.

"In case it's not obvious, that's another insult," I add. I turn back to the fire and focus my attention on it.

Pestilence lingers for a minute or so, and a part of me is curious what he's doing back there. Hopefully dying of humiliation, though I doubt it.

Eventually, the horseman leaves the living room, the clanking of his armor growing fainter and fainter. A door closes, and then I hear bathwater running.

I could use a bath too. I smell like horse and sweat, and who knows how dirty my bandages are. But taking a bath means asking for help removing my bandages, and I'm just not ready to go groveling to Pestilence at the moment.

I light the paper shoved between the logs, then I sit to watch the fire grow.

For the first time since I drew the burnt match, I have a moment to myself not fueled by adrenaline or fear or pain. I try not to think about what that means. It's easier to understand where things stand between me and the horseman when he's actively seeking to hurt me. It's not so easy when he's just irksome.

For a long time, my thoughts are aimless. You'd think I'd use the time wisely—to plot my escape or think of ways to incapacitate the horseman, but no. My mind is oddly empty.

There's a collection of fine porcelain figurines lining the mantel. One by one I scrutinize the painted faces. It's such a specific interest—to collect these little figurines—and it's just another reminder of how many people are out there in the world. Right now, whole cities of them are fleeing for their lives.

I imagine all the lonely corners of Canada, each one now home to thousands of displaced individuals waiting for the horseman to pass through. We're playing a lethal game of *Whac-A-Mole*, and we're all the vermin.

I stare down at my mom jeans and outdated shirt. Among all those thousands of people are my parents.

My heart lurches. I don't know why my mind keeps taking me back to them. Guilty conscience, I suppose.

The plan had been for us all to bunk down at my grandfather's hunting lodge—a hole-in-the-wall cabin located dozens of kilometers northwest of Whistler.

Deep down, I knew I'd never make it there.

The memory still stings.

"You go on ahead," I told my parents. "I need to finish evacuating the city."

"Don't be a hero," my dad said. "Everyone is leaving their post."

"I need to do my job."

"If you do your job, you'll die!" he shouted. He never shouted.

"You don't know that."

"Damn it, Sara, I do. You do. What is the survival rate of this thing?"

There wasn't a survival rate. People either avoided messianic fever, or they succumbed to it. I knew that; my dad knew that; the whole world knew that.

"Someone has to help those other families," I said.

My father stopped listening at that point. That was one of the only times I ever saw him openly cry.

He already believes I'm dead, I remember thinking.

And now, to the best of his understanding, I am.

Absently, I touch my cheek, feeling moisture there.

"What a surprise. I half thought you'd try to escape again."

Instinctively, my shoulders hike up at Pestilence's voice.

I clear my throat, then swipe quickly at my eyes. He doesn't get the pleasure of seeing me upset.

"I get that you don't think highly of people," I say, swiveling to him, "but that's just—*Jesus!*"

Standing across the room, his hair still dripping from the shower, is a very naked Pestilence.

CHAPTER 12

"Oh my God." I shield my eyes. "Put some clothes on! No one wants to see that!"

He frowns. "Your human sense of propriety is absolutely ridiculous."

For all this dude's knowledge, there are very obvious holes in his education—like, for instance, what makes humans uncomfortable as fuck.

"It doesn't change the fact that seeing you butt-ass naked is not on my short list of things to do during the apocalypse."

Not that it's a bad body or anything. I mean, if circumstances were different...

"Why you tell me these things when I want you to suffer is such a quandary," he says.

"Can you just put some pants on?"

Really, that's all I ask.

He comes up to me, every inch—and I mean *ev-er-ry* inch—on display. I take in those glowing amber tattoos that are so foreign and beautiful. My eyes move to his massive shoulders and his tapering torso; my gaze dips lower, to his abs, then to…

Maybe it's just sitting next to the fire, but suddenly the urge to fan myself is overwhelming.

"*Please*," I plead.

"When I begged you for mercy, did you grant it?"

This is *so* ridiculous. "No, but—"

"*No*," Pestilence agrees. "And for this reason, I too shall overlook your pleas."

He's not getting the fact that being shot in the face and staring at an impressive example of the male form are two *entirely* different tiers of suffering. No, scratch that, they're not even tiers. They're like homophones; they sound the same, but the words mean two totally different things.

"You're really all for this eye-for-an-eye justice," I mutter.

An Old Testament God is definitely running the show here.

"You're seriously going to make me look at you naked?" I ask.

"Where you look is your concern." He steps up to the fire, and seriously, I can't even stress how hard it is not to look *there*.

Really, really *hard*. (Bet the horseman wouldn't get *that* joke.)

My brain is slow to process the fact Pestilence is using the heat of the fire to dry himself off. Which means he's going to be standing here for a while.

Time for me to skedaddle.

Just as I'm about to leave, the horseman beats me to it. He turns and begins walking out of the room, his tightly coiled muscles rippling with the movement.

"Lie down on the couch and take off your shirt," he orders over his shoulder as he retreats.

I freeze at the command.

He's naked, and now he wants me to undress...

What in the world?

To be honest, I'm more baffled than anything else. I didn't get sexy-time vibes from Pestilence—even though he was happy to prance around in his birthday suit. Not that it stops me from grabbing the fireplace poker. I will beat the crap out of this guy if he does try anything.

I'm just...stupefied at the idea that he would.

I tense when I hear the horseman's footfalls coming closer. A moment later he enters the living room. My muscles relax an iota when I see he's donned his black clothing. He's even put his boots back on. The only thing missing is his gold regalia.

For all his threats about remaining naked, the horseman has poor follow-through.

In one of his hands, he clutches a small item.

Pestilence pauses when he sees me, my shirt very much on, iron poker in my hand.

He sighs. "So be it." Taking several long strides, he crosses the room.

I swipe at him, and just like all those senseless horror-movie victims, it does nothing. Pestilence plucks the poker from my hand and grabs the back of my neck before hauling me over to the couch. He throws me facedown onto the sofa, and then presses his knee against my back.

"Humans," he mutters.

My breathing is coming in heavy pants. I buck, but it gets me nowhere.

A moment later I hear material rip as Pestilence tears the back of my shirt open.

The horseman's fingers hook beneath my linen bandages,

the pressure causing me to jerk from a sudden burst of pain as my wounds wake up, and then he rips through those too. He tears the linen apart like it's nothing more than tissue paper.

The process *hurts*. I don't think Pestilence is deliberately trying to harm me, but every brush of his knuckles or tug against my skin aggravates my wounds.

At some point, it ends. Goose bumps break out across my skin as the cold air of the living room kisses my flesh.

There's a pause, and then the horseman's warm palm brushes against my skin. His touch is only there for a moment.

"Sit up," he orders.

What?

Clutching the tatters of my borrowed shirt to my chest, I do as he says.

"Shirt off," he says, sounding vaguely annoyed.

I let out a shuddering breath.

I don't want to do as he asks, if only because despite how open he is with nudity, I'm not. But now...I'm remembering the way my body dragged across that asphalt, and the remorseless look in Pestilence's eyes the last time I disobeyed him.

This is not a human I'm dealing with. He won't hesitate to hurt me more if I resist. And I'm tired of resisting. It just feels so...useless against this unstoppable force.

I shrug off my shirt, doing my best to cover my breasts with my arms.

Pestilence's hand moves to my back, his fingers splayed. His touch is gentle, but I jerk at the feel of it anyway.

"Hold this against your front," he says from behind me.

I glance down at what he's offering. It takes me a second to register that the white cloth he's holding out to me is gauze.

Bandages. He means to *bandage* me.

I let out a shuddering sigh that ends up sounding like a

sob. All right, maybe it was a sob. And that sob turns into a hiccupping laugh, which turns into another laugh. And then I can't stop laughing, even as tears slip out from my eyes and I'm no longer sure whether I'm laughing or crying, *because*.

Because.

Because, oh my fucking God, I shot a man and lit him on fire, and even now I want to throw up that I could do that to anyone, even a harbinger of the apocalypse. But the nightmare didn't end there. I was tied up and forced to run behind the same undying creature I thought I killed, the same creature that's killing us all off. And I was then dragged, and my arm was wrenched out of its socket, and my back feels like it was torn to bits—not to mention my legs—and I had to watch a man die the most horrific death, and now I'm being patched up when I thought I was going to be physically humiliated, and ugh, this nightmare is not going to end, because Pestilence is an ungodly monster who isn't satisfied with destroying life as we know it. He must make an example of mine along the way.

Now I'm no longer laughing, and I'm not even sure you can call this *crying*. It's a full-body sob, like my mind's trying to purge everything it witnessed.

"I hope you're enjoying this," I say through my tears.

"I am," Pestilence responds joylessly. "Here." He passes me the roll of gauze. Still shaking with the force of my emotions, I take the bandages and wrap the linen across my torso, then pass it back. The two of us do this over and over until he's re-dressed my wounds.

I wipe my eyes, clear my throat, and pull myself together. Deep breath.

It's all going to be okay—or it isn't, but that's okay too.

Once I trust myself to speak, I say over my shoulder,

"I appreciate what you're doing, but if I don't clean the wounds, they're going to get infected." I mean, they may not, but that's a gamble.

I suppose I should simply be grateful for this little bit of *kindness*.

"That's unnecessary," the horseman says.

"What do you mean 'that's unnecessary'?" I ask, trying to riddle out what he's implying.

"Your wounds won't become infected."

I swivel more fully to face him. "How do you know that?"

He looks heavenward, like he's trying to find both God and his patience in the rafters. "Because I control infection in *all* its forms."

Seriously? So, not only can he prevent me from catching the plague, but he also doesn't need to clean my wounds to keep infection at bay?

"Then why change the bandages at all?" I ask, facing forward again.

"An injury this large demands upkeep for it to heal properly," Pestilence says. He rips the gauze from the roll and ties it off. "Now give me your wrists."

I do so, oddly mesmerized by the situation—and by Pestilence, if I'm being honest.

He leans over my wrists, his wavy golden hair falling in front of his eyes as he unwinds the old gauze. At this angle, the horseman looks heart-wrenchingly innocent, which is an odd thing to say about a man, particularly one who has a healthy kill rate under his belt. Perhaps it's simply that he's being gentle for once, or that I'm finally getting a glimpse of his (vanishingly small) humanity.

My brow furrows as I stare at his bent head. "Why are you doing this?"

"Suffering is meant for the living."

I don't know why I expect a different answer. And, you know, I get it. I hurt him, so he hurts me. We're both just following a script. It's just *this* moment that I don't get. Watching him care for me, be tender with me. It's unsettling enough that I expect an answer beyond *I want to make you suffer*.

But if there's another explanation, I'm not going to get it.

CHAPTER 13

Baths are going to be a problem.

The next day, I stare Pestilence down, the tub at my back, the door at his. The two of us are crammed inside a small bathroom in the new house he decided to bed down in.

Like the last home we stayed at, this one is blessedly empty. And bonus: this house has electricity, which means hot water, which means my ass is getting *cleaned*.

The only snag is the bastard who thinks I'm going to run away despite the fact he's left me alone in a bathroom before—hell, he's left me alone in bedrooms and living rooms and kitchens. He knows he's broken my will to escape. So I don't understand why he thinks there's any need to stay in the bathroom with me.

"Okay, you *have* to leave," I say, staring at the giant man across from me.

He folds his arms over his golden armor. Horseman code for *make me, lady*.

"You may not know this, but people don't watch other

people take baths." I don't *think* they do at least. But maybe there's a whole sexually deviant underbelly to society that I don't know about. Stranger things have happened—case in point: the man in front of me.

"You want a longer leash, you're going to have to prove you deserve it," he says, his face haughty.

"How about all those other times when you left me alone to go to the bathroom?"

"You were too weak to disobey me," he says.

"I wasn't last night."

He just stares at me.

I throw up my arms. "I'm going to be naked and drenched in water. Do you know how cold it is outside?"

He doesn't respond.

"It's cold enough to freeze my tits off," I answer anyway.

No reaction. Not even a laugh. Figures. Pretty sure his sense of humor is nonexistent.

"Please." I'm shamelessly resorting to begging.

"*Please?*" he echoes. "Have you forgotten our history? I begged and you denied." He leans against the door. "Take your bath, human, or don't, but I'm not leaving this room without you."

I seriously consider forgoing the bath. I'm no prude, but I'm not exactly thrilled to be showing the goods to a creature trying to end civilization either.

But in the end, it comes down to practicality. I'm covered in blood and dirt and who knows what other bodily fluids. I'm a biohazard.

Giving Pestilence a dirty look, I turn on the hot water and begin removing my clothes.

He doesn't have a problem with nudity, I try to reassure myself as I shuck off my pants. I think back to the sight of him buck naked. *He doesn't even know he's supposed to be embarrassed.*

That reassures me only a little.

It's when I reach for the gauze covering my torso that I hit a snag. Wherever Pestilence tied off the linen bandages, it's beyond my reach. I tug fruitlessly at the wrappings until the horseman peels himself away from the door.

He knocks my hands away and turns my back to him. I'm about to protest when *rrrrrrip*—he tears the linen from my back.

Once he's finished, he bends to my ear. "You're welcome."

I make a face at the wall as he returns to the doorway.

By the time the bath is nearly full and blessedly heated, the rest of my clothes and bandages are gone.

Pestilence's eyes flick over my body in that same dispassionate way they did before. I could be a lamp, for all his interest.

I should be relieved. If he were to instead assess each imperfection of mine, I might die of embarrassment.

His indifference, however, still gets under my skin. I'm not sure if I want him to be impressed at the sight of my body (ew) or if it bothers me *that* he feels nothing when he sees a naked woman. Humans have a slew of opinions when it comes to the female body (can't get fuckers to shut up about it), and Pestilence's lack of reaction only serves to remind me that he's something else.

I step into the tub, the water almost scalding. I sigh as I sink into it.

On the other side of the bathroom, the horseman sets aside his bow and quiver, leaning the weapons against the nearby wall before resting his head against the door. His gaze crawls over me, not crude or creepy but curious and mildly interested.

I wonder if this is all strange and new for him. Women, nudity, bathtubs, running water—the whole shebang. He's not just some person who's been born into this world and takes all these things for granted.

I sink deeper into the water, soaking in the water's warmth.

Been so long since I took a decent bath.

Most of the time, it was an icy dousing that I had to rush through before I caught my death. Tonight I'm going to stay in here until my fingertips look like prunes.

"Where are you from?" I ask idly.

Pestilence narrows his eyes. "*Elsewhere.*"

Of course he is.

I grab a bar of homemade soap and a nearby folded washcloth and I wash myself off, starting with my toes. I make my way up my body, scouring my skin until it feels raw and clean. Bits of blood and dirt slough off me.

There's no shampoo or conditioner—not terribly surprising, considering they're extravagances—so I lather my hair with soap, scrubbing it the best I can with my fingers, knowing full well it's going to feel funky once it's dry.

Better than dirty, I suppose.

It's only after everything else is clean that I reluctantly attempt to wash my back. As soon as the cloth scrapes against them, the wounds cry out. Unfortunately, that's not even the biggest issue I have. There's a good portion of my back that I can't reach, no matter how hard I try.

And I'm trying my ass off.

I hear the clanking of metal as Pestilence moves.

I eye him warily as he kneels next to the tub. He takes the washcloth from me, and one of his hands grips my shoulder, causing me to tense up.

He looks me in the eye. "I'm only doing this because your weak attempts at hygiene are painful to watch," he warns. I part my lips, but before I get the chance to speak, he grabs the back of my neck. "Bend forward."

I hesitate, annoyed at the way he's treating me, but eventually I do lean forward, wrapping my hands around my calves.

His fingers brush my damp hair aside, the touch sending goose bumps down my arms.

It's just the chill air, I tell myself.

I clench my teeth as Pestilence cleans my wounds, his touch surprisingly gentle. It hurts anyway.

"How easily your kind breaks," he murmurs as the washcloth makes another pass over my wounded flesh.

It's the closest he's going to come to an apology, and I guess it's good enough. I mean, at least he didn't *try* to kill me like I tried to kill him.

Only because he wants you to suffer.

Once Pestilence is done, he gives me back the washcloth, then returns to the door and sits with his back against it. He grabs his bow and rests it on his lap, once more the prison guard.

The water is grimy and cooling fast, and yet I'm now hesitant to leave. My back still aches where Pestilence scoured it with the washcloth, and my nerves are rubbed even rawer.

I'm feeling a little weird toward him. I don't know whether it's weird good or weird bad—probably weird bad.

I pull my knees up to my chest, leaning my cheek against them. "You still don't know my name," I say.

"I don't need to," he says, brushing a stray lock of hair from his face. "*Human* is just fine."

"No, it's not."

He narrows his eyes.

"Sara," I say. "My name is Sara."

He frowns. "What does it matter what you're called?" he responds. "You're all the same."

"Gee, you know how to make a girl feel special."

His mouth turns down. "You aren't special. None of you are. You're all vile, violent things."

"Says the guy who's killing off people by the thousands."

"I don't enjoy it," he says.

"Neither did I." The memory of Pestilence bleeding in the road, bleeding and yet *alive*, still sets my teeth on edge.

"Could've fooled me," he says.

I force out a laugh. "Then you're not nearly as good at reading humans as you are at judging them."

He cocks his head. "Maybe," he agrees, "but then, I don't need to read them, do I?"

He just needs to kill them.

We're quiet for a while. The horseman is scrutinizing the pliancy of his bow, and I'm letting the water's chill sink into my skin.

"Do you have a name?" I ask. "Other than *Pestilence the Conqueror*?"

He sets his bow aside. "I was not named."

I don't dwell on how that statement implies someone else was around who *could've* named him.

"Why not?"

Pestilence's eyes sharpen on mine. "I do not need a name to have a purpose. Humans are the ones who demand names for every blade of grass on this good green earth."

Because naming things humanizes them. And once you humanize something, you are essentially recognizing its existence. But considering the horseman is on a mission to kill as many people as possible, I can see why he'd have a problem with humanizing anything.

He wasn't given a name. I let that sink in.

Setting aside my intense dislike for the man, there's a part of me that feels sorry for him. He doesn't even have a proper *name.*

Be happy, Sara. Otherwise, you risk humanizing him.

And wouldn't that be awful?

"So…it's fine to call you *Pestilence?*" I say.

He inclines his head. "It's just a name."

Just a name. How ironic, considering not a minute ago he insisted he *wasn't* named. Then again, maybe I'm the one thinking about this wrong. Pestilence the Conqueror was the name *we* gave *him.* It's not like it was emblazoned across his chest the day he arrived or something he declared as he massacred whole cities.

I stare at the horseman some more. He really hurts my eyes. It's a good thing I don't trust pretty men. Because this one is definitely the prettiest I've ever seen, and he's also the worst one of the lot—save for maybe his brethren, but since the world hasn't seen hide nor hair of them…he remains the worst.

Pestilence stands, slinging first his bow and then his quiver over his shoulders.

"Come," he says. He grabs a towel from the rack and throws it at me. I don't manage to catch it in time, and a good portion of it hits the water. "I know you've finished bathing," he continues, oblivious to the hostile look I'm giving him, "and I'm eager to leave this latrine."

"It's not a *latrine*," I say, standing and wrapping the towel around myself. "It's a *bathroom.*"

He shakes his head as he opens the door. "Bath-room."

He splits the word into two parts. "The irony of the term isn't lost on me."

"What do you mean?"

"Only you humans would think it wise to put your privy next to your bathing vessels."

Seems reasonable to me. I mean, you shit, and then you bathe. What's there not to like about the arrangement?

"Where would you put it?" I ask, tilting my head to towel off my hair.

He opens the door. "*Not* next to each other."

Oh, that's real helpful. "Of course you would bitch about a problem without actually having a solution," I say.

He glances at me over his shoulder, swaggering down the hall. "One doesn't need to have a solution to recognize a problem when they see one."

"Your solution would probably be to burn toilets everywhere. Right? 'They're vile, disgusting things. Just get rid of them!'"

Ahead of me Pestilence guffaws. "Only a human would come up with such a ridiculous solution."

"*I was mocking you!*"

"I thought mockery was supposed to be insulting?" he says as he glances back at me. "As far as I can tell, you are the one who likened your kind to privies."

Ugh. I did, didn't I?

"You're missing the point," I say.

"I fail to see how you have one."

This is never going to end. The two of us could keep going around and around like this until the end of time.

"Forget about it," I mutter, leaving the horseman to go search for clothes.

In the main bedroom, I find a shirt and pants and

everything else in between close to my size. It's all a little too short and tight, but I manage to find a pair of pants that don't make me feel like an overstuffed sausage and a shirt that covers all the important bits.

Once I'm dressed, I head back into the living room. My breath catches when I notice the horseman. The light from the setting sun shines through the windows, making his hair glitter like spun gold. My heart squeezes the same way it did when I saw pictures of the Sistine Chapel.

A beauty so staggering, it makes you feel physically close to God.

I forget that we've been bickering and he's the enemy. For one single second, I feel an odd ache beneath my rib cage.

So close to God...

A God that wants us all gone.

CHAPTER 14

"Try it."

"Absolutely not."

"C'mon, trrrrry it," I insist.

"I said no."

As far as mornings post-Pestilence are concerned, this one is off to a great start. The sun is painting the world around us in soft pink light (so pretty), my hands are mercifully unbound for once, and nestled within them is a thermos containing my own version of deliverance.

I nudge Pestilence, who sits behind me, with my elbow. "You know you're curious."

"I think I would know better than you *what I know*."

Someone takes everything way too literally.

I press the thermos closer to the horseman, not dissuaded in the least by his protests. I mean, it's hot chocolate I'm offering. Also I really want to see if this guy is capable of drinking fluids. I haven't seen him touch food or drink so far.

Pestilence's hand digs into my hip, where he holds me against him in the saddle. "If I try it, will you quiet?"

"No, but you know you don't really want me to be silent."

My words are punctuated by the steady *clop clop* of Pestilence's horse, whom I've secretly named Trixie Skillz. I'm pretty sure the steed is a male (haven't checked because unlike some people I know, respecting one's privacy is important), but no matter.

I have his whole story figured out too. Trixie Skillz, the noble steed, once lived a life of poverty and fear, turning tricks on the streets for carrots and grain until Pestilence saved him. Now the two are inseparable. The end.

Pestilence takes the thermos from me, lifting the container to better scrutinize it. "If this is poison, human, I will tie you to the back of the horse again and make you run."

I snort. "Pestilence, if it were poison, I'd have bigger problems than getting another asphalt massage." Problems like keeling over and dying.

He scowls at me, then scowls at the thermos. "I don't know why I'm encouraging this…*pestering*."

Because you like it, I want to say, but I don't. I really am pretty sure a part of Pestilence—perhaps an itty-bitty part of him, but a part of him nonetheless—is starting to enjoy my company, pestering and all.

All right, perhaps *tolerate* is a better word. We're tolerating each other despite openly hating each other's guts. It's an odd relationship, but since he refuses to die and won't kill me, we're stuck with each other.

After eyeing the ever-loving shit out of the thermos, Pestilence brings it close to his lips.

Holy crap, he's going to do it! He's finally going to drink something!

The horseman hesitates, then holds the thermos out at his side and overturns it, dumping its contents out.

For a second I stare in horror at the small brown stream petering out of the mouthpiece, then I jump into action.

"You *heathen!*" I snatch the thermos from him. "You could've just said no."

"I did."

"Well, you could've meant it."

"I did."

I check the warm canteen. There's still a decent amount of hot chocolate left. *Nice.*

Pestilence's hand settles back at my side as I resume drinking the warm beverage.

"Why don't you eat or drink?" I eventually ask.

"Because I don't have to," he answers curtly.

"So?"

"*So?*" he echoes, sounding affronted. He peers down at me, maybe to make sure I'm serious. "I'm confused. Why should I eat or drink if I don't need to?"

"Because it's fun and it tastes good—well, except for my aunt Milly's fruitcake. That shit tastes like a dirty asshole. But yeah, food tastes good, as does the hot chocolate you squandered a minute ago."

"Tell me," he says, "if I indulge like a human, how am I better than one?"

Oh geez. "Can we not make everything into some lofty battle between good and evil? It's just food."

He doesn't respond for so long I think he isn't going to, but then he finally says, "I will think over what you've told me."

After that, the two of us are quiet.

Hate the silence.

Don't get me wrong, I'm usually comfortable being alone in my own mind. There are always things like philosophy, literature, history, and politics to think about. And when those lofty subjects get dull, there's the normal slew of noise to fill my head, like remembering to do my taxes on time, or figuring out how to logistically host a family get-together in my matchbox apartment, or mulling over what used books I'm going to blow my paycheck on.

But right now, my mind isn't that reliable old friend it once was. Every time the silence roars in, my mind drifts to that plague victim I tended to or the fact more are dying with every kilometer we travel. Worst of all is when I ruminate on the man at my back. I'm still his prisoner, but the longer I'm around him, the more muddled my feelings are.

I press my hand against his horse's neck. "Deep into that darkness peering, long I stood there, wondering, fearing, / Doubting, dreaming dreams no mortal ever dared to dream before..." I murmur to myself.

"What are you speaking of?" Pestilence asks.

"I'm quoting 'The Raven.' It's a poem by Edgar Allan Poe."

Pestilence makes a noise at the back of his throat. "I should've known that brief flash of eloquence was not of your making."

"Do you even have the ability to speak without insulting me?" I say. I swear this bastard is just trying to kill my morning buzz.

"Of course." I can hear the smug smile in his voice. "It is just that there are so very many things about you worth insulting."

If this hot chocolate weren't so precious to me, I'd dump the rest of it on Pestilence's pig head, consequences be damned.

I think the horseman is waiting for me to clap back at him—to be perfectly honest, I think he enjoys verbally sparring with me—but he up and ruined Poe, so I'm not going to give him anything else.

When the silence stretches on, the horseman says softly, "I enjoyed that bit of poetry."

I let out a huff.

Not going to take the bait, pretty boy. Not even when I really want to—because *Poe.*

I stroke Trixie's mane, the horse's white hair silken beneath my fingertips.

"Tell me about yourself," Pestilence demands.

I bristle at his tone. Said so high-handedly, like I'm here to serve him. Not to mention that the last few times I tried to chat with him, he was rude.

"No."

That response gives him pause. I can almost feel him studying the back of my head.

"You are such an odd creature," he says. "One moment you tell me you won't stop talking, and the next you refuse to."

He's *so* trying to bait me. If I didn't know better, I'd say the horseman was quickly developing an appetite for conversation.

He sighs. "Human, you've piqued my interest—a rare accomplishment. Don't squander it."

"*Squander* it?" This *guy.* "You mean by refusing to talk to you?" That's real cute. "I'll tell you a rare accomplishment—pissing me off."

He guffaws. "You mean this hellcat nature of yours is atypical?"

He's bringing out all my stabby tendencies.

"You want to know about me?" I practically shout. "Fine. My full name is not *human*, it's Sara Burns. I'm twenty-one years old. And a week ago, I was taken by an *insufferable* horseman. Would you like to argue about that too?"

I'm so ready to duke it out with Pestilence.

"Hmmm" is all he says.

No scathing comments or smart-ass remarks. Just "hmmm."

I could kill a bitch right now.

"What is it you do to fill your days?" he asks.

I have to glance behind me to make sure I'm speaking to the same man who was taunting me literally seconds ago.

He stares at me, looking guileless.

I grimace. "*Did*," I bite out. I don't do anything at the moment, except (joyfully) slow the horseman down. (We all have to get our thrills somewhere.)

Facing forward, I add, "I was a firefighter."

His fingers drum against my waist. "Did you enjoy it?"

I lift a shoulder. "It was just a job. It didn't define me." Not the way it did some of my teammates, who dreamed of being firefighters their entire lives. I blow out a breath. "I always wanted to go to university and study English," I confess. I don't know *why* I'm admitting this.

"English?" Pestilence says quizzically. "But you speak it fine—if a little odd."

"Not English as in the language itself," I clarify, tipping back the last of the hot chocolate. I slide the thermos into one of the saddlebags. "English as in literature written in English. I wanted to study the works of Shakespeare and Lord Byron and"—my favorite—"Poe."

"Poe," the horseman repeats, no doubt remembering the name from earlier. "Why didn't you study these poets?"

Regret is a bitter taste at the back of my throat, and there's no more hot chocolate to wash it out.

"Four horsemen came to earth and made a mess of the world."

When we enter the town of Squamish, it's just as abandoned as I'd hoped it would be.

We pass by a gas station whose pumps are rusty with years of disuse but whose store is filled with rows of preserved produce, nuts, and sweets.

Farther in, recently installed gas lamps still burn, though the sun has been up for hours. The lamplighter must've evacuated before they could extinguish the light.

Like the gas station's store, the trading posts we pass are still full of goods, a sure sign their owners fled before they had a chance to stow their products. As a result, a few of them were broken into and their items were stolen.

Beneath my layers of clothing, my skin pricks. This all could've happened hours ago, and yet there's not a single soul to be seen. It's vastly unnerving to pass through a town that by all rights should be full of people. It feels...*haunted*.

What must Quebec and Ontario and all the rest of the provinces to the east look like now that Pestilence passed through them? What must the U.S.'s East Coast look like now?

Whether you make it out of this alive or not, the world is never going to be the same.

Pestilence turns off the main road and weaves through the town, and I have no idea what his game plan is. It's too early to squat in some poor soul's home, and so far that's the only time the horseman ever leaves the main highway.

It's not until we approach Squamish's hospital that I feel uneasy.

"What are you doing?" I ask.

"Your feeble body needs amenities."

I stare at the hospital with quickly rising horror. *Amenities like gauze.*

We ran out of the linen wrappings this morning.

"I don't need any more bandages," I rush to say.

"Yes, you do." Gently, Pestilence says, "Do you really think it takes me going to the hospital for them all to die? Come now, Sara, I merely need to walk through a city to see its doom."

I glance back at him. I know I should be processing his words, but I'm hung up on the fact he actually said my name.

He continues, dauntless. "Whether I enter a hospital matters not. The humans will still fall, there especially."

It's not like what he's saying is news to me; it's just that I don't want to see the faces of those too sick and feeble to flee as death incarnate walks among them.

There's a chance the town went to special lengths to remove the hospital's patients. It's possible. But it's also possible the weakest individuals were simply unable to evacuate.

I grab the horseman's forearm as a thought comes over me. "A general store," I say, like I've discovered the cure for cancer. "They'll have bandages at a general store."

Pestilence stares down at where I grip his arm. "Did you see a general store on our way here?"

"I saw at least three of them." These days there's a trading post or general store on every street corner, each one existing because they have some edge on the market.

The horseman squints at me. "And you think I should go there instead?"

"Absolutely."

"Then it is settled," he says with finality.

Was…was convincing him really that easy?

For an instant I almost believe it. But then Trixie Skillz keeps clomping forward, and the hospital looms ever closer.

"What about the general store?" I look over my shoulder at Pestilence.

His face is grim as his gaze meets mine. "I mean to make you suffer."

CHAPTER 15

Hospitals are always the first places to go. That's the one thing all those movies got right. As soon as people began to get sick, they swarmed the medical facilities, thinking surely modern medicine could cure this. Surely we were better off than the poor sods who caught the Black Death. All those centuries we spent studying illnesses and conquering them— surely we were equipped by now to stop an epidemic.

We were wrong.

Pestilence hops off his horse, bow and quiver at his back, eyeing the building. This close to it, I can see a couple of spooked faces staring out. One of them is a woman holding her rosary, her lips moving in prayer.

God's not going to save you, I want to tell her. *He's the one who wants you dead.*

Swiveling back to me, the horseman reaches for my waist. "Come, Sara, and gaze upon the faces of the soon-to-be departed."

"I hate you," I say as he lifts me off his steed.

"Ah, hate. Another distinctly human emotion." He sets me down.

I don't think it's a distinctly human emotion—the horseman seems to have plenty of it himself.

He strides ahead of me to the double doors, looking like a gallant knight in his armor. For once in his wretched life, he tries to open the doors the proper way. They don't budge.

That's not surprising; hospitals have lockdown procedures for this sort of thing.

The horseman rotates, his eyes meeting mine briefly, and they spark with defiance. In one rapid motion, he swivels back around. His fist shoots out, slamming into the door like a battering ram.

With a groan, the double doors buckle but, shockingly, they still hold fast. My heart pounds as I watch the horseman. This is a horror movie, one where the bad guy is getting inside the house to kill off all the kids. Only this is real life, movies are dead, and the horseman is a flesh-and-blood fiend.

His fist pounds into the door a second time with preternatural force, and with a metallic screech, the doors collapse inward.

Pestilence steps aside as hospital alarms go off, his frightening gaze meeting mine. "After you."

In some ways, the visit wasn't as bad as I feared it would be. In other ways, it was worse. It's too early for people to succumb to the fever, so the few people inside were just your average bunch of hospital patients and staff. But all those terrified expressions... My stomach churns at the memory of them as we head away from the hospital, the horseman's precious fucking gauze loaded into the packs that hang on either side of Trixie's saddle.

Pestilence made me look at each one of them. All those people slated for certain death. It would be a lie to say he enjoyed making me look—he was just as grim as I was—but does that really matter in the end? He still made me stare down those few people stuck inside, just because he knew it would hurt me.

"I hope you're satisfied," I say once the hospital is far behind us.

His hold on me tightens. "Human, don't you know? I am *never* satisfied, and so onward I ride."

I don't say anything to that. Sadness has a way of getting into your bones and settling in for the long haul. In the end, that's what I feel. Not anger at Pestilence—though I do harbor more than a little resentment—but sadness at those few faces that will simply cease to be in a few days. The sorrow swallows me.

I'm quiet for so long that it becomes noticeable.

"I don't mean for this experience to be pleasant, human. If it were pleasant, you'd be dead."

One would almost think the horseman was trying to rationalize his actions. But that would mean he feels remorseful about what he did, and I know that's not the case.

I stare straight ahead, my gaze falling on a rusted washing machine sitting on the side of the road.

"No cutting remarks for me?" Pestilence asks several minutes later when I still haven't responded. "I have to say, I'm almost disappointed."

What does he *want* from me? Isn't it enough that every one of these stops kills a little something inside me?

I don't speak even once Pestilence approaches a house,

this one nestled among dozens of others. No one's inside, but even then, I'm still in too dour a mood to really care.

He dismounts, the movement looking agitated as hell. Obediently I follow, not waiting for him to help me down. He prowls onto the front porch, his armor gleaming in the watery light.

Pestilence brings up a booted foot and kicks down the door in a single smooth stroke. He doesn't wait for me before heading inside, though I know if I tried to run he'd be on me in an instant. He probably wants that.

Once I follow him inside the empty home, he rounds on me. "Why won't you speak to me?"

Not so long ago, he wanted nothing more than for me to be silent. But that was when the horseman didn't know there were better things than riding in solitude.

"I don't want to talk to you," I say.

Taking a few quick strides, he closes the distance between us and grabs my jaw. "Last time I checked," he says, tapping my cheek with his finger, "I wasn't keeping you prisoner because you *wanted* it."

A bitter smile twists my face, but I still can't find it in me to fight with him.

He releases my jaw in a huff. "Fine. Pout, human. It will do you no good. They're still going to die."

Why does he have to keep bringing that up?

I rub my temples. "You wanted me to suffer, and I've been suffering. So take your victory and leave me be," I finally say.

Pestilence's eyes harden. "This isn't even the beginning of suffering, human. I could make this worse. So much worse."

I'm sure he could, but right now I don't really give a fuck.

I walk away from him. All I want is to find an empty room away from the horseman where I can curl up and pretend I'm not seeing those faces every time I close my eyes.

I'm just about out of the room when I pause. "For all your righteousness," I say over my shoulder, "you really are a heartless bastard."

CHAPTER 16

I've gotten used to stealing from Pestilence's victims. Every time we squat in someone's house, that's exactly what I'm doing. Stealing their beds, stealing their food and water, stealing their homes and—if they're unfortunate enough to linger—their time. Pestilence may take their lives, but I take everything else.

And I'm starting to be okay with this. Well, as okay as anyone can be in my situation.

I pad into the kitchen the next morning, eyeing the snowshoes and vintage skis hanging on the wall across the way. Outside, rain beats ferociously against the windows and wind shakes the trees.

I rub my arms, grateful for the roaring fire Pestilence started. The weather may be a mess outside, but in here, it's downright toasty.

The rainstorm nearly drowns out the sound of muffled splashing coming from down the hall. Pretty boy needs his monster baths.

Icy monster baths, I amend as I head over to the cupboards. The electricity—and thus the hot water—doesn't work here.

My stomach growls, reminding me I haven't eaten since yesterday. One by one I open the cupboards. In total, I find two jars of pickles, one can of beans, and a moldy onion.

Yum.

There's also a refrigerator in the kitchen, but judging from the fact the electricity is out, I doubt it works. Still, you never know; people have fashioned these things into good ol' iceboxes.

I open it up and—

"Whoa."

Moonshine. Rows and rows of moonshine. I stare at them all as a river of what was probably once ice spills onto the floor.

Out of curiosity I grab one of the bottles from the shelf and unscrewing the lid, sniff the contents.

I make a face. Not just moonshine but *bad* moonshine.

"And you expect me to willingly drink your beverages."

I shriek at Pestilence's voice, the bottle slipping out of my hand. Quick as lightning, the horseman lunges forward and catches the glass container, saving us both from being covered in fermented piss.

"Careful, Sara," he says as he straightens, setting the drink on a nearby counter.

That smoky, rolling voice of his twists my name into something intimate and exotic. I think I hate how lovely he makes it sound.

His hair is dripping with water, and I find myself staring first at the darkened strands, which are the color of wheat, before my attention moves to his high cheekbones, where a few droplets of that icy water kiss his skin. I dip my gaze to his mouth, to his full, sculpted lips.

My cheeks warm at the sight of them.

He moves beyond me, oblivious to my thoughts, checking out the kitchen with mild interest. His bare feet splash into the puddle of melted ice as he peers inside the fridge.

"Not much here, is there?" he says, moving the jars around. As he does so, I catch a glimpse of…

"Oh my God! *Pie!*"

It's mostly gone, probably older than my grandpa, and it's likely breaking at least three different etiquette rules to go for it before noon, but who gives a crap? It's *pie*.

I none-too-gently hip check Pestilence out of the way and grab it. Closer inspection reveals it's apple pie (my favorite because *duh*), and there's about a fourth of it left. Enough for a single girl to tuck away without too much guilt…

The horseman watches me carefully as I set it out on the kitchen table before leaving it only long enough to rummage around for a fork.

He follows my lead, grabbing a fork from the drawer and heading back to the table.

"What are you doing?" I ask when he sits across from me, the metal utensil in hand.

Pestilence studies my lips as he answers, "You wanted me to try your human food."

I move my eyes between the pie and his fork. "Are you serious?" I suppose this is his way of smoothing over yesterday's unpleasantness. My enthusiasm plummets at the thought.

You'd been ready to share your hot chocolate with him, Sara.

But apple pie is a cut above even hot chocolate.

He'll just take a bite. He won't even like it; he's just trying to prove a point.

Wordlessly, I push the pie over to his side of the table.

The horseman stares down at the pie for a moment before gingerly scooping out a forkful of it. He brings it to his lips like he's done this a thousand times before, and after a brief hesitation, he takes a bite of the apple pie.

I watch him with a strange sort of fascination. It takes a hell of a lot to distract me from pie, but Pestilence eating food for the first time just happens to be that. His face stays expressionless the entire time.

He doesn't like it. Praise Jesus, he doesn't like it.

He sets his fork down and looks at me, his face serious. "You were right."

I was? About what? I crinkle my forehead in confusion.

"Not needing something doesn't mean you can't enjoy it." With that, he picks his fork back up and scoops out another bite.

"What are you doing?" I'm embarrassed at how alarmed my voice sounds.

"Eating."

"So…you like it?" I probe.

"Do you want a formal apology?" Pestilence asks me. "Would you like for me to admit I was wrong?"

I'd like for you to not enjoy my stolen pie, thankyouverymuch.

"I thought you mentioned food was a slippery slope into mortal depravity?" I say, sliding the pie pan back to my side of the table and taking a bite of it.

It's a bit stale, and I prefer my pie hot, but it is, in a word, *heaven*.

The horseman drags the pie back to his side of the table. "I mused on the matter." He scoops another forkful. Another bite just…*gone* to this beast. "Food in and of itself is not wicked."

I slide the pan back to me. "Indulgence probably is."

Now that I know he can eat food, the suspense is over. *Just give me back my pie.* That's all I ask.

"Perhaps," he agrees. It doesn't stop him from continuing to eat the flaky dessert, and he happens to take the world's biggest freaking bites.

The pie quickly disappears, most of it going to the man across from me, the man who doesn't even need to eat.

This is such bullshit.

After he's finished, Pestilence sits back in his seat, slinging one booted foot over his other knee. There's something so terribly normal about this situation. A man and a woman sharing breakfast. It's easy to imagine the horseman without his golden crown and his armor and weapons. It's easy to imagine him as just a man.

And that's very, very dangerous.

"I was wrong," he says softly, his blue eyes finding mine.

"About what?" I ask distractedly, scraping up the crumbs from the bottom of the tin.

Yeah, I am that pathetic.

"Consumption."

I lift my eyes to his.

His stare is too direct. I don't know what he wants from me.

I lift a shoulder. "Cool."

Pestilence's eyes go to my lips. "You use such strange language sometimes."

This from a guy who calls the bathroom a *latrine.*

I break eye contact for no other reason than I'm noticing just how handsome he is when he's kind.

My gaze drifts to the storm outside. It's been raging this entire time. I know from experience that if it's as cold as I think it is outside, the rainwater will burn like ice.

"Please don't make us travel today." The request just kind of slips out of me.

"*Please?*" His eyes are alight with fire.

Crap. He just loves that word.

His chair scrapes back. "Human, I think you just decided our day for us."

CHAPTER 17

Eff the cold and the horseman along with it.

My teeth chatter nonstop as Trixie Skillz trots ever forward. Even under my layers of clothes and the wool blanket I wear, my body won't stop shaking.

I may be the one Canadian who can't stand the cold. Everyone else is like, *Hey look, I can see the sun today, and even though it's cold enough to freeze water, by God, I think this is T-shirt weather!* Meanwhile, I'm what happens when a human and an ice cube have a baby.

I'm pretty sure I was switched at birth.

"H–how much l–longer?" I ask, my shivers making a mess of my speech.

I'm going to get hypothermia and die out here. And wouldn't that be ironic? Pestilence's captive dies of exposure—not to the plague, but to the elements.

The horseman glances down from where he holds me fast against his unyielding metal armor. "I'm not sure," he says. "You could ask nicely and help me decide."

He means I could say *please* again and screw myself over.

"Or you can remain quiet and we can ride through the night."

I swivel to face him. "Y-you are the m-most prideful jerk I—I've ever m-met!" I face forward again, pulling my wet blanket closer around me.

Once this is all over, I'm moving to Mexico. I bet no one dies of the cold in Mexico.

If I thought Pestilence would react to my outburst, I was wrong. We continue on, the minutes passing laboriously. We pass a few settlements so small that if you sneezed you would miss them. The storm lets up briefly, only to then redouble its efforts.

At some point throughout the day, my shivers lessen, but it's not because I've managed to warm myself up. Distantly, I'm aware this is bad. My fingers are stiff and hard to move, and my eyes keep drooping.

It's only when my wool blanket slides off me and onto the street that I catch Pestilence's attention.

"I'm not going back for that," he says.

I sway in my seat, my eyelids drifting closed. *I don't care.* I'm not sure whether I think it or say it, only that the horseman's arm is suddenly the perfect place to rest my head.

I close my eyes, barely noticing how tense Pestilence is.

"Sara?"

"Mm?" I don't open my eyes.

"Sara."

Just going to drift off for a bit...

"Sara." He turns my face toward him. I blink up at him as his gaze scours my features, lingering on my lips.

He looks alarmed. "You're not all right."

I'm not, am I?

I think I hear him curse under his breath, then he clucks his tongue, tightening his grip on me. Trixie begins to gallop, his hooves spraying icy water against my legs.

"Why didn't you say anything?" Pestilence roars. Or maybe it's the wind and rain that's roaring…

"I'm s-supposed to suffer."

He huffs, and I swear I hear him say, "Not like this." But that's ridiculous because I'm supposed to suffer *exactly* like this.

At the next turnoff, the horseman tugs on the reins, turning his steed down a muddy dirt path.

I glance up at him, seeing rain and sleet plaster his hair to his face. So much for pretty boy's earlier bath.

"W-where are we going?" I ask. My tongue feels thick and clumsy in my mouth.

"It seems I've once again underestimated just how fragile you are."

It's the closest thing he gives me to an answer.

Maybe a kilometer or so later, I catch sight of a yellow house that's seen better days. Pestilence makes a beeline for it, not slowing until we're nearly at its doorway.

He swings off the horse and gathers me in his arms. In three long strides, he's at the door. His booted foot slams against the wood, kicking the thing inward.

Inside, I hear a flurry of screams.

No, not more people.

"Out of my way!" the horseman bellows.

I catch a brief glimpse of a middle-aged couple and, behind them, two curious children.

No.

Pestilence sets me in front of a wood-burning stove, holding me close as I shiver.

I clutch his upper arm and force my eyes to open. "We can't stay here," I say, my voice weak.

"I need blankets," he demands. He's not even looking at me.

My eyelids keep closing.

Body feels heavy. So heavy.

"Please," I murmur. I know it's the wrong thing to say, but I can't help it. How else should I plead for someone's life?

"Sshh. Blankets! And more wood while you're at it."

A hand brushes my hair back, and I want to look and see who the hand belongs to, but my eyelids are too heavy to pry open. I finally feel safe and taken care of, and that's all my body needs at the moment. I relax, my head finding the crook of an arm once more.

Such an oddly comfortable place to sleep.

The children!

I begin to sit up again, forcing myself to rouse.

"Sshh, Sara. I'm right here."

Who?

Not the children.

Not the children.

———

I come to gradually, getting my bearings bit by bit. A mound of blankets covers me, and in front of me is a wood-burning stove, a fire cheerily burning inside it. I stare at the flames like they hold the answers to all my questions.

I move slowly, feeling like I drank my weight in bad moonshine and then decided to run a marathon before getting hit by a freight train. Yesterday was not my best day.

I groan, beginning to roll away.

As soon as I shift, I feel the wind brush against my bare skin.

113

What in the world?

Am I *naked*?

An arm tightens around my stomach, feeling like a band of steel.

Waitonefuckingmoment.

My mind screeches to a halt.

No.

No, no, no, nonononono.

Nooooooooo.

I glance over my shoulder, and sure enough there's Pestilence, spooning me like we're lovers. From what I can tell, he doesn't have a shirt on.

Deep breath, Burns.

"Did we...?" I can't even finish that sentence.

"You were hypothermic."

Oh. Of course. That would be the logical sequence of events. Not screwing the world's most hated being. Because that would be so far out of the question that—

Why am I even dwelling on this?

I gather the blankets, clutching them against me, and sit up with as much modesty as I can manage.

"Where are we?"

Pestilence sits up next to me, and now it really looks like the two of us were up to some hanky-panky.

"In a house," he replies.

Ask a silly question...

In the distance I hear hushed voices.

"*No, you can't go out there.*"

"*But I'm hungry.*"

"*Is that really the horseman?*"

"*I want to pet his horse!*"

"*Go back to your rooms, both of you.*"

114

Little feet pitter-patter against the floor.

My stomach contracts. *Children*. That's right. I rub the heel of my hand against one of my eyes, willing the past twenty-four hours to just go away.

Children. Under the same roof as Pestilence.

"Don't let them die," I whisper.

"Everyone dies, Sara."

I close my eyes. Everything hurts *so damn much*. My body, my heart, my mind.

They're going to die.

I twist to face him, pressing the blanket close to me. It has race cars printed all over it. A little boy's blanket, sacrificed so I'd be warm. Sometimes it's the little details that cut the deepest.

"Honestly," I say, "that is the biggest load of horseshit I've heard from you."

He squints at me. "Every *human* dies," he amends, completely missing my point.

"It doesn't mean they need to die today!" I hiss, trying to keep my voice down for the family's sake.

"They won't. They still have a few days yet."

Suddenly, I can't look at him, and I can't stand to be near him.

He's going to kill children. *Children*.

Of course, he already *has* killed children. Thousands upon thousands of them. But now the reality of it is being shoved in my face, and I can't stand it.

Wordlessly, Pestilence hands me a pile of clothes, undoubtedly something he swiped from the owners. This may just be the worst part of the whole thing. The horseman can think to collect clothes for me even as he lets his damnable plague kill *kids*.

Pestilence settles back on his forearms, watching me as I dress, his eyes not quite as disinterested in my body as they were the last time he saw it.

I must be imagining things.

I finally meet his gaze. "Change your mind."

"No."

My jaw clenches as I stare at him, my eyes accusing. He meets my gaze unflinchingly.

"I am not here to please your every whim." Pestilence's voice is steady, unfeeling. "I am here to end the world."

CHAPTER 18

It takes three days for plague to kill a man. Four, if you're particularly unlucky.

This family is particularly unlucky.

I don't know if this is simply nature at work or if Pestilence is pulling the strings (either to punish me for pissing him off or to "compromise" with me and give this family a bit longer to live).

It takes four long, agonizing days of sickness before the entire family passes. Mother, father, son, and daughter. All of them taken by this senseless plague.

Four days I lingered in that house at Pestilence's insistence while I recovered, four days the horseman made himself scarce, four days that I cared for the family—against their wishes. They wished me gone. At least they did until they were too weak to take care of themselves.

"Why is he doing this?" the woman, Helen, asked me the day before she died.

I knelt next to her side of the bed. "I don't know."

"Why did he save you?" she pressed.

"I tried to kill him," I explained. "He's keeping me alive so he can punish me."

She shook her head. "I don't think so," she murmured. "He has his reasons, but I don't think punishment is one of them."

My skin prickled at her words, and for the first time I felt some uncertainty at my situation.

Why would the horseman keep me around if not to punish me?

I recalled the torture I'd endured, and my uncertainty vanished. Helen simply didn't know what Pestilence put me through. That was all.

Of all the members of this family, it's the father who goes first. He was a big, burly guy who was built like a tank, and out of all of them, I would've thought he'd hold out the longest. Instead, in the early hours of the fourth day he closed his eyes, gave one final rattling cough, and passed on in the big bed he shared with his wife.

By the time he died, Helen was too sick to move him from the bed. I managed to drag his sore-riddled body from it, but Helen wouldn't let me remove him from the room.

"The children shouldn't see him…like that," she weakly protested.

So I dragged him into the main bathroom, and Helen had to lie mere meters from his cooling, rotting corpse. And even though she was succumbing to her own death by then, she lived long enough to realize the horror of it.

Their son went next. Before he died, I brought him into his parents' room so Helen could hold him as he passed.

She followed two hours later.

The last one to go was Stacy, their tiny daughter who

died wearing unicorn pajamas, lying under a sky of glow-in-the-dark stars. She'd called out to her mom as fever took her, cried for her dad when the open sores along her body hurt more than she could bear.

I held her hand and stroked her hair the entire time, pretending to be her mother so that in her confusion, she'd at least know some peace. And then she went like the rest of her family. Quietly. Like stepping out of one room and into another, her chest rising and falling slower and slower until it stopped rising at all.

That was twenty minutes ago. Or maybe it was an hour. Time plays tricks on you when you least expect it.

I sit at the side of Stacy's bed and hold her hand even after I know she's gone. I've seen enough during my time as a firefighter to develop a thick skin, but this...this is something else altogether.

She was just a child. And she died *last*, with no one but me to see her out of this world.

Behind me, the door creaks open.

"It's time to go," Pestilence says at my back.

I brush a few stray tears from my cheeks. Placing Stacy's hand on her chest, I rise before heading to where he stands in the doorway.

I step so close to him, I can feel his body heat.

"Why do you have to take the children?" I whisper hoarsely.

His hand falls to my shoulder, steering me out of the room. "You'd prefer a slow death for them, is that it?"

"I'd prefer for them not to die at all."

"What do you think will happen, human, once their families die off? Once these kids are all alone? Think they can hunt for themselves? Forage for themselves?"

All my retorts are like rocks in my mouth, rolling over one another. In the end, I just glare at him.

"See," he says, "you know my words to be true, even if you despise them."

"Why do you have to kill at all?" I say as he leads me down the hall.

"Why did you have to ruin the world?" the horseman retorts.

"I *didn't*."

"You did. Just as I don't have to touch each man to kill him, nor do you have to personally light the world on fire to be the reason it burns."

I rub my eyes. Every time we talk, I feel like I'm banging my head against a wall, hurting myself and getting nowhere for all my effort.

"Why does it have to be so god-awful?" I whisper. "The lumps, the sores..."

"It's plague. It's not supposed to be enjoyable."

He leads me outside to where Trixie waits, the saddlebags laden with goods lifted from this house. Seeing all the odds and ends tucked away, I feel like a grave robber, looting from the dead. I know they no longer need food and jackets, but I still can't shake the wrongness of it all.

Woodenly, I get on the horse, Pestilence joining me a moment later. And just like that, the two of us leave the house and its tragic former occupants behind.

We've barely gone a kilometer when the horseman fishes a wrapped sandwich from one of the saddlebags and hands it to me. "You haven't eaten," he explains.

I turn the item over and over in my hand. "Did you... make this for me?"

"I like the taste of jam. I thought you might as well."

So, yes, he did make it for me. The same man who just delivered death made me a sandwich because he noticed I hadn't eaten.

I pinch my eyes shut and draw in a long breath. Why does this have to be so complicated? Why can't he just stay in the nice little box in my mind labeled *Evil* and let that be that? These brief flashes where he's considerate and tender, they're slowly breaking me.

Opening my eyes, I peel away the sandwich's packaging, and sure enough, between the two coarse slices of homemade bread is a generous helping of jam. And only jam.

It's not lost on me how very similar this is to a pie—two bready surfaces holding a sugary fruit filling. I bring it to my mouth and bite into it.

It's not bad. I don't know why I thought it would be. Maybe I assumed jam sandwiches ought to taste wrong. Maybe I thought that after the day I've had, anything would taste like dirt in my mouth.

Instead it tastes like an indulgence. As I eat it, I imagine Pestilence in that cluttered little kitchen we just left, making this for me right next to the refrigerator-turned-icebox that was scattered with stick-figure artwork and alphabet magnets. All while down the hall I watched a little girl draw her last breath.

The sugary-sweet taste of the sandwich sours in my mouth. I take a few deep breaths before I try another bite.

"I don't like watching them die," Pestilence admits behind me.

I lower the sandwich.

He was all but absent during those four days I stayed with the family. I thought perhaps there was some other reason for it.

"Why didn't you force us to keep moving?" This could've been avoided if he didn't linger in one place for any length of time.

"You needed the rest," he replies.

Absently, I touch one of the bandages covering my wrists.

He's only keeping me alive to punish me, I told Helen.

I don't think so, she said. *He has his reasons, but I don't think punishment is one of them.*

I keep my thoughts to myself.

"But you still infect them," I say.

"I still infect them," he agrees. "And I will continue to infect them until my time has passed. But I do not like watching them die."

———

The two of us ride for the rest of the day, passing through a series of small deserted settlements. My thighs have finally stopped being so saddle sore, and my back itches where my skin is healing.

The weather has also decided to give me a break, the weak winter sun shining brilliantly above us. It's still colder than a witch's tit, but hey, it's not raining. I'll take it.

Trees hedge the highway to our left, and to our right, the beautiful waters of the Howe Sound glitter. Speckled amid them are a series of islands, and beyond those is the other edge of the mainland. The sight would take your breath away if not for the rows and rows of rusted cars sitting between me and the view.

The dead automobiles lie abandoned on either side of the road. This must be one of the sites still waiting on the government-funded cleanup. The arrival that knocked out most of our power also stranded thousands upon thousands of people in their cars in the middle of the open road.

If I close my eyes, I can still see some of the gruesome images of the pileups, cars smashed to smithereens with their occupants still inside. We no longer talk about that first wave of fatalities, not since Pestilence reappeared, but so many, many people died that first day—from car crashes, from planes falling out of the sky, from life-support machines giving out, and so many strange scenarios no one ever saw coming.

Around me, the rusted cars sit as sad reminders of the day the world changed. Pestilence doesn't spare them a glance. He and Trixie only have eyes for the horizon.

We ride throughout the day, not even stopping to eat. I come to find that's because Pestilence made me not one but three jam sandwiches *and* packed me a jar of artichoke hearts and a can of anchovies. I don't have it in me to tell him he won't want to sit anywhere near me if I actually crack that can of fish open.

Then again, I could get him to try the fish…we'd see just how well he enjoyed human food then.

It's not until the sky is a deep blue that we turn off the highway. Pestilence passes several houses, some dark and others with oil lamps burning bright inside, before we finally head up the driveway of some unlucky soul's home.

The screen door bangs open and closed with the wind, making an eerie squealing noise. And now that I'm looking for it, I notice the windows are boarded up. It's clear that whoever lived here, they haven't for a long time.

Sights like this aren't uncommon. Maybe the well on the property dried up or the pump stopped working. Maybe the house was too far from civilization now that cars are obsolete. Maybe a relative took the previous owners in, or maybe they died and no one wanted to buy this house in the middle of nowhere. The stories behind homes like this one are all different, but they all lead to the same fate—abandonment.

I hear there are entire ghost towns where people once lived but do no longer. Las Vegas, Dubai...

The thought of all those once opulent cities sitting like bones in the desert, their glittery attractions dulled with dust and falling into disrepair, sends a shiver down my spine.

Death has reared himself a throne / In a strange city lying alone... Poe's words ring out in my mind.

My attention returns to the home in front of us. *I don't like watching them die*, Pestilence said. A part of me thinks maybe that's why he chose this place.

The horseman tends to Trixie while I enter the home. As soon as I step inside, I pat the darkened wall until I find a light switch. Once I find it, I flick it on, ever hopeful that this house will have electricity.

For one blinding moment, the entryway flares bright with light. Then, with a shattering pop, the light disappears just as suddenly as it came.

"Shit."

I guess I should be thankful the damage isn't worse. I've had to put out more electrical fires than wildfires over the past few years. All these creature comforts are on the fritz.

Pestilence comes in behind me, already unfastening his heavy armor. He drops his bow and quiver on a nearby side table, then each piece of his armor. Lastly, he sets his crown down, running a hand through his hair.

It's all so very human. I wonder if he knows that.

"Light?" he asks.

"It doesn't work." I head over to another switch and flip it on and off. Nothing happens. "Nope, definitely doesn't."

I grope around the living room, looking for candles, lamps, wicks, matches—anything that can illuminate this place now that the sun's gone down. Pestilence heads back outside, leaving me to fumble alone.

He comes in a few minutes later, carrying several items. He passes me before setting his haul in what looks to be the kitchen.

I hear the hiss of a match being struck, and a moment later, he lights a lantern he must've picked up at one of the last houses we stayed in.

He hands the lantern to me, then walks down the home's dark hallway. I watch him go, listening as he opens and shuts another door. The muffled sound of a garage door being manually lifted drifts in, then the steady sound of hooves clicking against cement as he leads Trixie out of the elements.

I lift the lantern, looking around at the house. Half the furniture is covered with ratty sheets, and what isn't covered is blanketed in a thick coat of dust.

I walk over to the fireplace. There are still pictures sitting on the mantel. I pick up one, using my thumb to rub away a coat of dust. Beneath it is a portrait of a woman in her early twenties, her hair permed, frizzed, and fluffed to within an inch of its life. I choose another photo at random before dusting it off enough to see a group of squinting kids in bathing suits, floaties pushed high up on their arms.

I set it down as my gooseflesh rises. There's an entire life here that appears to abruptly have stopped. Whether death or displacement took them, it took them swiftly.

Most cities will look like this in the future.

It won't just be Vegas and Dubai. It will be every place Pestilence visits. And in that dystopian future, someone like me will go from house to house, skirting around the decayed corpses that have been left unburied inside.

I shudder at the thought.

The door to the garage opens and shuts, and Pestilence's heavy footfalls grow louder as he makes his way back to the living room. When he appears, he has several dry logs with him. He eyes me before making his way over and beginning to stack the wood in the fireplace.

An hour later, a fire is going, half a dozen candles are flickering around the living room, and a mattress and a few moth-eaten blankets have been dragged out from a closet and laid out in the living room so I can sleep where it's warm.

I sit on the mattress, knees pulled up under my chin, sipping water out of an old earthenware mug (the well still works) and staring into the flames. Next to me, Pestilence lounges against the mattress, his legs crossed in front of him.

"Why do you help them?" he asks. His eyes find mine, the flames dancing in them. Even lit by fire, he looks like an angel.

The devil was also an angel.

"Help who?" I ask.

"That family. And the man before them."

Is he serious?

I study his features, my heart unwillingly picking up speed because my body has no sense and cannot discern evil mofo from hot human man.

"How can I not help them?" I finally say.

"You know they're going to die anyway," he says.

It's such cold, pragmatic reasoning. Like the means to an end is nothing next to the end itself.

"So?" I glance back at the flames. "If I can ease their discomfort, then I will."

I can feel his gaze on me, hotter than the fire.

"You don't just do it to ease their pain though, do you?" he says. "You also do it to ease your own."

What a clever little horseman he is.

I press my mouth together, frowning. "You're right," I say. "Suffering is for the living, and you have made me suffer." Watching those children succumb while drowning in their own fluids, having to listen to their cries... "And how I despise you for it."

"I expect nothing less from the human who burned me alive."

I turn on him, my anger rising. "So it's still about *your* suffering, is it? You've wiped out entire cities, but at the end of the day, you were hurt. You want to know something? I hunted you down like a fucking *animal* because you deserve it. And I would do it again and again and *again*."

Would I though? A small traitorous part of me isn't so sure.

Undaunted by that thought, I continue, "You're killing us all *cruelly*, and you hate us for it."

He says nothing to my outburst, just sits there, studying me.

"Part of living," I say, "is feeling pain, senseless pain." I could tell him a thousand stories about the sheer unfairness of the world. But why bother? He doesn't give a shit about our problems.

"I am what I am," he says, resolute. He sounds almost... defeated. "I came here with a task, and I will see it completed."

"Who gave you the task? God? The devil?" I throw my free hand up in the air. "The fucking Easter Bunny? I thought you were Pestilence the *Conqueror*, not someone's goddamned errand boy!"

"*Careful*, human," he warns, his voice dangerous.

"Careful? If you're so frightened of my words, then shut me up."

I went too far. I know that as soon as I've spoken.

Pestilence raises his eyebrows at my challenge. A second

later, he rips off a section of the dusty sheet that covers the nearby couch. Getting up, he twists the linen in his hands. The action looks ominous.

He kneels in front of me, his eyes meeting mine. And then he shoves the linen between my lips.

Never in my life has someone tried to *gag* me.

For a moment I'm dumbfounded, but then the moment passes and I'm a raging bull, dropping my mug of water and battling Pestilence as he ties the material securely behind my head. I don't manage much more than slapping his face before he grabs my shoulder and thrusts my head into the mattress. He presses his knee against my back.

I buck against him madly, trying to shake him off, but he's more solid than simple flesh and blood, and my efforts get me nowhere.

Behind me I hear another rip, and then he's grabbing my wrists and looping the material around them.

I'm shrieking into the makeshift gag. "Oooooouuu muuuffuughhrrr!" I roar.

He binds my wrists tight. Once he finishes, he sits me up and squats in front of me.

Mistake.

I lift my foot and slam it into his pretty-boy face.

He rocks back, catching my ankle between his hands. "Do I need to bind these too?"

"Ullll uuuuggghinnnn eeeenngggh ooooouuuuu!"

He holds my foot hostage, waiting for me like I'm a toddler having an unreasonable tantrum.

I give my foot a few useless jerks before I give up. This guy makes few empty threats, and I'm not all that interested in being completely restrained.

When I stop fighting him, he releases my foot, reaching a hand up to his face to rub it where I clocked him.

"You hit solidly for a human—I'll give you that."

"Uuuuugh oooo, aaaahuuulll."

"I'm surprised you're this mad. You're the one who suggested silencing you."

I shriek again.

"Calm yourself, little human. Maybe then I'll release you."

Little?

He goes back to his side of the fire and loses himself in the flames.

I sit there, across from him, seething, my breath coming out in hot, ragged pants.

Next chance I get, I'll kick him in his holy balls.

Some uncountable amount of time goes by like that, the two of us sitting close but mentally leagues apart.

Finally, Pestilence looks up at me. "Are you ready to be civilized?"

"Uuuuh oooo!"

"No? Hmmm, maybe I'll give you a little longer."

Pride is a lonely soldier, seeing out his watch when there's no one else there to care. I thought fire training had burned most of it out of me, but nope.

In the end, I cool myself down. Getting angry at one of the horsemen of the apocalypse for bringing about the end of man is like getting angry at ice for being cold.

I lie down on my side, ignoring the shooting pain as my weight settles on one of my bound hands.

Wordlessly, Pestilence gets up and loosens my bindings, first removing my gag, and then, when I don't immediately curse him out, removing the linens that bind my wrists.

He sits back down, staring at the fire. I look from him

to it, and then I turn my back on both, curling up on the mattress and drawing one of the musty blankets over me.

It's still early evening, but I'm over the day. Over Pestilence and his macabre task. Over grief and anger and all those other emotions that hang heavy inside of me.

I feel Pestilence's gaze on my back just as surely as if he placed a physical hand against it, but I don't acknowledge it. I close my eyes and will myself to sleep.

My body is more tired than I assume because within minutes I'm out.

CHAPTER 19

Vancouver 18 km.

I stare at the sign in growing horror.

Up until now, I've only ever seen the horseman pass through settlements and small towns. But Vancouver is another beast altogether.

Hundreds of thousands of people live there. Surely they've already posted evacuation notices. Surely the city is empty enough…

The two of us continue down the highway, and each hour that passes has me more and more tightly wound.

The wilderness gives way to ritzy neighborhoods. The houses are nestled on either side of the highway, most secreted away behind large trees and shrubs but still visible enough for the occupants to see the water on our right.

There's not a soul in sight.

The closer to the city we get, the smaller and more tightly packed the houses become. Here, in the outlying suburbs, I spot the first true signs of life. The sight of a biker off in the distance, the faint sounds of shouting.

The click of Trixie's hooves against the asphalt is suddenly deafening. It reminds me too much of the moment Pestilence rounded the corner into my neck of the woods.

So I shouldn't be surprised when a gunshot shatters the normal sounds of the day.

But I am. I nearly fall out of my seat at the noise.

The horseman's grip tightens. "Hold on."

He clucks his tongue, and Trixie takes off at a gallop.

We race down the highway at breakneck speed. Another gunshot follows the first, then several more as a few doomed individuals try their hand at vigilante justice.

None of the bullets, however, find their target. Even as the sound of gunshots fades in the distance, Pestilence races on.

The highway branches, the 99 separating from the 1. The horseman heads west, staying on the 99. I don't know if he is aware of this, but the decision is a good one.

We sprint down the highway, crossing the bridge before entering Stanley Park. Here the city is interrupted by a dense patch of wilderness. Still, my body is poised for another assault. In a city with this many inhabitants, there's bound to be more.

The park blurs by us, the trees blending to create a green backdrop.

On the other side of the park, blocks and blocks of high-rises loom ahead of us, and to our right their steel-and-glass frames glitter in the midday light. Between each block of them, I catch glimpses of the ocean.

That's all I notice before the gunshots resume.

Pestilence yanks on Trixie's reins to steer us off the highway and down a side street, making a beeline for the water. The Goliath structures stand like sentinels on each side of us as we dash down the road.

I can't hear much over the pounding of hoofbeats, just the steadily increasing sound of gunfire. If maneuvering us off the highway was supposed to solve our situation, it hasn't.

Like me, other people—many of them, by the sound of it—decided to sacrifice themselves in order to kill the horseman. I wonder if they too assumed the horseman could die.

A bullet whizzes by me. If things keep up like this, I'm going to get hit.

I notice the people lingering in the doorways of buildings or leaning out of windows. Others still are openly running toward us, guns in hand.

Now this, this is a true ambush.

Without warning, Pestilence shoves me off his steed. I'm so surprised I forget to scream as I fall.

I slam hard onto the street, my eyesight darkening at the impact. All my old wounds shriek at being so violently jostled.

Ahead of me, more gunshots ring out.

A few people rush around the street, trying to get a good aim on the horseman.

Ahead of me, Pestilence brandishes his bow and arrow. Now that his hands are free, he uses them to shoot arrow after arrow at his attackers. I see one man fall from a window three stories up and another slump forward from where he crouches behind a tree.

As he rides away from me, the horseman takes out his assailants, sometimes turning in his saddle to shoot backward. I watch him for some time before I remember myself.

You're a firefighter, Burns. Get up and act like one.

I force myself to stand, favoring one leg over the other. As far as I can tell nothing's broken, though I'm going to have one hell of a bruise where I landed on my thigh.

I begin moving, a slow limp that doesn't get me far fast, but then I'm not trying to flee. I scan the street, looking for the injured.

I head over to the closest victim, a wiry man whose hair (what little there is left of it) is more white than brown.

"Sir, are you—?" My voice cuts off when I see the raw, bloody flesh at his throat. It's not even the horseman who got this guy. One of the bullets that missed Pestilence found another victim.

He tries to talk to me, his mouth opening and closing, his eyes wide with shock. All that comes out are a few red bubbles that gather on his neck.

There's nothing to be done for him.

I take his hand, kicking his gun aside; he has no need for it now.

"You're all right," I say soothingly. We both know that's a lie. "I'm right here with you. I won't leave you."

His hand squeezes mine tight, and his lips keep moving. I lean in to try to hear him better, but all I hear is the wet gurgling that comes from his throat.

I nod anyway, acting as though I'm keenly aware of exactly what he's saying. His lips slow until he has nothing left to say. He still clutches my hand, but then his eyes move above me, beyond me, and his hand relaxes.

Fuck death. Seriously, fuck this horrible, horrible thing we all must endure.

I let go of him and stand, my eyes already looking for the next person.

Farther down, a woman is trying to get to her feet, one

of the horseman's golden arrows jutting from her chest. I jog over to her, ignoring the pain in my thigh.

Time blurs as I move from person to person, giving what aid I can, which isn't much, but it does catch the eye of a paramedic-turned-infantryman. He joins the effort, which in turn catches the eye of a doctor.

The longer we linger out in the street, the more people trickle out of whatever buildings they took shelter in to now lend a hand. My throat thickens at the sight.

This is what Pestilence misses in his quest to kill us off. That right alongside the worst of human nature is the best of it.

We all work somberly together. No one outright says it, but I can practically hear the thoughts around me.

Am I infected?

Is it already too late?

How long do I have?

When will I start to feel ill?

A series of screams punctuates the air.

I glance up from the man I'm kneeling next to, the paramedic at my side.

Off in the distance, Pestilence gallops back down the street on his white steed, his armor and face smeared with blood.

What has he done?

He holds his bow, an arrow nocked, ready to kill anyone who dares to rise against him.

I tense at the sight. I almost believed this was the end of our partnership.

Should've known better. Pestilence the Conqueror gets to have his cake and eat it too.

"What in the hell?" the paramedic utters next to me. "He's back?"

I stand, drawing a few eyes to me.

Pestilence's jaw is tight, his eyes scanning the street as he charges down the road. When the horseman sees me, his expression doesn't change, but I swear he relaxes.

Why does he want me so badly?

He surges forward, his steed's pace quickening as the two head straight for me.

Run, an irrational part of me thinks—like that would do a fat lot of good now that he's set his sights on me. Instead I move into the middle of the street, away from where the other people are.

"What are you doing?" the doctor calls to me.

I ignore him, my gaze trained on the horseman. Pestilence, for his part, now pays the last of his assailants no heed. Nor does he need to. The gunshots that punctuated the air earlier are now all silent.

The stillness squeezes my gut tight. The horseman effort-lessly cut all these people down. How does anyone make a stand against this sort of power? It's too great, unstoppable.

As he closes in on me, Pestilence leans deeply to the side of his saddle, not slowing. I don't realize what he means to do until his arm extends.

And now, even knowing I'm not going to get away, I bolt. I don't know what drives me to run. Maybe it's the punishing pace of Pestilence's steed, maybe it's the fierce look in the horseman's eyes. Or maybe it's that rider and mount look like they bathed in the blood of their enemies.

Pushing my aching thighs for all they're worth, I sprint down the street, back toward the highway. Trixie's hoofbeats sound louder and louder as the two close in on me. I pump my arms, forcing my legs to move faster.

I don't make it very far before Pestilence's arm wraps

around my back. With a jerk that has my nearly healed wounds screaming in protest, he lifts me off the ground before setting me smoothly on the seat in front of him.

"Secure yourself, Sara," he commands, not slowing.

Going as fast as we are, there's no way I can adjust myself from sitting sidesaddle, so I wrap my arms around Pestilence's midsection, holding on tight to him as he directs us toward the water. His arm rests almost possessively around me, further securing me to him.

We speed by the large buildings for a second time, and as we race down the street, I catch sight of a few more fallen shooters lying in pools of their own blood, their bodies riddled with arrows. I stop looking when I see one of the golden arrows protruding from a dead man's eye. The whole thing is so ghastly and violent and sad.

Pestilence didn't spare them. Not like he spared me. And he may think I have the worse fate, but at the end of it all, I feel lucky to be sitting here on the horseman's steed rather than finding out what lies on the other side of death.

Abruptly, the buildings give way to sand, and I have a clear view of the inlet I've kept catching glimpses of. I stare out at the water and, beyond it, Vancouver Island.

Trixie's strides pound against the sand, his hooves spraying the fine grains against me. It's been years since I've been this close to the sea, but I don't get the chance to enjoy it. The dry sand gives way to wet, and still the horse doesn't slow.

"What are you doing?" I yell at Pestilence over the pounding of hooves, not quite able to tear my gaze from the water.

Other than securing me even closer against him, Pestilence doesn't respond.

My breath catches as the beach ends, and then, quite suddenly, we're thundering through the water.

Wait, that's not quite right...

I glance down.

"Oh my God," I say, staring at the rippling waves. "Oh my *God*." The steed is not wading through the water, he's galloping on *top* of it.

Trixie's hooves splash against the water's surface as though the inlet were nothing more than a puddle, kicking up a few stray droplets of sea spray onto me and the horseman.

We're riding on water.

I squeeze my eyes shut, then open them again.

Still on top of the water.

I don't know why I'm surprised. Pestilence can spread plague just by moving through a city, and he's impervious to death. What's one more freakish power?

Once we're well away from land, Pestilence's steed slows to a reasonable gait. Only now am I able to—awkwardly—throw one of my legs over the saddle and face forward. (I still nearly fall off in the process.)

Land hedges us in on all sides as we move across the water, chilly droplets splashing against my thighs.

Pestilence leans against me, his chest pressing against my back with enough force to make me lean forward.

Goddamn but he's heavy.

"Can you let up a little?" I say. *So close to elbowing his ass.*

He ignores my request.

Typical.

As the minutes tick away, a little more of his weight presses down on me. It happens so gradually that I'm bent substantially forward before I realize this may not be intentional.

"Pestilence?"

No response.

"Pestilence?" I say, a bit more urgently this time.

Nothing.

Damn me, but my stomach is churning with worry.

I rotate when I notice the blood dripping off the wrist that holds the reins.

Something is wrong with him. Very wrong.

I face him as best I can. His eyes are closed, his face is slack, and his crown sits slightly askew on his head. This last one makes him look—contradictorily—both more rakish and more innocent.

I put my fingers to his neck, searching for a pulse, but I can't get a read on him with the way our bodies are rocking on his horse.

"Pestilence, can you hear me?" I try to pull him away enough to get a response.

His head rolls backward until it appears he's staring at the sky, and I catch his crown before it slides off.

His body sways in his seat, then he pitches forward again, his face burying itself in the crook of my neck. I wrap my arms around him as his body lists sideways.

What happens if he falls off? Will he land on top of the water, or will he sink? What will happen to Trixie—and to me—if he does so?

Really don't want to find out.

I cradle him awkwardly in my arms as I steer his steed toward a nearby island. Of course, once the land looms large enough for me to see the details, I can make out streets and buildings—lots and lots of them.

Shit.

I tug on the reins, changing our trajectory, all while

trying to stabilize Pestilence, who may or may not be dead. *Temporarily* dead, but dead nonetheless.

How had I missed this until now? I heard the gunshots and saw the smeared blood on him when he came for me. And now that I'm looking for it, I can see he's bleeding from a dozen different wounds, and the fluid is all over him and all over me.

For Christ's sake, he was *bleeding* on me and I was still unaware. Lulled by the steady trod of his horse's gait and distracted by the fact we were traveling on water.

Eventually, Trixie heads toward another section of land. By the time the horse nears the shore, my arms shake from the strain of keeping Pestilence in his saddle.

It's only once his horse is clomping through the sand that I allow myself to relax my hold. The horseman's body cants to the side, and then the two of us topple off his mount.

Pestilence groans weakly when we hit the sand, our limbs tangling.

Alive.

I let out a breath, relief flowing through me. I don't know what else I expected from an immortal man.

And I definitely don't know why, of all things, I feel *relief.*

I drag my body from under his, then lay him out on the sand before pulling his weaponry off him and tossing it aside. He's in even worse shape than I thought, his clothes saturated in blood. It seeps out from beneath his armor and drips onto the sand. And his armor…

Some of those bullets blew straight through the metal, making the golden breastplate look like a slice of Swiss cheese.

Piece by piece, I unfasten the armor, grimacing as previously trapped blood drips onto the sand. My gaze moves to Pestilence's face. The normally tan skin is now pale and wan.

I skim my fingers over his cheek, feeling the chill that now clings to his flesh.

His chest rises and falls as he takes shallow breaths. At least he's breathing.

Since when do you want him to breathe?

I peel back what I can of the horseman's wet clothes. Bullet holes litter his arms, his legs, and his chest. His face, however, was left untouched. That's why I didn't notice. I was so transfixed by his beauty and his intensity—intensity he focused on me—that I didn't notice.

I pause when I see blood congealing in the sand around his head.

Dare I?

Before I can think twice about it, I lift his head and probe the back of his skull. I nearly gag as I touch something soft. He makes a plaintive noise at my touch. It's clearly painful for him.

Of course it's painful—it's a head wound you're poking, genius.

"I'm sorry," I whisper, not sure why I'm whispering.

I glance around. Trixie Skillz is lingering nearby, and like his owner, the horse is dotted with bullet wounds.

And still the horse carried not one but two riders across a sea.

I take a shuddering breath and look down the beach. On either side of me, the shoreline is thick with trees. Far down the beach to my left, a lone house is nestled among them.

At least there's a place to stay if we need it.

I move Pestilence's head so it rests in my lap. I don't know why I do that or why I remove his crown so I can stroke his matted hair. Even with blood and seawater tangling it, the blond locks are so soft, softer than hair has any right to be.

I smooth a thumb over one of his annoyingly perfect eyebrows. Battered and broken like he is, my reckless heart actually aches for him.

It's just because he's ridiculously pretty, I tell myself.

I run my knuckles over his brow.

"I'm sorry they did this to you," I admit. Just as I'm sorry for everything *he* has done to *them*. It's a catch-22.

I continue to stroke his hair, waiting for him to heal himself.

You could escape right now—vanish while he's recovering. Then you'd never have to answer to him again.

My legs stay folded beneath his head.

I'm slowing Pestilence down, I reason with myself. *I'm giving people more time to escape.* The world is caught in a hopeless game of cat and mouse, and I know that in the end the horseman will make his rounds and kill us all anyway, but I'm slowing his progress. That counts for something, right?

The shadows have deepened by the time the first of the bullets makes its way out of Pestilence's body. It wiggles out of his lower leg for a few seconds, then tumbles harmlessly into the sand.

Several minutes later, the horseman shifts for the first time, a pained breath escaping him.

"I'm right here," I murmur, continuing to run my fingers through his hair. "I've got you."

Pestilence stills.

"...Sara?" He seems to force his eyes open. They're unfocused as he gazes up at me.

"Hi."

He reaches up, his bloody fingers touching my cheek. "You didn't run."

I let out a laugh that's far too shaky for my liking. "I probably should've," I say.

"Probably," he agrees.

His hand drops, and he closes his eyes again.

"Pestilence? *Pestilence.*" But he's unconscious once more.

CHAPTER 20

After two more bullets pop out of his flesh, I decide it's time to move. The sun dipped behind the horizon twenty minutes ago, and I'm freezing my butt off.

I cast a few furtive glances toward the beach house just down the way. I can barely make out the dark structure. The lack of light is probably a good thing, seeing as how I'm going to be forcing my way in.

After shimmying out from under Pestilence, I grab his battered breastplate and settle it loosely over my chest. Even without the aid of a mirror, I know I look ridiculous. The breastplate swamps my torso, giving off the illusion that I'm petite. I'm not; it's the horseman who's freaking monster-sized.

I decide to leave the rest of his armor and weapons where they lie in the sand. He'll have to grab them once he's recovered.

After I put Pestilence's crown on my head (motherfucking queen right here), I hook my arms under his shoulders. I brace myself, taking a few fortifying breaths. "This is probably going to hurt," I warn him—not that he can hear me.

I move, shuffling us back bit by bit toward the house. Pestilence groans, fighting my hold weakly.

"If you can walk, then be my guest," I say. "Otherwise stop moving, unless you want me to drop you."

He does stop moving, but even without him resisting my efforts, it takes damn near an eternity to reach the beach house. My God is he heavy. I trip twice along the way, jarring the horseman awake each time. Behind us, Trixie Skillz plods along like the faithful steed he is.

Once I get to the house, I set Pestilence down and survey the place. There's no light coming from inside, and pine needles litter the stoop. Whoever owns this place hasn't been here for a while.

Probably someone's summer home.

I head over to the decorative door. Four square glass panes offer a glimpse inside. Seems cozy. Too bad it's going to look like a triple homicide by the time we're done with it.

I try the knob—I mean, you never know. People in my neck of the woods rarely lock their doors. This one doesn't budge.

My gaze drops to the glass panes.

Going to have to do this the hard way.

I shrug off my jacket and wrap it around my fist. Here's to hoping this isn't tempered glass I'm dealing with. Otherwise, this bright idea of mine may not go so well.

With one smooth stroke, I strike the glass.

"*Motherfucker!*" I shout, shaking out my fist. Even with the jacket as a buffer, my hand throbs from the impact. I glare at the intact windowpane.

Freaking tempered glass.

And god*damn* did that hurt.

Behind me, I hear laborious breathing and stumbling footfalls. "Move, Sara."

I swivel around and take the horseman in with wide eyes. I don't know whether I feel more shock or relief at the sight of him up and awake.

I step aside as Pestilence drags himself to the door before leaning most of his weight against the wall and leaving a smear of blood against the siding.

He reaches out and grabs the knob. With a swift jerk of his wrist, he breaks the lock, and the door swings open.

Annoying how easily he broke it—like it was nothing.

I help him inside, letting him lean his significant weight on me as I maneuver him to a plaid couch. Trixie clomps inside after us.

I lay the horseman out on the couch, then remove the breastplate and crown I wear, letting the items clatter onto the floor next to me. In front of me, Pestilence's eyes slide shut, and his breaths even out as he fades from consciousness once more.

After hooking my fingers in the damp cloth of his shirt, I rip it open, then push it off him as best I can. His torso is still a mottled mess of bruises and bullet holes, the injuries distorting the shimmering markings that ring his pecs. I find the other gunshot wounds that dot his shoulders, chest, neck, arms, legs, and in one case just above his collarbone. I lightly touch the skin beneath this last one.

At the press of my fingers, Pestilence's eyes flutter open, focusing on me.

"What are you doing?" he asks. There's both confusion and suspicion written all over his features.

Aside from poking him?

"I'm taking care of you."

The moment I speak the words, it really registers. *I'm helping the horseman recover.* Helping him, when only a short while ago I was the person pulling the trigger. I can hardly believe it.

The shock on his face must mirror my own.

He catches my hand, his eyes burning bright as he looks at me. "I'm fine, Sara."

He doesn't *want* my help. Didn't see that one coming.

"No, you're not. You got plugged with a small army's worth of ammunition."

He begins to sit up. "I've endured worse."

Yeah, I know. I was there. Being burned alive has got to top the Shitty Situations of the Year list.

I head back to Trixie, and after flipping on a switch and watching the overhead light sputter to life, I rummage through the horseman's saddlebags. As I do so, one of the bullets drops out of his mount's side before landing on the floor with a heavy *clink*. Poor horsey.

Eventually, my hand wraps around a bottle of Red Label I lifted from one of our stops. It takes a little longer to find the roll of gauze, but once I do, I return to the couch where the horseman is sprawled.

Pestilence's eyes drop to the items in my hands. "Those are *yours*," he says pointedly, like he doesn't want a thing to do with them.

Mayhap Pestilence is more afraid of my kindness than even I am of his.

"Well, tonight I feel like sharing," I say, unraveling the gauze as I move back to him.

He begins to push himself up, but I don't let him get very far. Grabbing his shoulder, I force him back down to the couch.

"I will heal on my own," he insists, scowling first at the gauze then the liquor that rest on the nearby coffee table.

"Yeah, you will." I grab a chair from the kitchen and drag it over. Then I sit on the chair in front of him and unscrew the cap of the whiskey, my eyes trained on his wounds.

"I don't agree with this," he says, but he's no longer trying to flee. In fact, if I didn't know better, I'd say I see curiosity sparkling in Pestilence's eyes.

No one's ever tended to him.

"I didn't ask whether you did," I say, grabbing the roll of gauze and pouring some of the whiskey onto it.

"Vexing woman."

I lift my brows and begrudgingly nod in agreement. I can totally be vexing.

"Don't you want me to suffer?" he asks ruefully, tracking each of my movements.

"I've never wanted you to suffer," I say. "Not even when I shot you down."

I move the alcohol-soaked linen to the first of his wounds.

He hisses as it touches his exposed flesh. "You lie, human. *This* is suffering."

He gets shot up a dozen times, and yet he complains about a little alcohol in his wounds?

"This is disinfectant."

"I can clean my wounds well enough without your crude methods."

Oh, that's right.

"Fine." I stand and go to the kitchen, where I rifle through the cupboards until I find two glasses. I bring them back. After pouring a shot into one of them, I hand the glass to him.

He takes it, giving the liquor a tentative whiff before wincing.

"To help with the pain," I explain.

"What does it matter?" he says, lowering his glass. "It will be over with eventually."

"Oh, for the love of—" I pour myself a double shot and take a deep swallow of it. I top my drink off, then set the whiskey aside.

Pestilence absolutely sucks at playing patient.

I grab the roll of gauze once more, intending to at least bandage his wounds. But as I reach out for him, he catches my wrist. "Sara," he says softly, "cease this. I appreciate the gesture, but it is in vain."

As he speaks, a bullet at his throat oozes out of the hole it burrowed into him.

So freaky.

My eyes meet his. "All right." Not going to twist his arm trying to help him if he doesn't want it.

I get up, grabbing the bottle of Red Label and my glass.

I'm halfway out of the living room when he calls out, "Where are you going?"

"To take a bath." *Need some goddamned alone time.*

I close my eyes and lean back against the tub, draping my arms over the rim and idly swirling my glass of whiskey. I can almost forget my life has gone to complete and utter cow shit.

Down the hall I hear the thump and scrape of Pestilence as he makes his way closer to me. A minute later the door creaks open. I crack my eyes just enough to see him limp into the bathroom holding his midsection gingerly, his still-full glass of whiskey in his other hand.

"I want to be alone," I say, closing my eyes once more. I don't bother covering myself. He's already seen me naked.

149

More than once. Also I doubt he's feeling all that lusty when he's barely holding himself together.

"Human, you have clearly forgotten that you're my prisoner."

Once, I was—and he had to stand guard over me to make sure I didn't bolt. But I don't know if I am any longer. That should bother me, but right now I have no more fucks to give.

I snort. "Do you really think I'm going to run?"

"You did in Vancouver."

Not going to open my eyes and let him ruin this moment I'm having.

"You would've too if you were about to be trampled by a horseman."

He guffaws but then falls silent.

"This drink tastes horrible," he says after a moment.

So he tried it when I wasn't looking. Sneaky horseman.

"Common opinion is that you don't drink liquor because it tastes good." I take a swallow from my own glass.

He grunts.

I pry my eyes open just enough to see him polish off the shot I gave him.

I grab the bottle next to me and hold it out like a peace offering.

After a pause where he's surely considering the wickedness of alcohol and how stained his soul's quickly becoming, he takes the bottle from me before pouring himself another drink. He's heavy-handed, probably because he doesn't realize just how potent the stuff is.

He looks at the label afterward. "Johnnie Walker Red Label," he reads. His eyes flick to me. "I saw you give this to that dying man."

That first nameless man I watched die of plague, he means. Pestilence noticed me giving him liquor?

"Drinking it helps with the pain," I say.

"People don't drink it to take away their pain," he replies. It's a statement, and yet I get the distinct impression that he's probing.

"Sometimes they do." But then, it's not always physical pain they're numbing themselves to. "But no, not always." I bring the hand holding the glass to my temple and tap on the side of my head with my index finger. "Sometimes they do it simply to alter their state of mind."

Pestilence is quiet after that. I let my eyes drift closed and pretend like I'm still blissfully enjoying a good soak and not acutely aware of his presence.

"You took care of me the same way you did your humans," he eventually says. There's something in his voice…

I open my eyes and catch Pestilence studying my face, his own eyes bright with what looks like desire. At the sight, my chest rises and falls faster and faster.

What *is* this reaction? I don't like him—I *don't*. It's just that he's handsome, and it's been a while since anyone looked at me like that.

That's all.

Well, that and the fact his shirt is still hanging open from collar to navel, exposing his glowing tattoos and muscular torso. You'd have to be dead not to react to that sight.

He tears his gaze away to peer down at his drink. "I don't know how to feel about that."

He's got really nice eyelashes. They're thick and dark and long. I'm not sure I've ever noticed *anyone's* lashes.

Why am I noticing Pestilence's eyelashes?

I force my thoughts away from eyelashes and pretty God spawn.

"I'm not sure how I feel about that either," I echo. What are we even talking about right now?

He nods companionably and brings his drink to his lips, taking two long swallows before grimacing. "This really does taste awful."

I give a soft laugh. "Then why are you drinking it?"

He meets my eyes. There's a lot of weight in that gaze. "You have already altered my mind. I wish to alter it *back*."

That's not how it works, I want to say. Instead I take another drink. "I know what you mean."

He squints at me, swirling the amber liquid around and around in his glass. "You were supposed to kill me, not help me."

The lingering taste of whiskey sours in my mouth. I wash it down with the last bit of my drink.

"It won't change anything, you know," he adds.

"I know," I say so quietly that I can barely hear the words themselves.

He's still going to drive us onward, infecting city after city.

The bath is getting cold, and I haven't begun to wash off. I set my empty glass aside and scrub the blood and grime from my body, feeling Pestilence's eyes on me the entire time. This time he doesn't offer help to wash my back, and I don't bother asking him for it.

When I sneak a glance at him, he's staring at me in a way that is no longer clinically detached like it once was. In fact, it's a decidedly human look.

This is what longing looks like, I realize.

My alarm wars with this horrifying *giddiness*. It's the same emotion I felt when I heard a rumor that Tom Becker, my high school crush, wanted to ask me out. Turned out he wanted to ask out Sara*h* (such is life—it just loves to kick you in the happy sacs), but for a blissful twenty-four hours I felt like baby angels were fluttering around in my stomach.

Just like I do right now.

I've had a decent amount of whiskey, but not enough to block out the sober realization that enjoying Pestilence's gaze on my naked body is decidedly *not* an appropriate reaction.

He rubs his face, looking weary and in pain, just how a man recovering from gunshot wounds ought to. After lifting his drink, he downs the second glass he poured for himself (which consisted of at *least* three shots of hard liquor). He grabs the bottle of Red Label and his empty glass and stands, his legs a little shaky.

He grabs the door handle, then pauses, his back to me. "Don't try to run," he warns over his shoulder. "I'd hate to catch you. Enough blood has been spilled today."

CHAPTER 21

I got Pestilence shit-faced.

That much is clear by the time I'm done bathing. I find him sprawled on the couch, the now nearly empty bottle of whiskey in his hand, his glass nowhere to be found.

When a horseman falls, he falls hard.

His head rolls to me. "You were right," he says, holding up the bottle. "My mind is altered."

Well, at least he's still perceptive.

He stares at the label for a second. "Doesn't even taste that bad anymore."

How many hell points did I just gain, getting this guy drunk?

When his gaze returns to me, his eyes drop to my clothes. The look he gives them can't be complimentary.

I managed to fish out an outfit from the closet in the main bedroom. By all appearances, the owners were a well-to-do older couple. The man liked his khakis pressed and pleated, and the woman liked her clothes to drape and glitter.

I'm practically swimming in the slinky black top I wear,

and I've had to cinch the pair of studded purple jeans to within an inch of their life to keep them from sliding off.

It was the best I could do.

I continue past Pestilence, heading for the kitchen, my stomach cramping with hunger. I pass Trixie along the way; the horse has managed to lay himself down in a side room, getting blood all over the owners' throw rug.

Definitely going to leave this place looking like a crime scene.

The kitchen tile is chilly against my bare feet when I enter the room.

Now to see if this place has anything to eat.

I only have to open the pantry to realize there's plenty. The deep shelves are nearly spilling over with canned and jarred goods, dried grains, and a staggering stash of liquor. The two of us could hunker down here for a good several weeks if we needed to—not that Pestilence would ever stay stationary for that long.

As I rummage around, grabbing pasta noodles and a can of red sauce, the horseman limps over to a chair in the kitchen. He's rapidly healing now, the exposed bullet wounds looking more like pitted red scars than bloody holes. He's shrugged off his tattered shirt, and his sculpted, tapered torso is now fully on display.

He watches me for a long time, not saying anything as I boil noodles and heat up the pasta sauce. (Electricity works here, woo!) It's only after I finish preparing the meal and pull out another bottle of liquor (bourbon this time) that I join Pestilence at the table.

He doesn't bother going for the plate of pasta I put in front of him, choosing instead to pour himself a generous helping of bourbon. He drinks deeply from it.

Dude's cruising for a bruising the way he's going at the alcohol.

He levels his gaze on me. "Why didn't you leave me?" he asks, looking almost desperate for an answer. "You could have."

My gut tightens in a queasy way, and I forget I have a steaming plate of pasta right in front of me.

He keeps circling back to this damn subject. I hoped he'd let it go.

"Were you afraid I'd find you and hurt you?" Pestilence presses.

I could lie. He probably wouldn't realize I'd fed him a fib. The only problem is that no good excuse is coming to me.

I open my mouth, and then I choose instead to pour myself another drink. What the hell—he's not doing this sober; I shouldn't have to either.

Taking several deep swallows, I down the bourbon, then set the empty glass down hard on the table.

"I don't know," I answer, pouring myself another drink before I set the bottle aside. "That's the truth." I stare at my scabbed wrists. "Back in Vancouver, all I could think of was helping those people who'd been hurt in the chaos." I take a breath and forge on, my eyes reluctantly rising to his turbulent blue ones. "And once we landed on the beach, all I could think of was helping you."

He frowns at me. If he was looking for solace in my explanation, I gave him none.

"Why did you come back for me?" I ask. "In Vancouver."

He looks affronted by the question. "You are my prisoner. I do not mean to let you go."

"You pushed me off your horse," I state.

His expression gives me nothing.

156

"You did that so that I wouldn't get shot, didn't you?" I ask, peering at him.

If Pestilence is disturbed by the fact I stayed with him and tended to his wounds (or tried to, at least), then I'm most unnerved by the fact he spared me from pain.

"You're no good to me dead, Sara."

"Why is that?" I ask, searching his face. "Why am I alive and here with you while your other attackers lie dead on the streets of Vancouver?"

His mouth tightens. "Because I deemed it so."

I take another drink of my bourbon. "That's not an answer."

"It's the only one you're going to get."

Damn him, this question is going to bother me.

Begrudgingly, I turn my attention to the pasta, swirling my fork in the noodles and scooping up a bite. As soon as it hits my tongue, I take a moment to savor it.

Lord Almighty, I forgot how good food is when you have a little liquor in your system. If I'm not careful, that two weeks' worth of food is going to be polished off by the end of the night—particularly if everything else tastes as good as this does.

Across from me, the horseman's gaze is riveted to my mouth. He tears his gaze away to look down at his plate. Lifting his fork, he tries to take a bite himself, but the thin pasta noodles slide uselessly between the metal tines.

I can't help it, I laugh. I get up and come over to his side of the table. He glances at me, his eyes bright and perhaps a little vulnerable. I think the alcohol is getting to us both.

Leaning over his shoulder and trying not to notice how pretty his torso is (for shame, Sara, he's still hurt), I take the hand holding the fork.

"What are you doing?" he asks, staring at our joined hands. There's a note in his voice...

"Here, turn your fork like this." Awkwardly, I maneuver the utensil in a circle. "Then scoop." I lift the fork, strands of pasta now wrapped around it. "This is how you eat it."

I can't see his expression, and he doesn't say anything in response, so I return to my seat, feeling like I overstepped, which is ridiculous in light of everything we've been through.

Pestilence takes a tentative bite of the pasta. If I hoped for some sort of amazing reaction, I'm sorely disappointed. He simply glowers at the dish as he chews.

"I shouldn't be eating this."

I don't bother to ask him why not. I already know it's his weird hang-up on "mortal vices." I think he's finding out the hard way that despite how willing a horseman's spirit is, even their flesh is weak.

Speaking of horseman...

"Where are your other three riders?" I ask. This is one of the many questions that haunt the world—where the other three horsemen are. It's too much to assume they're somehow gone; if Pestilence exists, so do the others.

Pestilence pokes at his pasta before tentatively twisting his fork around on his plate. "My brothers still sleep," he says, frowning as he takes another bite off his plate.

Sleep?

"Uh, when will they wake?"

He doesn't look up. "When it is time."

Go figure that even buzzed, Pestilence still manages to answer questions as cryptically as possible.

Despite feeling guilty about partaking in food and drink, the horseman makes quick work of his meal and most of his bourbon.

I move through the liquor considerably slower than him. I'm what you affectionately call a cheap date. If I can stretch my drinks out, I will.

I lean back in my seat. "After you arrived here on earth, did you also sleep?" There were, after all, five years when he was unaccounted for.

He nods, pushing his plate away.

I sort of want to ask him where he managed to sleep for five years undetected.

"Why sleep at all?" Why *wait* at all?

"There was the possibility..." He trails off, lost in some thought.

"What possibility?" I prod.

He rouses himself. "The possibility humanity would redeem itself." He grabs his glass and swirls it. "But alas, not even the end of days can alter the depraved nature of your cursed kind."

Ah, this spiel again. Just when I thought the horseman was done harping on humans for a while too.

Pestilence lifts his cup and stares at the little liquid that remains, his eyelids looking a little heavy. "This is poison," he says, out of the blue.

"Mm-hmm," I agree. I mean, technically, it is.

His eyes slide to me. "Was that your plan all along? To poison me?"

Oh God, and now this poison business. How senseless must he think I am to try to poison an undying man?

"You're the one pouring," I say.

That logic seems to mollify him. Somewhat.

All of a sudden, Pestilence stands before grabbing his chair and dragging it around the table so it's next to mine. He sits on it backward, unaware of just how sexy my traitorous mind finds him. He gives me one of his piercing stares.

I lean away from him nervously. "What?"

"I don't know," he admits. "I feel...*something* when I look at you."

My mind flashes back to the bathroom and the heated expression on his face. A blush creeps up my neck, the alcohol making it burn hotter and spread wider than it would if I were sober. I force my eyes to stay on his face when all they really want to do is dip to his torso.

"I cannot figure out what that something is," he continues. "And hear me, Sara, it is *aggravating* me."

Join the motherfucking club. We're taking applicants.

"You're human," he says. "I don't like your kind. I'm not supposed to like *you*."

I don't breathe for a second.

Don't ask the question, Burns. Don't—

"But you do?" I say.

His eyes drop to my mouth. He touches my lower lip with his thumb, rubbing it gently. "God forgive me, *I do*."

CHAPTER 22

I swallow, feeling that unnerving lightness in my belly. This close, Pestilence takes up my entire vision. I can see his thick golden hair, which is still matted with blood and sea spray, and the remains of the bullet wound just above his collarbone. It doesn't at all take away from the glory of him. I can see the ocean in his eyes—his blue, blue eyes—and the thick lashes that surround them.

And now I'm staring at his mouth and that full upper lip that gives him a perpetually pouty look.

He has no idea how good-looking he is. Scratch that—*good-looking* is a term reserved for humans who are attractive, imperfections and all. This inhuman thing, with his angelic features, isn't good-looking. He's blinding, breathtaking. He's perfection incarnate. And isn't that just cosmically unfair? He's a harbinger of the apocalypse. He doesn't need to be attractive, but he is.

His eyes continue to take in my lips. There's something raw and powerful in his expression, like liquor has made him hunger for other forbidden things. Human things.

He moves his thumb over my lower lip again, and I feel that simple touch *everywhere*.

Lowering his hand, he leans in. I'm not sure he's even aware he's doing it—moving toward the mouth he's fixated on.

Over the course of our association, I've been close to Pestilence, but not like this.

Not like this.

He's so close, our breaths are mingling.

My pulse hammers away at me until it's all I can hear. *Tha-thump, tha-thump, tha-thump.*

He's going to kiss me.

That warm flush spreads out from my stomach.

Shouldn't do this.

Can't do it.

Won't.

His hand slides to my neck, tilting my jaw up, his gaze still pinned to my lips.

Our mouths are so very close.

Just one taste, I reason. That's not so bad, right? Just one taste. No one could blame me for being curious. This horseman is supposedly God's justice and vengeance. How can I be doing anything wrong if I let His horseman touch me?

I half believe my wild musings. Right now, with the bourbon warming my insides and softening my resolve, I'll bend just about any logic to let this happen.

Pestilence hesitates. Unlike me, I imagine he may be having one final moment to talk himself out of—rather than into—this.

In that one moment, I come to my senses.

My eyelids lower, and I stare at his lips.

"*Please*," I whisper.

The hand on my neck presses into my skin, and then at once, it's gone.

Spell's broken.

"Please?" Pestilence pulls away to give me a look of disgust. "You say this to me now?" He runs a hand over his mouth and jaw, then looks around, like he's waking from a dream.

He stands, and I can only stare up at him. I have nothing to say. No words to ameliorate the situation because I knowingly drove it here.

I begin to stand as well, but Pestilence places a hand on my shoulder to keep me in my seat, almost as though I were now the one pursuing him.

He sighs, suddenly looking every inch as exhausted as he should be, considering the day he had.

"It's late, Sara," he says. "You'd best get some sleep. We ride early tomorrow."

With that he leaves me and the bourbon and this troubling emotion I'm pretty sure is regret.

I know I should feel relieved—triumphant even. But like the Good Book says, though the spirit may be willing, the flesh is, indeed, weak.

CHAPTER 23

Hangovers are the worst.

The next morning I force down the pancakes I made, hating that I can hardly enjoy them over my nausea.

This is why I don't drink regularly.

Well, that and the fact I can only afford moonshine most of the time. You don't even need to get drunk on that sour piss to get a hangover.

I pet Pestilence's horse, who spent the night inside and is now standing in the kitchen, snuffling the pancakes like he would like a taste.

Abandoning the pancakes, I stand and focus my attention on the horseman's mount.

I run a hand down the steed's neck. "You know, beneath your hardened exterior is just a lady who wants love and acceptance," I say to Trixie.

"My steed is a *man*," Pestilence says as he enters the room.

I tense at his voice. This is the first time today the two of us have shared the same space.

He comes up next to me to place a cursory hand on the horse, and damn my body, but I am aware of every inch of him.

"Don't listen to him, Trixie," I say to the horse, ignoring the man next to me.

"You *named* him?" Pestilence says incredulously.

He won't look at me. I mean, I won't look at him either, but he was the one who walked away from me last night, so...

I'm not looking at him first.

Apparently, hangovers make me childish.

I pet Trixie's white coat. It's such a pure color, like fallen snow. "He needed a name."

"*Tricksy?*" Disapproval drips from Pestilence's voice. "My steed isn't tricksy. He's a noble, loyal beast."

That...is not the reason I named his pet Trixie.

"You don't get to judge how I name him," I say, "when you won't name him at all."

The horseman rotates to me, and sweet baby angels, just the feel of his gaze is flipping my stomach.

I finally gather the courage to look at Pestilence. He's back in his full regalia, his black clothes whole and unstained once more. His armor is now smooth and unblemished. His bow and quiver are at his back, the latter full of arrows when I was sure that yesterday it was nearly empty. It's a neat trick how more than just his body can piece itself back together. Neat—and eerie.

Pestilence's gaze drops to my outfit—the lime-green top and flowing floral pants make me look like the love child of a diva and a hippie—but then it rises, stopping at my mouth.

Remembering last night.

I can still feel the press of his thumb there, feel the ghost of that almost-kiss. We have shared all sorts of small intimacies, each one backed by a different emotion, but those that passed between us last night... My cheeks heat a little. Those are going to linger with me.

Pestilence looks regretful, but I have no way of knowing what exactly it is that he regrets.

"Have you eaten?" he asks.

I clear my throat. "Yup," I say, happy to focus on something other than us.

There is no us, Burns.

"I packed up some food as well," I add.

The saddlebags are stuffed with the goods. I also packed up more liquor, despite last night's little soiree.

"Good, then let's be on our way."

We head out of the house and back to the beach, Trixie trotting behind us. I can't help casting a glance toward the area where I held Pestilence. It's too far away for me to make out the bits of blood that still surely stain the sand.

I turn to the horseman, his steed at my back. "Should we talk about last night?" I ask.

He clenches his jaw, and one second ticks by. Then two, three, four—

"What is there to talk about, human?" he finally says.

Ah. So the lines have been redrawn this morning. In the harsh light of day, I am once more Pestilence's archnemesis, and he mine.

I stare at him for a moment, then sigh. I don't know what I want, but I don't think it's this.

I swivel to face Trixie, but then he grabs my waist. For a minute, my wild imagination takes off. I even feel that damn fluttering in my stomach.

The horseman doesn't want things to be how we left them either.

But then, rather than pulling me into an embrace, he hoists me onto his steed before joining me seconds later.

Just as quickly as my heart soared, it now plummets.

Why do I *care*? Fuck him and this soft, weak thing I feel toward him. I can't believe I had the audacity to feel sorry for him and his wounds yesterday, as if he'd been a victim rather than the instigator.

As usual, Pestilence uses one of his hands to secure me to him, but today it feels all wrong. Impersonal and cold. Even when he hated me, he burned hot with the emotion. Now there's an indifference to his touch, and I'd rather gouge my eyes out than leave things like *this*.

The horseman clucks his tongue, and Trixie races down the beach toward the sea. I barely have time to register that we're going to be traveling over the ocean again before we make it to the water.

A wave of vertigo passes over me as I stare down at it, watching the way its surface ripples. I keep waiting for the ocean to start obeying the laws of physics and swallow us up, but it remains steadfastly solid.

It's only once we're out past the tumbling surf that I realize the vertigo wasn't all mental.

Oh God, horses and hangovers don't mix.

The roll of Trixie's body is sloshing everything in my stomach right, then left, then right again.

Stay down, I silently order the pancakes in my stomach.

I breathe through my nose. This will just pass, this will just…

Noitwon'titwon'tstopstopstop—

I lunge for the side of the horse. The sudden violent motion throws my body out of balance, and rather than vomiting, I slide off the horse.

"Sara!"

I hit the water with a smack, and the first thing I can think as I gasp in salt water is how blindingly cold the Pacific is. Cruelly cold. Water doesn't have a right to be this cold. It makes the icy baths I've had to take since the world ended seem mild in comparison.

It's only as I sink into the dark depths, paralyzed by the chill, that I realize I *am* sinking, the water no longer obeying whatever supernatural force allowed the horseman to ride over it.

If anything, it feels like the sea is greedy to pull me under, like I'm the tithe it requires for the horseman to cross unscathed.

I kick madly for the surface, my gaudy clothes dragging me down.

In my panic, I barely notice the arm that winds around my waist, tugging me away from the darkness.

It's not until I'm dragged back onto shore that I realize the horseman saved me. I don't have much time to concentrate on that little detail before I turn on my side and start retching up the contents of my stomach along with all the salt water I sucked in.

Bye, pancakes.

I sick myself until there is nothing left in my system. Even then, my body only half believes it, my stomach still contracting.

"You do *not* get to kill yourself!" Pestilence all but roars, sea water dripping off his hair. He looks wild with anger, and his eyes are so vividly blue.

I rub my neck, my throat raw. "I wasn't trying to," I say hoarsely, sitting up.

"Lies!" he bellows. "I saw you throw yourself from the horse."

"I needed to puke." The words come out scratchy. "That's all." I clear my throat, focusing on him. "Why are you so concerned, anyway?" I ask, rising to stand on shaky legs. I squint at him. "You've made it plenty clear today you don't care much about me."

Those last two lines were supposed to stay firmly inside my mouth.

The horseman glares at me, his brow furrowed. "Suffering is—"

My shoulders slump. "For the living. Yeah, yeah, I know."

He grabs my chin, forcing me to look at him. His eyes search mine, and they're raging with anger.

All at once, he jerks my face forward and kisses me.

CHAPTER 24

It's harsh. Angry. Almost violent. I suppose this is the only kind of kiss that's fitting for us.

And then it hits me that Pestilence *is* kissing me, his lips are crashing against mine, his touch feverish as he crushes me to him.

Unwittingly, I grab the horseman's forearms with my icy hands, using him to stabilize me.

He's kissing me.

I don't have the breath or the will left in me to tell him *please* again, to force his hand and stop this from happening.

Don't want it to stop.

After the first few seconds pass, it's clear Pestilence doesn't know what lips are supposed to do in a kiss. All his (hateful) enthusiasm is there, but it's being held up by the rigid set of his mouth.

I'm the one who ends up leading the way, my lips gliding over his. He follows my movements, all his anger making his mouth almost bruising in its ferocity.

It feels like I'm drowning all over again, the taste and touch of him sucking me under. Everything is harsh—the chill of my skin, the achy burn of my throat, the brutal brush of his lips against mine. Salt water drips down our faces, mingling with our kiss.

I don't know how long the two of us are locked together like that before I realize I'm wet and freezing and I just retched. (To be fair, he doesn't seem to mind.) And, oh yeah, I'm kissing *Pestilence*.

Still, it takes a surprising amount of willpower to tear myself away. I stumble back, and I pretend it's just the sand that has me weak in the knees.

Pestilence is breathing hard, his chest rising and falling laboriously. He takes a step forward, his eyes locked on my mouth.

Wants to pick up where we left off.

At the last second, he seems to come to himself. He scowls, his icy-blue eyes meeting mine. "You will not try to kill yourself again."

"I wasn't trying—"

"Do not defy me, Sara!" he bellows. Then, softer: "I won't let you die."

Pointless to explain myself. Pestilence is willing to believe I tried to poison him with alcohol, but he won't connect the very obvious dots that I poisoned myself with the stuff.

"Fine," I say, my voice twisting over the words. "It won't happen again."

He nods, his eyes going back to my lips. "Good—*good*."

Try number two to leave the island goes better than the first one. This, of course, is after we make our way back to the house and I warm myself up with another hot bath and another set of dry clothes—all on Pestilence's insistence.

It comes as a particularly unpleasant shock to me that the horseman cares about my well-being. I mean, I've known since he took me captive that he wants me alive, but this feels…different. And I'm not sure I like it.

I run my fingers over my lips. I can still feel the press of his mouth against mine, and though the two of us haven't talked about What Went Down, it's right there between us, lingering like an unwanted guest.

After we leave the beach house, we resume our travels along the water. Pestilence makes a big deal about keeping one arm firmly locked around my midsection. It's as hilarious as it is ridiculous.

If I wanted to kill myself "again," I'd hardly try the same failed tactic.

The wind tears at us, and even though I'm wearing layers of warm clothes, the chill somehow manages to wriggle its way in. It's made all the worse by the fact my torso is no longer cloaked in layers of bandages, my back injury healed enough for me to forgo them. I hadn't realized until now that the gauze somewhat insulated me.

I shiver, the action causing Pestilence to pull me closer.

"You will tell me if you get too cold," he orders, his breath warming one of my ears.

I give him a thumbs-up. "Sure thing." Not going to fight him on that one.

We hug the coastline as we head south, staying far enough away from land to avoid direct contact with people but close enough to make out the details of the shore to our left. Every so often, we see a sailboat or a canoe, but even those are a ways off.

It's late afternoon by the time the clouds part and the sun shines down on us. It heats my hair and reflects off the water, and before long my scalp and face feel tight. I wouldn't be surprised if by nightfall my skin is a particularly unflattering shade of red. And that's not the only thing bothering me.

I shift uncomfortably on Trixie Skillz.

"Hey, Pestilence," I say, "I need to use the shitter."

His hand squeezes my hip. "Human, you are speaking in tongues."

"The *latrine*," I clarify, my voice mocking.

"Ah." He totally misses the fact I'm making fun of him.

He tugs on the reins, turning his horse toward land. Twenty minutes later, the rippling water beneath Trixie's hooves is replaced with solid ground. I breathe a little sigh of relief to be back on land.

Around us, evergreens stretch as far as the eye can see. Wherever we are, there's not a hint of human life to be found.

I'm just accepting the fact I'm going to have to pee in the woods, when we find a paved road and then, a short while later, an outpost.

The woman manning it takes one look at us and bolts, nearly tripping over herself trying to get on her bike.

I find a sad excuse for a bathroom behind the building and use it. When I come back out, Pestilence is strapping blankets and what look like tent poles to the back of Trixie's saddle.

"What are you doing?" I ask, eyeing his horse. Right now, his steed looks less like the unearthly driving force behind the Pestilence's plague and more like a packhorse.

"Collecting supplies."

I glance at the outpost. This one has all sorts of survival

gear, from water jugs to homemade sunscreen, a fire-starting kit to dehydrated food.

All right. "Why?"

"In case we don't find shelter," he says, tightening one of the saddle's straps.

That's never been a problem before, but then again, up until today we were traveling along the highway. We're essentially off the grid now.

I glance at the horizon, where thick dark clouds are chasing down the sun.

Really not a good day for camping.

Pestilence heads back into the outpost and makes his way to the hunting section of the store. An entire wall is dedicated to various types of guns and ammo.

He strides right up to them. Calmly, he lifts a rifle from the wall then stares down at it, one hand wrapped around the barrel, the other near its wooden base.

My entire body tightens at the sight of the gun in his hands. I don't know what exactly it is that I feel. Surely it's not fear? Pestilence doesn't need a weapon to kill. He's plenty lethal as is. Maybe it's simply the alien way he's looking at the thing in his hands, his expression unreadable.

His grip on the rifle tightens, his arm muscles flexing, and then the metal groans as he *bends* the barrel of it, folding the gun nearly in half.

I stare dumbly at him, my mind taking a ridiculously long time to come to terms with the fact the horseman is strong enough to manipulate metal.

He drops the rifle to the floor, the thing utterly forgotten as he reaches for another. Pestilence doesn't stop until he's destroyed every last one of the guns the outpost was selling— hell, he even manages to find the one hidden beneath the counter before ruining that one too. There's a nice pile of them in the back.

Owner's going to lose their shit when they see someone folded their guns in half.

Once Pestilence is done, he leaves the store just as serenely as he entered it. "Ready to ride out?" he asks as he passes me.

I take one last look at the ruined weapons littering the store. "Uh…sure."

It's not until we're far away from the outpost, Trixie weaving us through a dense coastal forest, that either of us speaks again.

"It's my regret that though many things were destroyed by my arrival on earth, guns were not one of them."

I raise my eyebrows at his words. "I'm surprised," I say.

"Why would my opinion surprise you?"

I half turn my head in his direction. "Don't you want humans to kill each other?"

I wait a long time for him to answer.

"Hmmm," he eventually says, "I will have to mull this over."

And he must, because the last bit of our ride goes by in silence.

By the time the sky is an ominous gray-purple and the shadows are long, Pestilence and I still haven't come across a house. The horseman directs Trixie off the road to a relatively flat area nestled between mossy evergreens.

"We will stop here for the night," Pestilence announces, pulling his horse to a stop.

The two of us spend the next hour setting up camp. First comes a paltry fire, which is more for looks than anything else since the wood we burn is far too green to do much besides smoke and sizzle. Which is unfortunate, considering the first drops of rain hit me right as we finish lighting it.

Next comes the tent, and it's pretty obvious from the start that this piece of equipment is old. The material is that synthetic waterproof stuff no one makes anymore, and the color of it is a time-faded gray and maroon. The aluminum poles that go with it are nicked and bent.

Still, I bet the thing was one of the priciest pieces in that outpost. Shame we'll probably discard it in the next city we come to.

I frown at the structure once we finish setting it up.

Not only is the thing old, it's *small*. That means Pestilence and I will have to snuggle.

My heart gives a traitorous leap at the possibility.

"You did this on purpose," I accuse.

"I did what?" the horseman asks, rising to his feet on the other side of the tent. He dusts his hands off.

"Found us a small tent."

He comes around to where I stand and assesses the tent before us, his muscled arms folded over each other. His armor and weaponry sit off to the side, and the silky black material of his shirt seems to hug his broad shoulders and tapered waist.

"It could be bigger," Pestilence agrees. And then he moves away, unloading the rest of our supplies.

That's it?

I worry my lower lip. The rain falls in a steady patter, and I know it's only going to get worse. No way am I going to sleep outside tonight. As it is, there aren't nearly enough blankets.

I really am going to have to snuggle with the horseman. The idea makes me distinctly nervous, especially when I can still feel the memory of his kiss on my lips.

I cast a sidelong glance at Pestilence. He crouches in front of our meager campfire, the wood hissing and sputtering as he tends to it.

Why isn't he affected by this?

Likely feeling the weight of my gaze on him, he glances up at me, his blue eyes piercing. He straightens a little when he takes in my expression. "What is it, Sara?"

Sara. He says my name like it's a prayer.

"Nothing," I say, rubbing my arms, where beneath my layers of clothing goose bumps pucker along my skin.

He notices the action, his brow furrowing. "It's not nothing." Pestilence stands, glancing around. "What are you frightened of?"

I'm not having this conversation. I'm *not.*

I brush my hair away from my face. "I just…thought I heard something."

Pestilence frowns. "Anyone who tries to get close to us is doomed. You are safe, Sara."

But I'm not. Not from him and not from my own heart.

CHAPTER 25

I pull my coat closer as I stare at the sputtering flames between me and Pestilence. The night brought with it a biting chill that not even a halfway-decent campfire could ward off.

And this is no halfway-decent campfire.

The rain steadily falls, but it's not yet bad enough to drive me into the Tent of Doom.

The last of our meal sits comfortably in my stomach.

Not our *meal, I correct.* Your *meal.*

Pestilence hadn't been willing to eat any of the food we were carrying, nor to drink any of the water.

I do not need it, Sara, he said when I offered it to him. *You do.*

He may not have needed it, but his eyes still lingered on the food the same way they'd been coming back to my lips again and again.

He may not need these things, but he's developed a taste for them.

I hold my tin mug tightly between my hands, the tea keeping the cold from my fingers.

Across the fire, Pestilence's gaze is like the stroke of a lover. I feel it as though it were soft fingers brushing along my bare skin.

My eyes move up to his.

The hazy smoke distorts the horseman's features, but I can still make out his sharp jaw and wavy golden hair. One leg is sprawled in front of him, the other drawn up to his chest.

If the cold is affecting him at all, he doesn't let on.

He stares at me, the look in his eyes both familiar and strange. It's the kind of look that has me ducking my head and tucking a strand of hair behind my ear, like I'm some coquettish thing. It's the kind of look that reminds me that, regardless of his intentions, Pestilence is still a man, and a damn good-looking one at that.

"What?" I ask, swirling my tea around and around in my dented mug.

It's not fucking wine, Burns. You don't need to aerate it.

"I don't understand your question," he says.

Of course he doesn't.

"You're staring at me," I explain. "I want to know why."

"Can I not stare at you without having to explain myself?"

"It's rude to stare at someone." I still won't look at him.

"Are you offended?" he asks, curious.

I'm flattered. And *that* offends me.

"Unsettled," I say. "I feel unsettled by it."

"Why am I not surprised?" he mutters to himself. "You want me to understand your kind, and yet when I show any interest, you condemn my curiosity."

I literally have nothing to say to that. I don't even know whether he's right or if he just strung enough pretty words together that he appears right.

Not going to psychoanalyze that one.

"Fine," I say, taking a sip of my tea and meeting his gaze. "Look your fill."

He stares unwaveringly back at me. "I will."

I'm about to look away because it does feel horribly weird to have someone openly appraising you, but then—*fuck* that. If he's going to stare, then so am I.

I take him in from the arched tips of his golden crown to his dark shirt and soft leather boots. My gaze shifts to his hands—he has oddly attractive hands for a man.

Of course he does, Sara. Everything about him is attractive. It's you who's only starting to notice the fine details.

Pestilence smiles as my eyes rove over him, and I swear he presses his shoulders back just a little at my inspection.

"Are you enjoying what you're looking at?" I ask, even as I drink him in. The comment is supposed to be snarky, but it comes off more like bait for a compliment.

"Your form *is* oddly pleasing to me."

Like just about everything else Pestilence says, his words bring out two opposing emotions. My blood heats, and yet..."pleasing"? A painting is *pleasing*. And *oddly*?

A woman should not be "oddly pleasing." She should be a ball-busting, skull-crushing, badass motherfucker who's impossible to forget.

A line forms between Pestilence's brows. "I hadn't expected that—to enjoy the sight of you—just as I hadn't expected food to entice me or your liquor to enthrall me."

I take another sip of my tea. "What had you expected?"

"To be unmoved and unaffected by all human ways."

It should fill me with hope that Pestilence *is* affected by those things, and it *does*, but... I chew on my lower lip. The thing is it goes both ways. As much as I'm affecting his view of humans, he's affecting my view of horsemen.

"You haven't mentioned God yet," I say.

Pestilence looks at me quizzically.

"You keep mentioning how much you hate humans, how it's your job to end them, and how shocking it is to like the same things they do, but in all our conversations, you haven't really mentioned God."

He frowns. "Why would I?"

I lift a shoulder. "Isn't that what this is all about? God's wrath?"

"This isn't about God," Pestilence says evenly. "It's about humans and their poisonous nature."

I grab a nearby stick and distractedly poke the logs, causing the fire to jump and spark. "I just figured He was behind your existence," I say.

The horseman stares at me, eyes narrowed. "It is not for me to discuss with you the reasons I'm here."

"So God *does* unequivocally exist?" I prod. "And He's a man? And He put you up to this?" It's not like he said these things, but he didn't deny them either when *I* mentioned them.

"Sara," Pestilence says with some exasperation, "surely you know by now that something beyond this mortal world exists. Am I not proof enough?"

Well, yeah, but he could at least confirm it for the record and all.

"As far as gender goes," he adds, "only the feeble human mind could imagine a superior being, then have the audacity to shape that being in their own image—and to give it a gender."

Pestilence continues, "God isn't a man or a woman. He's something else entirely."

"Then why do you keep using male pronouns?" I ask.

"Because *you* do."

I give him a quizzical look.

"How do I know English?" he says. "Or wield a bow and arrow? Why do I wear breeches and a breastplate and look like a human? I, like God, have been fashioned into something you can understand.

"But this"—he gestures to his body—"is not what I really am."

"It's…not?" Having trouble with this one.

"I am *pestilence*, Sara," he says softly. "Not a man. I have a body and a voice and a sentience not for my own benefit but for yours."

Not going to lie, this may be the weirdest conversation I've ever had.

"So…" I say, to bring this full circle, "God isn't a man."

His tilts his head. "You seem surprised."

Do I? I shift uncomfortably. "I'm not *surprised*. It's just…"

"It's just what?" Pestilence asks when I don't finish the sentence. For once he's being halfway open with me.

"I don't know," I say. I prod at the fire with the stick I still hold. "Is He—or She, or They—even Christian?" The Four Horsemen, after all, were mentioned in the Bible.

Pestilence gives me a disparaging look. "You humans and your hang-ups with names and labels. God isn't Christian—just as God isn't Jewish or Muslim or Buddhist or any other denomination. God is God."

An answer that will appease pretty much no one.

The horseman leans back and appraises me. "What do *you* believe, Sara?"

I drop the stick and take a sip of my cooling tea. "Before you came to earth, I didn't believe in anything."

"You believed in *nothing*?" Pestilence is looking at me like he wants an explanation.

Knowing how he feels about the World Before, I really don't want to give him this part of me.

"We had science, and that was its own kind of religion," I say. "At least for me it was. It explained why the world worked the way it did—it answered the mystery of it all."

"I know enough about your science, Sara. It never answered the most important *mysteries*, as you call them. What is a soul, where it goes when you die, what lies beyond—"

I put a hand up. "Point taken, buddy."

He frowns at the endearment.

"I didn't *need* answers to those questions. I assumed this life was all anyone got and we were all deluding ourselves to think there was more."

"But you've changed your mind?" he prods.

I give him a sad smile. "It's hard not to when the Four Horsemen show up and all the world goes to hell."

I can hear the fire station's TV in my head, the unending newsreel playing. Political pundits were replaced with religious leaders and scholars, each one explaining their take on the Bible, the Quran and the Hadith, the Sutras, the Vedas, the Tanakh, the Mishnah, the Talmud and midrash, and a thousand other texts that suddenly pointed The Way to redemption. I half listened as each preacher and priest, rabbi and imam beseeched the world to find God before it was too late.

"It's just...religion up until now has been a matter of *faith*. It hardly seems like religion for me to believe now that there's proof."

What I don't say is that it's still hard for me to believe in religion now that our proof comes in the form of four beings who want to *kill* us. If we're suddenly all lambs up for slaughter, what's the point of life? And more importantly, if a painful and untimely death is what I'm to expect from life, then what should I expect from the afterlife?

I half assume Pestilence is going to proselytize to me, but he doesn't. He just continues to give me that unnerving stare of his.

I meet his gaze, and I hold it. The smoke makes sleek ribbons between us, and the rain dapples our clothing. Even in the firelight, I can see his blue eyes clearly. They're an appropriate color; I feel like I'm drowning in them, in him.

A bubbly, warm sensation spreads beneath my skin.

I once heard you can fall in love with someone simply by staring them in the eyes long enough. This is not that (please, God, let it not be that), but it *is* something.

Like lightning striking, the realization hits me: despite every wound we've inflicted on each other, despite him trying to end my world and my world trying to end him, he wants me...

And I want him.

I don't know who moves first, only that I've set my tea aside and he's getting to his feet. There's no rush to our movements.

I've had plenty of those nights when you can't possibly move fast enough because the moment you slow the rush, you'll realize what you're doing is desperate and impulsive, and you really think the other person is annoying but you just want to feel the press of their skin against yours, so you'll forgive it all until morning.

Both of us have plenty of time to turn away. To draw that line in the sand where he's some biblical entity that's come to end the world and I'm a human simply trying to stop him. But right now, he doesn't hate humans nearly so much as he wants to believe, and I don't wish to defy him as much as I want to believe.

Before I have a chance to get up, he kneels in front of me. The fire that was once a barrier between us now sits like a sentinel at our side.

"I cannot decide if you are a toxin or a tonic," he says, lifting a hand to my cheek. "Only that you plague my thoughts and fill my veins."

Pestilence really could work on his compliments.

His thumb strokes over my skin. "Tell me you feel the same way."

"I'm your prisoner," I say, sidestepping an answer.

"That is the least of the wrongs between us." He leans in closer. "Tell me," he repeats.

Without thinking, I press my mouth to his.

For one long agonizing moment, he freezes beneath my lips.

Just when I expect him to pull away, he lets out a small noise, something that sounds like want and defeat and surprise all wrapped into one. And then his lips press back against mine, meeting me stroke for stroke.

Hesitantly, he threads his hands into my hair. He cradles my face, his kiss soft, so exceedingly soft.

Taking my cue from him, I place my palm against his jaw, my fingers brushing the skin of his cheek.

He pulls away, his eyes bright with heat.

"Sara…"

My skin puckers, even as my eyes meet his.

I didn't mean to do that. That's what I'm supposed to say.

But the words stay locked inside me.

His gaze returns to my mouth, and whatever restraint he has left now crumbles. His lips are back on mine, stronger and surer than before.

The previous kiss could be called a mistake, but not this one.

He kisses me eagerly, leaning into me until his warm chest presses against mine. I let my hands drift over his face like I'm trying to memorize him by feel. My thumbs brush over his closed eyes and those enviable lashes, and they skim over his temples and cheekbones.

The smells of earth and smoke and pine needles fill my nose, the falling rain chilling my exposed skin. We're so far from humanity that right now Pestilence feels more like magic than some ancient blight.

His arms go around me, and without breaking the kiss, he carries me to the tent. I don't have time to fear that small space before he brushes the flaps aside and lays me down on the blankets. He kneels between my legs, taking a moment to set aside his crown, his gaze rooted to my face.

Languidly, he drapes himself over my body, his mouth finding mine once more. I nearly moan as his weight settles over me. It's been so long—far *too* long—since I've done this, and I find I'm aching for that comfort and connection.

The horseman's hands tremble as they brush over me, cautiously exploring. I wonder if this is taboo for him—touching a woman, a victim he's been sparing. I wonder how he feels about that.

I wonder how he simply *feels*. How he thinks. I don't know when I began caring, but now, with him so close to me, it seems important.

My lips part his, and I explore his mouth.

Another sound escapes him, this one less surprised and more primal. He crushes his mouth to mine, and our sweet kiss turns darker, hungrier. His hips grind against mine, and I break away from the kiss to sigh out my need.

"Sara," he says, nearly breathless, "I feel…I feel I am losing myself to this sensation—to you." His eyes search mine. "Is this…is this love?"

I sober up *fast*.

My hands had made their way to the small of his back, pressing his body flush against mine, and somehow my legs wound their way around him.

Got more than a little carried away…

I sit up, gently pushing him off me. Reluctantly, he rolls away. I lick my lips, tasting him on my mouth.

The last of that sensual haze retreats completely, leaving a creeping coldness in its wake. I made out with Pestilence—and I'd been ready to do more.

I shake my head. "No, this is not love."

He looks…disappointed. I think.

I can't exactly say what it is *I* am feeling or why. It's some sick combo between want and wistfulness and the deep certainty that this is *wrong*. Very, very wrong.

"Then what is it?"

"Lust," I say simply.

I can't sleep. Not in these woods as the icy sleet pummels our tent. The chill has claws, and I feel them digging into my skin through my blanket and all my layers of clothing.

I lie in my makeshift bed, shivering and feeling utterly miserable.

I mean for you to suffer. I can hear Pestilence's words clear as day. Pestilence, who wandered off hours ago and still hasn't returned. Pestilence, who didn't like what I had to say earlier, either because lust is not nearly so lofty an emotion as love or because feeling anything at all is simply problematic for him.

He's been gone for hours, and in all likelihood, he's probably waiting just out of sight for me to bolt so he can punish me in some cruel and unusual way and force things back to how they once were.

I think it would do us both good to have things go back to the way they were. But there's no way that'll happen. You can't unmake a kiss or unsee a look. We're both so screwed.

It's late by the time Pestilence returns, and the rain has all but stopped. I hear his boots as he crosses over pine needles. He doesn't try to mask his approach.

A moment later the tent flaps are thrown open, and the space fills with his unearthly presence. For several long seconds, he doesn't move.

Eventually, the horseman kneels next to me. He painstakingly takes off his armor and his crown for the second time that evening. And then he slides into the space beside me.

"I assumed you didn't sleep," I say. My voice seems to echo in the silence.

There's a pause. After a moment, he says, "I do not need it, but I can."

He moves closer to me, and after a hesitant second, the horseman drapes an arm over my body and pulls me close.

I close my eyes at the sensation, torn between enjoying his touch and knowing I shouldn't. I shake against him, shivering at the temperature.

"You're cold," he says, surprise coloring his voice.

I'm more than just cold; I'm pretty much a human Popsicle at this point. "I'm fine."

He tucks me even closer into him, throwing one of his legs over mine, pinning me against his body. *Motherfucking snuggling.* I don't even have the dignity to be upset by this because I'm so bloody grateful for Pestilence's heat.

You also like the way he fits against you…

"Try to sleep," he says, his voice deep. "Tomorrow we leave at first light."

Awesome.

Freaking hate waking up early—along with the cold.

Once this is all over, I'm moving to Mexico and sleeping in as long as I want.

Pressed against the human furnace otherwise known as Pestilence, my frigid body soon warms. Not long after, my eyes droop.

Just as I'm on the very edge of sleep, I think I hear Pestilence murmur against my hair, "This is not lust I feel, dear Sara. And I hope you are half as frightened of it as I am."

But I was probably just dreaming.

CHAPTER 26

I wake slowly, languidly, a delicious heat enveloping me. I stretch, my spine cracking as I arch my back. The arm around my waist tightens, the hand stroking up and down my back.

I open my eyes and stare into two blue ones.

My body goes rigid. Pestilence's face is only inches from mine, and the rest of him is pressed against me. The edges of sleep cling to his expression, and his hair is mussed. It pains me how attractive I find that.

Unlike me, the horseman doesn't look surprised to find us so close. He watches me, his gaze both wary and fascinated. Slowly, he releases me.

Kissing, snuggling, and now sleeping together.

Moving awfully fast, Burns.

Technically, this isn't the first time we've slept together. There was that instance back when I was hypothermic.

Feeling somewhat reassured, I push myself out of his arms and run a hand through my wavy brown hair. I don't look at him as I collect myself, but damn it, I can feel his presence all around me.

Got to get out of this tent.

Shoving on my boots, I slip out of the small space without giving the horseman another look.

Outside, the sun sits high in the sky.

So much for leaving at first light…

The tent flaps open behind me, and the horseman comes striding out. His mouth is set in a grim line, and his eyes are sad when they meet mine. The monster that is my horseman is a lonely, melancholy being.

He grabs his armor and straps it on, moving away from me and toward where Trixie waits.

"Come, Sara," he calls over his shoulder. "The hour of our departure grows late."

I glance back at our tent, realizing he doesn't mean to take any of our unpacked supplies with him. So I hurry to grab what few things I can't bear to part with and head after him.

He doesn't look at me as he slings on his bow and quiver. Nor as I stow away the items I grabbed from our camp. Nor even as he hoists me onto Trixie.

He won't acknowledge me just as I didn't want to acknowledge him when I fled the tent. I'm getting a taste of my own medicine, and it's fucking *effective*. There's so much reassurance and connection in a look. Having him withhold it only makes me want it more.

"You're sure we shouldn't pack the tent?" I ask, throwing one final look at the thing. It looks so lonely next to the remains of our fire. There's a chance we'll still be in the middle of nowhere when we stop later today.

Pestilence follows my gaze, giving it a black look. "We

won't be needing it again. Tonight we'll find a house to sleep in—or we won't sleep at all."

———————

There's more than one way to hurt a person. This time I didn't have to shoot the horseman or light him on fire to cause him pain. All I had to do was act like last night was a mistake.

And was it?

I *want* it to be a mistake, and Lord knows I feel bad right now—but not because I kissed the horseman. Or because I snuggled with him. I feel like crap right now because he's *still* giving me the same silent treatment hours later, and it's freaking *working*.

To break the silence, I told him random stories from my childhood, like the time I chipped my tooth because I literally tripped over my own shoelace or about how my friends and I had an annual tradition of jumping into Cheakamus Lake as soon as the ice melted from it. I even admitted to him how I developed stage fright. (I fell in front of my *entire* middle school class as I walked up to the podium—I couldn't get a word out after that.)

He didn't react to a single one, though I know he was listening raptly by the way his hand would tense and relax as it gripped me.

So I try poetry for a change.

"Once upon a midnight dreary, while I pondered, weak and weary…'" I begin, quoting Poe's "The Raven." I recite the whole poem, and again I can tell just by the way Pestilence holds himself that he's listening to me.

But like my stories, he says nothing after I finish reciting it.

I move from "The Raven" to *Hamlet*. "To be, or not to be, that is the question…"

I quote the play for as long as I can, but eventually, the lines get jumbled in my mind and I have to abandon the soliloquy.

Still nothing from Pestilence.

I recite Lord Byron ("Darkness") and Emily Dickinson ("Because I could not stop for Death") and more Poe ("Annabel Lee"), and the entire time, the horseman doesn't utter one word. Not even to tell me to shut the hell up.

I give up.

"What are you thinking?" I finally ask.

He doesn't respond.

I lay my hand over the one that presses against my stomach, securing him to me. "Pestilence?"

He flexes his hand. "Last night I could not decide which you were—a tonic or a toxin," he says. "Today I've discovered you're both."

I wince a little at his words.

"You have woken in me things I did not know slumbered," he continues. "Now that I am aware of them, I cannot ignore their existence. I fear I am becoming...like you. Human and full of want. I *need* this longing to go away."

"'*Longing*'?" I almost choke the word out.

"Don't tell me I am mistaken in this too," he says bitterly. "Love, lust, longing—you cannot refashion my feelings. I know my heart, Sara, even if it's alien to you."

What did I walk myself into?

"What do you want from me?" I ask.

"Nothing! Everything! *Fuck*," he swears, the profanity shocking coming from his tongue. "This is so *confusing*."

I'm about to speak when he cuts in. "I want to taste your lips again. I want to hold you like I did in the tent. I don't understand why I want these things, only that I do."

193

My face heats. Is it wrong to feel flattered when Pestilence is clearly having an existential crisis?

No?

All right.

"Love, affection, compassion—these are the few redeeming qualities your kind has," he says, "and now I'm being *tempted* by them, and it is breaking me in two."

Ever been stuck in a situation you desperately want to get out of, but there's no escape? That's this moment, sitting here on Trixie Skillz and listening to Pestilence tell me about all his feels.

"I can sense you drawing away from me," he says. "The more I want from you, the more reluctant you are to give it. And I don't know what to do."

I do. "Stop spreading plague."

He laughs humorlessly. "I cannot help what I am any more than you can help what you are."

Is that really true though? He spared me, which means he has at least a tiny bit of control over his lethal ability.

"We are locked into these roles, you and I," he says, "and I do not know what to make of this misery."

He sounds so desolate, so hopeless.

I squeeze his hand.

My heart hurts again. This man is so much worse than all the other men I've ever known, and yet I feel chafed raw by him.

I reach up and tilt his head down to mine, and then I brush a kiss against his lips.

I can feel his sweet agony in the kiss. He leans his forehead against mine. "This is misery, Sara," he repeats. "But it is the sweetest misery I have ever felt. I don't want it to stop."

I hate myself a little when I say, "It won't."

It's the middle of the night before we come across a house. We've already passed by a city, so it's not like there weren't other options, but driven by whatever supernatural force controls him, Pestilence pressed on without stopping.

As I dismount, I squint into the distance. Perhaps it's just my imagination, but I swear I see faint specks of light. Another city? At the thought, some residual fear from Vancouver rises in me. I can still hear the gunshots, see the panic, and feel Pestilence's warm blood against my skin.

The horseman passes me, his armor and weaponry clanking dully as he makes his way to the front of the house.

He grabs the doorknob and twists, cleanly breaking the lock. The creaky door swings open.

"You know, you could always try knocking," I say.

"And allow your fellow humans to grab their guns? I think not, dear Sara." Pestilence steps inside, not bothering to mask his entrance.

Farther in, I hear furious whispering and then stumbling footfalls.

"Whoever you are," a man hollers, "you have one minute to get the hell out of my house. Otherwise, I'll blow a fucking hole in your head."

I glance at Pestilence's form. "Seems like the guy's going to grab his gun anyway."

It's too dark to see the horseman's reaction, but I already know he wears a grim look. I hear rather than see Pestilence grab his bow and nock an arrow into it.

The stranger's footfalls get louder as he gets closer. He must be carrying an oil lamp because our surroundings subtly brighten. I can make out a cluttered living room with odds and ends stuffed into every nook and cranny.

Just as the man steps into the entryway, his oil lamp coming into full view, Pestilence's bow makes a small *twang*. A second later, the man across from us lets out a shout, dropping something heavy—something that sounds suspiciously like a gun.

"What the fuck!" he yells.

With another slick sound, a second arrow is nocked into Pestilence's bow. "Move for the weapon, and my aim will be a little better."

The man lifts his lamp a higher, getting a good look at the horseman. He curses as he recognizes him.

"Get the hell out of my house!" he roars.

I take a step back, the force of his words enough to drive me out into the night. Pestilence grips my upper arm, keeping me in place.

"We mean to stay," the horseman says.

"Like hell you do!"

From the hallway I hear more voices. I close my eyes when I realize this is another family. More children I'll have to watch die. Another set of footsteps heads our way.

"The devil will dance on my grave before I host *you*," the man says to Pestilence. His eyes slide to me. He gives me a cruel, mean look, like I'm less than the dirt on his boot. "You and your whore."

In the next instant, Pestilence takes two strides to the man. After grabbing him by the neck, the horseman slams him against the wall, causing the drywall to buckle.

A woman—clearly this man's wife—steps into the foyer, a scream catching in her throat as she takes in Pestilence and then her husband, who's currently in his clutches. She covers her mouth, her eyes darting back down the hallway where her children are.

"It is one thing for you to insult me," Pestilence growls, ignoring the woman altogether, "another for you to insult *her*." He jerks his head my way. "One will earn you my ire, the other a painful death." He squeezes the man's neck tight enough to hear him choke. "Do you understand?"

"Get—out," the man says.

Pestilence shakes him a little. "Do you understand?" he repeats, a dangerous edge entering his voice.

The man glares at Pestilence, his expression full of malice, but he holds his tongue and nods.

All at once, the horseman drops him, and the man crumples to the floor.

"Now," Pestilence says, turning to the woman who's still watching all this with her hands covering her mouth, "my companion needs food and a bed."

"We have no food or beds to spare," the man says coldly from where he lies, rubbing his neck.

At that point, I decide to walk out of the house. Behind me I can hear more threats coming from the horseman. I just don't have it in me to watch as we ruin yet another family's life.

I find a large boulder on the edge of the front yard, and I sit there until my hands and nose go numb.

I hate that I'm seen as in league with Pestilence. I may be attracted to the horseman, but I by no means agree with what he's doing.

Eventually, I hear heavy footfalls making their way to me.

"There's a bed and a hot meal waiting for you inside," Pestilence says.

I toe a bit of grass. "I'm fine."

"So you're just going to stay out here all night?" he asks, squinting up at the stars.

If my body were as tough as my will, I would.

"Why do you have to invade people's homes?" I ask instead.

I know even as I say it that the horseman doesn't do this because he wants to; he does it because I'm the one who needs food and rest. It's me he dotes on, even at the expense of his victims.

"All the world is mine," Pestilence says. "Even this ogre's house." He scowls back at the place.

Maybe this sick feeling is survivor's guilt. Or maybe it's remorse for my shifting loyalties. Either way, the horseman's words worm under my skin.

All the world is mine. Of course, Pestilence the Conqueror would believe that.

"Is it not enough to die by your hand?" I say. "Do we also have to kiss it on our way out?"

Because that's essentially what the horseman is doing when he forces these people to do his bidding.

"You rather enjoyed the act, last I remember," he says softly, his eyes dipping to my lips.

I'm happy Pestilence can't see the flush that spreads across my cheeks. I glance away.

"Are you mad at me?" he asks.

I sigh. "No. I just… This is misery," I say, harkening back to the horseman's earlier words.

He studies me for several seconds. "Come inside," he says gently.

I move my gaze back to him slowly. When he looks at me now, I notice more than just a pretty face. I see the first stirrings of compassion in his eyes.

That's new.

All my resolve folds under the ardor in Pestilence's eyes.

No one's ever looked at me that way. I stand, entranced by the look. A whisper of a smile touches the corners of his mouth as I let him lead me back inside.

The horseman has learned how to feel. Nothing good can come of this.

Nothing at all.

CHAPTER 27

*Nick Jameson is a mean, mean man. He didn't need a horse-*man to drop on his doorstep for that to be the case.

Our host's one redeeming quality, as far as I can tell, is that he loves his family, though even this is a possessive, selfish sort of love. More than once I've seen the whites of his sons' eyes as they dart quick glances at their father, and most of the time his wife keeps her head ducked and her gaze downcast.

All the next day, Nick watches me, his hate so clearly carved across his face, his lips pressed into a thin line. Pestilence may be the man responsible for spreading plague, but it's clear who Nick Jameson blames.

I don't see anything besides that hate until late in the afternoon. Nick's wife—Amelia, I think her name is—finds me outside, standing just opposite their icebox, petting Trixie.

"Sara," she calls, coming closer.

I pause, my hand resting against Trixie's striking white coat.

"Yes?" My gaze reluctantly falls on her. Amelia's face

is flushed with the first signs of fever. Like the rest of the family, the plague is already sinking its talons in her.

"How did you...how did you come to be in the horseman's company?" she asks, coming to my side.

I turn back to Trixie, my hand moving over the horse's neck once more. "I tried to kill him," I say emotionlessly. "He doesn't die," I add, just in case Amelia or Nick were getting ideas.

Amelia sidles in closer. "How long ago was that?" she asks.

"Weeks." It seems like lifetimes ago.

"How are you still alive?" she asks, almost wondrously.

I dig my fingers into Trixie's mane. "It's his way of punishing me."

After several seconds, she says, "So you tried to kill him?"

I can hear it in her voice, a plan forming.

I swivel fully to face Amelia. Her eyes are red and puffy, and her cheeks are so pink they look freshly slapped.

"It won't work," I say.

"What won't—?"

"Trying to get him to spare you or your family. If you think he'll save you from death like he has me, I'm here to tell you he won't. Since he took me, he's killed everyone else who's tried to end his life."

Her eyes search mine. "Why did he spare you?"

I shake my head. "I don't know."

I mean, he keeps saying I need to suffer, but it's been a while since he's actually *made* me suffer.

"So there's no hope?" she presses. "There's no way to help my family?"

"He doesn't know mercy," I tell her.

But does he? He feels hate and lust and longing—perhaps he's felt merciful a time or two...

Amelia rubs her eyes. "I *can't* watch my children die," she says. "Don't you understand? I gave them life. I held them inside me, then in my arms. All these years I've protected them—so if there's a way to save them, any way at all, please tell me."

Grief once again has me in its grip. I wonder when I'll get over it, when I'll be desensitized to all the pain and suffering around me.

Her eyes search mine. "Was there something you did, a deal you made…?"

I swallow. I think I know what she's getting at.

"Amelia, if there were something I could do, I *would*." If giving my body over to the horseman would pay for their lives, I'd gladly do it. But it won't.

A tear slips from the corner of her eye.

I take her by the arm. "You need to get inside—"

"What does it *matter*?" she says, frustration coating her words.

She has a point, though I don't bother saying as much. Instead I escort her back to her bedroom.

"Rest," I tell her, lingering in the doorway. Nick is nowhere to be seen. "I'll get you and your boys a glass of water."

The house is eerily silent as I wander back to the kitchen. If I didn't know better, I'd say I'm the only one inside the house. It's only as I pass one of the sons' bedrooms that I hear husky, masculine weeping behind the closed door. I know without peering inside that it's Nick, broken by his grief.

Shortly after I enter the kitchen, I hear the front door open and then the heavy footfalls of Pestilence, clad in his full regalia. My reckless heart speeds up at the sound. This slow burn I feel for the horseman is agony. Raw, exquisite agony.

As I grab glasses from the cupboard, Pestilence comes up

behind me. Sweeping my hair out of the way, he brushes a tender kiss to the back of my neck, his lips lingering.

I forget myself for a minute. A long minute.

"You let him touch you?"

I startle, nearly dropping the glass cups at the sound of Nick's voice. I swivel around to look past the horseman.

Nick stands at the other end of the kitchen, his eyes bright with the beginnings of fever. There's such disgust in his expression.

Unwillingly, my gaze moves to Pestilence, who for once doesn't wear his usual stoic expression. The horseman looks vulnerable and guileless and even a little unsure of himself.

He meets my eyes, and I see he thinks he's done something wrong.

That gets to me.

I touch his face. *It's okay*, I want to tell him.

"Un-fucking-believable."

Now my eyes move back to Nick. He may be sick and weak, but he's lucid enough, and there is open loathing in his eyes.

"I thought maybe you were just fucking the freak," he says, "which is bad enough—"

Pestilence steps in front of me. "You walk a fine line, Nick," he says, cutting the man off. "I hope you haven't forgotten my earlier words."

Nick gives me a look that lets me know this matter is far from settled, and then he retreats down the hall.

I take a deep breath. I have to go back there to bring his wife and sons water, which means I'm going to have to interact with the man again.

"Every time you shake my belief in human wickedness,

a man like that invariably reminds me just why I must elimi-
nate your kind," the horseman says.

I have several objections to that, but I voice none of them.

"We should go, Pestilence," I say instead. "We don't
belong here."

Not *you* don't belong here but *we*.

"No, Sara. We stay until the deed is done."

*He wants you to suffer, even now, after you've tended to him,
held him, kissed him.*

"So that's how it is?" I say.

"You are my prisoner."

*What a fool you are, Burns, to care for someone who has so
little regard for you.*

What I feel for this man *is* agony. Terrible crushing agony.

I rotate to face Pestilence. "If that's the way things are,
then keep your hands and your mouth to your fucking self."

Pestilence is the enemy. I can never forget that.

CHAPTER 28

It's two nights later when a burning-hot hand presses over my mouth, rousing me from sleep.

"Not a word," the gruff voice commands.

I blink my groggy eyes open.

What's going on?

I squint into the darkness, half expecting to make out Pestilence's striking features. But it's another man who glares down at me, his face coarser, meatier, and frankly *uglier* than the horseman's.

I feel the cool bite of metal under my jaw.

"Get up," Nick demands, his voice hushed.

My mind is furiously trying to catch up with what's going on. Gun. Nick. Waking me up in the middle of the night.

Throwing off the ratty wool blanket, I carefully slip off the futon.

He pushes me forward across the living room and toward a door that leads to his backyard. "Out the door, quietly."

Fear rattles through my bones, but the emotion is so very

weak. I've lived through too many fires to be frightened of death. The only thing that keeps me moving toward the front door is the ridiculous worry that Nick's sons or wife could get drawn into this—or have to bear witness to it.

Behind me, in one of the far-off rooms, I hear a wet, rattling cough.

They have enough worries as it is.

I let Nick lead me outside, my bare feet going numb as I walk over fresh snow. More flakes of it drift down, kissing my face and tangling in my hair.

Ahead of me, there's no back fence to enclose Nick's yard from the thick forest pressing in on it. I can just make out the icebox and the area where Trixie was secured earlier. The horse is gone, presumably with its rider—whom I haven't seen since dinner.

Nick pushes me forward with the barrel of his gun. "Keep walking."

If tonight goes according to this guy's plans, I know how it will end. Nick and I take a stroll into the woods, and only one of us leaves.

I'm not going to let that happen.

"Where's Pestilence?" I ask.

"You mean your boyfriend?" he says, his voice dripping with malice. Nothing and no one in the world can take the ugly hatred out of this man.

"He's not my boyfriend."

Just need to bide my time until we reach the forest. It's hard to shoot someone when there's a tree in the way.

"No?" Nick says, feigning surprise. "So you're just whoring your body out to that thing to buy yourself a little time?"

This guy's family is on the brink of death, and he's worried about my sex life?

"You know, I don't even blame him all that much," Nick continues behind me. "Who wouldn't want to tap a piece of fine ass if they got the chance? But you," he says accusingly, "you're the one who turned your back on your own fucking kind when you started screwing that monster."

I don't even bother telling him I'm not "screwing that monster." The truth won't save me.

"What do you possibly hope to accomplish by killing me?" I ask, stepping past the first of the evergreen trees that border the property. I can barely feel my feet at this point.

Need to make a move, and soon.

"Vengeance for my family."

I raise my eyebrows even though he can't see the action. I know the horseman likes kissing me, but I doubt my death would shake him all that much. "Pestilence won't care," I say. "You'll just be killing me to kill me."

Nick's boot slams into my back, sending me sprawling into the snow.

Whatever chance I had to escape, it's gone now. My feet are too cold, my body too prone. I squandered the time I had chatting with this angry man.

"What's one more death?" he asks, staring down at me. "We're all fucking dying here anyway. I'll be glad to rid the world of one traitorous whore."

Up until now, the horsemen, the plague, the dying electronics—none of it had truly felt apocalyptic. Not even seeing those empty cities Pestilence and I passed through, their occupants hidden.

It's *this* moment, lying in the snow, a gun at my back, where it sinks in. This truly is the end of days. Because even with all its hardships, in the world I grew up in we didn't turn on each other. Not like this.

I flip over and stare at the rifle.

Nick pulls the bolt back, sliding a bullet into place.

Shit, he's really going to do this.

There are worse deaths than gunshot wounds, I think, staring down the barrel.

"Put the gun down." The stoic voice comes from the forest behind me.

Both Nick and I glance over my shoulder.

Standing in a patch of moonlight, looking ever so much like a deity, Pestilence holds his bow at the ready, his crown gleaming in the dim light.

Nick readjusts his hold on the weapon. "Save my family, and I'll let her go."

"I don't bargain with mortals." Pestilence takes a step forward, his aim never wavering.

"Stay back!" Nick calls. "If you want her to live, keep your distance, horseman!"

It's all playing out wrong, like a loose string unraveling cloth.

"I assure you, I won't."

I take a steadying breath. Just staring at the horseman's cool demeanor calms me.

"I'll shoot her!" Nick threatens, his anger morphing into panic as his moment of revenge slips further and further from his reach.

"Do so at your own peril."

My eyes cut to Nick's, and I see the moment he decides killing me is still the better option.

I never see his finger pull the trigger.

The air stirs next to my ear, then—

Thwump—BOOM!

My entire body jerks at the sound.

Dear God.

My hand moves to my chest. But the pain I expect to feel never comes. It's only after I take in several frightened breaths that I realize I haven't been hit.

Thwump. Thwump—thwump—thwump.

Faster than I can react, Nick's body seems to dance as it's riddled with arrows. He grunts, dropping his gun and falling to his knees. His fingers go to his chest, where the arrows protrude.

I look over my shoulder at Pestilence, who's striding toward us, his face filled with grim determination. "She is not yours to kill," he says.

Turning back around, I crawl over to Nick and push the rifle out of his reach. I look over his injuries, and my paramedic training kicks in. It doesn't matter that I have a serious hate-on for Nick; I assess his injuries all the same.

"Don't...touch me...plague fucker," Nick says between laborious breaths. "You're nothing but...a goddamned...whore."

I hear the strain of oiled wood, and when I look up, Pestilence has another arrow already nocked, the point of it trained on Nick. "I let your poisonous words pass the first time," the horseman says, "but I won't a second."

Nick heaves in a breath, the sound wet. "You and I... both know...it's true. How many times...did she have...to suck your...cock before—"

The arrow hits him in the shoulder with a solid *thwump*. He lets out a garbled shriek.

"Test me again, human."

"Do it," Nick goads. "It would be...a faster...death than...what you've...given my family."

"Don't," I say to the horseman. He stopped Nick from shooting me. Nick is no longer any sort of threat.

Pestilence walks over to the man and stares down at him, arrow still pointed. "If I know any mercy," he says, "it's Sara's doing."

If I know any mercy, it's Sara's doing.

Only days ago, I told Amelia the horseman was incapable of it.

You're changing him just as he's changing you.

Nick must want death because he says, "Fuck you and this cunt—"

The final arrow rips through Nick's throat, and now he's choking on his words, drowning in them.

"Vile human," Pestilence says, looming over the dying man. "You could've spent your final breaths pleading for your family, but I see only hate in your heart."

I can't hear what Nick says, but I doubt whatever he mouthed at the horseman was particularly kind. It takes less than a minute for Nick to bleed out, and he leaves the world with a glare in his eyes.

I slump with exhaustion.

Pestilence slings his bow over his shoulder and kneels next to me, his hands skimming over my body. "Are you hurt?" he asks, concerned.

I shake my head, pushing myself to my feet. "I'm fine."

The horseman takes me by the arm. "I was wrong, Sara, this cursed home is no place for even my wrath. Come." He leads me to Trixie.

I eye the horse, then glance down at my icy feet. "Um, I need shoes…and my coat…and a bra. And everything else."

Pestilence looks me over, from my borrowed pajamas down to my toes. I swear I can see him putting together what happened—how I was pulled from bed and led into the woods for a midnight execution.

Does he realize Nick wanted to kill me to hurt him? Does he understand human motives well enough to piece that together? And if Nick had been successful, would the horseman have even cared that I died?

Without another word Pestilence scoops me up.

I yelp as I swing into his arms. "What are you doing?"

"Helping you," he says, carrying me back into the house. He sets me down on the floor of the living room, where the fire is nothing more than a few dying embers. Kneeling in front of me, he takes my feet and one by one rubs heat back into them.

"Why are you doing this?" I ask, watching him carefully.

He shakes his head but doesn't answer me.

Once I'm warm again, I grab my clothes and slip them on. All the while, the rest of the house is utterly still.

We leave shortly after that. And even though it's the middle of the night and the snow is coming down harder, I'm so freaking relieved—to be alive, to be leaving that house, to feel Pestilence at my back, his arm gripping me tightly.

We've barely made it to the highway when Pestilence jerks on the reins, bringing Trixie up short.

I look around in confusion. "What are we…?"

Pestilence tilts my jaw, and then his mouth slams down on mine, his other arm crushing me to him. It's the kiss of a desperate man. Like he's trying to inhale me into himself. Whatever initial clumsiness he had with the act is gone, replaced by this ferocity.

He eventually breaks away, his lips swollen.

Pestilence's blue eyes are luminous. "You came…too close to death for my liking."

It's like he's only now processing it. And right here is the answer to my earlier question—my death would have affected the horseman.

Discreetly, I press a hand to my hammering heart. I mean something to him. What a shock.

He casts his gaze to the dark horizon and clucks his tongue, and we resume our punishing pace once more.

"How long do you plan on keeping me captive?" It's an almost-hilarious question, considering how muddled our roles have become.

Pestilence is quiet.

I glance up, only to see him staring down at me, his eyes deep blue.

"Until my task is complete, you and I shall ride together," he says.

Until his task is complete. That's such a simple statement, but it encompasses a vast, nearly unimaginable task ahead of us. To travel the entire world on horseback, watching millions fall to plague. How many months would it take? How many people would I have to watch die before my mind broke? How many more brushes with death would I have to face?

It would be unendurable.

"So I'm going to travel the entire globe?"

"Yes." He sounds pleased.

I'm going to die.

Not by Pestilence's hand, perhaps, but there will be someone in some city who will do what Nick could not.

That was always the plan, Sara. From the moment you pulled out that matchstick, you knew you were a dead woman walking. Don't get remorseful now.

Of course, my continued existence bothers me nearly as much as my impending death.

I search his face in the darkness. "Of all the people whose paths you crossed, why did you pick me?"

He's quiet for a long time. So long, in fact, that I assume he's not going to answer. It's only as I'm about to face forward that he does.

"I felt God's hand move me to spare you," he says.

Surprise washes through me. I imagined he might feed me his story about making an example of me. But this…

God told him to spare me. I have *no idea* how to feel about that.

He frowns. "I thought…I came to this world to mete out His wrath, but that night, and every one since then, I have wondered…"

I wait for him to finish the sentence, but this time the silence stretches on until I realize that's all I'm getting. It's a whole lot more than he's given me in the past, so I'll take it.

"What's God like?" I ask.

"That is not a subject I can discuss with mortals."

Of course it isn't.

"Well, then can you at least tell me what it's like?" I ask.

"What what's like?" Pestilence's grip has moved so he's now cupping my arm, his thumb rubbing circles onto my flesh.

"I don't know—death. The great beyond." I hold out my hand to catch a flake of snow.

"It would be easier to explain sight to those born blind," Pestilence says. "It can't be understood by description alone, it must be experienced."

What's the use of having a horseman around if he won't answer any of the fun questions?

I drop my hand back into my lap. "Can you at least tell me whether humans have souls or not?"

"Of course humans have souls, Sara." I can hear the amusement in his voice. "I wouldn't be here if they didn't."

213

Pestilence's hand moves back to its usual spot—pressed against my stomach—and I can just make out a ring he wears on his index finger, a round dark stone at its center.

Not for the first time, I realize there is so much to this man I'm completely unaware of, despite kissing him, sleeping with him, living and riding with him.

Ever so gently, I run my hand over his ring. He flexes his fingers at the touch.

"Tell me about your life," I say distractedly, still focused on the ring and the hand that wears it.

"What is there to tell?" Pestilence's voice rumbles behind me.

"I don't know, tell me a memory." Anything to know him by so he's not just some otherworldly horseman.

"My memories would disturb you," he says curtly.

As opposed to my reality, where people die painful, tormented deaths?

"I still want to hear about them."

He takes a deep breath. I don't know how he does it, but he manages to make something as simple as drawing in air ripe with reluctance.

"What do you want to know? Shall I tell you about man's first cities? I remember stirring awake, my attention caught on their attempts to elevate themselves from other creatures. I saw them divert water from rivers and plant the first crops. I watched them build crude houses and tame wild beasts. I admit, I was awestruck at the sight of man molding nature into something pleasing, something he could use.

"Then came towns and cities, kings and law. The world moved faster as man built and created and innovated and *conquered*. I was there for it all, and I've been here ever since.

"I've stood in ancient bazaars. I've walked through city centers. I've lingered in castles and alleyways and everything in between. I've stayed in a thousand different houses, and I've kissed the brows of countless humans, and I've laid my hand on each one.

"I came to earth and I touched, and the world knew terror."

Jesus.

"I am Pestilence, and my memory is longer than recorded history—it is even longer than man. I came before him, and, dear Sara, I will outlive his end."

CHAPTER 29

It's still dark out when Pestilence stops Trixie in front of another house. Just the sight of it has my heart galloping. I don't want to face another family so soon.

The horseman swings off his steed. "Wait here," he commands.

He heads over to the darkened house, opening the gate to the side yard before disappearing.

I rub Trixie's neck as I wait for the horseman. What could he possibly be up to now?

A minute later the front door opens, and Pestilence strides back to me.

"We will stay here tonight," he says.

I hop off Trixie and warily follow him inside the house. It's only as I catch a whiff of garbage that's been sitting out too long that I realize the place is empty. My muscles relax.

I head over to a light switch and flick it on. Above me, the entryway light sputters to life.

Electricity. Score.

Tentatively, I explore the house, flipping on lights here and there as I do so. The place is a shrine to junk; heaps of it are piled everywhere. Old prescription bottles and magazines, weather-damaged paperbacks and moth-eaten clothes—all stacked into precarious mounds.

I bet whoever lived here had to practically be pried out of their home when the evacuation orders went out. No one spends this much time hoarding junk to leave it all behind.

I wrinkle my nose at the ripe smell in the air. It isn't just old garbage; it's also the smell of animals. I move into the kitchen, where I spot several aluminum bowls, one filled with water and the rest empty.

Mystery solved.

Owner has a dog or three.

Pestilence rises from where he knelt in front of the hearth, dusting off his hands, a fire taking shape behind him. Backlit by flames, he looks formidable and perhaps a little sinister. He grabs his bow and quiver from where he set them aside and heads past me.

"Sleep, Sara," he says over his shoulder. His tone is so brusque that had he not kissed the life out of me a short while ago, I would say I angered him.

"Where are you going?" I ask, restless at the idea of him leaving.

He pauses, rotating to face me. "To patrol the area," he says. "There are always humans who hunt me. They wait in the quiet hours to spring their traps."

"Is that where you were before, when Nick...?"

Pestilence's face darkens at the reminder. "Unfortunately, this night I missed the danger right in front of me."

I think that's his weird way of apologizing.

I bite my inner cheek and nod. "Well...be careful." The

words sound horribly awkward. Why do I even want my inhuman and undying captor to be careful? What could possibly happen to him?

Pestilence hesitates, his features softening at my words. "I cannot die, Sara," he says gently.

"You can still get hurt."

Really, where is all this sentimentality coming from?

The corner of his mouth curves up. "I swear I will do my utmost to not get hurt. Now rest. I know you need it."

I do. My body feels leaden now that the last of the adrenaline is finally exiting my system.

Once Pestilence leaves, I peer into each of the bedrooms. There are two beds, both of which I can use, but there's just something about them that's intensely unappealing. Maybe it's the strong smell of dog coming from them or the moldering piles of old clothes, broken plates and scraggly dolls heaped around them. I don't particularly want to sleep in either of these rooms.

I grab a few blankets I find folded on the couch and lie down in front of the wood-burning stove.

You'd think after the night I had, I'd be lying awake for hours, replaying those fateful minutes in the woods behind Nick's house. But no sooner have I lain down than I drift off.

―――――――

I don't know how long I sleep for, only that I'm awakened by the sound of footsteps.

Going to kill you. He's going to kill you.

A burst of fear floods my system, and I scramble to sit up, forcing my eyes to focus on the noise.

Pestilence comes over to me, a towel wrapped around

218

his waist. "Be calm," he says, kneeling at my side. He tucks a strand of my chestnut hair behind my ear. "It's only me."

It's only Pestilence, the one being the rest of the world fears. And the sight of him brings me an embarrassing amount of relief.

I take a deep, stuttering breath. "It's been a long day."

The horseman's wet hair drips between us, and rivulets of water cut down his chest. I feel a rush of heat at the sight of his bare skin. The firelight caresses every dip and curve, and not for the first time, I notice the exquisiteness of his form. His high cheekbones and full lips look all the more extreme as shadows dance along them. And then there's the rest of him, which is all so distinctly masculine, from his powerful sculpted shoulders to his thick cut biceps.

My eyes drop to his chest, where his rounded pecs flow into rippling abs. But it's impossible to look at his torso without noticing the strange glowing marks that shimmer in the darkness, illuminating the surrounding skin.

I reach out and run my fingers over the letters that curve beneath his collarbones like a necklace. They glow with a golden fire, their form odd and beautiful.

Beneath my touch, Pestilence's skin jumps. He holds very still, letting me explore his body.

"What are these?" I ask. It's obvious it's writing, but it's a language unlike anything I've ever seen.

He stares down at me, his eyes bright. "My purpose, written into flesh."

The horseman places a hand over mine, effectively trapping it against one of the symbols. Steering my hand with his, he has me trace the marking.

"This one means *divinely ordained*," he explains, releasing his grip.

I raise my eyebrows at him before my attention drops back to his chest. I move my hand over several characters, stopping on one to the left of his heart.

"And this one?" I ask.

"Breath of God."

I trace the word. Beneath my touch, Pestilence's skin pebbles.

"What language is this?" I ask.

"A holy one." His eyes are on me, tracking my movements.

If I had a little more courage, my hand would drop lower, where another band of characters rings his hips, the lowest of the symbols dipping well beneath his towel.

But alas, my courage fails me.

"Can you speak it?" I ask.

His hand presses over mine once more, holding my palm against his heart. "Sara, it is my native tongue."

I stare at the writing wondrously. I feel a presence here in this dark room. It presses in close. I can see it in the back of the horseman's steady gaze, and I can feel it in the very beat of his heart.

My gaze lifts to his. "Say something for me."

His eyes shine. "I cannot," he says gently. "To speak the holy language is to press divine will upon the world."

I pull my hand away, removing myself from him. "Isn't that what you're already doing?" How else am I supposed to interpret Pestilence riding across the world and spreading his plague?

He leans forward, looking lupine and feral as he comes in close. "What is spoken cannot be unheard. It is not for mortal ears. But...I am not above sharing a word or two with you."

I forget to breathe as his own breath fans against my

cheeks, his lips—and the rest of his nearly unclad body—so very, very close.

Just when I think he's going to share one of these sacred words, he says, "Go back to sleep. I will watch over you."

I don't want to sleep, not when I still feel the press of his supple skin beneath my fingers, marked with figures strange and holy. I'm unbearably lonely, my body aching at the lack of a partner, and damn it all but the partner it wants is him. *I* want him. All of him. In me, around me, next to me, filling my mind, my body, my life—and that's so many different kinds of fucked up, and I'm so over it, so over feeling torn.

Pestilence stands before backing away into the darkened recesses of the house. I nearly call out to him. It would be so easy to coax him toward me, to remove that towel and pull him down and feel his weight settle on me.

To my shame, it isn't my loyalty to humankind that stops me from calling him back. It's the deep fear that he'll refuse my advances.

There are only so many shitty things a girl can take in a single day.

CHAPTER 30

The good news: this house comes stocked with every food imaginable to man. The bad news: everything apparently expired seven years ago.

That's what we get for squatting in a hoarder's home.

At least there's coffee—and powdered creamer. I greedily drink my cup while sitting in the house's breakfast nook, the space packed with dirty dishes, mail, and a few more of those empty prescription bottles.

I stare out the window, taking in the yard with its thin dusting of snow, warming my hands on the mug I hold. My gaze drifts from the window to the nearest pile of junk. Resting at the top of it is a flyer with a drawing of Pestilence.

Warning! Pestilence is Coming!

The words are emblazoned in red. Beneath it in smaller print is a paragraph detailing his movements and urging residents to evacuate, preferably for at least a week.

I flip the page over and nearly balk. Staring back at me is my face. It's not particularly accurate; it has that same look that police sketches have. My face is wider, my cheeks fuller, and my chin pointier, but it's still me.

Traveling with a Mystery Woman!

The paragraph beneath it says that while evidence suggests I'm Pestilence's prisoner, I'm likely working for the horseman and to keep a wide berth.

Lastly, the page has a map of North America, a red line drawn up the East Coast before cutting across Canada and ending with the tip of the line curved downward, suggesting the horseman and I are traveling down the West Coast, which seems accurate enough.

Behind me, the door opens, jerking me to attention. I shove the paper away.

Likely working for the horseman. The warning replays itself over and over in my mind, and I feel every inch the turncoat. Because that flyer nailed my situation, hadn't it?

"Sara!" Pestilence calls, his heavy footfalls making their way to the kitchen.

He grins when his eyes alight on me, the expression so foreign and wonderful that even in the mood I'm in, my heart skips at the sight.

"Knew I'd find you in here," he says.

I give him a watery smile back.

It only takes him a few moments to see I'm troubled.

His grin falls away. "What's wrong?"

We're supposed to be enemies, but despite everything, I kind of like you. Oh, and the rest of humanity has figured that bit out too.

I shake my head. "Just...tired."

He comes over to me, clad in all his accoutrements. There's nothing like seeing Pestilence dressed in his finery to make a girl feel like three-day-old roadkill.

He bends down and, studying my face, presses his thumb right beneath my eye.

"You're getting exhausted," he notes.

Scratch that—*seven*-day-old roadkill. We're talking the really fucked-up bits of critters that remain plastered to the asphalt long after they've expired.

"All the traveling has taken a toll on me," I admit.

The stress, the long days stuck in the saddle, my mounting injuries, the relentless winter chill, the unreliable meals—I've done my best to muscle my way through it, but it only takes Pestilence's notice for it all to come crashing back into my awareness.

Exhaustion probably won't be what kills you, I remind myself.

Pestilence frowns. "Then you shall rest. We'll linger here for"—he glances out the window, taking in the weak winter sun—"two more days."

I don't have the heart to tell him two more days won't make much difference. That resting hasn't *made* much of a difference. We've been pausing for days at a time.

It's never going to get easier with Pestilence. Care though he may, he's always going to be impervious to the things that will kill me, and so he'll always push me harder than what I'm capable of.

But I don't say these things. Instead I nod and give him another weak smile.

His frown deepens. "I don't like this look," he says, studying my features. "You lie to me with your face. Do you need more time? Three days? Four? You shall have it—only remove this sad, defeated look. I cannot stand it."

I don't think anyone has ever told me anything so genuinely frank and kind.

On a whim, I pull him to me, hugging the horseman tightly. At first, he's stiff in my arms, but as the seconds tick by, he hesitantly wraps his own arms around me, and I feel utterly engulfed by him.

"You're a good man, Pestilence," I admit.

And therein lies my problem. He's not a nice man, he's not a peaceful man, but he's a *good* man.

I close my eyes and breathe him in. He smells like cheap soap and, beneath that, divinity. (Didn't even know one could literally smell divine, but there you have it.)

His lips brush my ear. "You forget, I am no man, Sara."

A laugh escapes me. "Fine. You're a good harbinger of the apocalypse."

He holds me tighter, his cheek brushing against my temple. "And you are a compassionate woman." I feel him finger a lock of my hair. "Far *too* compassionate, if I'm being honest," he says under his breath.

I take some solace in the fact that whatever this is I'm beginning to feel, Pestilence is experiencing it as well. And we may each be bulldozing our morals, but at the very least we're doing it together.

We end up leaving the house two days later. That's about all the time I could take in that messy place. I'm no paragon of cleanliness, but that house… Even now, kilometers away, my skin crawls at the thought of it.

I'm pulled from my thoughts when I catch sight of a sign in front of us. After we fled Vancouver, we traveled through mostly backroads and places off the beaten path, but inevitably, Pestilence made his way back to the main highways. And now I see something I missed.

I suck in my breath.

Seattle 54 mi.

"What is it?" Pestilence asks.

"We're in America."

Somewhere between Pestilence getting attacked in Vancouver and my own brush with death a few days ago, I didn't even realize we crossed *countries*.

"Ah, *America*," Pestilence says with distaste, dragging me back to the present. "Here they are made particularly mean."

A ridiculous wave of fear washes through me at that. "Pestilence, we need to get off the main road."

"Whatever for?" he asks, genuinely curious.

I can still feel the ruin of his head cradled in my lap. I'm not ready to go through that again.

"There's a large city coming up," I say. "Bigger than the last one." There were dozens of people waiting for Pestilence in Vancouver; how many would there be in Seattle? "Let's go around it."

"I will not be driven off my course by the presence of humans."

That's the last he says on the subject.

My dread mounts as we close in on the metropolis. Something bad is going to happen. I can feel it the way you can feel a storm coming; the very air is ripe with it.

Like Vancouver, the slide into Seattle is gradual. First we pass through a sleepy satellite city, which gives way to another that's a little denser. And then another. A wave of déjà vu washes over me as we pass through the same types of communities we did in Vancouver.

Pestilence's arm tightens around my waist. Can he feel it too? The promise of violence flavors the very air.

I pull my jacket tighter around me. It's only going to get worse the farther south we travel. Portland, San Francisco, Los Angeles… The nightmare we encountered in Vancouver will repeat itself over and over. And even once we're through with the West Coast, there are entire other countries to cross.

The shadows are just beginning to stretch their spindly fingers across the land when Pestilence leaves the highway, leading Trixie into a neighborhood of tired-looking houses that appear as though they've settled their old bones in for a long rest.

Pestilence turns Trixie onto the driveway of a darkened house, the horse's hooves clacking against the cracked concrete. The pale green paint of the place looks timeworn and faded.

We ride right up to the door before Pestilence swings off his mount. After grabbing the doorknob, he twists, breaking the lock and shoving the door open.

I'm just stepping off Trixie Skillz when I notice the hazy glow of an oil lamp coming from inside, the flame turned way down low. Reclining on the couch next to it is an old woman, her white hair cropped close to her head, her spectacles perched low on her nose. She peers over them at us, the book in her hands entirely forgotten.

We crashed the house of someone's *grandma*. Just when I thought we were fresh out of horrors, another one comes.

"We have nothing of any value, I assure you," she says, her voice surprisingly steady for someone who thinks their home is being invaded.

"I am not here for your *things*," Pestilence says. "I am here for your hospitality."

The woman squints curiously at the horseman. Setting her book aside, she rises to her feet. Age has made her soft and plump, but there's a quiet strength to her.

"Ruth," a thin, raspy voice calls from another room in the house, "who's at the door?"

Did he miss the part where we broke into their home?

Ruth's gaze stays on Pestilence for a long time, moving from his bow and quiver to his crown before settling on his face. "I believe it's one of the Four Horsemen, dear." Her eyes flick to me. "And he's brought with him a lady friend."

"What in the—?" Shuffling sounds come from the back room.

Whatever shock came over Ruth moments ago now dissipates. All at once, she moves, hurrying over. "Well, come now, you both must be cold. Come in, come in—and for the love of the good Lord, shut the door behind you."

Pestilence looks quizzically from her to the doorknob, which hangs at a funny angle. I push the door closed behind him.

Ruth comes to me and helps remove my coat. Her dry hands brush against mine. "Heavens, girl!" she exclaims, cupping one. "You're going to catch your death out there. You're as cold as ice." Ruth clucks her tongue at Pestilence. "Shame on you for letting her get cold."

The horseman stares at Ruth in shock, and I try not to smile. It's clear he's never encountered a sweet old lady before.

Just then, an elderly man limps out from a hallway branching off to the left. He comes to a stuttering stop.

"Lord Almighty!" He places a hand over his heart. "You weren't kidding, Ruthie," he says, staring at Pestilence.

Warily, he steps closer, his eyes drinking in the horseman. "Truly, you are real?"

Pestilence's chin is lifted at a haughty angle, though his expression is more piqued than arrogant.

"Of course I am," he says calmly.

Out of nowhere, the old man lets out a husky whoop. "Well, I'll be damned. Come, sit. *Mi casa es su casa*," he says.

This has got to be the weirdest situation I've ever been in. And considering the past few weeks of my life, that's saying something.

The two of us follow the elderly couple into their kitchen, Pestilence with far more reluctance than me. He stares at the couple suspiciously, his hand edging toward his bow. He clearly doesn't know what to make of this hospitality. Truth be told, neither do I.

Ruth bustles over to the stove, warming a pot of tea while the man gestures to a worn wooden table. "Please, you must be tired." He glances out the window. "Bad weather to travel in."

I nearly cry, taking a grateful seat. It's been so long since another human being treated me with any kind of genuine care. I almost forgot that people do this.

The old man limps his way to the other side of the kitchen, where Ruth is grabbing mugs.

"Sit, love, let me do this," he says.

She guffaws. "You're the one who needs to sit," she says. "That knee is going to give you trouble tonight."

"Bah! Everything gives me trouble these days." He glances my way and winks at me, the gesture causing Pestilence to look between the two of us.

Ruth grabs a spatula and swats at her husband, who's now attempting to bodily move her. "I've got this. Now stop feeling me up in front of our guests and go sit down."

The man grumbles, saying louder, "I'll take my affection where I can get it."

His wife throws him a warm look over her shoulder as he takes a seat across from us.

The horseman watches the entire exchange with the utmost fascination.

"I'm Rob, and that's Ruth," the old man says, settling into his chair as he makes introductions.

Pestilence inclines his head. "I am Pestilence, and this is Sara," he says, gesturing to me.

"Pestilence," Rob repeats, his eyes bright with awe. Remembering himself, he turns to me and nods. "And Sara. Pleasure to meet you both."

I glance between everyone, nearly as shaken as the horseman is. We've come to expect a certain dialogue between us and our hosts, and this one has veered wildly off script.

"Is it though?" Pestilence asks, assessing the man. "A pleasure to meet us, that is?"

"Well, of course it is!" Rob says, slapping his palm against the tabletop for emphasis. "How often does one of the Four Horsemen arrive on your doorstep?"

Ruth shuffles over with several steaming cups of tea.

"Thank you," I murmur when she hands me a mug.

Pestilence frowns at his own drink, his nostrils flaring at the smell.

Rob pats Ruth's side as she takes a seat next to him. "Thank you for the tea." His gaze lingers on her, and it's an intimate enough look that I avert my eyes.

Pushing his drink away, Pestilence leans back in his seat, his expression caught somewhere between troubled and hopeful. "Most mortals do not take kindly to my presence."

"Does it look like I fear death?" Rob asks.

The horseman's eyes narrow shrewdly.

"I'm old, my body hurts, and my wits are half-gone." He glances at Ruth. "Our children have grown up and left us, and now their children are nearly full-grown. If the end has come, well, I'm happy to be leaving it alongside my wife."

A wrinkle mars Pestilence's brow. "It is not a good death," he admits.

I don't know why he's even bothering to make himself look bad. These people *want* to like him.

"Far better than losing your mind, memory by memory," Ruth says. She shudders. "That's how my own mother went. It's awful enough to lose someone, but to watch death take them piece by piece until there's nothing left but a husk..." She shakes her head. "No, there are far worse ways to go than plague."

"We mean to stay here for several days," Pestilence says. "Sara will need a bed, and food, and water."

Again Pestilence seems to want to aggravate the elderly couple. His efforts, however, seem to be in vain. When their eyes move to me, their expressions are kind.

"That's not a problem," Rob responds. "As I said, *mi casa es su casa.*"

I take in Pestilence's glowering profile when it hits me. No one's ever just *liked* him before. Not until now. He doesn't trust Ruth or Rob because why should he? People *hate* Pestilence, the spreader of plague.

I grab the horseman's hand, an action that draws the elderly couple's eyes to me.

Ignoring them, I lean in to Pestilence. "Can I speak to you alone for a moment?"

His eyes flick to our joined hands, then to my face. Without a word, his chair scrapes back and he unfolds all six-plus feet of himself.

Pestilence follows me back into the entryway. When I swivel to face him, he stands close, his clothes brushing against mine.

"What is it, Sara?" he asks, touching a lock of my hair like he can't help himself.

"These people aren't trying to deceive you, Pestilence. They're genuinely excited you're here." Which is batshit wild if you ask me, but hey, no one is asking, so—

"How do you know this?" he asks, not bothering to deny the fact he's skeptical.

I lift my arms helplessly. "I just do."

He studies me, rubbing his jaw absently as he thinks on it. I try not to dwell on how sexy that small action is.

Finally, he nods. "All right. I will…work to trust these people because you do."

I take his hand again and squeeze it. I'm about to let it go when his grip tightens.

"Sara," he says. His other hand joins the first; he clasps my hand like it's a gift.

One look at his eyes has me quaking. His gaze is too deep, his face is too sincere… Whatever he's about to say, my heart's not ready for it.

I pull my hand from his and head back into the kitchen, not waiting for him to follow.

Several seconds after I take a seat, I hear his heavy footfalls. His eyes are locked on me as he sits. I can all but sense the words he needs to say, the ones I ran from.

His gaze lingers on me for a short while longer, but eventually his body relaxes, and he drapes an arm casually over my seat back. I swear every inch of me is acutely aware of that arm.

The entire time, Ruth and Rob watch us impassively. It makes my palms sweat, knowing what they may be seeing.

"So what brings you to our home?" Ruth asks cheerily.

"Sara needs to rest and recuperate," Pestilence says. I can feel his gaze everywhere. "The long days of travel take their toll on her."

"Ah," Ruth says, taking in his words and his demeanor. "And how about you? Will you need a bed?"

Pestilence lounges in his seat, his large legs splayed. "I am Pestilence the Conqueror, the first of the Four Horsemen come to claim your world. I am eternal, and my task unwavering. I do not require anything to sustain me."

All riiiight then.

Ruth raises her eyebrows pleasantly. "Well, there's an extra bed if you need it. Now," she says, getting comfortable in her chair. "How did you two meet?" She looks between the horseman and me as she takes a sip of her drink.

She's a sly one, this Ruth. Pretending like she's not mapping out my strange relationship with Pestilence.

"I attempted to kill the horseman," I say.

Ruth sets down her tea, her mug clattering against the table, clearly shocked by the answer.

"I shot him with my grandfather's shotgun," I continue, "and then I lit his body on fire."

Both of our hosts are at a loss for words.

Probably didn't need to go into that much detail…

I guess Pestilence isn't the only one trying to sabotage this couple's hospitality.

"She's my prisoner," the horseman explains.

I grimace into my mug. The statement rings decidedly untrue to my ears.

"If you don't mind me asking, what do you plan on doing with her?" Rob asks the question pleasantly enough, but I can tell he's ready to throw Pestilence out if given the wrong answer.

I squeeze my cup a little tighter. I hadn't expected strangers to care about me, especially ones who are eager to host a horseman of the apocalypse.

"I'm keeping her," Pestilence says.

Again that *look* from the horseman. My stomach bottoms out, and I try to tell myself it's dread, but I can't fool myself.

You're anticipating what's to come, Burns.

Neither Ruth nor Rob object to Pestilence's answer, but I can see it bothers them. Had I tried to kill a human—well, we have justice systems that deal with those sorts of crimes. But to punish me by keeping me prisoner...that's just not done.

The horseman pushes his chair back and stands. "I need to attend to my steed. Entertain yourselves in my absence."

Said like he's the fucking king of the castle and not what the cat dragged in.

Without another word, he stalks out of the house. In his absence, the kitchen falls very, very silent.

Finally: "Are you okay, dear?" Ruth asks.

I rub my thumb over the edge of the mug. "Yeah, I am." I glance up. "I mean, it's all relative at this point, but I'm not dead, and that's more than can be said for everyone else." My voice breaks. It doesn't escape me that I'm sitting at a table with two more of Pestilence's victims.

Ruth leans forward to place one of her hands over mine. She gives it a squeeze. "You're going to be just fine," she reassures me.

I didn't know I needed to hear those words until I feel my eyes prick. I nod at her, drawing strength from what she said.

Wrong to be taking her kindness and courage when she's the one who truly needs it.

"I'm sorry," I whisper hoarsely. "About...everything." I'm apologizing for more than just crashing into Rob and Ruth's life alongside Pestilence. I'm apologizing for all those families whose lives we upended. I'm apologizing for failing to finish off the horseman, for now *liking* the monster. I'm apologizing for every little wrong, fucked-up thing that's happened since God decided it was time for us all to pay the piper.

Rob waves that away. "We received evacuation orders. We knew what staying meant," he says, trying to absolve me of guilt.

"The horseman," Ruth begins, "he's not"—she seemingly searches for the right words—"*forcing* you to do anything against your will, is he?"

Rape, she means. She's worried he's been raping me.

"No—*no*," I rush to say. Pestilence may be brutal, but he's also gallant in his own odd way. He'd sooner cut off his hand than take me against my will. "He doesn't really think like that," I admit. "His understanding of human nature is limited to what he's seen from his travels and from what he's learned from me."

But is that really true? There's so much I still don't know about him.

"If you don't mind me speaking bluntly," Ruth says, "the horseman may say you're his prisoner, but he doesn't treat you like one."

My breath catches in my throat. I don't want to hear her next words.

"He treats you like…well, like he's interested in you."

My stomach tightens uncomfortably. "I know," I say quietly. I don't have the balls to admit the interest isn't one-sided.

Just then the front door opens, and Pestilence strides back in. His eyes find mine immediately, and there's such naked longing in them.

When did we go from hating each other to *this*?

He takes a seat next to me before pulling his chair closer to mine. "Are you hungry?" he asks, all his attention focused on me.

"I'm fine."

"That's not a true answer," he says.

"It's the only one you're getting," I say tartly.

Of course, that's all Ruth needs to hear before she bustles away to put together a platter of nuts, fruits, and cheeses.

Rob leans forward. "How much can you tell us of your origins?" he asks, changing the subject altogether.

Pestilence's attention reluctantly moves off me.

"That question has several answers," the horseman responds. As he speaks, he removes his bow, then shrugs off his quiver.

"Are you a Christian entity?" Rob presses.

I should've anticipated this line of questioning from the cross hanging over the kitchen table.

Pestilence kicks his big-ass boots up on the table before crossing his feet at the ankles. I have no idea whether he knows it's rude to do so, but he seems comfortable enough. He rests his arm over my chair again.

"Christian, Muslim, Jewish, Buddhist—they're all wrong and they're all right," he says. "It's not the details that are important. It's the overall message."

I feel the horseman's fingers playing with my hair, the sensation making me want to lean into the touch—I'm a sucker for head scratches.

"Morality, and not faith," he continues, "is what matters to God."

Rob's eyes are alight with joy. "Of course," he says. He gives a startled laugh, like the entire conversation is just so

236

surprising, which—*yeah, no shit, Burns*—it is. "Ah, I never thought this day would come. I am the luckiest man, to be sitting here with proof of His existence. And how much do you know about the Bible?"

"The Bible is a work of man, not God. What use have I for something that's more wrong than right?"

I tense, expecting Ruth or Rob to bristle, but they don't. I'm pretty sure Pestilence could fart and they'd find it enchanting.

"And what *is* right?" Ruth asks, coming back with the tray of finger foods, settling herself into her chair.

"That I and my brothers have come to conquer this land, and unless humans change, all will be laid waste and your day of judgment will fall swiftly upon you."

He should really lube us up for entry rather than just shove shit like that at us.

Rob leans forward. "How do we change?"

"Your natures are corrupted," Pestilence says. "Your hearts are hard, and your minds are set on a selfish, destructive course. You have killed off countless creatures, you've made a mockery of nature, you've turned your backs on one another. Unless your ways change, you will be eliminated."

Rob runs a hand over his close-cropped white hair. "That's a tall order for our lot," he says sadly.

"That is why humankind will perish." Pestilence says this with such certainty that I have to tamp down a shiver.

He doesn't believe we can change.

Rob leans forward. "But there's a chance we won't?"

Pestilence hesitates. "Yes," he finally says. "There is a chance. Until Death has ridden across the earth and deemed it unworthy—until God Himself has called us back—there is a chance."

I lie awake for a long time that night, my mind slow to turn off. Even once it does, my sleep is fairly light. A peel of laughter or a gruff word from the other end of the house is enough to rouse me.

Pestilence stays up late with the elderly couple, talking about things I can't quite make out. Bits and pieces of conversation drift in, and it's just enough for me to figure out they're talking about God and religion. I get the impression the horseman is far freer with his words around them than he is with me.

Startlingly, I feel a spark of jealousy. I don't even *want* to talk to Pestilence about God, so I don't know why it bothers me.

You want him to share his most private thoughts with you and you alone.

To think he's telling this couple things he won't utter in front of me…beneath the jealousy and annoyance is hurt.

You're his prisoner, something you seem to forget over and over.

After what feels like an eternity of restless sleep, I hear chairs scrape back, then the shuffle of soft footfalls as Ruth and Rob make their way to the back of their house. I strain to hear anything else, each passing second waking me further, but there's nothing.

Is Pestilence sitting alone in the darkness?

It's not until sometime later, when the sound of a chair sliding back wakes me for the five millionth time, that I hear the horseman's signature footfalls. He heads down the hall toward my room.

My heart patters as he nears.

Is he coming for me?

The thought that once filled me with revulsion now fills me with excitement.

I hear him pause outside my door, the silence stretching on and on.

What's he doing?

The doorknob turns and he steps inside. I can barely make him out in the darkness. He's just one larger shadow among the rest of them, his form looking staggering as it fills the doorway.

He moves to the right of the bed before taking a seat on the floor and resting his back against the wall.

I don't know what to do with myself—I'm supposed to be asleep but I'm not, and that feels like such a big lie. Pestilence *must* realize I'm awake, right? I'm sure I'm breathing too loudly or lying too still.

"Among my growing list of flaws is cowardice," Pestilence says in the darkness. "I come to you now like a thief in the night, for I fear you'll never listen to me under the light of day"—his voice is whisper-soft—"and I must confess all the things in my heart."

Allll right. This should be interesting. And now I'm fucking *wide awake*.

"I find you beautiful, dear Sara, so beautiful. But it's such a sharp, scathing beauty—like the edge of my arrowheads—because I remember you are not like me. One day you will die, and I grow anxious of that fact."

I force myself to breathe and to hold back the awkward choking sound that really wants to escape my lungs. No one has ever spoken to me like this—no one has ever even *thought* of me like this.

"I admit," he continues, "I have no idea what's come over me. Never in my long existence have I felt this way. Not until I came to your world in this form could I feel. And before I met you, even that was limited to the vitriol that burned thick in my belly. All I once wanted was to raze civilization to the ground.

"It was not until I met you, hated though you were, that I understood the meaning of God's words. Of *mercy*." He says this as though it's of paramount importance. "And now I understand why there is hope yet for your kind. Because along with the bad, there is *this*."

Okay, I'm pretty sure this dude has no effing clue I'm awake.

"And I cannot figure out what this *is*," he continues, "only that I feel it when I see you and when I think of you. When we ride together and I hold you, I feel as though all is right. And when you laugh, I think I may truly die. This is an agonizing sort of pleasure, and it's ever so perplexing. I don't understand how pain and affection can coexist."

He sighs, tipping his head up to stare at the ceiling.

"When you ignore me, I burn with restlessness. It feels as though the sun has turned its back on the world. And when you smile at me—when you gaze at me like you can see my soul—I feel...I feel like I am lit on fire, like *you* have been called by God to raze *my* world."

He is breaking me wide open—and I have no defense against it.

He rises to his feet then and walks to the door. He pauses there. "For good or for ill," he says over his shoulder, "I have been indelibly changed by you."

It's only once Pestilence's footfalls fade away that I release my choked sob.

It's bad enough that I want his body. If only the attraction ended there. But my heart is giving way to the horseman's words, and I'm afraid that in the end, it may be just one more of the horseman's conquests.

CHAPTER 31

The next morning, I shuffle into the kitchen, noting the cold plate of scrambled eggs and ham left on the table alongside an empty mug, a tea bag, and a thermos full of hot water.

My finger idly touches the rim of the mug as I glance out a nearby window. The sun is already high in the sky. I rub my head, mussing my brown hair.

Slept too long—long enough for our dying hosts to make me breakfast.

The sound of Pestilence's heavy steps has my entire body going haywire. It can't decide whether I should squeal or bolt from the room.

"Good morning, Sara."

I force myself to turn and look normal and not like I eavesdropped on things last night that I shouldn't have. "Um, morning."

The horseman's gaze is deep, his eyes full of all those things he was waxing poetic on last night.

Don't act like you didn't tuck away each one of those compliments to savor later.

"Where are Rob and Ruth?" I ask, grabbing the thermos and busying myself making a cup of tea.

Pestilence's face turns somber. "The plague has begun to exact its toll."

My skin burns hot with guilt, and for an instant, I feel just as sick as they must. I'm eating their breakfast and sleeping in their bed like Goldilocks while they die from the plague I literally brought to their doorstep.

The horseman steps in closer, staring down at the tea I'm steeping.

When you laugh, I think I may truly die.

"I understand alcohol, but I do not understand coffee, and I most definitely do not understand tea," he says, completely unaware of my thoughts.

I shrug.

"It tastes and smells *acrid*."

"You actually tasted it?" I ask, raising my eyebrows as I bring the cup to my lips.

He grimaces. "Last night, after you went to sleep, Ruth and Rob insisted I try it."

I snicker. "You let them pressure you into trying tea when I couldn't even get you to drink hot chocolate?"

What a sucker.

Pestilence glowers at me.

I take another swallow of tea to hide my smile. Despite our casual conversation, the hand that holds the mug trembles.

I find you beautiful, dear Sara, so beautiful.

His words from last night surround me; I can't just be normal around him. Ugh. I'm all wound up.

My eyes drift to the breakfast laid out for me. Between

242

Ruth and Rob's sickness and Pestilence's attention, the thought of eating is twisting my stomach into knots.

I feel like I am lit on fire, like you *have been called by God to raze* my *world.*

On an impulse, I swivel to him and brush a kiss against his lips.

Pestilence's hands move to my waist and he reels me in, and what was meant to be a brief peck turns into a long, languid kiss.

For several seconds I give in and let myself be consumed by it. But then, somewhere along the way, I remember myself.

I break the kiss off as shame smolders low in my belly. Will it ever go away, or will I have to deal with it day after day, city after city, until all the world has burned down and only I remain?

Still staring at my lips, the horseman takes a step forward, ready to resume the kiss.

I place a hand on his chest.

He glances down at it. "Am I to believe you no longer want my affection when not a minute ago you sought it out?"

Do I tell him the truth?

"Pestilence, I..." I can't do this here. *Not when a couple is dying in the next room over and you're responsible.* I clear my throat. "I need to go tend to Rob and Ruth."

The horseman's eyes drift in the direction of their room, his face pinching with strain. Without another word, he leaves the house, the sound of the closing door echoing long after he's gone.

CHAPTER 32

This time, when I care for the elderly couple, Pestilence decides to assist me. He's endearingly bad at it and more hindrance than help, but he actually cares enough to try and that's good enough for me.

Of course, it's not just the tasks he's bad at. He's sullen and moody as he helps the couple sit up in bed so they can eat and drink what little they can. His temper further worsens anytime Rob thanks him or Ruth lovingly pats his hand.

If I didn't know better, I'd say the horseman is particularly agonized watching his plague take this couple.

At the end of day two, hours after Pestilence left the house and never returned, I wander into Ruth and Rob's room. The two of them are in bed, their bodies turned to face each other. Their hands are locked together, and their eyes are closed. From what little I can see of their skin—and what I can smell—the sores are already opening on their bodies.

"Lord, we ask that you bring your horseman some level of peace, for he is struggling with this mortal coil," Rob says, his voice strained and weak. "And we ask that you give strength to Sara, the girl you have placed at his side. She is upholding the role you have tasked her with, and she is doing so with grace, but nonetheless she is profoundly affected by her circumstances…"

I don't hear any more than that. Like a coward, I flee the room. Their kindness was already too much, but this is something else altogether.

I can't do this. Even as they're asking their god to give me strength, I'm breaking because I can't fucking *do* this. I can't eat their food and sleep under their roof and watch them die horrifying deaths while they pray for me and Pestilence.

I want to laugh at that last one. They're praying for the one man impervious to God's wrath.

But is he? It's a quiet thought and an easy enough one to push away.

In the distance, I hear the door open and then the heavy footsteps of the horseman. Of all the moments for Pestilence to come back, it has to be now.

He enters the guest room silently, finding me sitting on the edge of the bed. One hand covers my eyes as my shoulders shake.

"Sara?" he says hesitantly.

I drop my hand from my eyes and instead stare down at it.

"Don't let them die," I say, my voice cracking. I can't look at him.

He steps into the room before closing the door behind him. "What is this?" he asks.

"They're good people," I say, the words catching as they come out. "They don't deserve to die this way."

"Life doesn't take fairness into account," Pestilence says. "I assumed you of all people knew that."

"Damn it, Pestilence, you saved me!" I say, my temper flaring. "You can save them too!"

There's a long pause. Then: "I will not."

I force myself to look up at him. I have to ignore the agonized look in his eyes.

"*Please.*"

He glances away. "That damnable word."

I forgot how much he dislikes it until that moment. Guilt and heartache rush in. He's going to kill them now simply because I said it. He's going to enjoy it too.

But for once, that doesn't happen. Instead maybe for the first time ever, he appears *torn*.

I can physically see him pulling himself together.

"No," he says, resolute. "Do not ask me this again."

I stand, my despair transforming into something hotter, meaner, as I stare down the sentient thing that *could* take away their illness.

"Or else what?" I ask, stepping up to him. I push at his torso. "Will you tie me up again? Drag me behind your horse until I'm within an inch of death? Expose me to the elements until I get hypothermia?"

He narrows his eyes. "All great suggestions."

"Why save me but not them?"

"I intend to make you—"

"*Suffer.* I know. God, do I know." I back away from him and sit wearily on the bed once more.

He stares at me for a long moment, then he takes a step forward. I tense, and he must notice because he stops. Then, defiantly, he closes the rest of the distance between us.

Pestilence sits beside me, his body dwarfing mine. I'm about to get up when he puts an arm around my shoulders.

I should be pushing him away. I should be yelling at him

or storming out of the room. I should be doing a hundred different things. Instead I lean into his embrace and bury my head in his shoulder. My body shakes as I cry great, heaving sobs. His other arm comes around me, and he pulls me onto his lap, cradling me against his massive torso. I take perverse comfort from him, even though he's the very thing responsible for my grief.

He presses his cheek to my temple, holding me so tightly that I wonder whether he too is taking comfort from the embrace.

"Don't be sad," he says, his lips brushing against my skin.

I shake my head against his chest. What he's asking is impossible. And yet the longer he holds me, the better I feel.

I breathe him in. "I'm not going to survive this." I whisper my greatest fear to him.

Pestilence's body locks up.

"You will," he insists, "because you must."

I pull away long enough to stare him in the eyes. "I won't," I say again. "I'm going to die before you're finished with this world."

And then Pestilence will be the only one left to suffer.

CHAPTER 33

You can feel the end coming, like a wave rushing in. It moves over you, makes itself at home beneath your skin. It settles into your lungs and slips into your heart and eventually inserts itself into your mind. This terrible, awful thing called *death* goes from being a distant eventuality to a sudden certainty.

As the evening stretches on, Ruth and Rob need more and more care, and it's somewhere during that time that I feel death join our little party, lingering in the shadows, waiting for the right moment to collect these souls. The elderly couple must feel it too because even though they're weak and in increasing amounts of pain, they manage to move into each other's arms.

Pestilence stares at them curiously, as though he's never seen anything like this before.

Their skin is old, their bones are old, their hearts are old. And they've loved each other for a long, long time. And yet it's clear that even after all the years they've had together, this parting is too soon.

Far too soon.

My throat clogs. This is...personal. Really, really personal. And heartbreaking—and not for my eyes. I bow my head and eventually slip out of the room.

The horseman doesn't follow me, choosing instead to be an interloper. Five minutes pass, then ten.

What could he possibly be doing in there?

Finally, when it seems like an eternity has passed, I open the door again and peek in. Pestilence sits next to the bed, his large frame dwarfing the side chair. He watches the couple with a confounded look on his face.

Ugh, need to remember this guy has zero social skills.

After slipping inside, I take his hand and tug him off the chair and out of the room. He appears just as confused by this new turn of events as he did about the couple he was staring creepily at.

"What is it, Sara?" he asks when I shut the door behind us.

"These are their last hours. I'm sure they want to spend them alone."

His gaze wanders back to the closed door. "How do you know they want to be...*alone*?"

I can tell he finds my word choice strange—*alone* is traveling through a foreign land for weeks on end and never once speaking to another soul. It's most definitely not holding another human being while murmuring in low tones about things only lovers know.

Pestilence is staring at me, waiting for my answer.

How to put this? I never thought I'd have to explain something this obvious to someone else.

"I mean they want to be alone together," I say. "They want to share their final time enjoying each other's company, not ours."

The horseman is still looking at me with no small amount of confusion, so I elaborate. "We only get so many minutes alive," I say. "When you find someone worth spending that time with, you don't want to share those minutes with anyone else." Particularly not your final few minutes.

For a long moment, Pestilence digests this. Eventually, he inclines his head. "Then I will leave them...*alone.*"

I peer closely at him. "Why were you watching them, anyway?"

Pestilence doesn't really like watching people die, for all the death he delivers.

He hesitates before saying, "They are in love."

Now it's me who isn't following.

When Pestilence sees this, he explains, "This is the first time I've seen humans in love. It's...curious, *compelling*, to see a side of human nature that has been previously hidden from me."

I don't know what to make of that. "But you've been alive to witness thousands of years of human history. You must've seen love at some point during all that time." After all, he's the one who waxed on about how ageless he is.

"Yes," he says slowly. "But not like this."

Not as a living, breathing, *feeling* thing. And somehow that makes all the difference.

CHAPTER 34

Rob goes first. It's a bleak cold morning, the day he dies.

Ruth's weak cry wakes me. Though the sound of it is faint, there's something to it that hits me low in the gut, and I just know he's gone. The great love of her life is gone.

I hurry to her bedroom, even though there's no reason to rush at this point. Pestilence is already there, Rob's frail and pockmarked form cradled in his arms.

The horseman's sorrowful eyes meet mine, and he looks so hopelessly adrift. I can't make sense of his emotion, this horseman who insisted they must die.

After moving past him, I kneel at Ruth's side. Even in the middle of her fever, she cries weakly. I pull up a chair to her bedside, and I stay with her, clutching her hand in mine as her grief works its way through her system.

You'd think that after a lifetime with him, Ruth would be inconsolable, but not an hour after I entered her room, her sadness has passed like a storm moving through a city.

"I'll be with him soon enough," she tells me. "It really is

a blessing to leave this world together. And to live in an age when I know, without a shadow of a doubt, that I'll see him again—and so soon. I can almost pretend he simply left the house on an errand."

Only, Rob's not coming back.

Her eyes grow distant and sad. "I just can't believe it's over..."

Just then, Pestilence reenters the room, his presence like that of the Grim Reaper. But maybe that's just me because when Ruth sees him, she has a smile ready for the horseman.

Instead of returning the look, Pestilence glances my way, his brow wrinkling with concern as he frowns. He stops well away from the bed.

"Don't be a stranger *now*," Ruth chastises him. "Come closer."

The horseman moves toward Ruth like she's a cobra set to strike. It's almost laughable to see formidable Pestilence wary of soft, loving Ruth.

She pats the bed next to her. I wince at even that small action. I can imagine how unbelievably painful the sores must make movement.

Gently, Pestilence sits where she indicates.

The old woman reaches out to him and cups his cheek. "I forgive you, dear."

Pestilence looks blindsided. "For what?"

But he knows. I can see it on his face. He knows exactly what she's forgiving him for, and he's covering up the fact he—is—*shaken*.

"You don't have an easy task ahead of you," she says. "For whatever reason, the Lord deemed fit for you to feel what it is to be human—the loss, the heartbreak, all of it."

Suddenly, Pestilence appears very young.

Only now do I see in him what Ruth does: he is one of

us even as he stands apart. He's not insulated to our pain and torment the way I'd like to believe he is. He has to bear it like some kind of penance.

With that one realization, the entire axis of my world shifts. *He is every bit a victim of this apocalypse as I am.*

Noble, gallant Pestilence, who must watch us all die, who must *make* us all die, even though death greatly bothers him. No wonder he hates us so much. He *has* to. Otherwise, he's murdering thousands and thousands of people for no good reason other than the fact he was told to do so.

"You're going to be okay. You walk in His light," Ruth says like the straight-baller she is. I mean, holy shit, this woman is on her deathbed and she's comforting the dude who put her there. If that's not badass, I don't know what is.

Pestilence's nostrils flare as though he's holding back some strong emotion.

"Rob's not here to say it," Ruth continues, "so I will say it for him: You take care of that little lady you're with, all right?"

He stares at her the same way he did that first night, like he's never encountered a Ruth before.

Slowly, he nods. "With my life, I swear it."

Something warm and uncomfortable spreads through me.

She gives him another one of her sweet smiles. "Now, if you would be a dear, I'm awfully thirsty."

She has no more than to utter the request for Pestilence to do her bidding. The two of us watch him leave, and it's only after he closes the door behind him that Ruth calls out to me.

"Come closer, Sara."

I almost don't. Now that it's my turn to sit on the bed and hear Ruth's final words, I find I really don't want to. A childish part of me believes that if I avoid doing so she may live longer, like this ailment is a spell that can be broken.

Reluctantly, I sit on the mattress and take her hand in mine.

She peers at me closely. "My, are you young."

Now that we're alone, she seems fainter, weaker. No matter how many deaths I sit through, I always forget how alarmingly fast the end comes to the plague's victims.

"Only on the outside," I say. It feels as though I lived a hundred different lives, each of them violent and bloody. I guess that's what sorrow does to you—it fast-tracks your soul.

Ruth gives a sad chuckle. "If that isn't the truth..." Her gaze wanders off before returning to me. She squeezes my hand, her grip surprisingly strong. "What you're doing..." she begins.

Immediately, my pulse hammers away. I have a horrible feeling I know where she's going with this.

"It's...good," she finishes.

"I don't know what you're talking about." Just like Pestilence, I'm hiding from the truth in Ruth's words. And just like Pestilence, I'm shaken by how perceptive she is.

Ruth gives me a sly look. "But I think you do."

I squirm under her gaze.

"I've been around long enough to see the signs," she continues.

The signs of *what*?

"It's all right to care about him—even to love him," Ruth says.

"I *don't* love him," I say too fervently. My words ring false even to my own ears, and I don't know why. I am *not* in love with him.

She pats my hand. "Well, in case that you eventually do, you should know it's not wrong, and it's definitely not something to feel guilty about."

But isn't it? To love the thing destroying your world? That seems tasteless at best, unforgiveable at worst.

"Love is the greatest gift we can give or receive," Ruth continues, unaware of my turbulent thoughts, "and I have a feeling," she says quietly, "love is the only thing that can get us out of this mess." She squints. "Do you understand me?"

Of course I understand her. It's the slogan every religious busybody has been bleating from the top of their lungs since the horsemen's arrival. Except because it's Ruth, a woman who doesn't just utter the sentiment but has lived it, I finally take the words somewhat seriously.

She nods to the door. "That boy out there"—only Ruth would have the wherewithal to call ageless Pestilence a *boy*—"has seen a lot of human nature, the bulk of it ugly. He's only now seeing the beauty of it, and largely through you."

She gives my hand another squeeze. "Show him what we shine with. Show him humanity is worthy of redemption."

CHAPTER 35

Ruth expires less than two hours after our talk. She gives in to death almost eagerly, like an old friend reunited at last.

As soon as she's gone, the house feels cold and lonely, as though its soul slipped away with those of its owners.

Unlike the other families we stayed with, Pestilence won't allow Rob and Ruth's bodies to molder in their own homes. Instead I see him out in their backyard, a shovel in his hand, as he digs one large grave.

I walk out there and help him move their bodies into the ground. The hairs on the back of my neck stand on edge as I touch their corpses. The dead feel perverse. Now that whatever forces animated Ruth and Rob are gone, I find what's left of them nearly unbearable to touch.

"It's all right, Sara," Pestilence says, seeing my unease. "Go inside. I will finish tending to them."

My gaze travels to the bodies, their forms entwined. I should be thinking of how appropriate it is that they're buried in each other's arms, but the sight has me swallowing bile.

Pestilence's hand clasps my shoulder. "Go inside," he repeats, gentler than before.

Now I'm the weak one, the one who can't stomach the sight, and Pestilence is the strong, steady one.

I do as he says and go inside, and I end up making a bath for myself in Rob and Ruth's bathroom. The process takes a ridiculously long time since I have to boil water to heat the tub. On the flip side, the lack of electricity gives me an excuse to gather all the candles and lamps I can find and scatter them around the bathroom.

I sigh when I finally slip into the tub, the water just on this side of scalding. I filled the large basin excessively full because today I'm fucking treating myself.

Right in the middle of my bath, Pestilence comes back inside. He must be looking for me because he eventually makes his way to the main bathroom.

My first thought when I see him is that it's just not fair to be that good-looking. Even covered with streaks of mud, he's the most handsome thing I've ever laid eyes on.

His gaze softens when he sees me. "Are you feeling better?"

I shrug, and the action draws his eyes down. The first time he saw me naked, there was a clinical sort of detachment in his gaze.

Definitely not the case now. The longer he stares, the more wistful his expression becomes.

Fuck it.

"Do you want to join me?" I ask, because—treating myself.

Rather than respond, he unfastens his armor.

Taking that as a yes.

This may be my best or my worst idea yet.

Pestilence's eyes are on me when he takes off the last of his clothing. He's perfect, his body flowing from one sculpted contour to the next. And now I'm sure I'm the one wearing a wistful expression.

Pestilence steps into the tub, the water darkening with the mud that rolls off him.

I thought there was plenty of room for the two of us, but as soon as the horseman sits, I realize just how large he is, even folded up.

My foot brushes his hip, and his legs have me pinned in place. All sorts of skin is touching, and it is *majorly* distracting. Idly, he runs his hand up and down my leg, slowly setting me on fire. My foot jerks the moment his knuckles graze the arch of it.

"What are you thinking of, dear Sara?" he finally says.

That I am one bad decision away from jumping your bones.

"Why did you bury them?" I ask instead.

Pestilence picks up my leg, studying it before he places it in his lap. "Let's not talk about sad things right now." He deliberately runs a thumb over the arch of my foot, grinning a little when my leg jerks again in response. "Do most humans take baths together?" he asks.

Just the harebrained ones.

"No."

He squeezes my foot. "Then why did you invite me in?"

"Because I like being close to you," I say, my voice hushed.

He raises his eyebrows at the admission. I think we're both surprised by my honesty.

"Are you going to regret this tomorrow?"

"Probably," I answer.

His gaze returns to my leg. For a long moment, he runs his hand up and down it. Every time his fingers move high on my thigh, I tense.

"How does a human choose a mate?" Pestilence asks, out of the blue.

Rob and Ruth clearly got under his skin.

"Well, first," I say, "we don't call them 'mates'—well, not usually at least. We have all sorts of names for significant others—boyfriend, girlfriend, husband, wife, spouse, lover, soul mate."

He narrows his eyes in a way that suggests he's taking my words way too seriously.

All the while his hand moves up and down my leg. Up and down. By the seventh stroke, my nipples are fit to cut glass and my core aches.

Does he know how wild his touch is driving me?

"How does one find a...significant other?"

I pat the water with my hand—anything to distract myself from Pestilence's attention. It's already problematic for my hormones, but in light of what we're talking about... well, he's reminding me that it's a lonely world and this girl hasn't gotten any in a *long* time.

"I don't know," I say, "anywhere, I guess. It doesn't really matter how or where or why you meet. It's more about how they make you feel."

"And how should they make you feel?"

The tone of his voice raises my gooseflesh, and I can't help but peer up at him.

A mistake.

His eyes glitter in a way that is decidedly not helping my heart rate. My gaze keeps drifting to his naked torso, his muscled body painfully pleasing to look at.

Focus, Burns.

"Um...they should make you feel good." I run my hands over the surface of the water. "But, again, dating someone—having a girlfriend or boyfriend or lover—is not the same as what Ruth and Rob had. They were soul mates, and as far as I can tell, soul mates bring out the best in each other." Unlike all my exes, who brought out my worst traits.

"They're the ones you want to spend all your minutes with," Pestilence adds, connecting this conversation to the earlier one we had. He looks at me like he's having a light bulb moment.

"Uh, yeah," I agree. I didn't realize how carefully he's been hanging on to my words. "I think when you find the one, you want to spend all the minutes you have with them."

"And how does one know when they've found...the one?" Pestilence probes, his gaze searching mine.

I give him a hopeless look. "Beats the hell out of me. I've never met a man who's made me feel like that."

Liar, a traitorous part of my brain whispers. This conversation is getting dangerously close to Things that Make Sara Burns Wickedly Uncomfortable.

Pestilence scowls at that answer.

Abruptly, I rearrange my body, my leg sliding out of the horseman's grip. At the action, his gaze drops to my exposed breasts.

He looks utterly transfixed by the sight of them.

You know, it ain't half bad being the first woman this dude has come across. My body is riddled with flaws, yet he stares at it like it was crafted by a master hand.

What would happen if I gave in to that look?

It's all right to care about him—even to love him. Ruth's words echo through my head.

This isn't love, but it *is* something.

Acting on impulse, I move my slick body onto his thighs.

Don't overthink this.

Leaning forward, I brush a kiss across his lips.

His hands skim up my torso, his thumbs grazing the underside of my breasts. But that's as far as he'll go. I bite back an impatient moan. Moving myself onto his lap should be evidence enough that I want things to progress, but Pestilence doesn't understand cues, and even if he did, I'm not sure the noble horseman would act on this one anyway.

Going to have to spearhead this.

I take his hands and place them over my breasts.

He sucks in a breath. "Sara—"

"You can touch me," I say. "I would like it if you touched me."

His hands remain unmoving.

Okay, if he doesn't do something in the next few seconds, I may die of mortification.

"*Please.*" It slips out, completely by accident.

Oh, motherfuckery.

Pestilence lets out a groan.

"I shouldn't," he says, his eyes transfixed on my chest, "not when you fling that word at me and not when you offer up your flesh. But I find...I do not have it in me...to resist this plea."

Bless all the freaking saints, I nearly climax at the feel of his hands kneading my breasts.

"Never imagined they'd be this soft," he murmurs. He's looking at my breasts like he's a thirteen-year-old discovering his father's skin mags for the first time.

On what seems like a whim, he leans forward and takes one peak into his mouth. A shocked gasp slips out of me at the sensation. The tip of his cock brushes against me, and it feels rock-hard. All sorts of illicit thoughts cross my mind.

What would it be like to have all this pressed down on

me? I'm almost mindless with the need to find out. The two of us are playing a dangerous game. Scratch that, *I'm* playing a dangerous game. Pestilence probably isn't even aware there's a game being played.

Take it slow, if not for your sake, then for his.

His hands are drifting down when I pull away, moving back to my end of the tub. His expression still smolders, and he appears to be debating whether to prowl after me or not.

"We shouldn't be doing this," I say, fully aware I'm giving this guy mixed signals. "Not here anyway," I add, like this place is somehow sacrosanct when a minute ago I gave zero fucks.

"What care do the dead have?" Pestilence says. "They are beyond these things."

Good point.

Still, there's no rush.

I pick up Pestilence's hand and press his knuckles to my cheek. Some of the fevered want in his eyes softens. He tugs on my hand and pulls me to him, but rather than continue our little tryst, he simply holds me close. Somehow, despite what we were doing seconds ago, the embrace manages to be affectionate, loving.

It's hard for him too, I remember. *He still has this task, but he understands the horror of it and now the loss.*

And yet he's giving me comfort. I lean into him and let him hold me. He cradles my head to him, and I feel him brush a kiss along my hairline. I didn't even know this was what I wanted the entire time, but it is.

"Be at ease, Sara."

And the terrible truth is that, in his arms, I am.

CHAPTER 36

By the time we leave Ruth and Rob's house, there's a stillness to the surrounding neighborhoods and a faint scent of rot in the air. This is death settling in for a long stay. It's unnerving as fucking hell.

It rains as we ride out—which really isn't all that surprising considering we're traveling along the Pacific Northwest, the birthplace of the rainstorm.

When the horseman and I are alone, we can pretend away each other's faults. He can be my dashing noble knight, and I can be his strange companion, but once we're on the open road, where it's impossible to ignore signs of the apocalypse, we both remember how things really are.

For the millionth time, I hope my parents are all right. I've resigned myself to the reality that I'll never see them again, but now, after watching Ruth and Rob die, I'm more aware than ever that my mom and dad could've endured the same fate. And that possibility utterly terrifies me, so I choose instead to hope they escaped the fever unscathed.

Pestilence drives Trixie Skillz at a gallop, forcing the tireless horse to race kilometers on end. That's how we enter Seattle proper—with houses and streetlamps, newly abandoned stables and long-dead storefronts all whizzing by in a blur.

I appreciate the speed. Most of my focus is on remaining on the horse rather than what sort of nasty welcome is waiting for us in one of the U.S.'s big cities. Yet despite the distraction, I can't fool my body into relaxing. My muscles are locked up to the point of pain, and my limbs shake—both from the dreadful chill and from my mounting anxiety.

The longer the two of us go without something—*anything*—happening, the more apprehensive I become. There's not a soul in sight. Not a single frightened soul.

It's not until the squat, run-down buildings and defunct shopping centers give way to the taller decaying skyscrapers that I realize this is unusual. Really, really unusual. Evacuated cities are livelier than this, especially when they're this big. You're bound to run into *someone*.

"Where is everybody?" I ask.

Probably waiting to ambush your ass, Burns.

At my back, Pestilence is quiet, almost contemplative. A wave of trepidation washes through me. Did something change while the two of us stayed at Ruth and Rob's house? Did the Big Man throw in the towel and decide none of us were worth redeeming?

If that were true, Einstein, you'd be dead too.

Eventually, I see a man with a scraggly beard and dirty brown hair leaning against the wall of a high-rise. I feel so oddly relieved just to see another human being that it takes me a minute to realize something is still very wrong. There are several open sores on his face, and he stares listlessly at the street.

"Stop the horse." I'm surprised by the vehemence in my voice.

Pestilence pulls on the reins, and Trixie halts. After slipping off the steed, I run for the man.

Even several feet away, he smells like rot and bodily fluids, and his eyes don't move from the street.

Dead. That's my professional assessment.

Only, when I place two fingers against his neck, his pulse beats weakly.

I rock back on my feet.

Shit, he's alive.

Though not for long.

His fevered eyes slowly move to mine, and his cracked lips move. "*Help.*"

My gut clenches at his plea. I don't have the heart to tell him there isn't much I can do at this point.

Instead I head back to Trixie and grab a few painkillers I swiped from Ruth and Rob's place, along with a canteen of water.

When I return to the man, I show him the pills. "They won't heal you," I explain, "but they may take the edge off the pain."

He opens his mouth weakly, too tired to even reach for the medicine. I place them on his tongue, then hold my canteen to his mouth. Behind me, I hear Trixie's impatient whinny, and I sense Pestilence's burning gaze.

The man takes a few weak swallows, nearly choking in the process. I'm just about to stand when he grips my hand with surprising force. His feverish eyes are pinned to mine.

"I see him," he says.

My brow furrows. "Who?"

Shouldn't indulge the man. Fever is likely making him

265

hallucinate, and his disheveled state suggests he might not have been all that healthy *before* the plague struck.

"*Winged Death*," he hisses.

I try not to be spooked, but my skin pebbles anyway. This is year five of the horsemen. The supernatural exists, and it is *wrathful*.

Death still sleeps.

Giving his hand a final squeeze, I pull away from the man and make my way back to Pestilence. He still sits on his mount, waiting solicitously for me.

"He's coming for me!" the man shouts at my back. "He's coming for us all—" His words cut off as a hacking fit starts up.

My eyes meet Pestilence's. "You've already been here," I say.

The truth is written all over the dying man.

The horseman inclines his head. "I rode here a few nights ago," he admits. "I did not want a repeat of Vancouver."

I don't know how I feel about that. Grateful, I suppose. I know he did it more for my benefit than for his. But then, what kind of person does that make me to feel grateful for death coming early to these people?

Dazed, I get back onto his steed.

The two of us ride deeper into Seattle, the city's ominous silence settling into my bones. A few sheets of paper scatter in the wind. I catch a glimpse of one. *Evacuate Now*, it reads in thick red font before blowing away.

The place gives me the heebie-jeebies. You can feel Death here, his hand pressed to the walls of this place, his shadow eclipsing the sun. I see several more individuals— some leaning against the wall like the last man, others collapsed in the middle of the road, like their bodies gave out before they could get where they needed to go. Already I smell rot on the wind.

For every person I come across, I have Pestilence stop his horse so I can give them aid—if they're alive to receive it. Most aren't.

Trixie's hoofbeats echo off the sides of buildings as we move through the abandoned streets.

"I would've thought there'd be more...bodies," I eventually say.

Maybe it's macabre of me, but now knowing Pestilence has already made his way through Seattle, I keep expecting to see the dead everywhere. Hundreds, maybe even thousands, of people had to have stayed behind in a city this big. Where are their bodies?

"Humans prefer quiet corners to die," Pestilence says.

At his words, my skin pricks, and my gaze moves up to the buildings towering around us. Logically, I know no one lives that high up any longer—the elevators are all busted—but I can't help but wonder just how many bodies are sequestered in these Goliath structures, bodies that will rot and stink and infect the living for who knows how long.

Pestilence tightens his hold and clucks his tongue. Trixie's steady trot morphs into a gallop, and the towering structures blur by.

Up the street is another prone body, but this time, the horseman shows no signs of stopping.

"Pesti—"

"Enough, Sara. You cannot help everyone."

Obviously, I can't. I already tried that route, and it landed me here, in the company of a trick-turning horse and his tragic, monstrous master.

My stomach twists as we pass the person by—an elderly woman.

She looks dead, I reassure myself.

But not all of them do. Some cry out as we pass, begging for help or death—whichever they prefer. It hurts a deep and fundamental part of me to do nothing.

In the end, that's exactly what happens. We leave the city of Seattle and the horrible icy rainstorm behind, until the people are nothing more than a grim shadow at our backs.

CHAPTER 37

The next week is a miserable series of days as we move south from Seattle to Tacoma to Olympia, the endless stretch of cityscape keeping me on edge.

At night, most of the houses Pestilence and I bunk down in are empty, but in one instance the recently deceased was still lying in her bed, her body a wasteland of sores.

As Pestilence and I travel through the unending urban centers and I come across more dead and dying people speckling the streets, it becomes clear the horseman is making a habit of leaving me after I fall asleep to race ahead and spread his damnable plague. He makes no further mention of it, but he doesn't need to—the proof is right in front of me.

It's not until Olympia is far behind us and fields and forests replace the dilapidated buildings that I feel I can breathe again.

That night, the cabin we squat in is obviously a bachelor pad. There are posters of sports teams and half naked women and beer brands all over the place. Shit from before the horsemen's arrival.

Real tasteful.

Pestilence eyes it all with a mixture of curiosity and revulsion.

At least the owner made himself motherfucking scarce. He may like his titties to look like flotation devices, but the dude's got enough practical sense to get the hell out of town before the reaper comes knocking. Literally.

After I light the few candles and oil lamps I can find, I move to the kitchen. Unfortunately, Bachelor Dude only has a jar of beets (seriously, man—beets? *Beets*?), some greasy leftovers in his icebox that will definitely give me food poisoning, Tabasco sauce, and beer. Lots and lots of alcohol. Moonshine, fancy ales, bottled brews, and even some pop-top pre-arrival stuff.

Welp, guess I know what I'm having for dinner.

While I rummage around, Pestilence forgoes starting a fire and instead heads out to the back of the house, where a huge balcony showcases a view of the thick evergreens that skirt the property.

I keep an eye on the horseman as I grab things from the kitchen. He hasn't said much all day. In fact, if I didn't know better, I'd say Pestilence is a bit…melancholy.

It's hard to pity the very force that's ruined your world, yet that's exactly what I feel. He sits at the edge of the balcony, letting his feet dangle through the rails. I can't read his emotions based on that broad back of his, but I have a feeling they're stormy.

After grabbing the goods I've gathered, I head outside. A chill wind rustles my hair, carrying with it the scent of pine. I sit next to Pestilence and hand him a beer, the cap already popped off. It's been a long day. Beers are good for these kinds of things.

"You don't like killing people, do you?" I ask.

It's an almost unfathomable thought, but I don't know, Pestilence just seems...upset.

He frowns at the tree line. "It's not about what I like."

It's about the task he was sent to complete.

"You don't have to do it," I say so very, very softly.

"And what do you know about my choices?" He turns to me, his expression tumultuous.

"I know you have them," I say.

We *all* have them. Even I do. That's why I carry this guilt around even though the situation was thrust upon me. Because I have been complacent when I don't need to be.

"Do I?" Pestilence says it challengingly, as though I don't have the first fresh shit of an idea what choice he actually has in the matter. He glares down at the bottle in his hands, like he only just realized it was there. "What am I supposed to do with this?" he asks, lifting it.

I shrug. "Drink it, pour it out, blow a freaking tune across its rim. I don't really care," I answer, bringing my own beer to my lips.

Done giving advice to Pestilence; it only ever backfires anyway.

The anger fades from his expression, leaving him looking bleak. He watches me with those sorrowful blue eyes before facing forward again. After a moment, he brings the beer to his lips and takes a long swallow of it. He winces at the taste, then takes an even longer pull from the bottle.

He lowers it. "I cannot let my feelings get in the way of my task."

Of course he can't.

"But it is kind of you to care about my feelings, no matter your motives," he adds.

The wind whistling through the trees fills the silence that follows.

I rub my thumb over the glass shoulder of my beer. "Who are you, really?" I ask, my gaze rising to meet his.

The horseman is right, I do care about his feelings. I care about him, and I want to get to know him and understand why he cannot waver from his purpose. Maybe then it will make sense to me. Maybe then I'll stop pushing him.

His brow furrows. "That is a strange question, Sara."

He always says my name with such strange inflection, and I always get a small thrill from it.

"I am Pestilence," he finally answers.

"No, that isn't *who* you are, that's just"—I struggle to find the right words—"your task."

Those full lips of his pull down at the corners. "I do not work like you think I do," he says, his features troubled. "My past is a series of impressions completely removed from this body and experience. And since I came to earth in this form, well, I *am* my task, and it is me—it is the sum total of my existence."

But it *isn't*, and it hasn't been for who knows how long. Probably ever since the horseman picked me up and started getting a taste for the very things he's destroying.

And that makes me wonder: *Is* Pestilence impervious to God's wrath? Ever since Ruth brought the topic up, I keep coming back to this question. I mean, Pestilence is carrying out the Big Dude's task, so he should be, and yet…his deeds *are* weighing on him. I can see it now more than ever. There's uncertainty there, like he's no longer sure whether what he's doing *is* right. Even though God must've decreed it and even though it's been branded onto his skin, Pestilence is wavering.

On a whim, I take his hand and squeeze it before threading my fingers through his.

He glances down at our joined hands, then lets out a breath.

His eyes meet mine. "My favorite possession is my steed."

At first I don't really understand what he's saying. But then it clicks.

I soften. He's *trying*. Trying to tell me about himself.

"The steed you won't name?" I ask.

"The steed you already *have*," he corrects. "And you've given him a terribly ignoble name at that." He takes a drink of his beer, clearly unsettled about having an opinion and voicing it.

"And why is Trixie Skillz your favorite thing?" I prod.

He sets his beer down. "Because he is a faithful, steady, and constant companion."

"Those are good reasons," I say.

"You're talking down to me," he says, his eyes narrowing.

"I'm not." I'm really not.

He must see the truth because his attention turns to the view, and he continues, "I love the dawn—the birth of day. Snow makes everything easier on the eyes. Human food is either surprisingly terrible or surprisingly good." He lifts his beer. "Though sometimes, I will admit, it can be both at the same time.

"I find human clothes coarse, I like making fires, falling asleep is a troubling experience—but it is oddly enjoyable when you have someone to hold—"

Color rises in my cheeks.

"—and my favorite person is you."

Now my face is flaming in the darkness.

"I'm the *only* person you know," I respond. I could be the shittiest person out there and I might still be his favorite.

"I have met *many* people. I assure you, you haven't won the title by default."

I don't know what to say in the face of that kind of flattery. Not to mention that every time Pestilence admits something like this, my body goes haywire.

Hate having a crush.

But this is more than just some crush and there's no pretending otherwise. I like the way Pestilence talks, the way he thinks. I like his compliments, his consideration. I like his gallantry, his gentleness. I like him even though he's bringing about the end of the world—and that is immensely troubling.

He looks down at his drink. "I don't want to talk about myself anymore," he says. His focus swivels to me.

"What?" I say.

"It's your turn to tell me about yourself."

Shit, he's putting me on the spot.

I rub my thumb over the neck of my beer bottle. "You already know so much about me." I talk about myself all the time when we're in the saddle together, often simply to fill the silence. "What else could you possibly want to know?"

"Quote me more of your favorite poems. Tell me more of your life. It is all so very fascinating."

See, that right there is proof this dude needs to get out more.

"It's not that fascinating. *I* am not that fascinating."

Even in the darkness, I see Pestilence's eyes squint as he scrutinizes me. "Do you honestly believe that?"

Do I?

Sure, I had a cool job as a firefighter, but what was there to my life other than work and my humble collection of books?

I let out a gruff laugh. "Yeah, I do."

"Then you are wrong." Pestilence states this with such certainty. "You are compassionate to even the worst of your lot. You give aid to the dying. You care fiercely, so fiercely. These are no ordinary feats. And this is not touching on what you mean to me."

My breath hitches.

"You have managed what no one else has: You have awoken my heart. So, yes, Sara, of all the words I'd use to describe you, *fascinating* would definitely be one of them."

CHAPTER 38

You have awoken my heart.

There it is, out in the open, what I have desperately been running from.

A shiver runs through me as I take in Pestilence's form. He's not the only one who's been affected by the other's presence.

I lean toward him, ready to do all sorts of ill-advised things because I'm just so tired of fighting this.

Before I get the chance, the horseman reaches out and runs a hand up and down my arm. "You're cold," he says. "Forgive me, Sara, the elements do not affect me the same way." He rises to his feet, then reaches for me.

After grabbing my beer, I let him help me up and I follow him inside, my body tightly wound in anticipation. It doesn't dissipate—not when Pestilence leaves my side to start a fire, not when I move the candles and oil lamps into the living room. The only thing that seems to have any effect on my giddy nerves is my beer…and I wouldn't exactly say it's helping the situation either.

Not that it stops me from grabbing another two from the icebox—one for me, one for Pestilence.

By the time I return to the living room, the fire is blooming.

I pass the horseman one of the drinks, feeling a twinge of guilt for giving him a taste for the stuff. But then my eyes meet his and my nerves rise, and I praise God in all His wrathful glory that alcohol exists.

Taking a long swallow, I sit next to the fire. Pestilence lounges across from me, leaning his weight on one of his forearms, his new beer sitting untouched next to him. His gaze moves from the fire to me, flames dancing in his eyes.

"Do you ever wish things were different?" I ask. "That you and I weren't supposed to be mortal enemies?"

"What good does wishing do, Sara?" he says.

I want to tell him wishing makes all the difference, but it sounds too cheesy, like something people used to say before the Four Horsemen landed, back when the world made sense. Wishing doesn't fill your belly or stop your house from burning down. It doesn't make your car drive or save you from the plague.

"I don't know," I finally say. "I just want to stop feeling this way." I hate this guilt that's eating me up. "When I looked at you, I used to see a monster"—a beautiful monster, but a monster nonetheless—"but I don't anymore."

"What *do* you see when you look at me?"

Rather than answer him, I lean forward and brush my lips softly against his. He seems content with that, his hand coming up to cup my cheek.

Gently, I push his shoulder back until he falls against the floor. He pulls me down with him, our bodies pressed together.

My mouth finds his once more, and suddenly the fire isn't simply at my back. It's beneath me, in me, searing through my veins.

I pause to run a finger down the horseman's face. He really is problematically beautiful, with his high cheekbones, sharp jaw, and guileless eyes.

"Right now," I say, finally ready to answer his question, "I see a man."

A man to kiss, to touch, to lose myself in.

"I am ageless, Sara."

If that's supposed to make any sort of sense, then it's lost on me. Maybe that's his way of protesting my answer. Whatever.

I return to his lips and fall into the kiss. He may be ageless, he may be a force of nature rather than a human, but in the end I don't really care. Pestilence is Pestilence, and that's all that really matters to me right now.

The hard planes of his body fit just right against mine, and his touch feels like it was made for me. I reach for the straps of his armor, hopelessly confused about how to remove it. His hand covers mine, and for a split second my stomach plummets.

He's going to stop me.

Instead Pestilence moves my hand and unfastens his metal breastplate himself. He makes quick work of the rest of the armor until it all litters the floor around us.

The problem with armor, I've now come to realize, is that even after all the fanfare of getting it off, there are *still* his clothes to deal with.

Then again, the longer it takes to undress him, the greater the anticipation...

He watches me wonderingly as I grab the edge of his shirt and slip it over his head.

Glorious man. I could stare at him for hours, trying to memorize every inch of his strange, beautiful skin.

Tentatively, he reaches for my jacket, and I help him shrug it off. The two of us make quick work of my layers of clothing until I'm down to just a bra and jeans. I slide the straps off my shoulders, then reach around and unclasp the hooks holding it fast.

Pestilence stares at my bare chest, and a part of me is dying to know what he's thinking. Reaching out, he tentatively runs his hands over my breasts. Heat floods his expression. He may say he's not a man, but he's aroused all the same.

I lean in and press a kiss to his chest, right over one of the angelic markings. "What does this one mean?" I ask, my breath fanning over the foreign word.

He gives me an odd look. "Pestilence."

His name.

I move my attention down, where another band of golden markings dips beneath his waistline. I've caught a glimpse of the entire spread before, but I've never had a chance to really look at these lower characters. Even now, they're hidden from sight.

My hand moves for his pants. Pestilence catches my wrist, his chest rising and falling with obvious want.

I think he knows this is different. *Tonight* is different. It's one thing to kiss and admire—to even touch—but it's another to pursue this.

He stares at me for what feels like an eternity. Then, coming to some decision, he rises to his feet.

I think this is where I get turned down.

Only, it never happens.

He reaches for his boots and pulls them off. Then the horseman's hands go to his pants. He hesitates for only an instant before he unfastens them. The entire time his eyes are on me.

Pestilence steps out of the last of his clothes, leaving him as gloriously naked as the day he was born...er, *created*.

It's physically difficult to look at the perfection of him in the firelight. It makes his skin glint like muted gold and his markings to glow all the brighter.

He stares at me with such intensity. "I didn't tell you the full truth, Sara."

I stare at him quizzically. "What do you mean?"

For a moment, all I hear is the crackle of the fire.

Looking as though he's coming to some great decision, Pestilence draws in a breath.

"That day in the woods, the day I found you, I *intended* to kill you."

A good dose of my desire dampens at his admission. Nothing like hearing your post-apocalyptic boyfriend once wanted to murder you to throw a wrench in the mood.

I sit back on my haunches. "What changed your mind?"

He kneels in front of me. "The light that filtered through the trees that night cast strange shadows on your tent, and one of them was this one." He takes my hand and moves it low on his pelvis, right over one of the curving characters. It takes a hell of a lot of effort to stare at the glowing word rather than let my eyes continue downward.

I stroke the skin softly. "What does it mean?"

"*Mercy*," he breathes.

Something superstitious ripples down my spine, drawing out the gooseflesh. "And so you didn't kill me," I say, my gaze finding his.

"And so I didn't kill you," he agrees, the firelight glittering in his eyes.

All this time I was hating on God, when He (or She—let's be less patriarchal here) was the very thing that stopped the horseman from killing me all those weeks ago.

And now here we are.

His hands go to my jeans.

He hesitates, probably waiting for me to change my mind. And maybe after that admission, I should change my mind.

But I don't.

I lift my pelvis, angling my body to better help him remove my pants.

Pestilence does so, reverently looking at each patch of exposed skin as it's unveiled. He traces a finger along the edge of my ill-fitting panties.

"I wished to be convinced of human depravity," he says under his breath, "but instead...*this*."

His fingers hook around the underwear, and then he's pulling it off me. And with that, the last bit of clothing between us is gone.

Moving agonizingly slowly, Pestilence drapes himself over my skin. I almost sigh at the sensation of his weight and warmth against me. My hands come around his back, gliding over the thick bands of his muscles. I pull him closer to me, feeling his cock trapped between us.

Pestilence the Conqueror hasn't tasted conquest at its most carnal. Not until now.

He hooks an arm around one of my legs and lifts it indecently. He glances down between us, and even though I'm certain he simply intended to see how our anatomy lined up, his gaze catches on my core, and there it stays.

Whatever he sees causes his cock to jerk.

I reach between us and wrap my hand around it, pulling a groan from him.

"Sara, this is…beyond words."

And we haven't even gotten to the best part yet.

I guide him to my opening. For several agonizing seconds he stays there, immobile, soaking up the moment.

"Please," I finally say. My hands move to the small of his back and urge him on.

"*Please,*" he repeats, letting out a pained laugh. "I should deny you, *but I cannot.*"

His breaths are coming faster, his blue eyes piercing me even as his cock pushes its way in.

I release a breath at the sensation of him entering me. He feels…*sublime.*

Pestilence has only partially sheathed himself when he pauses, his forehead dropping to my shoulder.

He releases a shuddering breath, then lifts his head once more to stare at my face as he fills me up, his expression one of rapture. His gaze continues to brighten until he's fully seated inside me.

"This is suffering," he says. "Exquisite suffering."

God, is he right. This is that place where pain and pleasure meet.

I reach for him. My fingers brush his crown, which somehow managed to stay on his head this entire time. Gently, I set it aside.

He tracks my every movement but doesn't protest.

Can't believe he's inside me.

If he was breathtaking before, now, this close to me, he's almost unbearable to look at—like trying to stare down the sun.

Slowly, he pulls out of me, then thrusts forward. A groan slips out of him. "Cannot unknow this sensation…surely it will haunt me for all my days."

He starts out slow, savoring each stroke of his hips like I do good chocolate. But like good chocolate, the savoring gives way to indulgence. His pace picks up, and soon he's not gently stroking me but fucking me in a frenzy, his hands finding my hips and pulling me closer, closer.

He stares at me like he's never experienced anything so wonderful. "Sara, I am…I am in you. A part of you."

I swallow thickly.

The idea that Pestilence can reach inside me and touch something deep and intimate—if only in the most physical sense—should bother me, but I am decidedly *not* bothered.

In fact, everything about this feels painfully *right*, as though this is where he's always belonged.

I cup his cheek. "You are." I bite back a moan as his thick girth slides in and out of me, our bodies making slick sounds as they come together.

He leans his head against mine. "I've wanted to be this close to you," he says. "Close enough to feel your heart beating against my skin."

I press my hand to his chest, right over his own heart. Beneath my palm, it pounds away.

He closes his eyes at the sensation. When he opens them, they glint with so many emotions. "Never want to leave."

I don't want you to either.

I give him a soft smile. "You don't have to yet."

He marvels at me as I writhe beneath him. I clutch him tight, forcing each one of his strokes to go deeper as my core clenches around him.

Pestilence groans at the sensation, the deep sound heightening my pleasure.

I feel myself building, building…

"Oh my God," I breathe. *Meant to hold out longer.* "Oh my God, *oh my God.*"

The horseman pauses, staring down at me with concern.

"*Don't—stop,*" I plead.

He resumes with thrust after powerful thrust and—

Oh—my—God.

I cry out as my orgasm takes me suddenly. My back arches as it lashes through me, blinding me briefly.

Pestilence's strokes deepen until he's slamming himself home. He hikes up his eyebrows, staring at me in glorious shock as he's pulled toward his own climax.

I feel his cock thicken, and with a deep groan, he comes inside me. My body quakes at the sensation.

He stares down at me, entranced, as his strokes gradually slow. "That was…" He says a word that breathes along my skin, and it's like God is in the room with us for a moment.

Angelic—whatever the word was, it was spoken in Angelic.

"What does that mean?" I ask, aware of how reluctant he's been to share his native tongue with me.

Pestilence gives me a deep look. "Heavenly. That was *heavenly.*"

CHAPTER 39

Note to self: Pestilence doesn't do casual sex.

Quick flings clearly aren't a thing for him. Though to be fair, sex in any of its forms really isn't a thing for him. At least not until I fucking corrupted him. I can't decide if that makes me feel particularly proud of myself or a bit despicable.

I think, if I'm being truthful, I'm feeling a bit of both.

He's not going to be chill about it either, I can already tell.

After we finished last night, he took me to bed. I don't remember much except the warm press of his body behind mine, holding me close. He woke me up twice with his roving lips, and after a bit more exploration, he fit himself inside me and screwed me until I was calling out his name.

That wasn't what was bad. I have no complaints at all about bumping uglies. It's everything that's happened since then.

Like him bringing me breakfast in bed—breakfast he most definitely lifted from someone else's house because this homeowner didn't have bacon and eggs. Also, I didn't know Pestilence could *cook*.

He could've forced someone else to cook this breakfast for you.

I shut that thought down before I can imagine just what scenario could've led to *that* outcome.

He's also been pulling me aside all morning to steal quick kisses or confess all those things he already admitted to me that night I was "asleep."

Don't get me wrong, they're nice gestures, gestures that make my heart soar and fill my stomach with those silly little butterflies, but last night was simply a bout of quick and dirty sex and nothing more.

Absolutely nothing more.

Long after we've left the bachelor-pad-turned-love-shack behind, after I've quoted Pestilence some Poe (*Is all that we see or seem / But a dream within a dream?*), I think the worst of his adoration has blown over.

Until he leads us to a church.

I stare uncomprehending at the building, with its severe spire and the marquee that states: *God's chosen can never truly die.*

"What are you doing?" I ask.

"Sara, you gave yourself to me wholly and completely. I want to show you my commitment."

I scrunch my features, his meaning not immediately coming to me. It takes several ridiculously long seconds to put it all together. But then—

He wants…he wants…to *marry* me? After last night?

Shit on a motherfucking stick. I mean, I know I'm a decent lay, but I'm not *that* good.

I glance over my shoulder at him. "Is this a pity proposal?"

He squints. "I don't follow."

I sigh, facing the church once more. It's seriously doubtful there's an ordained minister inside to oversee the ceremony…

Why am I even thinking about this?

286

"I don't want to marry you," I say.

Several silent seconds tick by.

Finally: "Whyever not?" Pestilence sounds offended. "Are you *ashamed* of me?"

"Huh?" I'm completely confused. I turn back to him. "You know people don't just…" *Get married.*

Except plenty of people *do* just get married—people who know each other less well than we do and for reasons far less solid than *I fucked you, so you're now mine.*

It's just that I, Sara Burns, need slightly more motivation before I marry a freaking horseman of the apocalypse.

"Why do you want to marry me?" I ask.

This is not a conversation I ever imagined having.

"You gave yourself over to me, as I did you," Pestilence says. "You are mine, mind, spirit, *flesh.*"

Ugh. *Definitely* working with an Old Testament God here. Pestilence probably expects two cows and four goats from my father too.

"So because I'm the first woman who ever spread her legs for you, you want to put a ring on my finger?" I say, just to make sure I understand the situation correctly.

"Don't talk about it like that."

"You mean about spreading my legs?" I'm still eyeing the church with no little distaste. "Why not?"

"It's lewd, and what we did last night was not lewd."

"The term you're looking for is *made love*," I say.

"Made love," he echoes, sounding pleased.

"And Pestilence," I continue, "sorry to burst your bubble, but what we did last night wasn't lovemaking. That was fucking if I ever felt it."

Liar, liar, pants on fire. That was about as intimate as I ever get when it comes to sex, but he doesn't need to know that.

When I look over my shoulder at the horseman, his expression has darkened with discontent.

He tilts his head as a thought comes to him. "Have you done it before?" he asks, scrutinizing me.

"Done what?" I respond, knowing damn well what he's talking about.

"Lovemaking. Have you ever done it with another?"

"Errr...not *lovemaking*." Per se.

"*Fucking*," Pestilence amends, curling his lip a little as he says the word. "Have you?"

Why do I feel like I'm playing catch with a live grenade? Oh, I know: because we're having the Exes Talk hours after I took Pestilence's virginity.

Fuck my life.

Or not. Fucking is clearly getting me into a lot of trouble.

And I need to stop thinking about that word. *Fucking.* Gah.

"Yesss..." I say reluctantly.

His dark mood only worsens. "Of course you have. Why I expected any better of you is a testament to my cursed idealism."

"Keep talking like that, Pestilence, and I will push you off this horse."

He laughs. "You couldn't dismount me if you tried, human."

So we're back to "human."

"You're being an asshole."

"*Is nothing sacred?*" he bellows. "I was *inside* you. Inside *you*. I felt you move around me. I gave you my essence. And you're treating it, all of it, as though we merely danced together."

This is really not how I imagined this whole conversation playing out. I feel myself flushing.

He clears his throat. "You will not be with another," he states.

"Are you fucking *kidding* me?" I all but shout.

Dear God, stop with the word *fucking*, Sara.

"I will not share you like what we did was meaningless—even *if* you seem to think so."

I want to throttle this man. "Who I have sex with is not your decision to make."

"I will not share you!" he roars. "Even if that means chaining you to me, I will not!"

"And I will not marry your archaic ass!" I shout back at him. "Even if that means being hog-tied and dragged behind your damn horse for the rest of my life!"

His grip tightens. "Don't tempt me, human."

"And stop calling me 'human'!" I add heatedly. "I have a name!"

"One I only like to use when I'm overly fond of you, which I'm not right now."

"Big surprise, Captain Obvious. I'm not too fond of you either."

He seethes behind me.

"Fine," he says after several seconds. "I will not marry you today. But this discussion isn't over."

"The hell it's not!" I need to hit something.

We ride in silence after that. Thank fuck.

Ugh. Stop with that *word*.

CHAPTER 40

We've only traveled a kilometer or so past the church when I hear the gun blast.

I don't have time to think about the fact the horseman must've stopped riding ahead at night. I jolt just as the air stirs violently next to my left temple. In the next instant, Pestilence's body whips back, his hold on me slackening even as his blood mists against my skin.

Someone shot my horseman. Oh God, someone shot him.

I swivel in the saddle. "Pestilence?"

His body sways, and I have to catch him to keep the horseman from sliding off his steed.

Pestilence's head rocks forward, and I see the blood, the blood and—

Oh God, oh God, oh God. Where the left side of his face should be, now there's only a mangled crater.

Going to be sick…

His blood drips everywhere. So much blood.

People in gas masks begin circling us. Trixie rears up,

pawing at the air. I scream when I feel the horseman slip through my clutches. He falls off the saddle behind me, hitting the ground with a dull, wet thump. At the sound, I nearly lose the breakfast Pestilence made for me.

I stare down at his prone, *lifeless* body, unable to rip my eyes away.

"It's all right, he's gone."

"He can't harm you anymore."

The townspeople's words are faint and distorted behind their masks. They're coming closer, looking strange and sinister.

They *hurt* him.

Coming to the side of Trixie, they forcibly remove me from the horse. I lunge for Pestilence, only to have them pull me away.

My last words to the horseman were oaths shouted in anger.

I'm fighting to get to his ruined body, but these people hold me back.

You'd think I'd be used to the sight of him like this, but no matter how much I reassure myself that he'll be all right, my eyes tell me otherwise.

From the ground he groans.

Jesus. Even though half his face is gone, he's still *aware.* I let out a shriek. He's *aware.*

Pain must be unbearable.

Someone shoots him again—and again, and again— trying to kill an unkillable thing.

I scream at the sound of each bullet, horrified at the way his body dances beneath the gunfire.

I'm still shouting as I'm forced away from the road and into a nearby building. It's only after someone's pushed me into a pew that I realize they dragged me to a *church.*

He had wanted to marry me!

I squeeze my eyes shut. Maybe the morning would've gone differently had I said yes to Pestilence's proposal. He was so eager, and I threw it in his face like what we did last night didn't matter when it did. God, it did.

I take in a shuddering breath and glance around. One by one the people who led me here disappear into another room to remove their masks. When they return, they no longer appear so menacing.

The men and women that fill the church are civilians, civilians who decided to sacrifice their lives to take down the horseman. Civilians who are bringing me blankets and coffee—civilians who are *helping* me, an ex-firefighter, the best they can.

Doesn't change the fact they hurt him. That they may be hurting him still.

I stand, the woolen blanket sliding off my shoulders, feeling like my emotions have been pushed through a meat grinder.

Where is he?

"The others are dealing with him," someone says, and that's the first I realize I've spoken out loud.

"We heard about you, you know," says one of the women milling about. "The reports kept mentioning he had a prisoner."

"She didn't look like his prisoner," someone else mutters.

"Shhh!" another hisses.

I wipe my eyes and glance around me. There are eight women and three men, all between the ages of twenty and sixty. All of them now slated to die. (The gas masks were a cute accessory, but not even they can stop Pestilence's plague.)

When will the media figure out the horseman cannot be

killed? When will people stop sacrificing their lives to end an immortal thing?

An immortal thing I happen to care for.

Got to get to him.

Got to *save* him.

I make my way down the center aisle, heading for the exit.

I've only gone several feet when I'm intercepted by one of the men. He's a big, burly guy with a white handlebar mustache and a firearm holstered at his hip.

"Let's sit you back down," he says, his tone so damn condescending.

After taking my upper arm, he leads me back to a pew.

"Am I under arrest?" I ask.

"Of course not," he says, "but you've had a trying morning. Why don't you rest a little?"

I glance at him, then at the others.

They're not going to let me go. I can see it on their faces.

I don't know why they care. Then it dawns on me—

I survived the plague. They must be aware of that.

And who wouldn't want to keep someone like that around? I could know the cure; hell, they may think I *am* the cure.

I return to the pew like a good little girl (ugh), and sit there, letting everyone believe I'm meek.

Five minutes tick by agonizingly slowly.

In the distance, I hear a faint neigh.

Trixie.

I mean to wait longer, but hearing Pestilence's horse is what breaks the last of my patience. I can't keep sitting here when I have no idea what's happening to my horseman.

I push myself out of the pew again.

Handlebar Mustache tenses when he sees me back on my feet. Before I can so much as exit the pew, he heads me off.

Don't look at his belt.

"Is there something you need?" he asks, folding his arms over his chest.

"Yeah, there is."

Before he has a chance to respond, I grab for his gun. My hand cradles cold metal just as he lets out a surprised shout.

I level the firearm at him and flip off the safety. "Get out of my way."

Around me, I hear gasps.

The man lifts his arms. "Now wait just a second there. Let's not do anything hasty. We're just trying to help you."

I must not look nearly as threatening as I feel because several other people creep in.

Better make your stand before this unravels.

Raising the gun to the air, I fire off a shot. The sound, already deafening, is made all the louder by the church's acoustics.

People scream, several covering their heads. Above me, plaster rains down.

I train the gun once more on the man I stole it from.

"I'm leaving," I say. "And you can *help* me by getting out of my fucking way."

Handlebar Mustache must see there's just a little too much ferocity in my eyes for his own well-being. He steps aside.

I swing the gun toward the other people who stand between me and the exit. They back up, their arms in the air.

The church is uncomfortably silent, the only sound my muted footfalls on the worn carpet.

I'm nearly to the double doors when Handlebar Mustache calls out to me, "Why have you forsaken your own people for that thing?"

He has the audacity to ask the question while standing in a church.

I turn back to face the man, my gaze sweeping over the rest of the wide-eyed men and women who watch me.

"I haven't forsaken you," I say. "God has."

CHAPTER 41

Trixie lingers right outside the church. As soon as he sees me, Pestilence's steed shuffles over, his muzzle nudging my cheek. I can almost imagine he's greeting me fondly.

I brush my hand over his face, frowning at the dark stain down his side.

The horseman's blood.

I hoist myself into the saddle and stroke the steed's neck. "Take me to Pestilence."

We were ambushed just around the corner from the church, so it doesn't take long to return to the site. Still, by the time we arrive Pestilence is already half buried in a shallow grave off to the side of the road.

The people in gas masks stand around the grave, dumping shovelfuls of dirt into it.

The stolen gun is still hot in my hand. By the time the first man lifts his head in my direction, I'm already aiming it at him. He makes a surprised noise, dropping his shovel. The other men glance at him before looking around in confusion.

They too startle when they see me astride Pestilence's horse, weapon in hand.

Now that I have their attention—

"You all have five seconds to make yourselves scarce. Then I start shooting."

No one budges.

"One—"

Now people begin to scramble.

"Two—"

One of the men reaches for his gun.

I fire off a warning shot, the gun kicking back in my hand.

They drop their shovels and abandon the grave. A few of them take off running, but some loiter, not ready to let a woman scare them off.

"Three—"

The masked men move onto the street, backing away from me, a couple with their hands in the air.

Like that's going to placate me.

"Four—"

They move back a little faster.

"*Five.*"

I cluck my tongue, attempting the sound Pestilence makes. Beneath me, Trixie leaps forward, charging down the street.

Now the last of the masked men sprint for their lives. Nothing like having an undead steed running you down to get you going. I fire another shot just to give them a good scare.

Halfway down the street, I pull on the reins, letting the men get away from us, watching their forms grow smaller and smaller.

These people knew before they saw me that I'm traveling with Pestilence.

A foreboding shiver passes over me.

If today's events get back to the media, the world will soon know I'm no longer his captive.

I force back a cry when I stare down at Pestilence's makeshift grave. He's nearly unidentifiable, his body awash in blood, dirt, and pulpy, fleshy things.

I don't want to move him out of fear that I'll hurt him.

Townspeople will come back. You may only have minutes.

That's what gets me going.

Setting the gun aside, I crouch next to the grave and hook my arms beneath Pestilence's armpits.

"I'm so sorry," I whisper.

And then I pull.

He lets out an agonized cry, the sound garbled by his ruin of a mouth, as I heave him out of his tomb. A silent tear trickles out at the noise.

If only my earlier self could see me now. How far I've fallen, crying over a thing that can't die. Over the very thing I was supposed to kill. And look at me now—I'm pointing guns at anyone who tries to take him from me.

Ever so slowly, I tug Pestilence out of the earth. Trixie kneels next to me, the steed anticipating his rider's needs. I drag the horseman's body onto the saddle.

Not going to be very comfortable, but it will have to do.

Settling myself behind him, I again cluck my tongue. Trixie rises to his feet, the two of us balanced on his back, then the steed takes off.

Several shots ring out, and I flatten myself over the horseman as the bullets whiz by me. I glance over my shoulder. The men I so recently drove off now run back into the street from wherever they tucked themselves away, training their guns on us.

Shit.

I jerk on one side of the reins, pulling Trixie's head to the side, steering us off course. Pestilence's body slides a little, and it takes most of my strength to keep the horseman on his horse. But at least the bullets meant for me and Trixie miss us.

I yank on the other side of the reins, forcing the horse to change trajectory again, zigzagging across the road until the gunshots fall to silence. When I look over my shoulder again, the men in gas masks are out of range.

Safe. We're safe—for now.

I don't dare slow the horse until the town is far behind us. Once I do, it's only so I can scour our surroundings for a house. Considering my shitty luck today, I'm probably going to choose a home with the meanest asshole living inside it. Without Pestilence to strike the fear of God in him, who knows just how bad the situation may get.

I suck in a deep breath. There's just no helping the situation.

I end up picking a home that's directly off the road, hoping whoever lives there is long gone. It takes an agonizingly long time to get inside, but on a positive note, the place has been vacated.

I lead Trixie through the door after me, careful to not jostle Pestilence's slumped body in the process. It's only once I move the steed next to the couch that I drag the horseman off. He slides into my arms, knocking me off-balance, and the two of us collapse in a heap on the couch.

Real smooth there, Burns.

I wiggle myself into a comfortable position beneath Pestilence, feeling blood from his various wounds seep into my clothing.

Now that I'm holding him, I find I can't let him go. His face is still mangled, and it's been further obscured by the dirt matted to his skin.

With a shaky hand, I run my knuckles over an intact section of cheek.

You fool. You've gone and fallen for this thing.

He moves in my arms, and I nearly yelp. I almost forgot *he's still in there.* Still aware of what's going on. My bile rises at the thought.

To think I did worse to Pestilence than even those men.

"Shhh," I say, gently maneuvering myself out from under him. I arrange him on the couch, his long form barely fitting.

I take one of his hands in mine, brushing a kiss along his dirt-covered knuckles. "Try to sleep," I say. "I'll be right here."

Pestilence mumbles something—I don't even know *how* he's making noise.

I shush him again, and he quiets, settling into something that, if not sleep, must be somewhat like it.

I make good on my promise; I stay by his side—leaving only to start a fire and dig up rags and water, which I use to wipe us down the best I can. Once I finish, I take his hand in mine, holding it close to me.

As the hours tick by, I watch the slow but miraculous evolution of the horseman from something that ought to be dead to a beautiful sleeping man.

Looks like something straight out of a fairy tale.

With a metallic groan, Pestilence's hole-riddled breast-plate bends back into place, the golden armor ever so slowly returning to its original seamless surface. Just as wondrously, I watch his face rebuild itself from sinew and bone to muscle and tendons and skin. Eventually, I even see the horseman's long eyelashes sprout along his newly formed eyelid.

This is magic. This is faith. This is the barest glimpse of the leviathan that is God.

Even after his body has all but healed, Pestilence doesn't wake. Beneath his closed lids, his eyes move back and forth.

What do horsemen dream about?

It makes me ache to think of him dreaming. He's so much more human than I ever imagined him to be.

I had a hand in that—more than a hand if I'm being honest. He eats food because I gave him a taste for it, drinks beer because I offered it to him.

Makes love to me because I opened myself up to him.

Makes love. I worry my lower lip at the phrasing.

The hand I hold now tightens, scattering my thoughts. When I glance up, Pestilence's eyes flutter open.

I sit up straighter, bringing our clasped hands to my lips.

A smile blooms on his face, but then it's wiped away, his brow creasing instead. "Are you okay?"

Those are his first words. Just when I thought this man couldn't gut me any more.

I pinch my lips together so the truth doesn't leak out. Because no, I'm not okay. I haven't been okay since Pestilence was shot off his horse. Even before then, I'm not sure how okay I was.

I'm having more than a little trouble dealing with ~~loving~~ *liking* this horseman.

He begins to sit up, looking increasingly alarmed when he sees the blood on me. "Where are you hu—?"

"It's not my blood, it's yours. They...*shot you.*" I whisper

301

this last part because emotion is choking up my vocal cords. Already my tear ducts are coming online; as I blink, a couple slip out. Now that Pestilence is awake, I'm having trouble staying strong.

He sits up, a frown on his face as he takes in my hazel eyes.

"Are you crying…for me?" he asks, his voice laced with disbelief.

I want to say something snarky. Instead I wipe my cheeks. "Maybe."

Pestilence eyes me as though he can't make sense of the sight. "You know I can't be killed," he says quietly.

"But you can be hurt." And they hurt him so badly.

"That bothers you?" His voice gentles.

I gesture to my wet cheeks and red eyes. "Yes."

His gaze goes soft. "*Sara.*" He says my name lovingly, and it's what undoes me.

I lean forward, and my lips are on his. His arms come around me, half pulling me onto him as his mouth responds to mine, devouring me just as eagerly.

It's easy to forget how strong he is when he's hurt, but now that he's regenerated, I feel his strength as it envelops me.

Still, he's bloody and I hate that. And I hate that I hate that, but not nearly enough, and I'm making no sense, but honestly, absolutely nothing in my life makes sense right now, so…

"I'm sorry," I say. "I'm sorry for what those people did to you, and for what I did to you—and for what everyone else has done to you since you arrived."

Pestilence came here with a grisly task, and he armored himself against the atrocity of it by convincing himself humans were monsters. And we proved him right every time we attacked him.

That's what hate does—it brings out your worst.

He's only caught glimpses of our goodness, and yet that's all it's taken for his deeds to weigh on him.

Because that's what compassion does—it brings out your best nature.

"I'm sorry for every thoughtless thing I said earlier," I continue. "What we did together meant something to me. *You* mean something to me."

Pestilence holds me close. "Does this mean you're going to marry me?"

I laugh through my tears. "No, I don't do pity proposals. But I'm open to makeup sex."

Pestilence kisses me again, sliding one of his hands reverently up my cheek and into my hair.

"It wasn't a pity proposal, dear Sara," he murmurs.

He sits up, my body tucked tightly against him, then stands, cradling me in his arms. His lips find mine once more, and we resume the kiss. I'm barely aware that we're moving through the house until Pestilence lays me out on the bed in the main suite.

I shiver at the sight of the horseman above me as he removes his refashioned armor, his gaze searing me the entire time. He takes his crown off last before setting it on the bedside table.

Stripped bare of his golden adornments, he's no longer my noble, otherworldly Pestilence but my flesh-and-blood lover.

He comes back to me, fitting his body over mine.

"Sara, Sara, Sara," he breathes, kissing my eyelids, my cheeks, my lips, my chin. "I confess your earlier apologies moved me, but they are unnecessary all the same. You needn't ask for my forgiveness—you already have it and more, if you'll but take what I offer."

I think he means marriage…and for the first time, the thought intrigues the crap out of me.

I could marry him.

He kisses the column of my throat, right down to the hollow at the base of it. "You have my mercy, my mind, my adoration, my body, my…*life*."

I could've sworn that for a moment he was about to say another four-letter *L* word, but maybe that's just my imagination.

And for the first time, I'm *disappointed* he didn't say it. But that makes no sense.

Life is a big enough promise coming from an immortal man.

I'm just a greedy bitch.

Pestilence makes quick work of removing his shirt. I almost sigh at the sight of his thick arm muscles and his tapered torso. My hands move first to his pecs, then to his abs, for once ignoring the markings that ring his skin. Beneath my fingertips, his muscles tense, like his skin is hypersensitive to my touch.

The horseman flashes me a purely masculine smile, enjoying my exploration. He sinks back down onto me, lifting my shirt to expose my belly.

I shiver at the feel of chilly air along the band of bared flesh, but then Pestilence's warm hands move over it, and his lips claim it kiss by kiss.

"Once again I have you to thank for protecting me—*saving* me," he says against my skin.

Saving, that's a big word coming from him, the man who is impervious to death and believes he's too powerful to need rescuing—or at least he used to believe that. I don't know when things shifted in his mind, only that they have.

"Tell me, dear Sara," he continues, "how may I repay you?"

I shake my head, staring up at him. "That's not something you ever need to repay me for. I didn't do it to make you owe me. I did it because I care about you."

His eyes find mine, soft and bright and burning with so much…*love*.

Or am I imagining this too? All I know is the look is too tender to be lust and too passionate to be kindness or compassion.

No, my eyes aren't deceiving me. Now and only now am I seeing his feelings for what they truly are.

Love.

I have bound this man to me. I've cultivated a very human appetite in him, and this is the result. Love.

I should be frightened at the thought, but a strange sort of thrill rushes through me.

This time, it's Pestilence who takes the lead. His hands rove over me, tossing away my blood-soaked clothes one piece at a time, his touch strong and sure.

My passion rises; along with it is this delicious *uncertainty*—like the horseman knows forbidden things that I don't and tonight he's going to introduce me to them.

I think Pestilence means to move slowly—I know I do—but in the end, our movements are hurried. The last of our clothes come off, and then it's just leagues and leagues of glorious skin.

His tanned arms bulge as he dips lower and lower on my torso, kissing a trail down my body. He pauses when he gets to my core, staring at it for a long second. Then he kisses that too.

Involuntarily, my hips rise off the bed.

Whoa.

Pestilence spreads my legs wide, giving himself an unobstructed view of me. He drinks the sight in before moving back up my body and settling his hips between my thighs.

I feel him thick against me, his cock pressed to my entrance. Without warning, Pestilence drives himself inside. I nearly moan as he fills me, coating himself in my wetness.

"I missed this," he says as he pulls out. He thrusts into me hard again, his movements deep and demanding.

I run my hands up his back, drawing out goose bumps along his flesh. "Me too."

Now that he's this close to me, this alive, I can finally, *finally* banish the last thoughts of this morning to the hinterlands of my mind.

Pestilence cups my face. "This is *not* fucking."

He chooses *now* to make his point?

He stares at me as he works my core, and I realize he expects an answer.

Can't remember my own damn name at this point.

"Mmm," I say. That's noncommittal enough.

His hips piston, in and out, in and out.

"This is lovemaking," he states—no, *demands*.

He's really latched on to that term with gusto.

"Tell me your thoughts," he all but orders. "I need to hear them."

How can he even *think* right now? But one look in his eyes has me sobering up real quick. This is important to him.

"This isn't fucking," I agree, and I mean it. There's far too much emotional subtext here between us. Each rushed touch is filled with longing, with *lov*—

"It's lovemaking," Pestilence agrees, like the two of us are on the same page.

I shake my head. Am I in denial? No? Yes?

"Lovemaking is slower, more reverent..." That's all I've got.

The horseman's brow furrows, and his pace—*damn it*—his pace slows. But his thrusts deepen, his cock thick and throbbing inside me, and he unshutters his gaze so everything he feels is right there staring down at me. He's gazing at me as though I'm *beloved*.

He brushes his thumb over my cheekbone. "Like this?" he asks as he pumps slowly in and out of me.

"Yeah," I say, unnerved as hell because the full force of that adoring gaze is staggering, "just like this."

His eyes dip to my lips, even as he moves deep inside me. "And if I kiss you, will I still be making love to you?"

I nearly forget to breathe. "It's all about your intent."

His mouth follows his gaze until I feel the sweet brush of his lips against mine. The very sweep of them as they pass over my mouth seems tender, *loving*. And when he coaxes my lips open and our tongues touch, that too seems to be done as though he reveres even the very taste of me.

He pulls away. "Was my intent clear?"

"Very."

Pestilence goes slow and deep for a while, but then, perhaps in response to my own feverish need for more of him, he speeds up, his thrusts becoming fast and rough.

"Want to keep making love to you, but I cannot resist this *need*—"

"*Then don't.*"

My words are permission enough. He takes my mouth again, and this time his kiss is brutal. His pace doubles, as though he can't help but move deeper, faster, until the headboard rocks against the wall.

I twine my legs around his, needing to touch as much of him as possible.

Each stroke makes me burn hotter and brighter. It's like I unleashed a storm. I guess that's what you get when you fit a force of nature into the body of a man.

His eyes lock with mine. The moment stretches on and on. Something passes between us, something I won't put a name to, but something that comes from me every bit as much as it comes from him.

Something that worries me deeply.

I hold on until I can no longer, but that *look*. I'm powerless against it.

With a cry, I come, sensation lashing through me as I call out his name. He bellows when I tighten around him, his own climax riding on mine. Pestilence grips my hands in his, pinning them to the bed as his harsh final thrusts batter me.

And then the moment's over.

Pestilence gathers me to him; even after he's no longer inside me, he still seems keen to keep me close.

He brushes his lips against my forehead. "I like making love to you, Sara Burns."

My stomach somersaults.

"I think it may be my new favorite thing in the world, next to this." His hold briefly tightens.

I run my hand over his chest and down his abs, smiling softly. "You prefer this to my wicked conversational skills?" I tease.

"Ask me again tomorrow when we're in the saddle," he says, grinning. "I'm sure my answer will change."

That smile! The sight of it causes my breath to hitch.

"You're just saying that to get on my good side."

"Sara, you only *have* good sides. I'm saying this because each moment with you is my new favorite."

You'd think I'd start to get used to his flattery, but like always, Pestilence's words have a way of overwhelming me.

The two of us are quiet for a while, and I'm blissfully happy simply lying against him, enjoying how his hand lazily strokes my back.

But the longer I lie there, the more worrisome my thoughts become. This morning bubbles back up, even more gruesome now that Pestilence is in my arms, and I feel the weight of my emotions pressing in from all sides.

These attacks will keep happening. I know it as certainly as I'm sure Pestilence does. I'm not sure why this is some sobering revelation now. I was, after all, one of those people who tried to take him out. Of course it's going to keep happening.

Humankind is desperate enough, reckless enough, courageous, self-sacrificing enough—

Vindictive enough.

Because at the end of the day, even if humans can't stop him, they can at the very least make him regret landing on God's green earth.

They. The pronoun stops me cold. That last thought—I said *they*, not *we*. I cut myself out of the group.

It's another one of those moments where the axis of my world tilts.

This whole time I've been so focused on how I've changed the horseman that I haven't been paying attention to how he's changed me.

"I'm not your prisoner," I whisper.

Pestilence's touch stills. He doesn't respond.

"I'm not," I insist. "Not anymore." I'm drawing a line in the sand.

The edge of his mouth curves up. "Accept my proposal then."

His mood is light—sex has a way of doing that—but I'm somber.

"I'm serious, Pestilence. Earlier today I stole a man's gun and threatened him with it. I would've killed for you if I needed to." That admission hurts coming out. "So, no, I am not your prisoner," I reiterate, "not any longer."

For a long moment, he says nothing.

"All right," Pestilence finally agrees. "You're no longer my prisoner."

The truth is, I don't think either of us knows *what* I am. I may no longer be his prisoner, but I doubt I could freely walk away from him either. At this point, I'm conceding to the realization that I don't *want* to walk away, that I care for this terrible, wonderful being.

"What've you done to me?" I whisper, searching his face.

I set out to destroy this man, not to *protect* him.

"The same thing you have done to me, I imagine," Pestilence says, brushing a lock of my hair aside. "You want your people to live, but you're unwilling for me to be harmed. I want your people to die, but I cannot harm you. Each of us is trapped between our minds and our hearts."

"It's not the same," I say, hoarsely. "You're only saving me because God sent you a sign."

Pestilence brushes a kiss against my temple. He's shockingly good at cuddling.

"God might've interceded on your behalf once," he says, "but He hasn't needed to since. You are mine, and nothing—*nothing*—will change that."

CHAPTER 42

We're out by dawn, and not long after that Pestilence starts prodding me to recite another poem.

What are the chances I'd find a man who likes poetry?

Since he liked "The Raven," I dredge up "Lenore."

"…Come! let the burial rite be read—the funeral song be sung!—/ An anthem for the queenliest dead that ever died so young…"

I don't even get all the way through the end of the second stanza of Poe's "Lenore" before I realize Pestilence isn't paying attention. And after he made such a fuss about hearing a poem too.

"And so," I continue, "the banging chick Lenore died and people apparently weren't super sad because she was the shit and they hated her for that and now you want to kill everyone because we're all a-holes of epic proportions."

I pause, waiting for Pestilence to say something, *anything*, but he doesn't.

I sigh.

The horseman strokes my belly absently with his thumb, lost in thought.

"Have you thought about children?" he says, rousing from his reverie.

The question takes me by surprise. "I'm sorry?"

"Children," he repeats.

"What are you talking about?"

"We've had unprotected sex—twice. I may be new to these parts, but even I know the purpose of reproduction is to *reproduce*."

A sick wave of vertigo washes over me. I put a hand to my head.

I hadn't once thought about using protection.

And now...

Oh, *shit*.

"Can that happen?" I ask. "Between us, I mean."

He's not human, I reassure myself, and a bit of my unease retreats. Biologically, we're not programmed the same way.

Right?

"I don't see why it can't," he says. "I can eat and drink and make love just like a mortal. Perhaps I can sire a child just like one too."

Welp, there goes my nice, calm morning.

"But you don't *know*?" I ask, my voice rising.

There's a brief silence, then: "Sara, I sense you're afraid of the possibility."

Ding—ding—ding! You guessed correctly.

He continues, "For a woman who so eagerly takes my flesh into hers—"

Jesus. My cheeks heat.

"—you're awfully reluctant to deal with everything else that comes with the act."

I am, aren't I? But in my defense, we're talking about a *child*.

He would protect them, just as he has you.

That's beside the point, brain. Don't go soft on me now.

Awesome, I'm debating with myself.

"Have you thought about it?" I ask Pestilence, rather than addressing his comment.

"I have."

I wait, but he doesn't say more. "And?" I finally prompt.

"And I find the possibility...*thrilling*."

It thrills him? My lady parts are waaaay too happy about that.

"As you may imagine," he says, "my excitement greatly disturbs me. I am *killing* your kind. What happens if I am father to one?"

I really want to clear my throat because, uh, dude's also banging one, and isn't that reason enough?

"They could be immortal," I say, though I'm more asking this than anything else.

"They could be," he agrees, and my stomach bottoms out at that.

I could give birth to a deity-thingy. A god spawn.

Nope. Nope, nope, *nope*. Noooooooooope.

This conversation is quickly going from uncomfortable waters to my-vagina-is-mutinying-it-doesn't-matter-that-you're-sex-on-legs-well-okay-maybe-it-does-a-little-never-mind-my-vagina-is-cool-with-it.

That's what happens when you're upsettingly pretty. My libido forgives *a lot*.

"But it could also be mortal. Human," he says. "And I will have created it. I, who am tasked with the destruction of your kind."

That boy out there has seen a lot of human nature, the bulk of it ugly. He's only now seeing the beauty of it, and largely through you... Show him humanity is worthy of redemption.

Ruth's final words ring in my ears.

Pestilence is straddling two warring natures—his divine one, which demands we all die, and his mortal one, which doesn't want to kill us and perhaps even wants to *save* us... And each day he's with me, his mortal nature strengthens. *I* strengthen it. The thought fills me with no little wonder.

"So what are you going to do about it?" I ask.

His lips brush the shell of my ear. "What shall come to pass is to be seen. One thing is certain: I cannot stay away from you."

My stomach clenches at that.

Nor I you.

I'm debating whether I should state my opinion when Pestilence's hold tightens on me. I look up at him, but he's staring ahead of us.

I follow his gaze, and my eyes widen. In the distance, between the boarded-up buildings that speckle the sides of the highway, is a sea of people all dressed in white.

As we get closer, I stare in wonder at the hordes of them. They line the street, their bodies bowed in supplication.

Bowed for Pestilence.

They waited for him, willingly giving up their lives for this demonstration.

I glance at the horseman just in time to see his upper lip curl in disgust. "Praying to false idols," he says. "They deserve the plague that will take them."

Did I think even a second ago that I was making inroads on his bloodlust? Apologies, I was mistaken.

"The same one I deserve?" I say.

"You were touched by the hand of God," he responds smoothly.

Four more white-robed people stand in the middle of the road, obstructing our way. One of them is an older man with wild eyes and ashen hair. Next to him are three *beautiful* youthful women.

When we get close enough, the man steps forward, bringing Trixie to a halt. I can feel Pestilence seething at my back, but the horseman doesn't try to get his mount to move again.

"I, the Prophet Ezekiel, come to you in our hour of darkness," the man says. "I give unto you, the Conqueror, these three women to have and to hold."

To have and to hold?

Ick.

Ezekiel looks so magnanimous about his offer too, like we should give him a cookie for the effort he went through to procure these women.

The holy roller comes forward, the women at his heels. Something dark and possessive rises in me at the way the women are looking at Pestilence. They seem a little too eager to be the horseman's servants.

"What is this?" Pestilence asks, his gaze sweeping over the sea of robed men and women.

"We have long awaited your arrival," wild-eyed Ezekiel says.

Behind me, the horseman grunts. "And them?" Pestilence juts his chin to the women.

"They are yours," Ezekiel says.

"What am I supposed to do with them?" Pestilence asks, pinching his brows in confusion. Out of the six of us here, he's clearly the only one not understanding the delicate subtext of this situation.

He wants you to take them to Bone Town. Obviously.

But I keep my mouth shut because I really want a now slightly uncomfortable Ezekiel to spell it out himself.

"Whatever it is you please," the prophet (ha!) says smoothly. He flicks his eyes to me just as Pestilence tightens his grip on my torso. I see Ezekiel smother a frown.

Awww, was he hoping the horseman would trade up? Too bad Pestilence enjoys his old model just fine.

"If you were me, what would you do with them?" the horseman asks.

"It is not for me to assume," the prophet says humbly. At least he thinks he's being humble and demure, with his eyes turned to the ground and his head bowed.

The women are beginning to fidget. I think all of them imagined this exchange going a little differently.

"And in return?" Pestilence presses. "What do you want in return for these women?"

I tense. The horseman is not seriously considering this, is he?

Ezekiel's eyes rise. They glint with avarice. "I would hope you would spare us"—his hand sweeps over the sea of people—"your most loyal followers."

The horseman's gaze scrutinizes the crowd. "Hmmm."

The prophet looks thrilled at Pestilence's deliberation.

Finally, the horseman's attention falls once more to Ezekiel. "You presume a great deal, holding me up as you have," Pestilence says, his voice calm.

Ezekiel's face flushes.

"As for the barter," the horseman continues, his voice hardening, "you wish to give me three humans in exchange for hundreds—do you think me a fool?"

For the first time since we happened upon him, the prophet looks a bit unsure of himself. "N-no—"

"Your women would be nothing more than a hindrance to me," Pestilence says, talking over him. "As for the rest of your people, you should know by now I cannot *save*. I can only kill."

My skin prickles at his words.

"If you believe in a God, which you appear to," the horseman continues, "I would suggest you pray to Him. He's the only one who can save you all now."

CHAPTER 43

"I understood Ezekiel's intent," *Pestilence says, once the* prophet and his people are far behind us. "There is much about this world that baffles me, but *that* did not."

So he *did* understand the women were meant as sexual offerings.

And just when the horseman's gotten a taste for a woman's flesh...

Ezekiel must've heard whispers that Pestilence kept a captive woman, one who didn't succumb to the fever. He must've thought that if he offered up a few more women, he could arrange for his chosen people to live.

Bet he thought he was pretty clever too.

We pass through several successive towns quickly, only stopping once at an outpost so I can go to the bathroom and Pestilence can swipe a tent and a few other odds and ends.

Guess we're camping again tonight.

And naturally, as the day ends, the heavens decide to unleash yet another torrential downpour. Because camping isn't shit-sucking enough.

By nightfall, rain batters outside our tent, and not even the waterproof material is enough to keep it all out. It seeps in from the muddy ground outside and through the tent's seams. The flimsy structure shivers and shakes as it gets pummeled.

The horseman and I are twined together in the darkness.

"So, this is fun," I say.

Pestilence huffs out a laugh. "It isn't our worst night together."

No, technically it's not. What a depressing thought.

I can't see him in the darkness, but his warmth is everywhere.

"Poor Trixie," I say.

He's still out there. Shortly after we dismounted, Pestilence gave the horse a pat on the flank, and the creature trotted away into the woods.

"My steed is undying. I assure you he is fine." The horseman's breath brushes against my cheek. "You still haven't finished reciting that Edgar Allan Poe poem."

From this morning? He actually remembers that?

"You weren't listening."

"I was, though I'm not sure your macabre poet is the type to pen *a-holes* into his work."

I smile in the darkness, remembering when I went off script to get the horseman's attention. "Poe has a sassy mouth."

"Does he?" I can hear the grin in Pestilence's voice. "What other well-kept secrets of the universe do you know?"

"Hmmm." I pretend to ponder this. "Wednesday is the most underrated day of the week. Hot baths can take away just about any ailment. *Phlegm* is the most horrible word in existence—not *moist*, like my mother insists. The world is worth saving, and I want to call you by something other than *Pestilence* because despite what you say, names do matter."

I hadn't meant for the conversation to suddenly get deep or for me to get preachy, but there you go.

Pestilence stiffens around me. "I do not seek to change you. Why must you try to change me?"

Because you're destroying my world.

"I can't change you, Pestilence—only you can do that."

"Hear me, Sara: I *won't* change."

Now it's my turn to stiffen in his arms.

He turns us so he can gaze down at me. "I am merely pretending to be a man, nothing more," he says. "My body does not need food, nor water, nor sleep, nor all the mysteries of the flesh. I indulge in them because I indulge in you."

"Oh, and that's the only reason?" I say just a wee bit snidely.

I mean, give me a goddamned break. He indulges in all those things because he enjoys the taste of food and strong spirits and the feel of his body close to mine. Pestilence may not be a man, but he very desperately wishes to be one.

"Enough of this," he says, sharp like a knife. "Do you want to know why I wear this crown?"

I can already tell by his tone that he means to hurt me, to scare me, to remind me of the monster he is. Should I tell him that this too is a human trait? How we mortals love to push each other away to protect ourselves from our own pain?

"I am the First Horseman," he continues, "the one tasked with toppling your old way of living. You and your foolish brethren believed you could outpace God. You built and innovated, and in your quest you robbed the earth of its purity and forgot you all had another master.

"You all turned your backs on God—yes, even you, dear Sara—and I am here to *make you remember.*

"I am your mortality. I am the ugly truth that your bodies are impermanent, feeble, *corrupt.* I am the reminder that all men must face a great and fearsome reckoning." The rain thunders along with his voice. "This is who I have always been and will always be—undying, unchanging."

He falls silent.

"That is *such* horseshit."

I feel, rather than see, his surprise. "You think I'm lying?"

"You're acting like you can't change, but to live *is* to change, and right now you're *alive.* Even though you can't die, you still walk among us. You love like us and you feel pain like us."

He doesn't say anything to that, so I plow on.

"Maybe the world has forgotten God and you're supposed to rain down His righteousness, but don't act like it isn't a choice. Every time you pass through a city, you *choose* to infect it. You choose to kill, and no god you stand behind can protect you from that truth."

Several seconds pass, the violent patter of rain against our tent the only sound between us.

"If I am such a monster," Pestilence finally says, "then what does that make you, who have willingly fallen into my arms?"

"A fool," I say, "but that's nothing new."

"I will not stop."

I could swear he sounds bothered, but I can't say which part of our conversation got under his skin.

"And I won't shut up about it until you do."

"You cannot hope to win this," he warns.

"If you think this is about *winning,*" I say, "then you haven't been listening to me at all."

"Hmmm," he muses, stroking his hand down my arm while he gazes down at me. "You have given me much to think about."

Wait, something I said actually got *through* to him? And just when I'd assumed I'd have more sway talking to a wall.

"Enough of this for tonight. I want to feel those foolish, wicked lips of yours on mine and your body beneath me—for such is the price of my companionship," he says, his breath fanning against me.

"Awfully optimistic of you to think about getting boned after that little speech of yours..."

"Boned?"

"I'll explain it later."

"Good. I'm tired of making war with that mouth of yours." He leans in. "Show me the other side to living."

And so I do.

CHAPTER 44

I should be wary of days like today, when the sun burns bright and the sky is a blinding shade of blue—the kind of day that hurts your eyes and squeezes your heart. It's the kind of day that, even in the heart of winter, reminds you what summer feels like.

It's a fucking liar of a day, and just like all painfully beautiful things, I should know better than to trust it.

Last night's campsite is far behind us when Pestilence and I enter our first town of the day, the two of us soaking up the morning sun as we chat.

"...I heard a noise beneath my sink," I tell him, right in the middle of my story, "and when I went to check it out, there was not one but *three* rats." I pause dramatically.

"I don't understand how this led to the...*fire alarm* going off," he says, hesitating a little before repeating the term. I only just explained to him what a fire alarm is and how the one in my apartment escaped the horsemen's arrival unscathed.

"They ran at me!" I exclaim.

"So?"

"So?" Rats don't *run* at people. Particularly not in an age when people will *eat* said rats. "So I grabbed a can of hair spray and a match, and I made a flamethrower."

No one drives this bitch out of her home.

At that, the horseman throws his head back and laughs. I stop speaking just so I can turn in the saddle and stare at him.

Only Pestilence could outshine the sun.

"Don't tell me you tried to hurt the creatures?" he asks when his chuckles die down.

"You know, that's real precious coming from you."

He starts laughing again, and new life goal: Get Pestilence to laugh more.

"Did it work?" he asks.

"Of course it didn't work."

That only makes him laugh harder.

"Well, *I* didn't think it was very funny at the time," I say, but I can't keep a straight face. It's impossible when he lights up like this.

He manages to smother his laughter enough to say, "Isn't your job to put out fires, not—?"

BOOM!

My body is violently thrown forward as the world explodes around me. I feel the heat, the terrible scorching heat, at my back as I tumble through the air. It sizzles against my skin, though Pestilence's body shields me from the worst of it.

I slam into the ground, my side flaring in pain at the impact. All around me, sizzling bits of asphalt and dirt rain down, singeing me in a dozen different places.

I lie on the ground for several seconds, breathing hard as thick smoke billows through the air.

What the hell just happened?

On the other side of the road, Pestilence lies pinned beneath Trixie, a pool of blood spreading out from the back of the horseman's head. His horse's body is partially gone, and what remains is bloody and singed.

I let out a whimper at the sight.

Pushing my torso up, I drag myself to them, my limbs screaming in protest.

Some of the road has been blown away, and it's that more than Pestilence's unconscious form or Trixie's ruined body that makes me realize we just survived an *explosion*.

Someone planted a bomb.

Dear God.

They come out of the woods as I crawl to the horseman, their forms quiet and sinister. There are at least a dozen of them, maybe more, and unlike the last ambush, these people don't bother wearing masks.

Know they're going to die.

They do, however, dress in a similar fashion. Lots of black leather and camo print.

Gang, my mind fills in.

Their hate is visceral; it contorts their faces and thickens the air.

They won't be like the others.

I'm not going to survive this.

"Pestilence," I try to call out to him, but my voice is too hoarse from pain and smoke.

Even though he can't possibly hear me, he slowly swivels his face to mine from where he's pinned.

His eyes are full of fear.

For me, I realize, as the men close in on us.

The group doesn't bother going for me first. Instead they

cluster around Pestilence. Deftly, they lift Trixie off him, and for a moment it almost looks like they're saving him from being crushed to death, but I know better. People are not nearly so altruistic when it comes to the horsemen.

One of them holds a pump-action shotgun at his hip, pointing it at Pestilence.

Again my horseman's gaze goes to me before moving to the people that surround him. "Spare my—"

BOOM!

The shotgun goes off, the cartridge blasting away Pestilence's face.

A shocked scream rips from my throat.

Someone breaks off from the group. A woman, I realize. She steps up to me and cocks her head, inspecting me like a bird would a worm. Whatever she sees, it causes her to frown.

With a swift kick, she slams her booted foot into my temple, and the world melts away.

CHAPTER 45

I wake with a groan. My head feels like it has its own heartbeat.

I try to reach up to touch my temple, but my wrists are secured behind my back. My legs too are bound at the ankles, pinning me in place. I blink away the last of my confusion.

Someone's propped me up against a tagged building, the paint weathered away. A few people linger next to me, but most gather around a nearby telephone pole.

I squint at them, trying to figure out what's going on. It takes me several seconds, but I finally make out the bloody body they're all staring at.

Pestilence.

A burly man is tying him to the base of the telephone pole, the rope wrapped a dizzying number of times around the horseman's ruined form. At Pestilence's feet are piles of firewood.

Pestilence's face is nearly gone, and most of his back must be burned away from the explosion. If he were mortal, the horseman would be dead five times over, and tying him up would be pointless. The fact these people are restraining him means they know he can't die.

Someone besides me finally learned the terrible truth.

And now these people are using it against him.

I let out a hopeless cry.

Once the man finishes securing Pestilence to the telephone pole, the nails and hammers come out.

Even as they bring the items up to his body, I can't comprehend what they're going to do; my mind won't let me. It's only when they hammer the first nail into Pestilence's skin that I understand.

They mean to crucify him.

Pestilence's body gives a jerk from the pain. A second nail quickly follows the first and then comes a third and a fourth. His body shudders again and again.

I scream, and once I start, I find I can't stop.

In my line of business, I'm used to seeing compassion, sacrifice. I've seen men hospitalized because they ran into a burning house to rescue a dog. I've seen neighbors empty their pantries and open their homes to victims because they wanted to help people in need. I've seen so much goodness. My job always showed me that even in the worst of circumstances, humans can be their very best. We as a people are good. We are.

So it's all the more shocking to see this side of human nature. The cold, cruel side of it. So shocking that the only word that comes to mind is *in*human.

Several people assist in crucifying Pestilence while the others stand by, content to watch their comrades *torture* my horseman.

I scream myself hoarse, begging for them to stop.

"This cunt actually cries for the bastard," someone near me says, nodding in my direction.

One of the men comes up to me, a shotgun slung over his shoulder. Crouching in front of me, he peers at my face for a second, then backhands me.

I hear Pestilence's garbled roar as my head whips to the side.

"Fuck me, Jesus, this thing really doesn't die."

I roll my head back to face the man in front of me, my cheek throbbing from the hit. It's just one more pain to add to the rest.

"Stop hurting him," I whisper. My face is wet, and that's when I realize that this entire time, I've been crying.

The man in front of me squints, taking in my tears. "I think we got ourselves a couple here. The horseman and his human whore."

I stare miserably at him. It's a terrifying sight, looking into the eyes of someone who thrives off violence and hate. For all his carnage, Pestilence never *enjoyed* himself.

"Tell me, girl, how many times did you have to fuck that thing before he decided to keep you?"

Someone else calls out, "Maybe we should have a taste— see what's so special about her pussy."

A woman shouts, "I'm not going to stand here while you all fuck her. Keep to the plan, Mac."

Mac, the man in front of me, looks over his shoulder at the woman with annoyance.

After sliding his shotgun off his shoulder, Mac pulls out a wicked-looking knife from his belt. He grabs the bindings at my ankles and begins to saw through them.

"Try to kick me, girl," he says under his breath, "and I'll make sure everyone here enjoys that cunt of yours."

Kicking him *is* tempting, but my legs are far too weak to do any real damage.

Once he's cut away the ties, he grabs his gun and rises to his feet.

"Move," he commands, giving my calves a kick. He jerks the barrel of his shotgun to a vague section of the road about fifteen meters away.

Forcing my injured legs under me, I rise to my feet, then limp down the street, Mac at my back.

I've only taken ten or so steps when he kicks me to the ground. In the distance I hear laughter and, beyond that, an agonized moan.

Pestilence. Apparently, he has enough line of sight and good enough vision that he can see what's going on.

"Get up," Mac orders, amused.

I bite back a moan at the pain as I push myself to my feet, then resume walking. A few steps later, he kicks me back down.

Again people cackle and Pestilence cries out. And again Mac orders me up only to kick me down soon after. The whole scenario happens a few more times until the laughter dies off and the horseman's moans become one continuous wail. Then I simply hobble down the road, my heart sitting like an anvil in my chest.

I think this is what it feels like when your spirit breaks. When there's nothing left to believe in anymore. The unconquerable Pestilence has been conquered, these humans have lost their humanity, and I'm going to die on the most beautiful winter day.

When I reach my destination, Mac orders, "Stand there. Just so."

I turn and face him as he backs away from me, his shotgun held loosely in his hands. He's almost to his comrades, some of whom are now staring at us, when Mac trains his gun at my midsection. The group of them have arranged themselves so that, even tied up, the horseman can clearly see me.

Pestilence cries out weakly, and my eyes meet what's left of his.

"Don't forget your mercy," I tell him as Mac pumps his gun, loading a cartridge into place. "Or what you mean to me. I would've given everything up for you—"

"Hey!" Mac calls. "Why don't you shut the fuck up, skank? Oh," he adds, "and say hi to Satan for me."

BOOM!

I don't hear Pestilence's roar over the sound of the gun blast.

My body jerks as a spray of pellets tear through my torso. The pain is sudden and *everywhere*, blinding me and stealing my breath. It blooms from a dozen different places.

I fall to my knees.

Can't catch my breath.

I hear the horseman's bellow as I put my hand to my chest and watch my blood slip between my fingers.

All the king's horses and all the king's men couldn't put Humpty together again.

It's that senseless line that runs on repeat in my mind. And I know it's senseless and that my life is bleeding its way out of me, and these final seconds are more precious than whatever it is any of us hold dear anymore, but I can't shut my brain up from that ridiculous nursery rhyme.

Mac doesn't bother shooting me again. Instead he laughs with his comrades over his witty last line as he slings the shotgun over his shoulder. Someone begins to pour lighter fluid over dried wood piled at the horseman's feet.

They're going to burn Pestilence. Just like I did.

The last thing I smell is smoke.

I don't know how long I linger on the very edge of life.

The pellets must've missed the important bits, part of me thinks. Another part of me thinks maybe I already died. I mean, how do any of us really know what death is like?

"Sara…"

"Sara…"

"Sara…"

Someone keeps calling my name. I try to peel open my eyes, but what I see makes no sense.

The gang is gone. All that's left of them is a smoldering pile of ash. That and the stump of a man who's blindly dragging himself away from the remains of the fire.

Pestilence…

"Sara," he croaks. His body is blackened, and his face… it can't be called that. I can't make out any recognizable features, though obviously there's a mouth somewhere among it all since he's the one who's been calling out to me with the mangled remains of his throat.

I make some small sound. I don't have enough life in me to be sad or surprised or horrified.

My surroundings fade.

When they come into focus again, Pestilence has managed to drag what's left of himself to my side. He curls his charred body around mine, almost protectively.

"Sara, Sara, Sara…" This time his voice is stronger. Still hoarse, but now he sounds like he has a bad case of laryngitis rather than a charbroiled voice box. "Say something."

Speaking should be easier for me than it is for him, and yet all I manage is a low moan.

I feel an arm fit around my torso. I feel it tug me close. And then Pestilence's body begins to shake.

I never knew the horseman could cry. Not until I hear his sobs. The sound is awful, even more awful than his screams.

"Forgive me, Sara."

What's there to forgive?

That's what I want to say, but I can't seem to form the words. My mouth won't work properly; I'm pretty sure it's only my mind clinging to life. Even the pain isn't so bad anymore. It's just there, like a pulse.

And then I'm relieved I can't voice my thoughts because there's really so much that *does* need forgiving. His cruelty, mine, all that death and violence.

These violent delights have violent ends...

Before it was nursery rhymes; now it's Shakespeare running through my mind.

But Pestilence wasn't all that violent in the end, was he? He was sad and strange, and he came to earth with a purpose I caught him questioning a time or two.

God, please don't let me die.

Otherwise, Pestilence will be all alone, and that thought cuts deeper than my bullet wounds.

We lie there together, our limbs entwined. A peaceful sort of darkness licks at the edges of my vision. I rally against it.

But eventually, I lose the fight against the darkness, and I slip softly into it.

CHAPTER 46

I'm jostled awake by the pain. A cry slips out of me, weak and pitiful.

Can't be dead if it hurts. Right? You're not supposed to feel pain in death…

Unless I'm burning in the fiery pits of hell. That's always a possibility.

My eyes crack open, and I stare up at mottled skin.

It takes me a moment to focus my vision, and then I'm staring up at Pestilence's still very damaged face. His eyes have reformed but not his nose yet—it's just a blackened pit—and not much of his lips. But there are areas where the dark flakes of skin are sloughing off. Underneath them, his flesh is a healthy pinkish hue, which I know in a day will deepen into a golden tan.

My horseman.

He stares down at me. "Stay with me, Sara. Stay with me, beloved."

My body rocks again, the pain stealing my breath. It's

only then that I realize he's *walking*. I can't look down to see the burned remains of his legs and feet, but they must still be grisly. He's walking and—even more astounding—he's doing it while carrying me in his arms.

I still catch no sign of the people who hurt us, though they must be around here somewhere. Or maybe they're like my childhood dog who crawled beneath our deck to die, heading back to their own quiet corner of the universe to wash off the stench of murder and let the plague take them.

A pained whinny pulls me from my thoughts. I manage to turn my head just enough to see Pestilence's mount. Trixie Skillz lies on his side, his body mostly burned.

They didn't spare the horse?

Bastards.

Trixie is looking at his master, pawing weakly at the ground. I didn't think I had energy left in me to grieve, especially not for an undead horse, but I do. I pinch my eyes shut and lean into Pestilence's chest, my body screaming in protest as a silent sob racks my body.

The horseman's arms tighten around me. When he gets to Trixie's side, he lingers there for a moment. Then he begins to walk again, leaving his steed behind.

The world loses focus as I fall asleep and wake up, fall asleep and wake up.

I'm not sleeping. The thought cuts through my groggy mind. *I'm losing consciousness.*

At some point, the smell of smoke is replaced by that of strong antiseptic. I rouse at the odor, too weak to lift my head or open my eyes.

"…heal her…"

"…could, there's still infection to worry…"

"…care…or die…"

"No."

"*No?*" This from Pestilence.

I moan a little. In response, Pestilence's lips press to my forehead. "Stay with me, Sara," he whispers against my skin.

Weakly, I press a hand to his chest, my fingers touching the warm skin at the base of his throat.

I want to tell him I'm all right, to not worry about me, but there's a wall of pain I need to break through first, and I just can't seem to.

"Do you care about her?" the stranger's voice says.

"I *love* her."

My fingers flex against his skin.

I need to open my eyes. I need to see the look on his face as he says those words. I need to hear them again while he gazes down at me.

Despite my best efforts, my eyes stay firmly shut.

"You love her?"

"That's what I just said, human."

Through my dim awareness, I can already tell Pestilence is losing his temper.

"Then I hope it hurts to watch her die."

A horrible yawning silence follows.

"So be it," the horseman says solemnly.

Even through my haze of pain, I get chills from his tone.

The stranger—a woman, I think—begins to scream. The sound echoes down the corridor, gaining strength. Strength or…are those other voices?

Stop. I try to say it, but all that comes out is a moan.

And then the voices are in my head, giving sound to my pain. It builds and builds in my ears and beneath my skin, burning me from the inside out.

I fall into the darkness again, and this time, it's not so easy to claw my way awake.

I blink my eyes, taking in the muted light. It's everywhere—above me, below me, to either side of me.

I touch my stomach, but it no longer hurts. I'm no longer hurt; there's no blood, no broken skin, nothing.

"So this is the mortal my brother has fallen in love with."

I squint in front of me at the muted glow of light. From it, a shadow begins to appear, its outline blurry.

"Pestilence?" I call.

"Not quite."

With each passing second, the shadow deepens, its form sharpening until I can make out the dark shape of a disfigured man.

Wait, not disfigured, *I think as I take in the lumps at his back.* Winged.

Thanatos.

The Fourth Horseman.

He stares down at me, and that's when I realize that I'm lying on the ground—if you can call this insubstantial thing beneath my body ground.

After a moment, the horseman reaches out a hand for me.

"Am I dead?" I ask, ignoring his hand.

"Momentarily."

I'm...dead.

That should bother me—as should the frightening winged horseman in front of me—but for whatever odd reason, I don't mind the situation so much. Maybe it's this place.

Thanatos's hand is still extended, and reluctantly, I take it.

"I need to get back," I say as he pulls me to my feet. "Pestilence needs me."

"Does he, now?" Death cocks his head, his black hair shifting, the waves framing his face like a funeral shroud.

He's quite handsome, I realize. Just like his brother. Only Pestilence's beauty is overwhelming; Death has a tragic, cutting face.

He still hasn't released my hand.

"The last time I saw him, he needed no one." Thanatos continues to study me. "Seems he's...succumbed."

No idea what that means.

"And what about you?" Death asks. "Do you need him?"

Like air to breathe. "Yes."

Death's wings open wide, flapping a little, almost in agitation. "Your body doesn't want you back, Sara Burns."

How does he know my name?

Death's grip tightens, and his wings beat in earnest. Does he mean to carry me off?

"There are other things that await you," he says.

"I want to go back." I can't leave Pestilence. I won't.

Thanatos's onyx eyes search mine. "I could stop this now, and yet, I'm so very...curious." His wings close. "All right. So be it—"

He releases my hand, and I fall away from him.

I stare up at mighty Death the whole way down, even as his form shrinks and the muted light darkens.

I fall farther and farther down...

CHAPTER 47

My chest bows, and I take a sharp, shuddering breath.

Jesus, the pain! Like someone's holding a flaming torch against my chest.

I force my eyes open, taking in the sparse hospital room around me.

Not dead.

The thought seems preposterous after the gunshot wound I sustained.

I move my hand to my hospital gown. Then I shift it aside enough to look at my bandaged chest. There's not much to see besides the linen wrappings, but hot damn does the pain make up for it.

I'm most *definitely* in the land of the living. Being dead couldn't possibly ache this much, and I doubt the afterlife smells this god-awful. The air is thick with that chemical smell all hospitals have—like this is humanity's last rallying cry against disease. And judging by the scent of death that also stains the air, it's a weak rallying cry at that.

It's only then that I realize I have no idea how I came to be in this room, and there's no one else around to fill in the blanks for me.

I listen for a minute, straining my ears to hear anything beyond my room, but all is quiet. The whole place is just one long, terrible silence.

I kick off my sheets, then let out a hiss.

Christ, this injury hurts worse than being dragged behind Pestilence's horse. The pain is everywhere and in everything. Now that I've awakened it, it seems to surround me. I take several swallows of air, closing my eyes against the violent sting of it. When it finally abates, I move again, this time slowly and stiffly.

I clench my teeth against the pain when I make it to the door. Then I have to lean against it for several seconds, just catching my breath. I sway on my feet.

Not going to make it very far past this point.

I still grab for the knob. I turn the cool handle and open the door.

The smell hits me first. Like Death dropped his pants and took a shit.

My throat closes, unwilling to breathe in the fumes. My heart pounds madly as I step into the hallway.

That's when I see them. Dozens of bloated, rotting bodies slump against the walls and lie sprawled across the floor.

I gag at the sight. If there had been anything at all in my stomach, it would've come up.

Why didn't these people evacuate when they had the chance?

They were unwilling or unable to, Burns.

And so they died.

Clomp, clomp, clomp. Hooves click against linoleum. A

moment later, Pestilence rounds the corner, towing Trixie behind him.

I freeze at the sight of the horseman.

Unlike me, who must look like fresh shit (because I certainly feel like it), Pestilence is back to looking angelic—unstained, unsullied, untouchable.

The only thing about him that's different is the harsh set of his features. I didn't realize that hardness was missing from his expression—even when he hated me—until now. But as soon as he sees me, his face softens. Softens completely.

Pestilence releases his horse's reins and swiftly strides over to me. He cups my face and kisses me, his lips lingering. "You're awake—awake and *alive*." He pulls away, his eyes shining as they search mine.

I swallow. By all rights I should be dead.

I *was* dead…wasn't I?

For a moment my mind conjures a brief flash of wings, but then the image slips away.

"I meant to be here when you woke." Pestilence's hands glide over me, like they need to make sure I am, in fact, alive. "I did not leave your side, not until an hour ago when I retrieved Tricksy."

One of his palms moves over my heart. He rests it there, closing his eyes. "I thought you had *died*"—his voice breaks—"that you had slipped beyond my reach."

I touch his cheek. "You saved me."

Pestilence leans into the touch, his eyes opening. "I will *always* save you," he says fervently. "And what you went through will *never* happen again."

A chill runs through me as shadows enter his eyes. His gaze clears a moment later, and I think I might've imagined the whole thing.

Pestilence frowns. "You should not be out of bed, Sara."

I really shouldn't be.

"I'm fine," I say smoothly.

The horseman's frown deepens at the lie.

My gaze moves past his shoulder, where bloated bodies lie about. "What happened?" My voice is low and raspy.

Rather than respond, Pestilence ushers me toward Trixie. I try to stand against him, try to hold out until he gives me answers, but he's much too strong and much too stubborn, so I let him silently lead me back to his steed.

"Hey there," I weakly say to Trixie. Last time I saw the horse, he was all but dead. Now the beast drops his muzzle and nudges me.

Hitched behind Trixie is a wagon, the bed of it lined with a plush mattress, a pillow, and a blanket.

For me.

A hazy memory surfaces.

I love her.

That's what Pestilence said.

I grab his forearm. "I heard you." I swivel to look at Pestilence even as my heart rate picks up. It's not just pain that's now overwhelming me, it's all these exquisite emotions that are too big to fit beneath my skin.

The horseman looks at me quizzically. "Heard what, dear Sara?"

"You *love* me." My voice catches.

I don't question the sentiment like I once did, when he got confused between love and lust. Not after what the two of us just went through.

He pauses. At first I see some hesitancy in his gaze, as though he's not sure how I'm going to react to that news. But whatever expression I wear, it causes his eyes to shine.

"Yes, Sara, I do," he says resolutely. *Fiercely.* Like his love is here and it's here to stay.

Just as I'm about to smile, another memory comes back to me.

Then I hope it hurts to watch her die.

The words have my stomach knotting up.

Did a doctor say that? It seemed like it from the bits I remember of the conversation. And we *are* in a hospital. It would make sense that Pestilence spoke with a doctor...a doctor who wanted Pestilence to understand a thing or two about loss.

That's about when the screams began. I thought maybe they'd been in my head, those screams, but now I look around again. These people have blood coming out their ears and their eyes, their noses and their mouths. Plague victims don't look like that.

"What happened?" I repeat, staring at the bodies. Something is not right here.

"They would not heal you." Pestilence's voice is cold, so cold.

My gaze sweeps the hallway before returning to him. "*All* of them?"

"Enough."

My eyes linger on what used to be a nurse, her eyes, ears, and nose bloody. These deaths weren't from the plague. They were *revenge* killings.

I'm shaking, and I think it's from horror.

"If they all died, then who *did* heal me?" I ask.

"There were a handful I found, and I kept them alive long enough to tend to you."

Long enough.

"Come," he says, cutting off the rest of my questions so he can help me onto the cart.

343

He helps me lie down, and I have to pinch my eyes shut because he's being so gentle, so careful. Even though he recently exterminated a hospital, he handles me like I'm delicate.

"Don't do that, Sara," he says quietly.

He's not going to spare humanity, just me. "Do what?" I force my eyes open.

"Don't act like I'm the monster. They were going to let you die." His gaze burns, like he's still trapped in the flames.

"Not all of them," I whisper.

"Enough."

I glance away from the horseman.

"This is what I was created to do!" he says hotly. "They died fast. Doesn't that count for something?"

It does. And they would've died regardless. It's just that I saw all those bodies, and that is a sight I can never unsee.

It's one thing to watch a family die in their homes, to talk to them and care for them and witness their deaths. It's another to see a building full of rotting corpses, their faces awash with terror. I can't see them for the people they once were, and that makes them all the more grotesque.

I don't respond. Honestly, I'm too damn tired to argue with Pestilence right now.

"So be it," he says.

That's also what he said right before he pressed his will on a room full of doctors and nurses and sick people.

I shiver again, ignoring the frustrated growl that leaves his throat. He stalks back to his horse and swings himself into the saddle. Even the cluck of his tongue sounds irritated.

The cart bumps as it rolls over the bodies. I grimace as it jostles my injuries, the pain so intense it closes my throat, but it's the thought of all those bodies that causes me to dry heave.

He gave those people a quick death; I *shouldn't* be upset. It's just that this time, he was angry when he killed them.

And I'm to blame for that.

For the first time, a dark, insidious realization creeps up on me—

Pestilence's love for me may not save human lives. It may end them all the faster.

CHAPTER 48

The more kilometers we put between us and the hospital, the more my horror fades.

Now what I'm remembering most viscerally are Pestilence's cries as he was tortured and the way those people enjoyed his pain. I can still see the charred husk of the horseman moving toward me, calling to me from the wasteland of his body.

What unimaginable pain he must've been in, and still he clawed his way to me. But he did more than that. I can remember Pestilence's broken body as he carried me in his arms. Arms that were undoubtedly burned away completely in places.

He endured all that to *save* me.

By the time Pestilence pulls Trixie to a stop—in front of a mansion, no less—I'm feeling sorrowful, *penitent*.

When he makes his way to the back of the cart, I can tell he's expecting another argument. His shoulders are rigid, and his mouth is pressed shut. I can almost hear all the arguments and counterarguments he's spent the ride thinking about.

But I don't fight him.

Instead I open my arms.

He hesitates, clearly bewildered and unsure where I'm going with this. At last, he kneels and takes me into his arms, embracing me like I'm life itself. I hold him close, even though my chest feels like it's getting shot all over again.

"I've never been more scared in my life," I whisper.

He nods against me.

"For you, I mean."

He pulls away to meet my eyes.

"I never want to see that happen to you again," I say hoarsely.

Pestilence touches my cheek. "Nor I you." Softly he says, "I thought you were *dead*." His voice breaks upon the last word.

I might've been, I think, remembering the strange vision I had of Thanatos.

He searches my face. "Never have I felt such…fear. It's a horrible emotion."

It is.

"And never have I felt such *hate*."

I don't blame him—what those people did was sickening—and yet I quake at his words.

The horseman closes his eyes, leaning his forehead against mine. When he opens them, they're pained. "This saving and dying business is becoming a disturbing pattern between us."

"It is." But I don't want to dwell on that. I move my hand so I can stroke his pretty lips. "Say it again," I whisper.

His brow furrows. "Say what?"

"Tell me how you feel about me."

His face seems to come alive with realization, his lips curling into a rakish grin before he becomes solemn once more.

"I love you," he says. "Before I even understood the term, I loved you. I love your laughter and your bawdy humor. I love your compassion and your vivacity, your fierceness and your loyalty.

"I meant to make you suffer, and look at me now—desperate to keep you alive and in my arms."

The soft look on his face makes my stomach flip.

A gust of blustery wind tears through my clothes, forcing a shiver out of me, and that's enough to break the spell.

"Let's get you inside," Pestilence says.

"Only if you continue to tell me everything you feel," I say, greedy to hear it all.

"*Gladly*, dear Sara. There are many, many things I have yet to share. I wish for you to know them all."

He begins to slide his arms under my body, clearly meaning to carry me.

I put a hand on his chest. "I can stand," I insist.

Pestilence appears dubious but backs off.

Gingerly, I swing my legs out over the side of the cart, hissing a little as I do so. Black spots dance at the edge of my vision.

Push through it, Burns.

I force myself to my feet, my body screaming in protest, those black spots spreading.

Wasn't this bad at the hospital.

Pestilence stands in front of me, all his earlier tenderness gone, a disapproving frown growing on his face.

I take a step toward him and collapse in his arms.

Trying to walk was a mistake. I see that in hindsight.

Pestilence keeps me bedridden in the (evacuated) mansion

while he plays nursemaid. At first I assume the whole situation is a temporary one. But then one day turns into two, then three, then four, then five—six—seven—nine—thirteen...?

The days tick by as my wound heals, and time begins to bleed together until I can't remember how long we've been here. Long enough for me to discover Pestilence can be bossy and overprotective, particularly when I try to do anything that remotely resembles living.

"I don't remember you being like this when you came close to killing me," I say irritatedly, throwing back my covers on day fifteen—sixteen? twenty?

"Am I to be punished for caring too much?" Pestilence asks from where he stands next to the bed. "Is that what you're suggesting?"

Damn him for twisting my words.

"I am not staying in this shitty bed another hour." It's really not a shitty bed. Pain and idleness have just made me testy, that's all.

"By God, you are, and if I have to hold you down in it, so help me, Sara, I will."

Pushy horsemen also make me testy.

"I'm healed!"

"I fight infection off your body even now! You are *not.*"

"Just let me walk around!"

"So that you collapse on me again? I think not!"

"That was *weeks* ago."

It feels even longer. I *need* to move around.

"You're hardly better now than you were then! Your feeble body is still badly injured."

Feeble body? I seethe. "You're being a fucking bully!"

"I'm your *fucking* savior at the moment." Pestilence looks utterly done with me.

I don't remember being this combustible with him before.

He's scared of you dying, and you're scared of letting him in the way you want to.

He runs a hand through his hair, then glances over his shoulder at the door.

Pestilence seems to deflate. "I will not argue with you," he says. Gone is the heat from his voice. He backs up, then turns on his heel, making a hasty retreat for the exit.

"Wait," I call when he's nearly to the door of the main suite. I don't want to fight.

The horseman pauses.

"I'm sorry. Come back."

And he does, his imposing frame sitting on the mattress. All it takes is for me to show a tiny bit of vulnerability and Pestilence caves, trading in his tirade for soft touches and even softer kisses. He won't go further than that, but it doesn't matter. Right now, all I want to feel is the breadth of his love.

His *love*.

He gives it to me freely, and it feels like the warmth of the sun on my skin.

Our days go on and on like that, spiced with our little dramas and soothed by whispered confessions and touches that never quite go far enough. At the back of my mind, I keep waiting for the home's owners to return, but they never do, and so our stay goes on and on, falling into a pattern of sorts.

My bullet holes go from open wounds to raspberry-colored scars, the skin cratered and shiny. I now look like a creature of the apocalypse, my body a map of old wounds. I will never be like Pestilence, whose perfect form has recovered from brutalities without so much as a scar. A petty part of me mourns the sweet smoothness of my skin, but the tougher part of me, the Sara motherfucking Burns who fought fires and shot a horseman from his steed to protect her town, is simply happy to have escaped death.

I shouldn't have. Several times over I shouldn't have. And now I'm honest enough with myself to admit Pestilence has always been the reason why. He's saved my life over and over. And right now, his one reason for being here—to spread plague—has been put on hold.

All so Pestilence can care for me.

Love has a funny way of rearranging priorities. It's begun to rearrange mine.

And yet…I feel uneasy about this temporary respite. For as doting and infuriating and caring as Pestilence is, that hardness I first saw in the hospital still lingers in each one of his features.

We stay in that abandoned mansion for so long that the world thinks he's gone. I happen to know this because among other things the house has a functioning television.

Even more shocking than news of the horseman's "disappearance" is just how much reporters know about me. There are a couple of blurry photos of me and the horseman, one from when I was still officially his captive, my wrists cuffed, and a later one taken while I sat astride his horse.

The reporters don't know what to make of me. They don't know whether I am his prisoner or his lover (C, all of the above) or what happened to us. The whole thing appears terribly confusing for them—should they laud me or condemn me? They've settled on pity.

Pestilence comes into the bedroom where I'm cooped up—still in fucking bed—his large frame filling the doorway. He removes his bow and quiver and sets them down next to the doorway. Then off goes his armor. He leaves his crown on his head, his hair windswept beneath it.

I know without asking that he's been patrolling the grounds. Not that he needs to. Anyone who comes remotely close to this place will fall ill. I think he does it more because he's restless. The need to move through all the lands of man and spread disease must eat away at him.

He is not a patient man. Except, of course, when it comes to me and my oh-so-feeble human body.

He sits on the edge of the bed, the look in his eyes raising my gooseflesh. There's love there, but beneath it, there's that same coldness. I don't know what to make of it.

Pestilence lifts the edge of my shirt and runs a finger over the uneven flesh. He leans forward and kisses one of the scars. "To think that if just one of these projectiles hit somewhere else, it could've killed you."

I notice the very slight shiver that courses through his body at the mention.

"How do you feel?" he asks.

"Healed."

Pestilence narrows his eyes at me. It's the same answer I've been giving him every day for *weeks*.

And it's been true for a while, but try talking sense into a being who cannot die and does not intuitively know when a human is completely healed.

I grab his hand and tug him down next to me. For the first week or so that I was healing, he took to lying in bed with me, holding me close, his hand resting over my heart just so he could feel the steady beat of it. Even once he assured himself that I was going to pull through, he still would come into bed with me, pressing his body close and falling asleep when he let himself.

But sleeping and cuddling was *all* he dared to do with me. Now I roll onto him.

"Sara," he protests.

"I'm not a porcelain doll," I say, moving to straddle his hips. "I won't break that easily."

"You and I both know that's not tr—"

I silence him with a long slow kiss. I think he wants to resist, but Pestilence is still so shaken by *the mysteries of the flesh* (as he calls it) that he doesn't do much to stop this.

His hands come up to cradle my face as my lips part his. I spend a few seconds simply breathing him in before my tongue presses against his. The moment it does so, his hands slide to my upper arms, gripping me tightly.

My own hands delve into his hair, knocking his crown askew. He has enough sense to set it on the bedside table.

I roll my hips against him, and he lets out a groan. "Sara, you are still heal—"

"Do I look like I'm in pain?" I ask.

He frowns at me but doesn't argue. Nor does he fight me when I remove first his shirt, then the rest of his clothes. But he doesn't exactly help me either.

At some point, however, his tune changes. He begins to meet me touch for touch, kiss for kiss, until he's leading the charge. His hands rush over me, and there's just not enough skin for his rough palms to cover.

He hooks his arm around me and then he flips us, leaving me to gaze up at him.

So damn beautiful. I don't know if I'll ever get over the sight of him.

Expertly, Pestilence removes my clothes before tossing them carelessly aside.

Once I'm naked, his gaze rakes over my body, halting at the

juncture between my thighs. He dips down, pressing his lips to my core. Reflexively, I buck up against him. He spreads my legs apart and continues to kiss me right—between—my—thighs.

Christ.

"Wh-what are you doing?" I ask, breathless. I begin to sit up, only for him to push me back down to the bed.

"I assume it's obvious," he says. He nips at me, and oh Jesus, he is so fucking dirty. *Where* did he learn to be this dirty?

His tongue comes out, and he tastes me.

I moan, my back arching off the bed.

"This is how you kill me," I murmur.

He pulls away instantly. The moment he takes in my flushed cheeks and dazed look, his worried expression morphs into one of masculine satisfaction.

I'm pretty sure no one has given Pestilence anatomy lessons (aside from me), but he's figured out pretty quick that my clit is the source of all the goodness and wonder in the world.

The horseman returns to his ministrations, and his clever tongue has me bucking and writhing beneath him. His warm breath puffs against me as he laughs. Pestilence might've once been a newb at this, but the pupil is definitely surpassing the master in record time.

"Ugh," I moan. "Ssss—stop. Too much. Stop."

At my words, Pestilence hesitates.

"Oh God, *don't you dare stop,*" I say.

I feel the breath of his laughter again, and then he's back to sucking and licking, and this time he doesn't stop.

He keeps going and going and—

I let out a cry, my hips rising off the bed as sensation rips through me, blinding in its intensity.

Pestilence doesn't give me time to fully come down. He moves up my body. "You've convinced me."

"Huh?"

He wraps my legs around his waist. I feel his cock right at my opening, hard and insistent.

"You're healed."

And then he drives himself inside.

Another moan slips out of me as his thickness stretches me. It's been lifetimes since we did this. Pestilence has been so careful not to hurt me or jostle my wounds that it's a shock he's now suddenly *in* me.

It's an even bigger surprise to feel his frenetic energy. His movements are not slow and reverent or even playful and exploratory. He pistons into me like he can't drive himself deep enough, and he gathers me to him like he can't hold me tight enough. His mouth sears my skin as he kisses my shoulder, one of my bullet wounds, my throat, my lips.

He grips my legs, pulling me closer.

Thump—thump—thump!

The headboard smacks into the wall again and again and again until paint and a little bit of plaster chip away.

Pestilence's eyes glint brightly. And it's not wholly love I'm seeing. It's love and anguish and a possessive desperation and—strangest of all—an apology.

I can't make much of it now, however. Not with his cock filling me up and rubbing me down in all the right places.

For a second time, I tip over the edge. I clench around him, pulling him close to me. With a groan, he comes on the wings of my climax, rocking into me like his very life depends on it.

Once he begins to come down, he kisses me everywhere, his lips brushing over every bit of exposed flesh. All that raw masculine energy is converting into something painfully sweet and reverent.

He gathers me to him, cradling my body against his own. There's nothing like being pressed skin to skin with this man to make me feel utterly at ease with the world. My eyelids lower.

Still haven't figured out the contraception issue, I think lazily.

Pestilence brushes a kiss along my temple.

He'd make a good dad.

Can't believe I just had that thought…

I nestle closer to him as I let myself drift off.

One of his fingers traces over my stomach.

His body slides away from mine, and his voice filters in from the edge of sleep. "I'm sorry, Sara. I was waiting for this, and I thought maybe…maybe you getting better would change my mind, but it hasn't. It's only made me surer of what I need to do."

I grope for his hand, but it's gone.

CHAPTER 49

The next morning, I make my way into the kitchen, trying not to let Pestilence see just how fatigued that simple action makes me.

I shouldn't have bothered. For once the horseman isn't even paying attention. The television in the living room is on, and Pestilence stands in front of it, his arms folded, staring at the screen grimly.

I glance at the TV, just to see what has tied up his attention.

"Breaking news: virulent outbreak of messianic fever along the West Coast and Pacific Northwest, spreading into Mexico. State and local governments are rapidly trying to quarantine infected areas. No known sighting of the horseman yet. Please stay in your homes and avoid city centers. I repeat, please stay in your homes and avoid city centers. To all those affected: our prayers and thoughts are with you."

My stomach bottoms out.

I stand there for a long time, not talking, not reacting,

just…*staring* at the television dumbly. The report replays five different ways, the information regurgitated to fill the empty minutes. They show the pictures of Central Park taken after Pestilence passed through the city months ago, with its mass graves filled with bodies. Then images from Toronto and Montreal appear, the few photos anyone has of the fever. There are even a couple from Vancouver and Seattle, places I saw with my own two eyes.

But now new footage joins the old. A shaky video of a hospital in San Francisco appears, the place filled with the dying. Another from Los Angeles, where people lie in the streets, their eyes sunken and their faces flushed with the beginnings of fever.

San Francisco, Los Angeles. Those places are *states* away.

I grow cold.

I manage to rip my eyes away from the screen, and now, *now* Pestilence is looking at me. There's still that damn apology in his eyes but no remorse. *None.* In its place is a familiar coldness.

My throat works. I don't want to ask because asking makes it real, and this can't be real. The words come anyway.

"What did you do?" I whisper.

"My purpose."

CHAPTER 50

I can't breathe.

At this very moment, the entire West Coast of North America is a wasteland.

In my mind's eye, I see all those dead bodies lying in the hospital's hallway. I try to imagine a city's worth, two cities' worth—hell, entire *states'* worth—but I can't. The scale of that devastation is unimaginable. My mind won't let me comprehend that sort of loss.

Among all those millions are mothers, daughters, sons, brothers, friends, lovers, grandparents, children, babies. People who mean something to one another. Innocent, kind people. People deserving of life. Right now, they're all dying.

Pestilence couldn't have done this. Pestilence, who questions the morality of his actions. Pestilence, who loves me.

He couldn't have.

The two of us stare each other down. I expect to see something defensive in Pestilence's eyes—he always had to explain himself in the past—but there's nothing there. No guilt, no defensiveness, no stubborn tenacity.

His cool gaze is steady.

Because he *did* do this. More than that, he *planned* this. All the signs have been there. His dark moods, the ice in his blue eyes, the half-remembered apology he murmured to me yesterday when he left my side.

"*How?*" The scale of the devastation is so much larger than ever before. Before, Pestilence had to pass through a town to infect it. Now his reach seems boundless, stretching thousands of kilometers away from us.

He must understand what I'm asking because he says, "I've always had this reach. I just never felt the urge to exert it before."

Not until me. Somehow, I'm the spark that ignited this terrible deed.

"Undo it," I whisper.

"It's done," he says, his expression uncompromising.

I'm shaking my head. It can't be *done*. I *refuse* to believe that.

"You cured me of infection, you can undo this," I insist, my voice cracking.

I can't be the only human left alive along the West Coast. That's its own kind of hell.

"But I won't."

"*Please.*"

He flinches at that word—*please*. It started as a curse spoken between us, a plea voiced only so it could be denied. But somewhere along the way, *please* became redemptive.

Only now, Pestilence doesn't want to be redeemed.

Damn it, I can still feel a part of him between my thighs. I'm sore from all the places his body scoured mine today

360

and yesterday, his lovemaking as intense as it was passionate. He can't have left my side only to curse a good portion of North America.

"Please, Pestilence. Please...*love*."

Names mean so much. A rose may smell the same no matter what name you give it, but how you think of it may change. And I think of Pestilence differently—I have for a while. But to call him by a name of my own choosing, to give him an endearment and show him he's more than his namesake...I haven't been brave enough to do so until now.

But there's nothing left to fear anymore. Not in the face of this situation.

The horseman stills. I see that coldness crack in his eyes.

"You didn't expect that, did you?" I say. "Me loving you." I know I hadn't. And I don't know in what quiet hour the realization snuck up on me, but it did. "Maybe I'm a fool and a traitor, but I'm *yours*." I'm blinking back tears. "Damn it, you can't do this."

He takes a step toward me, then another, his eyes dying a little bit, like he wants to touch me but knows I won't let him. Not now, with all this blood on his hands.

Never bothered you before, Burns.

But that was back when I thought I could change him—stop him.

Should've known better.

"I could've lived with what those men did to me, cruel as it was," Pestilence says.

My mind flashes to the horseman tied to the phone pole, most of his face gone.

"But when they shot you—" His voice cuts off with emotion, and I realize my fatal error. "You should've never shown me love, dear Sara," he says.

This whole time, I assumed love would redeem the horseman and save us all. I should've known it would only ever damn us to our grisly fates.

"If you now understand loss," I say, "then you know what you're taking from these people."

He clenches his jaw. "It is no more than they deserve."

"No more than they *deserve*?" I say, aghast. "Who are you talking about? Rob? Ruth? *Me*?"

Pestilence's mouth thins. "You seem to think arguing about this will change these people's fate."

"You can change." I shake my head bitterly. "I don't know why you think you're incapable of it."

"People change, Sara, but horsemen don't. It doesn't matter what you think of me. I am and will always be Pestilence the Conqueror."

He's not going to bend. I can see it now. I should've seen it before, back when I could've protected my heart a little better.

"What happens now?" I ask. Immediately, I regret the question, my stomach roiling with dread.

"The world ends."

"And me?" I say, the desolation already creeping in.

"You will stay with me."

He doesn't ask it; he doesn't even say it as a challenge. It's spoken with complete authority.

I nod slowly.

Pestilence must sense something is wrong because he takes another step toward me.

"*Don't*," I say.

If he tries to make either of us feel better—I swear it will break the last of me. And there's so little left to break.

I glance around.

Can't be in the same room as him. I'm suffocating on all this tragedy.

I turn on my heel, eager to get away from him.

"Sara," he calls out before I can escape. His voice is so goddamned patient.

I pause. "You once told me names don't matter," I say, my back to him, "that what *I* called *you* doesn't matter."

I glance at Pestilence over my shoulder.

Love. I think we can both hear my earlier endearment in the air between us.

His expression is wary when he inclines his head. "I remember."

"You're wrong, you know," I say. "They do matter."

Pestilence is the very worst of his nature. I glimpsed the very best of it, but that part of him, that future, is no more than a whisper of a possibility, like smoke dissipating into the wind.

I leave him at that.

CHAPTER 51

I walk away from him long enough to grab my things—what little I have. It's hardly more than the shirt on my back.

I stare at the bedroom for a long time, feeling like my heart is unmaking itself one piece at a time.

Why couldn't you have fallen in love with a normal boy and then died a normal death alongside him? Why did you have to choose a horseman? Why did you have to insert yourself between him and the world?

My time with him has been a deadly tug-of-war between love and loyalty. How I ever deluded myself that it *wouldn't* come to this, I don't know.

I pull on my boots, grab my borrowed coat, and then head for the front door.

Pestilence is where I left him, still standing guard by the television, still consumed with his own wrath.

I walk right past him.

"Where are you going?" he calls out, his voice ringing with authority. He doesn't sound scared or lost or uncertain.

Does he seriously have no idea?

Ignoring him, I reach for the front door and slip out.

Outside—*fuck*, it's cold. I stagger a little at the temperature. It's a wet, biting chill that wriggles under your skin and seeps into you. Already my ears sting. I bring up the hood of my jacket.

You'll never survive this, weakened as you are. Ill-equipped as you are.

The door opens behind me. "*Where* are you going?"

I stop at Pestilence's voice. Now there's something to it besides pent-up rage. Something that is still too confident to be worry. I think it may be shock and a touch of confusion.

"To rejoin humanity," I say.

"I haven't released you."

"I wasn't aware I was your prisoner," I say.

Clearly, he seems to have forgotten this little detail.

"You are *mine*."

I pull my jacket closer to me. "I am *no one's*," I say vehemently.

The horseman scowls at that but doesn't try to argue the point.

I appraise him. "Just say I stayed. What will you do when all the people are gone?"

"I will endure."

"What will you do when *I'm* gone?"

"I will keep you alive," he insists.

I search his face. "Even if you could, even if you could protect me from every attempt on my life—because there will be more so long as I'm with you—you wouldn't be able to keep me alive forever. Eventually, I'd age. I'd age and die, and then you'd be alone again, only now there'd be no more humans, just you."

"And my brothers," he adds quietly.

I throw up my hands. "All right, you and your murderous brothers." Brothers who have been absent these long years. "But other than them, you'd be alone."

My body trembles from the cold, and Pestilence's eyes go right to the action. "Cease this foolishness, Sara. Come inside," he says gently. "I will warm you up."

I give him an incredulous look. "Do you still not get it? You're killing off *everyone*. Did you seriously think I would stay with you after something like this?"

"You stayed with me before," the horseman says heatedly, but I don't miss the spark of fear at the back of his eyes.

I let out a hollow laugh. "That was when I thought you hated what you were doing to my world."

Back when I thought you could change.

Isn't that the most horrible detail of all? I finally got what I wanted—Pestilence *did* change, just not for the better.

"I'm doing this to avenge you!"

"I never asked for your vengeance," I say. "I asked for your *mercy*."

Pestilence flinches at the word as though I slapped him. It's the very word that saved my life the night I tried to kill the horseman. The word that's saved me every night since.

Mercy.

"Did you ever think maybe your God's *mercy* was never meant for me?" I ask. "That maybe it was meant for everyone else?"

No, he hadn't, if his expression is anything to go by.

I turn, beginning to walk away, only to feel the warm press of Pestilence's fingers in the crook of my arm.

"If I have to tie you to me, I *will*," Pestilence says. "But I will not let you go."

I swivel to face him. For all his lofty demands, his face betrays his true feelings. I can see stark panic in his expression.

He hadn't anticipated this.

"Pestilence," I say, my voice calming, "you can force me to stay with you, but you can't make me want to be with you."

"But you do want to be with me," he insists. "You called me 'love.'"

I look away. "I did."

"And you love me."

My heart beats faster. I may not have said the three words, but the horseman speaks the truth. My eyes move to him. "I do," I agree. "And it is not enough."

He staggers back a step. "Not *enough*?"

I think I may be hurting him worse than any weapon ever did.

"It's not enough to overcome whatever else lies in your heart," I say. "You clearly hate humankind more than you care for me."

Pestilence's nostrils flare, but he bites back a response.

He doesn't deny it. Ouch.

"Love is supposed to bring out the best parts of you," I continue, reminding him of our talk shortly after Ruth and Rob passed. "Not the worst," I add quietly.

"I did this *because* I love you," he says fervently. There's more fear in his eyes than before.

"Love doesn't work like that."

But, of course, there are other things that go hand in hand with love—great, terrible things. Things that, for the first time ever, Pestilence is beginning to feel.

You let him into the Garden of Eden. You let him taste forbidden fruit. You gave him the knowledge of good and evil, and now you are both paying for it.

I take a step back, committing his face to memory.

Need to leave now, before you cave and return to him. I'd never forgive myself then.

My heart, however, feels like it's being ripped in two at the prospect of leaving.

"Goodbye, Pestilence."

After rotating around, I force myself to start down the steps leading away from the mansion.

I haven't taken more than five paces before the horseman is on me. He scoops me up and carries me inside, kicking the front door closed as he goes.

"What are you doing?" I protest, squirming in his arms.

No response.

Now I truly struggle. "Let me go."

He puts me down in the foyer. The room spins a little once I'm on my feet.

So weak. Too weak.

Can't stay here though.

I head back to the door, and again he picks me up and bodily moves me away.

Again, as soon as he sets me down, I move toward the door.

He cuts me off. "Sara, I cannot let you leave."

He's begging me with his eyes, and I know he sees what I feel: I'm not strong enough, *healed* enough. All those weeks of traveling, all those wounds, even with the rest, my body isn't ready for more. And still I drive it forward.

"Pestilence, don't make this worse than it already is," I practically plead. "I'm leaving, either with your blessing or against your will, but I won't stay here any longer."

The look on his face pulverizes the last of me. I can see his heart breaking. That raw grief lingers for just a moment, and then his features harden.

Without a word, he picks me up again.

"What are you doing?" I struggle in his arms. "Pestilence, put me down!"

Ignoring my demands, he moves into the main bedroom and deposits me onto the bed.

By the time I scramble off it—taking an extra few seconds to let the vertigo pass—he's already made it to the door. With a parting look, he slips out, closing it behind him.

Rushing after him, I grab the doorknob. I twist it, but the door won't open. The horseman must be holding it closed.

"Pestilence, let me go." My voice rises with panic.

He doesn't seriously mean to keep me here, does he?

"You *will* forgive me," he says quietly from the other side of the door.

"Let me go!" I shout louder.

But he doesn't.

———————

Pestilence boards up the main bedroom's windows and blockades all the doors leading out. Not before I rush outside a few times and he has to drag me back in, but eventually, he manages to bar all the exits, leaving me trapped inside.

And so I'm back to being his prisoner.

At least the horseman is smart enough to keep his distance. I only see him a few times throughout the rest of the day, when he drops off food and water, his eyes sad and haunted.

I think maybe whatever madness came over Pestilence will wear off. That he'll eventually unbar the windows and open the door and beg for my forgiveness.

But it never happens. One day melts into the next, and he stays away, coming to me only so he can feed me.

Not even at night does he slip into my room to express his tortured feelings for me or to fall asleep pressed against my back.

My body misses him; my heart misses him. The latter is dying beneath my rib cage, hating his betrayals yet wanting him still.

I don't try to escape. What's the use? I can't slip past Pestilence unnoticed.

I try not to think about all the millions of dead people that must be rotting right where they died. The TV stays off for that very reason. I can't bear to watch the news and see all those bodies. Not when I played a role (albeit unwittingly) in their deaths.

That leaves me to thumb through the few books in the room or to recite poetry aloud from memory.

Sometimes I can physically feel Pestilence nearby—listening to the sound of my voice, lingering outside my door. The air feels saturated with all the things left unspoken and unfinished between us. Things that have been left to decay alongside all those dead bodies.

Life goes on like this for days and then a whole week.

Is this truly going to become our new normal? Pestilence keeping me like a caged bird, fated neither to die nor to fully live?

When the door opens on day eight, Pestilence looks beaten down. His blue eyes are dim, and his golden-blond hair doesn't have its usual luster.

"I cannot do this anymore," he admits. "I surrender."

I freeze where I sit on the bed.

Pestilence the Conqueror *surrendering*?

He removes his crown from his head and tosses it on the floor between us. "It's yours," he says bitterly. "I may have laid claim to the world, but I've lost you, the only thing I ever really wanted."

My pulse gallops as I stare first at the discarded crown, then up at the man who wore it.

"You are free to leave," he says. "I will not stop you."

His eyes are bleak. Gone are the shadows in his eyes, but so is whatever spark of hope once lay in them. When they meet mine, he looks at me like he's drowning.

I should feel exalted, vindicated in some small way, but it's just one more pain to add to the rest.

For several seconds I don't move.

"Damn it, Sara, if you want your freedom, leave before I come to my senses."

I slide off the bed, grabbing my things one by one, keeping a wary eye on him. I half expect him to slam the door shut in my face at any moment. This must be some trick.

But it doesn't appear to be.

I step past the threshold to the room, pausing to face him.

"Go, and join your doomed race," he says, his gaze reluctantly meeting mine. How it now blisters! He has pain to match my own. "But don't expect me to kill you."

Too late, it seems, he's figured out the meaning of mercy.

After everything Pestilence has done, I don't expect leaving to hurt me so bad. I thought my heart had been abused enough to forget it belongs to the horseman.

I was wrong.

I don't look at Pestilence when I leave him at the house's entrance. Walking away from him pains me enough. Seeing whatever emotion fills his face could make me waver. The horseman no longer wears his crown. It still lies, forgotten, in the bedroom.

I head for the street, each step cutting me deeper and deeper. I've lost everything else—family, friends, neighbors. Leaving Pestilence is going to bleed out the last parts of me.

Where should I go? How many kilometers will I have to walk to get to the living? Will I die before then? I know Pestilence won't allow me to succumb to plague, but there are other ways to die. I could starve, perish from the elements.

And if I don't die, what then?

One step at a time, Burns.

It's only once I reach the road that I turn back around. The mansion we've been staying in perches on a small rise. Standing like a sentinel at its threshold is the horseman.

Pestilence watches me, his face solemn. For a moment, I think I see hope spark in his eyes.

He thinks I'm changing my mind.

Steeling myself, I face the street once more and walk away.

CHAPTER 52

I don't hear the news. Not for weeks and weeks.

Still, I should've known. The truth was so obviously in front of me.

Instead it takes an outpost owner near the Canadian border to convince me beyond a shadow of a doubt.

"That blighted horseman's gone. I swear it on the newly dead, he is," the man says, leaning on the pine countertop as he adds up my things.

The sight of the outpost owner himself, *alive* and bustling about his store, is surprising enough, but then again, I ran into others on my way back up the coast. I assumed their presence had to do with Pestilence spreading his plague *solely* southward.

Now I stare at the store owner, his news not computing.

The world thought Pestilence was gone when we were holed up inside that mansion, but once I left, I assumed he'd resume his travels.

"You mean there haven't been any new sightings of him?" I ask dumbly.

He shakes his head.

No new sightings of him. An unpleasant sensation twists my gut, but I can't say what causes it.

Maybe there's no longer anyone left alive *to* spot him. The territory from Washington to California is vast...vast and full of the dead.

"Have you not heard?" the owner asks when he notices my surprise.

"Last news I received was that Oregon, California, and parts of Mexico were infected," I say. Even now a chill slides through me at the thought. I played a role in that.

The man lets out a wheezy laugh, pulling a slim case from beneath his counter. After opening it, he takes the raw ingredients from inside and begins to hand roll a cigarette. "Oh, you've missed so much."

Intentionally.

I made a habit of avoiding small talk like this, the guilt its own sort of illness. But now that we're on the subject of Pestilence, a sick sort of curiosity comes over me. I find I need to know how much of the world still lives—and how my horseman fared.

Hearing Pestilence hasn't resurfaced since I left him...

The loss feels physical, like a limb's been lopped off.

The outpost owner finishes rolling his cigarette, licking the edge of the white paper to seal the seam. "Pleased to tell you that all the sick recovered." He shakes his head. "Damn miracle it is." The man strikes a match and holds the flame to the end of his smoke before inhaling a grateful drag. "I'm not a praying man myself, but even I sent one up when I heard the news. Thought He'd left us to die."

Wait—*what*?

I stare at him in shock.

All the sick recovered.

Can't seem to catch my breath.

"You mean...all the sick—they...*lived*?" I say incredulously.

It cannot be. I was *with* the horseman. I saw his anger, witnessed his unbending will.

No way had he changed his mind.

"Yep," the man says cheerily enough, blowing smoke out the side of his mouth. "Even us up north here recovered—news didn't bother mentioning that." He frowns, like that's some great travesty when, oh my God, all those millions *lived*.

"Fucking plague came back right as I was reopening my store," he continues. "Thought I'd caught my death."

There's a pain in my chest that's equal parts joy and anguish. I don't want to believe him because if I've misunderstood, the disappointment may crush me alive.

I brace my hands on the countertop as I sway a little.

My God.

Pestilence *retracted* his plague. I don't know how, but he did.

He must've done it while I was confined to that damn room. I thought the worst of him then, and all the while he was *curing* the plague he'd brought down upon the masses.

The only thing besides his love that I ever wanted. He gave it to me.

Had I but turned on the fucking TV, I would've seen this.

Pestilence stopped the plague, and I still left him.

I swallow back a choked cry.

Why didn't he tell me? By God, that would've changed *everything*.

"And the fever," I ask, somehow finding my voice, "has it spread since then?"

Have to be sure I understand this correctly.

The outpost owner frowns, considering my words. "Not that I've heard, though who knows where the world's at these days? It hasn't been back around these parts, and that's good enough for me."

I thank the man for the news and walk away from the outpost in a daze.

My last encounter with Pestilence fills my mind.

I surrender, he said, casting his crown aside.

He had already reversed the plague by then.

I may have laid claim to the world, but I've lost you, the only thing I ever really wanted.

Why didn't he say anything? Did he think I was watching the news in that room, that I'd learned he'd cured them all and still decided to walk away?

These thoughts gut me. Because I'm still in love with Pestilence, and now, after vindicating himself, he's gone.

CHAPTER 53

By the time I return to my hometown of Whistler, I hear enough reports and firsthand accounts to believe the incredible.

The plague really *did* disappear over the course of days.

Just...*poof*, gone, and the horseman with it. I try not to think about that. My heart aches enough as it is.

I learn that, like me, people didn't believe the news—not at first, at least. Weeks without incident had to pass before anyone dared to hope that the messianic fever was truly over and that the horseman had vanished.

Then people began to hope—in that ridiculous way we do—that other things would return to the way they once were. That electricity would work as it ought, that batteries would hold a charge, and perhaps even the internet would eventually come back.

They hoped in vain.

The world never went back to the way it was. I doubt it ever will.

Without the horseman by my side, no one recognizes me as the girl he kept. Despite the few blurry photos that once circulated, not a single person has connected the dots.

When I finally arrive home, I get a hero's welcome— the firefighter who took a stand against the horseman, the woman they all thought long dead.

My father holds me for a long time, and my mother openly weeps. I'm blubbering like a baby when I see them both alive.

Plague never got them.

Our reunion is touching and ridiculous and beautiful, and I just fucking love my parents.

When I return to the fire station, Luke is the first one to see me. It's almost comical the way the shock registers on his face.

"Holy motherfucking shit! *Burns!*" He nearly overturns the chair he sits in when he sees me. "You're alive!"

"So are you!"

It's startling to see him after all this time. He looks a little leaner, not that I should be surprised. Living through a Canadian winter post-arrival is difficult enough. Living through a Canadian winter *in* the frozen wilderness is nearly impossible. And that's what he and all these other survivors had to do to escape the plague.

Luke's exclamation draws the attention of others, who are soon thumping me on the back and pulling me into hugs, Felix among them. They all escaped with their lives, all of them except for...

"Briggs?" I ask, my eyes searching for him.

Could just be his day off.

Someone sobers up. "Didn't make it."

"He...didn't?" My mood plummets. I was supposed to be the one who kicked the bucket, not him.

Surely he had enough time to escape.

"They needed help at the hospital. He came back early to aid the sick."

And he died for it.

The more I look around, the more I notice other missing men. "Who else?"

"Sean and Rene. Blake. Foster."

So many.

"All died in the line of duty," someone else adds.

I should've known. First responders will always put their lives on the line for others.

I get that itchy feeling beneath my skin. *It should've been me.* A dozen times over.

Pestilence stopped the plague altogether because of you, a quiet voice whispers at the back of my mind. Of course, that thought comes with its own strange pain.

"How did you escape the horseman?" Felix asks.

They're all looking at me.

I've dreaded this question since I realized there would be survivors in Whistler. There's so much I have to answer for, and I don't know what to include and how much to say.

So I keep it simple. "The horseman…showed me mercy."

Surprisingly, life returns to normal. Or at least as normal as I can expect these days.

I move back into my apartment, though I spend an agonizing few weeks carting my belongings from my parents' house—where they were brought when I was presumed dead—back to my place.

In the wake of my return, people have questions—*so many questions.*

How did you survive the horseman?
Where have you been all these months?
Why did it take you so long to come home?

For most people, I get good at nonanswers. For those who matter, I give them half-truths. At some point, I can't *not*; the truth is suffocating the life out of me.

But even then, I don't share everything—like how I fell in love with a monster, or how in the end he saved all our miserable lives. How I recited poetry to him and felt him change from a nightmare into a man.

I can't shake the loneliness I now feel. I first noticed it on the road home, when I bunked in abandoned houses or trekked over kilometers of unbroken snow. And now that I'm home, it seems to rush in from all sides. I'm drowning in my loneliness, and no amount of company can banish the sensation.

Not even this, however, can compare to the horrible feeling of falling back into an old life when everything is now different. Like trying to fit a square peg into a round hole. I hate it, but there's nothing better for me anywhere else, and so I stay here in this drab apartment, and each day I go to the fire station and pretend I'm okay when I'm not.

I'm really not.

Sometimes my mind wanders to what impossibilities might have been if Pestilence were a human man. What it would be like to be with him without the baggage. But then, if he were human, Pestilence wouldn't be *Pestilence*, so I guess it doesn't do to ponder the possibility.

Some things are just not meant to be, I suppose.

Now, glass of home-brewed and very suspect wine in hand, I reread a much-loved book of mine. Pre-Pestilence, I might've flipped through my collection of Shakespeare or

Lord Byron (hard-core lit bitch right here), but the greats are ruined for me. Particularly Poe. His dark soul and macabre heart are too similar to mine.

A knock at the door has me setting my book aside.

While I nodded, nearly napping, suddenly there came a tapping, / As of some one gently rapping, rapping at my chamber door.

Shut up, Poe, no one asked for your commentary.

I may legit be losing my mind.

Standing, I glance from the wine in my hand to the shotgun propped against the edge of the couch. I have two hands, and I need one to open the door, so what will it be—the gun or the wine?

Tough decision. Night visitors are always suspect, and I'm not super trusting these days, but…in the end, *wine*.

Glass in hand, I open my front door.

"Sara."

I drop the wine, the sound of shattering glass barely registering.

Pestilence fills the doorway, his golden-blond hair framing his face like a corona. His crown is gone, his bow is gone, his golden armor is gone. Even his clothes are different, not dark and pristine. He wears a flannel shirt and jeans, and on his feet are scuffed *human* boots.

"*Pestilence*," I breathe, my heart thundering. *Can't be real.*

"I am Pestilence no longer," he says, continuing to stand there, not daring to come any closer.

It's so unbearably hard, staring at him. He still looks like an angel, even in human clothes. Will he ever *not* look like a divine thing?

But it's more than his sheer beauty. It took a long time to admit to myself just how far I fell for him. Too late I realized I loved everything about him—his heart, his mind, his very essence. But even as I realized it, I mourned it because by then he was gone.

And now I don't know what to do, whether to close the distance between us or keep away from him. I don't know in what state he's coming to me.

I left him...a broken thing.

I bite the inside of my cheek. "They said you just disappeared."

He searches my face, and maybe I'm just imagining it, but he looks like he's trying to memorize each one of my features.

"I can do many things, Sara, but disappear isn't one of them."

A surge of relief follows that statement. He can't just vanish and leave me.

I stand aside, opening the door wider. "Want to come in?"

Pestilence's gaze moves to the apartment beyond me, his eyes sparking with interest and a want so fierce, it makes my knees weak.

My horseman came back for me.

Carefully, he steps inside, glass crunching under his boot as he does so. His attention is everywhere, taking in each little piece of my humble life.

"Where are your things?" I ask softly as I close the door, my eyes scouring him again. The bow that's never more than an arm's span away from him, the crown that almost always decorates his head, the golden armor that makes him look ever so otherworldly—it's all gone.

I surrender, he said.

He swivels to face me. "My purpose is served."

What does that even mean? And why does that fill me with dread?

"And Trixie?" Had the creature served his purpose too? That would kill me.

Pestilence jerks his chin over his shoulder. Only now, when I manage to tear my eyes off the horseman, do I bother to look out my window. In the darkness beyond, I catch the barest shadow of his mount.

Trixie Skillz, the steed whose back I rode on all those weeks, snuffles in the darkness, his reins looped about a broken lamppost.

I turn back around only to find Pestilence standing close, his eyes devouring me like a starving man.

"How did you find me?" I ask.

"I never left you."

My brow furrows.

"Come now, Sara," he says at my confusion. "I wasn't just going to let you slip out of my life *that* easily. I'm far too stubborn and not nearly noble enough."

What is he saying? That the entire time I made my way back here, he shadowed me?

"Besides," he continues, "you were still recovering, and I didn't trust your fragile body to make the journey back."

I can't take in enough air.

He cared. Even when he thought I didn't, he never gave up.

"So you followed me?"

He nods.

And I never knew.

"Why didn't you ever show yourself?"

Pestilence glances down at his boots. "You made your decision. I wanted to respect that." He laughs self-deprecatingly, toeing a stray piece of broken glass. "But I couldn't, in the end."

And I'm so glad for it.

"You stopped the plague," I say.

He meets my gaze, his expression turning guarded. "I did."

"Why?" I ask, searching his face.

Pestilence's eyes are deep and true. "Because love brings out the best in you."

I swallow thickly. If the past couple of months have been a nightmare, this is some wonderful dream, one where I get everything I want.

I don't trust it. I've come to find that things that appear too good to be true often are. Why should the one thing I want more than any other follow a different logic?

"Back at that last house, why didn't you tell me you cured the sick?" I ask. That would've saved months of this agony.

Pestilence's gaze is tortured. "My mind was a mess at the time. I...had not committed to my actions, not even after I set them in motion. Nor after I let you go. It took weeks of contemplation for me to come to terms with my decision. My heart spoke first—my mind had to follow."

His expression turns fierce. "I should never have let you go. I should have listened to you, spoken with you, fought for you. I'm only now learning how very complex humans are."

My heart beats madly at his words. Hope surges through my veins, and that scares the crap out of me because all hope does is prime you for a letdown, and I'm not sure I can take another letdown.

"And the plague—it's gone for good?" I ask.

Pestilence gives me a sad smile. "Sara, there will always be sickness and disease—that I cannot change. But my divinely wrought plague will never infect another. I have...served my purpose," he says again.

And again that one sentence fills me with a strange sort of dread.

I tug on the sleeves of my shirt. "What happens to you now that you've served your purpose?" I'm proud that my voice doesn't tremble like the rest of my body is beginning to.

It shouldn't be possible to feel this much. Excitement and anxiety and fear are all churning inside me. But mostly fear, fear for my horseman. I never asked him what would happen if he simply *stopped* spreading the plague.

I probably should've.

Pestilence's blue eyes pierce mine. "Come with me and find out."

That ache in my chest expands, but now it hurts with something halfway between pain and pleasure.

"There are so many things between us," I say. So many insurmountable things. I want him so bad it hurts, but I swear it feels like he's the one thing I can't have, even after his wrongs have been righted.

Pestilence closes the last of the distance between us. Gently, he takes my hands, staring down at my knuckles. "I may no longer be Pestilence the Conqueror, but I *will* fight for what I want, and I want *you*." His eyes rise to mine. "Tell me you want me too."

I'm standing on the edge of a cliff. All I have to do is take a single step, and then everything can change. Everything *will* change.

He squeezes my hands. "Come back to me," he says. "Quote me Poe and Byron, Dickinson and Shakespeare. Tell me your human histories, share your memories with me. Let me taste your food, and let me drink your wine. Let me make love to you and hold you in my arms until dawn. Share your life with me."

I stand there, still frozen, still sure he's some vision made to haunt my days. Sure I'm going to wake.

Pestilence's hands move to cup my face. "I was wrong—about humanity. And I was wrong so many times when it came to you. Forgive me."

I press my eyes closed, then open them. He's still there, still gazing at me with his sad eyes.

"Come back to me, Sara," he repeats. "*Please.*"

That damn word.

The world distorts beyond my watery eyes.

"I'm still going to die someday," I whisper.

He nods solemnly. "I know."

"You're okay with that?"

He strokes my cheek with his thumb. "Sara, I don't know how many minutes you get or I get, but I do know I want to spend them all with you."

My heart hammers in my chest.

I look at his face, his angelic face with those sad, solemn eyes. He really could be an angel—maybe he *is* an angel, if such things exist. I don't know. I don't know much of anything except that joy is a strange thing, and I feel it now with him just as I have felt it a hundred times before in a hundred different little moments between us.

I reach up and wrap a hand around his wrist. "If you're no longer Pestilence the Conqueror, then what would you like me to call you?" I ask, leaning a little into his touch.

He gives me a shy, vulnerable smile. "*Love* has a nice ring to it."

"All right, love," I say, noticing his whisper of a smile at the endearment, "what minutes I have left—they are yours. *I* am yours."

There is a moment when it doesn't compute. My

horseman's eyes are still haunted, and he looks like hope utterly abandoned him somewhere back in Washington. But then it *does* register, and his whole face transforms.

First his gaze brightens, his eyebrows hiking up, and then a smile that could outpace the sun spreads across his face.

He leans down and takes my lips, and the kiss is an end and a beginning all at once.

CHAPTER 54

The kiss has only barely begun when it goes from sweet to wild and desperate. He's my oxygen, and I haven't been able to breathe for *months*.

I move my fingers to the buttons of his flannel shirt, but my hands shake so badly from need and want and all this goddamned adrenaline that I can't seem to undo a single one.

Pestilence pushes me up against the wall, his pelvis grinding into mine.

"Missed you so much," he says between kisses. "Love is *unendurable* when it spoils."

But, miracle of miracles, this love *didn't* spoil. It might've carved us up from the inside out, but in the end, it didn't twist us into monsters. It stopped Pestilence from killing the world, and it made me strong enough to walk away from him when he wasn't worthy.

And, in the end, it brought him back to me.

I go at Pestilence's buttons again while the horseman

peels my shirt off. The rest of our clothes quickly follow as I lead Pestilence to my bedroom.

Only a faint oil lamp flickers in the darkness here—well, it *and* my horseman's strange markings, the latter of which haven't dimmed in the least.

I touch them reverently as he lays me down on the bed. "They're still here," I say.

He trails kisses from my mouth, up my cheek, to my ear. "Of course they are, Sara. They can't just walk off me."

I turn and laugh into his lips. "Earth has given you a smart mouth."

"Earth has given me a smart woman, and *she* has given me a smart mouth."

His hand goes to my breast, and I gasp as he kneads the soft flesh.

Pestilence was right to call love "unendurable." I can't fathom how I managed to go this long without him touching me.

I wrap my legs around him, wanting more—*needing* more.

"It's been so long," I whisper, and my eyes prick.

Oh God, I'm going to cry. We're about to bone, and I'm going to cry.

But then Pestilence is there, his lips pressing first to the corner of one eye, then the corner of the other.

"Far too long," he agrees. "But that's all over now. There's no need for sadness anymore, Sara. Your people are safe, and you are in my arms."

His mouth moves lower, now too busy tasting my flesh to tell me all sorts of pretty things. Which is probably for the best because my core is throbbing something fierce.

He kisses my breasts, taking first one peak and then the other into my mouth. I writhe against him as his ministrations light me on fire.

All the while, Pestilence's cock burns against my thigh. How he has patience for foreplay right now is beyond me. Then again, I was always the kid who peeked at my Christmas presents before they were wrapped, so...maybe when it comes to fun shit, I'm just overzealous.

Pestilence draws away long enough to line us up. For one instant he looks backlit, his golden hair luminous, his body glimmering in the darkness. And in that instant, he's a heavenly thing. Then the moment passes, and he's a man once more.

He pushes into me, his cock thick, the pressure of it exquisite. I can feel him *everywhere*.

My horseman lets out a breath, staring down at me with beautiful, terrible eyes. "God Almighty," he whispers.

If I weren't feeling so damn emotional right now, I might've made some quip about not taking the Lord's name in vain. He learned that bad habit from me. I might've even laughed as I reveled in the intense connection between the two of us.

Instead I take his face, his glorious face, in my hands.

"I love you," I whisper. He needs to hear it. I need to say it. Those words have been trapped beneath my sternum for so long.

He moves in me, his eyes riveted to mine. "I love you too, Sara Burns."

And then he shows me just how much he means it.

Afterward, the two of us lie in a tangle of sheets, and I could stay right here forever, my ear pressed against his chest, his heart pounding beneath me.

He strokes my naked back. "There is one thing I kept,"

he says. "One thing my crown and armor were still good for. Would you like to see it?"

I nod against him, though I don't really have any idea what he's talking about. I'm just too unbearably happy to think about anything else except for the fact Pestilence is here in my arms.

Gently, Pestilence moves me aside so he can slip off the bed and pad into the living room. I can't imagine what's coming.

I gather the sheets to my body and sit up as Pestilence comes back into the room. He kneels next to the bed and lifts his hand, his fist tightly closed. One by one his fingers uncurl, and in his palm rests a small gold band.

His eyes glint. "Marry me, Sara. *Please*."

My breath hitches as I stare at the ring, which looks impossibly perfect.

Made from the last of his golden trappings.

My gaze rises to him. And then I smile. "Yes."

I'm going to marry a horseman of the apocalypse.

I extend my hand and let him slide the band onto my trembling finger.

I'm going to marry Pestilence.

"*Wait*," I say sharply.

My horseman raises his eyebrows. "Wait?" he repeats, looking incredulous. "Are you having…doubts?"

I can tell he has a hard time getting the last part of that sentence out.

"No, but…I want to call you something other than *Pestilence*. Not just an endearment but an actual name."

For better or for worse, he's a man. He needs a proper name.

"You mean like Tricksy?" he asks, completely serious.

God, no. Not like that. "Um, a human name."

I instantly regret mentioning the word *human*—it's one of his triggers. But Pestilence doesn't look repulsed by the idea.

In fact, he seems...intrigued.

He mulls it over for only a second or two before he says, "All right."

"All right?" I echo.

Seriously, it was that easy?

He laughs a little at my surprised expression. "I confess I have thought on this since we parted ways."

Last we spoke, he hadn't believed in personal names. He was Pestilence, and Pestilence was who he was. He was his purpose, and that was all anyone needed to know. Sometime during all those days and weeks we were separated, he changed his mind.

"What would you like to be called?" I ask.

His thumb twists the gold band around and around my finger.

"Victor," he says, a shadow of a smile creeping along his face.

I raise my eyebrows. I don't know what I was expecting. It's not like *Victor* is any less appropriate than any other given name. It's just that *Victor* is really...normal. I wasn't expecting normal.

"Victor," I repeat, grinning as I stare at him. I like it. A lot. "It's perfect."

His smile reaches his eyes.

"What made you choose it?" I ask.

He climbs into bed and takes me into his arms once more. I melt into the delicious heat of him.

This still feels like a dream. Will it ever not? Will I ever wake up one day and not be amazed at the force of nature I fell in love with?

"*Victor* is not so very different from *conqueror*, is it?" he says ponderously.

I tense at that.

Laughter rumbles deep in his chest. "Worry not, dear Sara," he says. "I am not clinging to my former ways." He takes my hand and presses it to his heart. The steady beat of it thumps against my palm.

"Rather, I am *your* victor. You see, I came to conquer this land and its people," he explains, "but instead one of its people conquered me."

I know my eyes have gone soft. It's a good reason—no, a *great* reason. One that makes my toes curl.

Pulling his head down to me, I kiss him, my lips making long, languorous work of the task.

Once the kiss ends, I ask, "What happens now?"

"We go away—or we stay and hope the world learns as I have learned. Either way, we do it together—for all the minutes we have left."

EPILOGUE

Year Ten of the Horseman

The sun is setting when it happens.

Victor drops his book, the spine hitting my legs, which are draped over his lap.

I glance up from my own novel, my gaze going from the book to his ashen face.

"What is it?"

Gently, Victor moves my legs aside and stands. He walks a few feet before he leans heavily against the nearby wall.

I set my own book aside, alarmed. I pretty much kick a path through the scattered children's toys to get to him.

"What's the matter?" I ask.

Is he having a heart attack?

Is that even possible?

When he meets my eyes, there's an old and familiar torment in them. "You may have stopped me all those years ago, Sara, but I am afraid…" His eyes go to our home's large balcony, which overlooks the Pacific. "I cannot stop my brothers."

A chill slides through me. We haven't talked about this subject in *months*. For it to come up now, and so ominously...

Victor heads outside, driven by some force I can't sense, and I'm helpless but to follow him.

He stands at the ledge, his hands gripping the railing so tightly I can hear the wood beginning to splinter. Amazing to think those hands that can hold me so gently can also do this.

"The wheel of fate has been set in motion," he says. "It still turns without my help."

Despite my unease, I smooth my fingers over his hand. Beneath my touch, his hold on the railing loosens.

"I can feel it," he says, not bothering to meet my gaze. His eyes move restlessly over the land. "My brother is waking."

I go cold all over. "*What?*"

He won't look at me, his body forced into a rigid stance.

"Pray for the world, dear Sara. War is coming."

WANT MORE OF
THE FOUR HORSEMAN?

READ ON FOR AN EXCERPT INTO THE NEXT BOOK

WAR

Year Thirteen of the Horsemen
Jerusalem, Filastin

The day starts off like most others. With a nightmare.

The explosion roars through my ears, the force of it knocking me into the water.

Darkness. Nothing. Then—

I gasp in a breath. There's water and fire and…and…and *the pain*—the pain, the pain, the pain. The sharp bite of it nearly steals my breath.

"Mom, Mom, Mom!"

Can't see her. Can't see anyone.

"Mom!"

The sky bobs above me. I cough in the smoke. My bag is wrapped around my ankle, and it's dragging me down, down, down.

No. I try to kick my way back up to the surface, but despite my efforts, it moves farther and farther from reach.

My lungs burn. The sunlight above me grows dim even as I struggle.

I open my mouth to cry for help.

The water rushes in—

I sit up in bed with a gasp.

My wall clock clicks away, the pendulum swinging back and forth, back and forth.

I touch the scar at the base of my throat as I steady my breathing. My sheets are twisted around my ankles. I disentangle myself and roll out of bed.

After grabbing a nearby box of matches, I light an oil lamp. Briefly, it illuminates a picture of my family before I raise it high enough to see the time on the clock.

It's 3:18 a.m.

Ugh. I rub my face.

I set the lamp down on my workbench, shoving aside the feathers, glass arrowheads, and scraps of plastic that litter its surface.

I glance longingly at my bed. There's no way I'm falling back asleep, which means I can work on my latest commission, or I can go scavenging. I glance at the walls, where some of my finished products hang—the oiled bows and painted arrows barely visible in the darkness.

Salvage-chic weaponry sells for a pretty penny these days.

It's too dark to make out the photos hanging alongside them, but my throat tightens at the thought of the images anyway.

Right now, on the wings of my dream, I don't want to keep company with the memories that haunt my apartment.

So scavenging it is.

———

My boots crunch along loose gravel as I wind my way through the streets of Jerusalem, outfitted with my bow, quiver, and the canvas bag I'll use to store my finds. I have a dagger at my hip and a small axe in my bag.

I pass a darkened mosque, which will be filled with people by the time I return. The synagogue down the street is dark and abandoned, several of its windows boarded up. It looks meek and repentant, like it didn't once proudly own that space.

No one else is out, save for the occasional Palestinian guard. They eye me grimly but leave me alone.

Life wasn't always this way.

I can vaguely remember my childhood. I had a happy one—or rather, I used to lack worries, and that's almost the same thing. Now worries stack like stones on my shoulders.

But that life is less real to me than even the dream that woke me.

I touch the hamsa charm on my wrist.

No, life wasn't always this way, but this has been my reality ever since the horsemen arrived.

I can see day one in my mind's eye like it's happening all over again.

How the lights in my fourth-grade classroom popped as they burned out, one after the other. My ears still ring from my classmates' screaming.

I had the misfortune of sitting near a window, so I saw firsthand how the cars lost power, their metal bodies crashing into whatever—or whoever—was nearest to them.

I saw a woman mowed down by a car, her eyes wide for that single second before impact. Sometimes, when I remember it, it's my father I see and not the woman.

I wonder if that's how it played out. I never saw his

mangled body—I just heard he'd been hit by a bus—so all that's left is to wonder.

People around here are fond of saying that life can change in an instant, and it's true. Birth, death, four strange men showing up one day with plans to destroy the world—all instant life changes.

But sometimes the most insidious change happens over time. Because day one ended and day two began. We were all expected to just continue to exist even when cars couldn't drive, and phones couldn't call, and computers couldn't compute, and so many beloved lives were lost. Eventually, this terrible new existence had to become normal. And that's how life's been for most of my twenty-two years.

I move west through the city, looking over my shoulder every so often. The moment I get a little too comfortable with my surroundings is the moment I get attacked.

I pass an aviary, the birds inside quiet at this hour. Once, you could get news almost instantaneously. Now carrier pigeon is the fastest way of sending messages…and there's no guarantee an outgoing message will get where it needs to go in one try. Birds, after all, are only so obedient and reliable.

The night is quiet. It's been like this for the past month. Not that it's ever particularly rowdy here at night, but this feels different. You can sense people's worry in the still air.

It must be the rumors.

There were…strange stories from the east, stories meant to scare you when you're huddled over a fire and the night seems especially terrifying.

Stories about entire cities going to the grave. About streets scattered with bones and cemeteries tilled like fields. And through it all, War, riding on his bloodred steed, his sword brandished.

I don't know how true they are—these days, so many things are hearsay—but Jerusalem has been more subdued than usual. A few people have even packed up and left.

I might've been one of those people, if I had enough money to get where I wanted to go. But I don't, so in Jerusalem I remain.

As I approach the Judaean Mountains that lie on the outskirts of the city, I hear the echoing footfalls of someone walking behind me. Could be the Muslim Brotherhood, could be the Palestinian police force, could be a raider like me or a sex worker looking to fill the last of their quota for the night.

It's probably nothing. Still, it doesn't stop me from going over my survival code, otherwise known as *Miriam Elmahdy's Guide to Staying the Fuck Alive*:

(1) Bend the rules—but don't break them.
(2) Stick to the truth.
(3) Avoid notice.
(4) Listen to your instincts.
(5) Be brave.

Five simple rules that, while not always easy to follow, have kept me alive for the past seven years.

I pick up my pace, hoping to put distance between me and the stranger. Less than a minute later, I hear the footsteps behind me quicken.

I sigh.

After sliding my bow off my shoulder, I remove an arrow from my quiver and nock it into place. Spinning around, I take aim at the dark shape.

"Move along," I say.

The shadowy figure is maybe ten meters away. They raise their hands, stepping forward a little.

"I just wanted to know what a girl like you was doing out this late," the man calls out.

So the individual's not a sex worker and probably not the police either. That leaves someone in the Muslim Brotherhood, a local gang member, or an ordinary civilian willing to pay for a woman's company. Of course, he could also be a fellow raider looking to poach my finds off me.

"I'm not selling anything," I call out.

"I didn't think you were."

So not a confused customer.

"If you're with the Brotherhood," I say, "I've paid my dues for the month." It's the cost of moving about the city with impunity.

"It's all right," the man says. "I'm not with the Brotherhood."

A raider then?

He takes a step toward me. Then another.

I pull my bowstring back, the wood of my bow groaning.

"I'm not going to hurt you." He says it so kindly that I *want* to believe him. But I've learned to trust what people do rather than what they say, and he's *not* backing off.

A criminal then. Honest people don't just sweet-talk their way into getting closer unless they want something from you.

And whatever he wants, I doubt I'm going to like it.

"If you come any closer, I will shoot," I warn.

His footfalls pause, and the two of us stand there for several seconds at an impasse.

He's standing in the shadows between the gaslit streetlamps, so it's hard to make out what he's doing, but I think he's going to leave. It would be the wise thing to do.

His footfalls resume—one, two, three—

I close my brown eyes briefly. This is no way to start a day.

The man picks up his pace as he gains more confidence that I won't shoot. He's completely unaware that I've done this before.

Forgive me.

I release the arrow.

I don't see quite where it lands in the darkness, but I do hear the man's choked gasp, and then I see him collapse.

For several seconds I stay where I am. Only reluctantly do I lower my bow and walk over to him, my hand hovering near the dagger at my hip.

As I get close, I see my arrow protruding from the man's throat, his blood darkening his skin and the ground beneath him. His breathing is wheezy and labored.

I stare at his face for several seconds as he grasps at the projectile. I don't recognize him—not that I assumed I would. I guess that's a relief. My gaze goes to the bag he was carrying.

Crouching, I open it up and rifle through his things. Rope, a crowbar, and a knife. A murderer's starter pack.

Unease skitters through me. Most people who do bad things have their motives—greed, power, lust, self-preservation. It's unnerving to cross paths with someone who plans on hurting you not as a means to an end but as the end itself.

The man's choking breaths slow, then stop altogether, his chest going still.

Once I'm sure he's gone, I remove my arrow from his body, wiping it off on his trousers before I slip it back into my quiver.

No one will bother to investigate what happened. No one will be punished, and by the time the sun is high in the sky, the body will be moved and the city will soon forget there was ever a corpse in the road to begin with.

Giving the man one final glance, I touch the hamsa on my bracelet and walk away.

I head out of the city and into the hills that lie to the west, trying not to think about the man I killed and what he wanted. Or that I barely paused before killing him.

I rub my forehead and then my mouth. Death is getting easier for me to dole out. That's...worrisome.

Once I've made my way into the rolling mountains, I veer off the road and toward the trees. The sky is starting to lighten, turning from navy to periwinkle as the sun gets closer to the horizon. Farther up the hill are the bones of a house, the cinder block and corrugated iron frame only partially complete before its owner abandoned the project.

I move toward it, the unfinished house a familiar sight. But it's not the building I'm seeking so much as the trees around it.

After heading over to a pine tree, I pull out my axe and begin to chop at a thick branch. The wood here makes for good bows and arrow shafts.

Fifteen minutes into my work, I hear...something.

I pause, my eyes going to the road. I strain my ears, but the wooded hills are quiet—

Wait.

There it is again. The sound is barely audible. I can't tell what it is, only that it's steady.

Probably a traveler.

I move to the nearby house before quietly slipping inside. I'd rather not get into a skirmish twice in one night.

Inside the abandoned structure, dirt, old leaves, and several cigarette butts litter the ground. By the looks of the place, it was built after the horsemen's arrival—there are no electrical outlets, nor are there any pipes to carry running water. We lost those luxuries shortly after the horsemen came, and try as we might, we haven't been able to get them back.

I move over to a framed window, keeping mostly to the shadows. I feel like a coward, hiding behind a wall because I *might've* heard something, but after my earlier run-in today, better to be a coward than a dead woman.

Ever so slowly the sound gets louder, until I can make it out distinctly.

Clop. Clop. Clop.

A mounted traveler.

I peer out the window, the sky now a rosy hue. There are trees and brush that partially obscure my view of the road, so I don't see the individual right away. But when I do—

I suck in a breath.

A monster of a man sits on a bloodred steed, a massive sword strapped to his back. There are gold rings in his dark hair, and kohl thickly lines his eyes. His cheekbones are high, and the scowl he wears makes him look absolutely *petrifying*.

For a moment, none of what I'm seeing really registers. Because what I'm seeing is *wrong*. No horse has a coat that red, and no man has that impressive a stature even when in the saddle.

Well, if the rumors are true, then maybe *one* person does...

I start to shake.

No.

By all that is holy, no.

Because if the rumors about his description are true, then it means the man I'm staring at may actually be War.

My lungs seize up at just the thought.

And if the rumors *are* true—

Then Jerusalem is fucked.

A small noise leaves my lips, and War—if that is, in fact, War—turns my way.

I duck.

Oh my God, oh my God, *ohmyGod*, I chant silently, invoking God's name again and again, even though doing so goes against one of the rules of my mother's faith. I gave up on following religious tenets long ago.

A horseman of the apocalypse may actually be standing twenty meters from me.

The hoofbeats pause, then leave the main road. Suddenly, I hear the *clop, clop, clop* of them heading up the hill toward me.

I cover my mouth, muffling my breathing, and I squeeze my eyes shut. I can hear the crunch of dry brush and the horse's noisy exhalations.

I don't know how close the horseman gets before he stops. It *seems* he's right outside the building, that if I stood and reached out the window, I could pet his steed. The hair on my arms rises.

I wait for the rider to dismount.

Could that really be War?

But why *wouldn't* it be him? Jerusalem has been the focus of several religions for centuries. It's a good place to bring about the end of the world—it's even been foretold by some that this *is* where the world ends on the Day of Judgment.

AUTHOR'S NOTE

Some book ideas are patient—some even coy. Then there are other book ideas, like the one I had for *Pestilence*, that simply pour out of you. This novel was the love child of months of sleepless nights and feverish writing. And yet, for all my excitement, this book wouldn't be what it is without the help of some amazing individuals.

Thank you first and foremost to my husband, who has always been my number one fan (on top of just literally being the best human out there). Special thanks also goes to my little June Bug, who probably did more to stall this book than anything else (hello half-time work) but whose utter existence is still so mind-blowing and amazing to me that it was inspiration enough.

Thank you to Leia Stone for you know what. Shannon Mayer, huge thanks for letting me pick your brain on really dull research stuff. You're the best.

To literally all the authors who've shown interest in this book—Grace Draven, Scarlett Dawn, Amber Lynn Natusch,

Kelly St. Clare, Linda Lee, and more—seriously, you all ~~are making me sweat and now I'm going to do a victory lap of editing~~ humble me.

Shout out to my beta readers and ARC reviewers, my street team, and all those wonderful book bloggers and bookstagrammers who have given this novel so much love. I heart you all so hard.

Lastly, thank you to you, the reader, who at this point is getting extra credit for making it all the way here to the end of my acknowledgments. I hope you enjoyed reading about these characters as much as I did writing them.

ABOUT THE AUTHOR

Found in the forest when she was young, Laura Thalassa was raised by fairies, kidnapped by werewolves, and given over to vampires as repayment for a hundred-year debt. She's been brought back to life twice, and with a single kiss, she woke her true love from eternal sleep. She now lives happily ever after with her undead prince in a castle in the woods.

...or something like that, anyway.

When not writing, Laura can be found scarfing down guacamole, hoarding chocolate for the apocalypse, or curled up on the couch with a good book.